Eyes of our Heart

NANCY MOSER

Overland Park, KS

The Books of Nancy Moser: www.nancymoser.com

Contemporary Books

Eyes of Our Heart
The Invitation (Book 1 of Mustard Seed Series)
The Quest (Book 2 of Mustard Seed Series)
The Temptation (Book 3 of Mustard Seed Series)
Crossroads
The Seat Beside Me (Book 1 of Steadfast Series)
A Steadfast Surrender (Book 2 of Steadfast Series)
The Ultimatum (Book 3 of Steadfast Series)
The Sister Circle (Book 1 of Sister Circle Series)
Round the Corner (Book 2 of Sister Circle Series)
An Undivided Heart (Book 3 of Sister Circle Series)
A Place to Belong (Book 4 of Sister Circle Series)
The Sister Circle Handbook (Book 5 of Sister Circle Series)
Time Lottery (Book 1 of Time Lottery Series)
Second Time Around (Book 2 of Time Lottery Series)
John 3:16
The Good Nearby
Solemnly Swear
Save Me, God! I Fell in the Carpool (Inspirational humor)
100 Verses of Encouragement (illustrated gift book)

Historical Books

Where Time Will Take Me (Book 1 of the Past Times Series)
Where Life Will Lead Me (Book 2 of the Past Times Series)
The Pattern Artist (Book 1 of the Pattern Artist Series)
The Fashion Designer (Book 2 of the Pattern Artist Series)
The Shop Keepers (Book 3 of the Pattern Artist Series)
Love of the Summerfields (Book 1 of Manor House Series)
Bride of the Summerfields (Book 2 of Manor House Series)
Rise of the Summerfields (Book 3 of Manor House Series)
Mozart's Sister (biographical novel of Nannerl Mozart)
Just Jane (biographical novel of Jane Austen)
Washington's Lady (bio-novel of Martha Washington)
How Do I Love Thee? (bio-novel of Elizabeth Barrett Browning)
Masquerade (Book 1 of the Gilded Age Series)
An Unlikely Suitor (Book 2 of the Gilded Age Series)
The Journey of Josephine Cain
A Patchwork Christmas (novella collection)
A Basket Brigade Christmas (novella collection)
Regency Brides (novella collection)
Christmas Stitches (novella collection)

Children's Picture Books

Maybe Later (Book 1 of the Doodle Art Series)
I Feel Amazing: the ABCs of Emotion (Book 2 of the Doodle Art Series)

Title: *Eyes of Our Heart*

ISBN 13: 978-1-7339830-5-1

Published by:
Mustard Seed Press
10605 W. 165 Street
Overland Park, KS 66221

Scripture quotations are taken from The Holy Bible, New International Version and English Standard Version.

Front cover design by Mustard Seed Press

Printed and bound in the United States of America

Dedication

Somehow I wrote it.
Thank You, God.

**

"I pray that the eyes of your heart may be enlightened
in order that you may know
the hope to which he has called you,
the riches of his glorious inheritance in his holy people."
Ephesians 1: 18

Note to Reader

All the Bible verses used in this novel
are listed by chapter in the
back of this book.

Enjoy the story
and enjoy His Word.

Chapter 1

Claire

"Whoever belongs to God hears what God says.
The reason you do not hear
is that you do not belong to God."
John 8: 46

"Surrender" was the word Claire Adams used to describe her obedience to the Almighty. It sounded better than "submission" though the effect was the same.

Claire always prayed before she went to sleep, and hoped she got credit for praying off and on during the day too. As a successful middle-aged woman she didn't pray out of need for a material this or that, or even an emotional that or this, but prayed to be a better person, a better child of God.

It wasn't that she considered herself holy (heaven forbid) but she'd had enough God-moments in her life to want to know Him on a deeper level and make Him proud. Long ago she'd given up the notion of getting her own way, or even wanting her own way. From experience—having had equal moments of saying yes and no to the God of the universe—she knew that His way was the best way and it was easier and far more beneficial to just give in. Surrender.

But on this particular summer night, as Claire went through her bedtime ritual of removing her makeup and slathering on three types of wrinkle cream, she knelt at the side of her bed and offered prayers out of need.

She needed money.

Claire prefaced her request by thanking God for His many gifts: her charming three-bedroom home in a tree-lined neighborhood in Kansas City; her good health (ignoring her aching knees as they were an expected part of getting older); her status as a single, independent woman; and her ability to create mosaic artwork that provided a modicum of fame and financial stability.

Until recently.

Business had been slow. There were fewer customers willing to shell out thousands for a large wall piece when they could buy a wrapped canvas made from their own photo of a waterfall they'd seen on vacation, or purchase a framed landscape for fifty-percent off from their local craft store. The lack of business was the main reason she'd succumbed to covering bowls, lamps, and boxes with tile because they could be sold at a price the masses would accept. She had a gallery, but online sales and seasonal art shows were the new way to reach customers. Yet mosaics were heavy and hard to ship.

She rested her forehead on her clasped hands. "Father? As You know, business is slow. I need to sell more art or I'm going to have to close the gallery, let Darla go, or . . ." She hated to say the next because she really didn't want to offer God the alternative, but since He knew all the details of her life anyway . . . "Or sell the house and move to a smaller place. I know You have a plan and You'll do what's best, so I'll leave You to work out the details. I trust You. In Jesus' name, amen."

With a nod at the heavenly transaction, and a grunt as she pushed herself to her feet, Claire slipped into bed, leaving God to do His stuff.

**

Immersed in a dream, Claire moaned and rolled over in her sleep.

The dream voice said, "Make this for us."

Us? Who is us?

Before the question was answered she woke up. The glow of her bedside clock emanated a green, otherworldly glow. She reached for the lamp and flooded her bedroom with its cozy light.

That was intense. She remembered the dream vividly and reached for the paper and pen she kept nearby. She quickly sketched the image before it faded.

A cross made of arrows pointing outward.

Doves.

Pink roses and white daisies?

She finished her sketch and looked at it. "What *is* this?" She did not ask the question with joyful enthusiasm but with confusion and even a bit of disdain. This was *not* the sort of mosaic she created. She was known for impressionistic murals. On a smaller scale she covered furniture tops and created wall and table art that leaned toward geometric, whimsical designs.

Her drawing was whimsical all right. Nonsensical. Bizarre. No one would buy such a design. It reminded her of the Byzantine mosaics she'd seen in Turkey because there was a sacred overtone to the design. Although Claire's faith in her art was strong, this piece . . . it was not something her customers typically purchased.

"I need to make money," she said to her empty house.

Claire looked at the drawing and the quick notes she'd made to match her dream image. The arrows were aqua, the center circular area at their junction was black, the roses pink, and of course, the doves were ivory. White daisies were scattered within the arms of the arrows. These were not her colors. At all. Claire hated pastels. She was drawn to bold jewel tones. Pink and aqua belonged in little girls' bedrooms, not in her art.

She looked at the clock. It was half-past one, far too early for even Claire to get up. She set aside the sketch, turned off her light, and snuggled into her pillows hoping to dream of something sensible.

**

Claire woke in the morning refreshed, having had a dreamless sleep for the second half of the night. She drove to her studio to work on her newest project, a royal blue and gray wall mosaic of waves. Or sky. She wasn't sure yet.

Her cell phone rang and she answered. It was Agnes from her favorite Kansas City antique mall.

"Have time to swing by, Claire? I have a present for you."

"I love presents."

"Then get yourself over here. Soon. I need to get the stuff out of the way."

"Stuff?"

"You'll see."

Claire detoured to the mall. Agnes often gave her a heads-up about old trash that Claire made into treasures. Adding mosaic tile to the top of a 1930s dresser or covering a tin platter with tiles was fun and usually profitable.

Ten minutes later, she arrived and found Agnes at the front counter. "Come with me." Agnes led her into the back room, to the overhead door. Just inside were five 12" x 12" boxes.

"What's inside?"

"See for yourself."

Claire opened a box to find thousands of white and ivory tiles. Tiny pieces, most no bigger than one-fourth of an inch wide. "Are the boxes all the same colors?"

"I didn't check."

Claire opened each box and found one filled with black tiles, one greens . . . All very usable. But the last two boxes made her pull up short. *No. No way.*

"What's wrong?" Agnes asked. "Those two full of gold or something?" She went to see for herself. "Pink and turquoise?"

"Aqua."

"Excuse me, Miss Artist. Aqua. They're pretty. Why are you staring at them like they're kryptonite?"

Long story. "Where did you get these?"

"I have no idea. They showed up outside this morning. I have no use for them. Thought of you. The price is right. Free?"

It took Claire a moment to respond. This was far too strange.

"I said they're free?" Agnes repeated. "You want them or not?"

"I want them. Thanks."

"Great," Agnes said. "Now come to the counter. I found a couple tin bowls you might like."

"Be there in a minute." Claire waited until Agnes had left, then stared at the tile. "Is this tile from You, Lord? Was the dream from You? Was the voice in the dream You?"

There was no other explanation.

Claire bowed her head, her thoughts a jumble. She let the implications rise and fall until she could breathe in a regular rhythm.

She lifted her gaze upward. “All right then. I have no idea why You want me to make this, but I’ll do it.”

Chapter 2

Claire

"After the Philistines had captured the ark of God . . .
they carried the ark into Dagon's temple
and set it beside Dagon . . .
When the people rose early the next day,
there was Dagon, fallen on his face on the ground
before the ark of the Lord!"
1 Samuel 5: 1-3

Claire did not like the way the doves were turning out in the mosaic. This was the fourth time she'd tried to get the various shades of ivory to look realistic.

She hung the three-foot cross mosaic on the wall and stepped back to check it out.

Her assistant Darla came in the studio and joined her.

"What do you think?" Claire asked.

"They still look cartoony."

Claire sighed. "Why can't I do this?"

"Because your style is more abstract. It's like forcing Picasso to paint the Mona Lisa."

"I'm Picasso?"

"More him than DaVinci."

She didn't take offense.

Darla pointed at the blue and gray abstract that hung nearby. "We could sell *that* one."

"I know."

"No one wants pink and aqua in their house," Darla said.

"I know."

"So maybe you should do what you do best and let this one go?"

Claire had been leaning in that direction for a few days. There was rent and utilities to pay for the studio, and Darla's wages, much less house expenses. It made no sense to finish this odd mosaic that no one would ever want to hang. Surely God understood basic accounting principles. Money-out only happened if there was money-in.

"You're right," she said. "I'll give it rest and come back to it. The Sunshine Art Fair is in two weeks. I need to finish some items we can sell."

"Smart move."

Claire left the arrow piece on the wall and went to work on the blue one.

**

Claire couldn't sleep—and Claire could always sleep. Every time she closed her eyes she saw images of aqua and pink tiles, arrows and doves and—

"Fine!" She bolted upright. "I'm going."

She got dressed and drove to the studio. Once inside she locked the door behind her. The place was windowless so she felt safe and wouldn't draw any attention.

She flipped on the lights and took two steps toward her workspace.

Then she saw it. On the floor was the blue and gray wall art. Hundreds of tiles were scattered across the floor.

Vandals? Who would do such a thing?

Then she noticed that the arrow piece was hanging just two feet away from where the blue one had hung. It was unscathed.

She squatted down to assess the damage. The background piece of metal was cracked in two places. But how? The fall from wall to floor would scatter the tiles, but damage the metal? It was strong. It had to be substantial to hold the weight of the tiles. She stood, holding the broken metal in her hands. "This doesn't make any sense. Why would one mosaic be destroyed and the other—?"

Her gaze moved to the cross mosaic. Then back to the destruction on the floor. Then back to the cross again.

She shivered and looked upward. "Message received."

Claire cleaned up the mess, then reverently took the cross down to finish it.

**

Claire didn't hear Darla come in the studio until she stood beside the worktable.

"Gracious!" Claire said with a hand to her chest. "You scared me."

"Sorry. When did you come in?"

"Early-early. What time is it?"

"Eight."

"I completely lost track."

Darla pointed at the cross piece. "I thought you set this one aside?"

"I did."

Darla looked at the blue and gray debris shoved aside on the floor. "What happened?"

"God happened."

"I don't get it."

"I came in and found that one on the ground. The metal is cracked and unusable."

"Why? How?"

Claire pointed upward.

"You're saying God destroyed the blue one?" Although Darla believed in God, she usually humored Claire's talk of God-happenings.

"I have no other explanation." She paused. "Do you?"

"An earthquake?"

"In Kansas City? That only affected one piece of art?"

"Maybe you didn't put it on the hook right."

"A possibility. But I prefer my explanation. God wanted me to work on the design *He* gave me. When I faltered, He brought me back to the task."

"Isn't that a little . . . dramatic?"

"And an earthquake wouldn't be dramatic?"

Darla stared at the tiles on the floor. "I'll clean it up. You finish the other one before He destroys anything else."

**

Claire's cell phone rang just as she finished creating a dove to her satisfaction.

"'Happy birthday to you . . .'"

Her best friend Michelle Jofsky sang the rest. Claire had completely forgotten it was her special day.

"Thank you, my dear," Claire said.

"How old are you?"

Ugh. "The big six-oh."

"Younger than me, so stop complaining."

Good point. Michelle had turned sixty-five a month earlier.

"I have a birthday muffin for you. I'll bring it over."

Claire made a quick decision. "I've already been at the studio for hours. I need to get out so I'll come to you. Are you at the shelter or the shop?"

"The shop. See you soon."

Claire grabbed her purse and keys and headed out.

Claire and Michelle had little in common other than their close proximity of age, and the fact that years ago they'd both given up everything to follow Jesus. Beyond that, their similarities diverged. After Claire's act of obedience—selling all her possessions and giving up her art—Claire had decided Jesus hadn't meant every *thing* as much as *any* thing that stood between her and full faith in the Almighty.

Michelle had continued her surrender of the material, devoting her life to helping others as the head of the dining room at Mercy Shelter in downtown KC and volunteering at the Nearly New Shop where proceeds circled back to the shelter.

They'd discussed their different applications of surrender many times and had come to the conclusion that both had pleased God, though Claire couldn't help but think Michelle was a lot more godly than herself.

Their looks were also as different as their professions. Michelle was six inches shorter than Claire and fifty pounds heavier. Her short hair was salt and pepper while Claire's was shoulder-length and a boxed ash-blonde.

Michelle was pensive and full of compassion, a keen observer, always willing to listen. Claire was feisty and full of wit, the life of any party. Together they made a whole.

Claire parked at the door to the shop. Her entrance inside was marked by the ding-ding of a bell on the door.

She looked around but the place was empty. "Yoo-hoo? Michelle? Olly oxen free."

Michelle came out from the storeroom holding a pink zipper jacket. "Look familiar?"

Claire rushed forward. "Well I'll be. I donated this ages ago. How did you know it was mine? I don't think you ever saw me wear it."

Michelle pointed at the tag on the inside edge of the collar. *Made Expressly for Claire Adams*.

"I'd forgotten about that. I donated it at least fifteen years ago. I wonder who's had it all these years. Do you know their name?"

"Does it matter?"

"Just curious."

Michelle put the jacket on a hanger. "Actually, I don't know who brought it in. We always ask if they want a donation receipt, but this woman didn't. In fact, all she donated was this jacket."

"Don't most people come in with a carload of stuff?"

"They do." Michelle began to hang it on a rack when she turned to Claire. "You want it back?"

"No can do. My body has shifted." She put a hand to her midsection. "Let someone else enjoy it."

Michelle hung it with the other outerwear and pointed toward the counter. "Your muffin awaits."

An enormous chocolate muffin sat on a paper plate with a single candle sticking out of it. Michelle struck a match and lit it. "You want me to sing again?"

"Thank you, but once is enough." Claire blew out the flame.

"Did you make a wish?"

"I always forget that part."

Michelle shrugged. "I bought myself a treat too." She pulled a donut from a bakery bag. They sat on the stools behind the counter and dug in. "Are you doing anything special to celebrate your milestone?"

"Ron offered to take me to dinner, but I said no."

"It was nice of him to ask."

Claire shrugged. "Celebrating my sixtieth with my ex is not appealing."

Michelle reached under the counter and brought out a gift bag. "Maybe this will help."

Claire was touched. "We don't give each other gifts."

"I couldn't resist. I found it in the pocket of the pink jacket. Actually, maybe it's been there all this time. Maybe it's yours."

Claire removed the tissue paper and found a small square jewelry box inside. She took the lid off.

And gasped.

"What's wrong?" Michelle asked. "Don't you like it?"

Claire couldn't speak. She held the pin with both hands as though it was weighty. It wasn't—physically. But spiritually?

It was a three inches in diameter and consisted of four arrows pointing outward forming an equal cross. Their depth was filled with tiny aqua tiles around white flowers. In the center was a black circle with two doves and a myriad of pink roses. Gold metal formed the frame of it, with scrolls connecting the outside of the crossed areas.

"Claire, please tell me what's wrong."

Claire drew in a deep breath, then let it out. "This is the same design as the wall mosaic I've been working on."

"Did you copy it?" Michelle pointed at the pin. "It's not your usual style."

She shook her head, staring at the pin. "God is definitely up to something."

"Why do you say that?"

Claire sat up straighter on the stool. "Something strange has been happening the past few weeks." She told Michelle about her dream and the tile materials appearing in all the right colors. "And now you give me this."

"So it's not yours?"

"I've never seen it before."

Michelle made a curlicue in front of Claire's face. "I can see there's more to the story."

"Like I said, I had the dream and started making the wall piece. But then I stopped working on it because I needed to work on something I could sell."

"Ye of little faith."

Guilty, as charged. "Early this morning I went to the studio where I found the sellable piece destroyed on the floor, while the God-piece was safely on the wall."

Michelle pressed a finger to her skirt, nabbing a stray crumb. "Right out of the Bible."

"Mosaics are in the Bible?"

"No, but there's the time the Ark of the Covenant was captured and placed next to a statue of a heathen god. In the morning the false god was found crashed on the floor, in pieces."

Claire shuddered. "*My* other piece wasn't a false god."

Michelle considered this a moment. "Why did you abandon work on the cross?"

She knew her reasoning would sound weak. "It's not a popular design or colors. And as I said, I needed to finish one that I . . . I could . . ."

"Sell."

The truth stabbed. "I chose the monetary piece over the God piece."

"It's one explanation."

It was heady stuff. "God clearly wants me to make this specific piece of art. But why? I've often felt He inspired my work, but this time it's so specific."

"I'm sure He'll let you know His plan. Eventually."

"Our plan." Claire pinned the piece of jewelry on her blouse. "He brought this pin to you. You're a part of it too."

Michelle squirmed on the stool.

"What?"

"Recently I've been feeling a stirring like I'm excited and scared at the same time."

"Like something's about to happen?"

She nodded at the pin. "Maybe something *is* happening."

"Maybe we're supposed to do something together—with the mosaic?" Claire asked.

"I've been praying for clarity. Have you?"

Sort of. Kind of. Not really.

Michelle put a hand on Claire's shoulder. "Let's pray now."

Claire was very willing to let her friend do the honors. They clasped hands and bowed their heads.

As usual, Michelle kept her prayers on-point. "Here we are, Lord. Send us."

"Send us." But as Claire repeated the words her stomach pulled ever so slightly.

Chapter 3

Claire

"Come, follow me," Jesus said,
"and I will send you out to fish for people."
Matthew 4: 19

Claire settled into a chair at the pay-table of her booth. For better or worse, the Sunshine Art Fair was officially open.

She spotted Michelle and waved her over.

"Here you are," Michelle said.

"Here I am. Thanks for volunteering to help out. I'm glad the shelter could spare you. Want some peach tea?"

"Of course." Michelle accepted an insulated glass of tea, adjusting the cover and plastic straw. She nodded toward a cooler and a box under the money table. "You came prepared?"

"I am fully supplied with totally un-nutritious but tasty food and all sorts of office supplies. I feel better when I'm overly ready-for-anything." She pointed to the cash box. "Between you and Darla . . . do you feel comfortable handling the money?"

Michelle opened the cashbox that already contained change. "Do you have a count of what's in here to start?"

"I do. This is not my first rodeo." Claire turned to Darla. "Five hundred, yes?"

"Yes."

"Most people will charge the purchase," Darla said. "No checks." She showed Michelle how to run the credit card machine then went off to finish setting up the art displayed on the tables.

Claire let herself relax for the last time that day. "Even though it's a lot of work this is my favorite art event of the year."

"I've come as a visitor, but I've never worked a booth. This should be fun."

"Let's hope so. I like having my work out where a lot of people can see it." Claire took a deep breath of the summer air which was already heavy with humidity. "I enjoy talking with people, letting them see what I do. What's the purpose of art if it's not seen?"

"We're not supposed to hide our light under a basket but let it shine for all the world to see?"

"Something like that."

Suddenly Michelle stared at a mosaic on the wall. "That's it. That's the God piece."

"Just finished it yesterday."

"Seeing the design larger, wow . . . arrows. Four arrows pointing outward."

"Yes . . ." Why did Michelle focus on the arrows?

Michelle stepped closer, gently touching it. "At the shelter this morning I spoke with a young man who had a tattoo on the top of his hand that had four outward-pointing arrows. Just like this. He got it a few days ago."

Claire felt her heart race. "Do you think it means something?"

Michelle pointed at Claire, then at herself. "We don't believe in coincidences. "

"The man was at the shelter? He's homeless?"

Michelle waffled a hand. "Transient is a better word. Transient and extraordinary. He travels around, going where God leads him, to do what God tells him to do."

"That is extraordinary."

Michelle nodded once. "He's our type of people, Claire. And he's here at the fair. I asked if he wanted to come and he agreed. I dropped him off at the entrance to roam around."

Claire felt a wave of panic. Her booth was at the far end, so it took a while for customers to get back to her. "If he's part of whatever it is we're doing I don't want to lose him. Maybe you should go look for him, bring him here."

Michelle linked her arm with Claire's. "If he's a part of it, it will happen naturally."

Claire knew she was speaking the truth, and yet, "What's he look like?"

"Trust, Claire. Trust."

As customers began to stroll by, Claire noticed a young man with longish wheat-colored hair standing at the entrance of the tent. He was staring straight ahead. At the mosaic.

"Good morning," she said.

Michelle stepped toward him. "Ryan! You found us."

He nodded, but his eyes were fixed on the cross.

Claire opened her mouth to speak, but Michelle raised a hand, stopping her. The young man walked closer to the art.

Finally he turned toward the ladies. "Sorry. I was just struck by . . ." He showed his tattoo to Claire. "Look. It's the same."

Her stomach did a back flip with excitement.

"I was supposed to come here."

Oh my. "It seems so."

He pointed at the mosaic. "I followed a dove here."

Oh my again. "You did?"

"The doves in your mosaic represent the Holy Spirit."

Michelle chimed in. "The dove can also represent the peace we find in Jesus."

Claire was amazed. "How about the roses?" *Tell me more.*

Ryan cocked his head. "They represent the beauty and grace of Jesus. Their aroma is the essence of Him. The white daisies represent the innocence of the baby Jesus."

Claire liked his take on it. "And the arrows?"

Ryan stroked his tattoo, his eyes still on the art. "I think it's clear they represent the Great Commission."

Claire hadn't thought of that. "Really?"

"Sure. Four arrows pointing in all four compass directions?"

Michelle stepped up. "Like the verse: 'Go and make disciples of all nations, baptizing them in the name of the Father and of the Son and of the Holy Spirit, and teaching them to obey everything I have commanded you.'"

"And of course, the whole thing is in the shape of a cross," he added.

Claire felt chills race up and down her arms. "You got all that symbolism from this one piece?"

For the first time, Ryan looked at her. "Didn't you mean for it to represent those things?"

She wanted to take credit but couldn't lie. "It wasn't so calculated. I got the idea and created the piece to match the image in my head. I didn't think about its symbolism."

Michelle laughed. "Only you could create a piece that represents the essence of Christianity and not even know it."

"Thank you?"

He held out his hand. "I'm Ryan Bauer."

She shook it. "Claire Adams. Very nice to meet you."

"Now what?" he asked.

"Excuse me?"

"I was prompted to get this tattoo and now I see it matches your art. God has a reason for everything. So, now what?"

Claire had to laugh.

But Ryan didn't smile. He seemed to be a serious young man. "How much are you selling it for?"

A price! She laughed. "I didn't put a price on it. Darla asked me earlier and I said I'd think about it." She reached under the table for her box of supplies. "How much should I charge?"

Michelle put a hand to her chin, staring at it. Ryan did the same, like two art critics assessing the worth of her work.

"All right, you two, how much should I charge?"

Michelle looked at her. "It's not for me to say."

"And obviously not me," Ryan said.

Claire glanced toward the aisles that were full of customers. "I need some guidance here."

"I think we know it needs to go to a special person," Michelle said, "but you're free to price it as you wish."

Free. You're free to price it as you wish. Free . . .

Suddenly, Claire knew what she had to do. She grabbed a pen and started to write on the price tag.

"Claire?" Michelle said.

"You're going to make it free, aren't you?" Ryan said.

Claire laughed and looked to the heavens. "Yes, I am." The rest of the idea materialized. "I'm going to give it away in a drawing. Not a raffle where people have to pay, but completely free."

"That's what I was thinking," Ryan said.

"Why didn't you say something?"

"It's your creation. You needed to figure it out."

"What if I'd put a price of $500 on it?"

Ryan smiled. "We'll never know now, will we?"

Claire could guess what would have happened. It wouldn't have sold. She remembered the piece in the studio that had fallen off the wall--a piece she *could* have sold. This mosaic had always been special.

And now it would be free. She let her mind move to practical matters. She needed something to put the entries in. She could put her supply box on the table, but that was ugly. Then across the fair's aisle she spotted the perfect receptacle in another booth. It was a basket that had an opening on top meant to cover a tall box of tissues. She walked over. "Can I buy this?"

"Of course."

Claire paid and took it back to her table. Then she quickly finished the two signs: *Enter the free drawing!* She put one on the table next to the basket and taped the other on the mosaic.

When she got back to the table, Michelle was already cutting paper into 2" x 3" rectangles. "We'll ask for their name and a phone number."

"How wise was I to bring along scissors and a ream of paper?"

"Brilliant."

Claire returned to her seat, feeling breathless. "Nothing like receiving inspiration at the last minute."

Michelle squeezed Claire's hand. "Now we can let God choose who gets the art."

"That's exciting."

"I agree," Ryan said.

The aisle in front of the booth filled with people. A couple strolled close and Michelle and Ryan backed out of the way. Claire restrained herself from standing. She knew it was best to let people enter on their own and look without interference.

"Morning," she said to them.

They came in the tent and stopped in front of the cross. The woman turned back to the pay desk. "There's a free drawing?"

"Yes, there is," Claire said. "On your way out, sign up right here."

She heard them murmuring to each other about how much they liked the piece.

It begins.

**

"Thanks for helping out, Ryan," Michelle said.

"No problem." He picked up a small table to carry to a customer's car.

Claire was glad for the few minutes alone with Michelle. "He's a nice young man."

"Yes, he is," Michelle said.

"He saw all sorts of symbolism in the mosaic."

"Yes, he did."

Claire balked at what she wanted to say.

"Just say it, Claire."

"I want to invite him to my house this evening."

Michelle's eyebrows rose.

Claire stepped aside so some customers could enter the booth easily. "You were the one who was drawn to him. You invited him here today. Why can't I invite him to my house?"

"Because it's your *house,* Claire. You've known him ten seconds."

Claire sighed. Then sighed again. "It feels right. Don't you feel anything?"

"Actually . . ."

"You do?"

Michelle bobbled her head. "Go ahead and ask him—as long as I'm invited too."

Claire drew her into a hug. "This is crazy."

"Or perfect."

One of the two.

**

When Ryan returned Claire was ready. She handed him one of her business cards with her address and home phone number written on the back.

"What's this?" he asked.

"I'd like to invite you to come to my house this evening—with Michelle—for a little gathering."

He looked at the card. "What kind of gathering?"

She hesitated. "I'm not sure."

He nodded. "God wants us to get together."

Claire chuckled. "*I* think He does but it sounds so strange I didn't think you'd go for it."

"I think He wants it too," Michelle said.

"Then I accept," Ryan said. "I'll help you pack up the booth when it's time to go."

How perfect was that?

**

A twenty-something blonde came in the tent. Her eyes immediately fixed on the cross. She walked close.

"We're giving it away in a drawing," Claire said. "We have an entry box on the front table."

The girl nodded but made no move to sign up.

"You like it?"

"I'm not sure."

Claire laughed.

The girl reddened. "You're not the artist, are you?"

Claire held out her hand. "Claire Adams, at your service. I'd like to hear your honest opinion, Miss . . .?"

"Peerbaugh. Summer Peerbaugh."

"And your opinion?"

Summer hesitated a moment. "I don't *dis*like it—at all. It's just an odd conglomeration of symbols."

"Hmm," Claire said, looking at her art. "Conglomeration. Not an encouraging term."

"Don't listen to me. I know nothing about art and don't have a single creative bone in my body."

Claire leaned closer. "No one knows anything about art. Its worth is in the eye of the beholder."

"I was drawn to the roses. Pink roses. Not red."

"Do pink roses—not red—hold some importance to you?"

She bit her lip. "I work at a flower shop and we got three pink roses tucked into a shipment of red—in addition to the red—and we didn't pay for them. It was very odd. I gave them to three important women in my life who live in a retirement home."

"There you go. The pink roses were a gift you passed along."

"I guess so. But I'm curious . . . in this mosaic, was there a reason for making them pink?"

"I wish I could say yes, but I can't. It just . . . happened."

"Beyond you."

"Hmm?"

Summer changed her weight from foot to foot. "I mean did it happen beyond you? Even in spite of you?"

She blinked twice. "Yes on both accounts. Very good, Miss Peerbaugh."

Summer continued to study it. "At the shop I was taught that pink roses symbolize gentleness and grace. Peace and happiness." She reached out and gently touched a rose. "I heard a story—unprovable of course—that roses were in the Garden of Eden. They didn't have thorns then. Man's sin created the thorns, marring their beauty."

Back from making the delivery, Ryan stepped close. "The crown of thorns was put on Jesus's head to mock Him as He was without sin." He smiled. "Not to interrupt . . ."

Claire took a step back, letting him into their conversation. "Ryan, meet Summer. Summer, Ryan."

"Pretty name," Ryan said. He nodded at the mosaic. "You're drawn to the roses?"

"And the dove," she said. "I've had some doves perched on the balcony of my apartment the past few days."

"I followed a dove here," Ryan said.

"That's odd."

"It is. I was sitting on a bench eating a sandwich and one landed nearby. It stared at me like it wanted my full attention."

"It wanted your sandwich," Claire said.

"Maybe. I tried to shoo it away but it kept coming back. Then it flew east. I followed it. All this happened right after I got the tattoo." He showed it to Summer. "Arrows. Just like the ones in the mosaic."

Her blue eyes grew wide. "I got roses, then saw a dove. And . . ." She pointed outside the tent. "Did you know you have a dozen doves sitting on top of this tent?"

"What?" Claire asked.

They all stepped outside and saw two dozen doves perched on the roof of the tent. Claire looked at the other tents. "The doves are only here."

"How cool." Ryan grinned. "Hey, Claire, can Summer come to your house too? She's obviously one of us."

"Us?" Summer said.

They heard a commotion to the left and saw people swarming around a handsome thirty-something man who was walking between the booths. They impeded his progress so he had to stop walking.

Summer recognized him. "That's Jered Manson!"

"Who?" Claire asked.

"He's a famous singer," Summer said.

"What kind of singer?"

"His music is a mix of Ed Sheeren and Neil Diamond," Ryan said.

"My kind of music." Claire stared at Jered. Then it hit her. "Jered Manson? Oh my goodness. I know him, or rather I knew him years ago back in Steadfast. He was just a kid, a struggling musician."

"He's not struggling anymore," Ryan said.

Jered signed a few autographs then looked toward them. His eyes moved upward and focused on the doves on the tent. The autographs were forgotten and he pressed through the fans and walked toward the booth.

He stopped out front. A red-haired woman walking beside him took his arm. "I see them, hon. There are so many."

"Excuse me, but why is this tent covered with doves?" he asked.

"We don't know," Claire said.

"Sure we do," Ryan said. He pointed inside. "Come inside and see."

They all went inside. They didn't coax Jered, or interfere, but let things play out as God intended.

Jered and the woman moved toward the cross. She took his arm and whispered. "Doves. And pink roses."

Claire's stomach flipped with excitement. "They mean something to you?"

The woman told a story about a dove flying onstage at Jered's concerts and some pink roses that had been delivered anonymously to the green rooms in different cities.

Ryan pointed at himself and Summer. "We were led here today because of doves, roses, and . . . arrows." He showed off his tattoo.

"Wow, man. That's drastic," Jered said.

Ryan gave Claire a look. She nodded and introduced everyone—including Michelle. And Jered's wife, Ivy.

When Claire was done she sighed. "It appears you were all brought here."

"Brought here?" Jered asked.

"Why?" Ivy asked.

"That's what we have to find out." Claire pulled two business cards from her pocket and wrote her address on the back. "I'd like all of you to come to my house tonight so we can discuss it further." She smiled at Jered. "We've met, you know."

"We have?"

It had been right after she'd given up everything. "In Steadfast? I knew your dad."

His look was noncommittal, but he nodded. "Nice to see you again."

"I hear you've made good on your music."

"I do okay."

"How's Bailey?" Claire asked.

He half-shrugged, like he'd purposely stopped the gesture. "Dad's still in Steadfast, running his restaurant I believe."

"You believe?"

"We don't stay in touch."

"That's too bad."

Jered seemed uncomfortable about the whole situation. He handed the card to Ivy. "I don't know about any of this meeting-up thing. I just finished a tour and I'm tired. And—" He shrugged. "It's too weird."

Ivy nodded, though she added, "But it's also fabulous. We'll be there."

Jered looked at her as if to say *We will?*

"Summer?" Ryan asked.

She seemed uncomfortable that they were looking at her. "I . . . I suppose I'll come."

"Very good," Claire said. "Seven sound all right?"

Seven, it was.

Chapter 4

Claire & Friends

"Again, truly I tell you
that if two of you on earth agree about anything they ask for,
it will be done for them by my Father in heaven.
For where two or three gather in my name,
there am I with them."
Matthew 18: 19-20

"Sit a minute, Claire," Ryan told her. "You're exhausted."

Claire stopped straightening the magazines on the coffee table and slumped onto the couch. "A full day at the art fair and now, guests. It is a lot."

"It's what you needed to do." Michelle finished the straightening, moving a copy of the newest *Art in America* magazine to the top. "Gathering everyone . . . it's fascinating," Ryan said.

Maybe. "But what do we do with you? Them?" Claire asked.

"*We* don't do anything," Michelle said.

"Great. Abandon me in my time of need. What do *I* do with them?"

Michelle sat beside her and took her hand, resting it in on the cushion between them. "Wrong *we*, my dear." She pointed at Claire and Ryan. "We don't do anything. This is God's party."

"Did He supply chips, because I'm pretty sure I'm out."

"You don't need chips," Ryan said.

Maybe not, but . . . Claire stood. "Coffee. I'll make coffee. And I have iced tea in the fridge."

Michelle yanked on her blouse, pulling her back down. "The beverages can wait two minutes." She scooted closer and patted the seat at the end. Ryan sat on the couch with them. "We need to take two minutes and pray about this."

Maybe three.

**

Jered parked the car in front of Claire's house. He and Ivy peered out the window.

"Nice house. Nice neighborhood," Ivy said.

"That doesn't make it any less weird."

She took his hand. "Let's go in and be weird together."

As if he had a choice?

When they were about to knock, Jered's stomach tightened. All he wanted to do was go home. If not for Ivy—

A yellow VW bug drove up. It was the girl from the fair.

"Her name is Summer," Ivy whispered.

Whatever.

They waited for her.

"Hi," she said. "I'm glad I'm not the only one who came."

"Let's do this thing," Ivy said.

Whatever this thing *is.*

Jered knocked and the mosaic lady answered the door. "Come in. Welcome."

The guy from the booth stood. "The gang's all here."

Jered let Ivy and Summer sit on a loveseat. He sat in a chair brought in from the dining room—close to the exit. There was a moment of awkward silence.

"Coffee anyone?" the woman asked. "Iced tea?"

Everyone declined.

"I told you you didn't need chips," the oldest lady said.

"Names?" Ivy said. "Could we exchange names again please?"

Thanks, Ive. He knew she was asking for his sake as he was horrible with names.

After figuring out who was who, Claire stood in front of a blue striped chair. She looked as nervous as Jered felt. "I'm glad you all came," she said.

No one said anything, so Jered took the lead. "Why are we here?"

"I'm not sure." Claire looked to Michelle for support. "But I think it has to do with God."

Jered's urge to leave intensified. He didn't do God.

Ryan chuckled. "Now *that's* a great intro."

Claire clasped her hands. "I think a little background is needed. From all of us. Perhaps we can go around and tell a little about ourselves."

"Good idea," Michelle said. "You sit too. You're making me nervous."

Claire sat. "I'll start." She moved a pillow to the floor so she could lean against the back cushions. "My name is Claire Adams and I'm a mosaic artist. Over fifteen years ago I felt God calling me to give up everything and follow Him." She gestured toward Jered. "So I did. I sold everything I owned, closed up my studio, and started over."

"That was brave of you," Summer said.

"Yes, I guess it was."

"You gave up everything?" Ivy asked.

"I did. Turns out I really didn't need to, but—"

"Didn't need to?" Ryan asked. "Didn't Jesus tell the rich man to do just that? And the rich man couldn't do it?"

"True. But the experience taught me the greater meaning to Jesus's direction is that we're supposed to give up whatever is most important to us—whatever comes between us and God—and follow Him. That *thing* may be possessions or money or a specific job or an attachment to a place . . ."

Jered looked around the tastefully decorated living room. "You obviously bought some of the stuff back."

"Don't be rude, Jer," Ivy said.

"It's okay," Claire said. "It's a valid point. The important part of my sacrifice was that it made me focus on God. I ended up in Steadfast, Kansas—where you lived with your father, Jered. I didn't have much money or a place to live so I hid out in the attic of the local library."

He remembered that. "People thought there was a library ghost."

"People do like the dramatic. But yes, some thought there was a ghost, but then I was discovered and . . ." She shook her head. "That's not important. What's important is that my faith was tested and strengthened. I grew closer to God." She put her hands on her knees. "There. That's my intro. Michelle? You want to go next?"

Michelle sat up straighter on the couch. "My name is Michelle Jofsky and I met Claire right before her Steadfast move. Virtually, the same sort of 'calling' happened to me. Long story short, God got my attention and I ended up working with the homeless." She gave a nod to Ryan. "Which is how Ryan and I met, just this morning."

"Seems like we've known each other longer than that."

"It does." She looked around the group. "The big life-lesson God's taught me is that we've all been created with a unique purpose. We've been placed in this unique time, in this unique position and place, in this unique set of circumstances to do something unique. We just have to find out what it is."

"This meeting is part of that purpose?" Summer asked.

"Maybe. Summer, you go next."

Summer ran her hands up and down her thighs. She was a bitty thing and with her long hair she barely looked twenty.

Her hands kept each other company. "I'm Summer Peerbaugh. I live in Carson Creek and . . ." She shrugged. "That's about it, really."

Ryan made a squawking sound like a game-show buzzer. "Sorry. That answer is not acceptable."

Jered felt sorry for her. "What do you do to make a living?"

"I . . . I work at a flower shop and I'm a server at a retirement home where my grandparents and two aunties live." Her eyebrows drooped, and she added, "They're not actually my aunties, but seem that way because I grew up in a boarding house where all of us lived together."

"Boarding house. See?" Ryan said. "That's interesting."

"Do you live with your parents?" Ivy asked.

She shook her head. "My mom and my step-dad moved to Nashville where he has family. I have my own place."

"Why didn't you move with them?" Michelle asked.

She looked shocked by the question. "I never even considered it."

"They didn't want you with them?" Jered asked.

He received another swat by Ivy.

"I would have been welcome. I just feel—have always felt—that I belong in Carson Creek. I'll probably live there 'til I die."

Now that's boring. But Jered decided to cut her some slack. "Did you go to college? Cuz I didn't."

She nodded. "I have a degree in social work. Not really using it yet, but . . . I like to work. I'm thinking of getting a third job. It's not about the money it's about . . ." She seemed to catch herself, like she would be embarrassed by the words she was going to say.

"If not for the money, why do it?" Jered asked.

Summer glanced at everyone, then at her lap. "I need to be around a lot of people so I . . . can serve them?"

"Serve?" Jered asked. That held no appeal.

She looked annoyed at herself, as though she was having trouble finding the right word. "I like to help people. It makes me feel good when I can help a bride plan the flowers for her wedding or when I can bring someone an extra piece of their favorite cake at the retirement home. I know it isn't much but it makes—"

"It's quite a lot," Claire said. "You have a 'servant's heart.'"

"That's what my grandma tells me."

Michelle was nodding. "'God loves a cheerful giver.'"

Summer smiled. "That's kind of my life-verse."

"You have a life verse?" Jered asked. It sounded too goody two-shoes. Contrived.

"I guess."

Claire said, "Mine is Proverbs 3: 5-6. 'Trust in the Lord with all your heart and lean not on your own understanding; in all your ways submit to him, and he will make your paths straight.'"

Ryan spoke up. "Mine is John 10: 27: "My sheep listen to my voice; I know them, and they follow me."

"Ooh," Michelle said. "I like that one. Mine is Psalm 143: 10. 'Teach me to do your will, for you are my God; may your good Spirit lead me on level ground.'"

This was getting way too strange. Jered glanced toward the door. Could he leave? He was *not* comfortable around Bible-thumpers.

But then Ivy said, "I don't know if this is my life-verse, but it's a favorite."

"Ive? What are you talking about?"

With a fresh breath her words spilled out. "It's Psalm 37: 4. 'Delight yourself in the Lord, and he will give you the desires of your heart.'" She glanced at Jered, then away. "I love that one."

"Since when do you have a life-verse?" Jered whispered.

"I didn't plan it. It's just a verse that comes up a lot and inspires me."

He stared at her as if she were a stranger. Then he got up and took a step toward the foyer. "Who are you people? Talking in verses—having life-verses—this isn't normal. You're all in la-la land."

Claire's voice was calm. "We don't mean to upset you. We're just talking."

"Talking in Bible verses."

Ryan raised his hands, looking heavenward. "'All I know is I know nothing.'"

"Stop it!" Jered said.

Ryan looked at him. "That wasn't from the Bible. That was Socrates."

Jered didn't like feeling stupid. "Ivy, let's go."

She hesitated, but only for a moment. "No, Jer. We need to stay. This is important." She crossed her arms, emphasizing her conviction to stay.

He took a step toward them, waving his arms. "What's important? Sitting around a room with strangers, sharing fancy talk about . . . about . . ."

"About God?" Michelle said.

Jered ran his hands through his hair. His head was going to burst. "This is crazy. No one does this."

"We do," Claire said.

Everyone nodded, even Ivy. She held out her hand. "Sit, please. Let's see where this goes."

"It's not *going* anywhere. It's a waste of time."

"But what if it isn't?" Ryan asked. "What if this is the first day of the rest of your life?"

He's doing it again.

Ryan smiled, "So saith the Sixties."

Ivy stood, an arm outstretched. "What if this is the most important day of the rest of *our* lives?"

Summer spoke next. "None of us knows why we're here. But we are. We were brought together to Claire's booth at the fair."

"Plus," Michelle said. "Claire and I have both felt something stirring, like something important was going to happen."

"I guarantee you, this is not important," Jered said.

Ivy gave him a pleading look. "It won't be unless you sit down and *let* it be. Sit. Please."

He never could deny her, so returned to his chair. She mouthed *thank you.*

Claire sighed deeply. "There now. Ivy? How about you go next?"

"I'm the wife of Jered, one of the most brilliant musicians in the world."

"Ive. Stop."

She continued. "We get to travel together to his concerts, but we live here in Kansas City. As Jered said, he just finished a tour."

"How did you two meet?" Summer asked.

"I was a waitress at a coffee shop—one of his early gigs. Ten years ago." She looked at her husband.

"About that."

"The place only held a couple dozen people."

"If that," Jered said.

"If that," she said. "I loved his music. I saw his passion. I brought him a pumpkin spice latte—it was October—and we started talking. In his spare time he gave music lessons. He loved helping kids."

"When they practiced." Jered sighed. It was nice to walk down memory lane, but in front of everyone?

"You loved helping them even when they didn't practice. You wouldn't guess it, but he's a real softie. I was completely smitten." Ivy gave him an adoring smile. "We've been married eight years." She looked at the others. "We're all talking about how God brought us together today, but I know He brought Jered and me together too." She looked back at him. "You know that's true, Jer."

He didn't like being put on the spot. "Yeah. I guess it's true."

She beamed. "We're talking about starting a family soon."

Michelle clapped her hands together. "That's wonderful."

"Can you take a baby on the road?" Summer asked.

"It's not ideal, but doable. At least until they get old enough for school."

Jered harrumphed. "My career will be dust by then and we'll have no choice but to stay home."

"That's a pessimistic view," Claire said.

"It's a realistic view," he said. "You know what they say: it takes years to be an overnight success but just a minute to be a has-been."

Ryan chuckled. "That's a good one. Not very inspirational, but I see your point. It's good to hold onto things loosely because you never know when it all will be taken away."

"*That's* depressing," Jered said.

"Not really. It makes life easier."

"Did you have everything taken away, Ryan?" Michelle asked. "You're transient. Homeless."

"Really?" Jered hadn't meant to comment. "Sorry, but . . . really?"

"Really." Ryan rubbed the palms of his hands against his jeans. "But unlike most, my situation is voluntary. I guess you could say I am a traveler for God. I go where He wants and do what He tells me to do."

It was Jered's turn to chuckle. "He talks to You?"

"Doesn't He talk to you?"

"No-o-o." He drew out the word.

Ryan held up a finger. "'God does speak—now one way, now another--though man may not perceive it.'"

It sounded like another verse, but Jered wasn't about to ask. "So He's speaking and I'm too stupid to hear?"

"I never said you were stupid."

"You implied it."

Ryan shook his head. "I did no such thing. But He does tell us to listen—it's the right thing to do." He raised a finger. "'Listen to my instruction and be wise; do not disregard it. Blessed are those who listen to me.'"

"It's something you can learn," Claire said.

"What if I don't want to learn?"

"Jer!"

He avoided Ivy's gaze. "I've got enough stuff rolling around in my head. I don't have room for more."

"But what if *that* stuff is drowning out *His* stuff?" Ryan asked.

Jered needed to change the subject. "So you just wander around?"

"Pretty much. God tells me where to go."

The guy was delusional. "And then what?"

Ryan took a cleansing breath. "Then I open the eyes of my heart and see what and who He puts in front of me." He smiled at Michelle. "Like Michelle here. This morning she sat beside me at the shelter and now look at us. We've found like-minded people and have gathered together."

"To do what?" Jered asked.

They all looked to Claire.

**

Claire looked back at the five faces peering at her with expectation—and skepticism. Jered's question was valid. They had been gathered together to do what?

Jered put his hands on his knees and pushed himself to standing. "See? Even she doesn't know. I'm done here."

"Jer . . ." Ivy said.

Ryan stood too. "That's it? That's all the time you give this? A few seconds?"

"I've been here a lot longer than that."

Ryan tossed his hands in the air. "Wow. A few minutes then." He looked toward heaven. "Sorry, Father. Maybe You should choose someone else to do Your work. This guy doesn't have the patience for it."

This wasn't productive. "Ryan. Don't be rude," Claire said.

"He's the one being rude. Brushing us off like he's better than us."

"Better at spotting a bunch of b—"

"Baloney," Ivy said.

"See? Ivy agrees with me."

"No, I don't," she said. "I just didn't want you to cuss." She pointed at his chair. "Please."

He reluctantly sat—as did Ryan—but the tension remained. Claire needed to say something to keep them there. *Please give me Your words.*

Summer did it for her. "We're all different," she said.

Jered rolled his eyes. "I'll say."

She traced the piping on the arm of the loveseat. "When I lived at the boarding house with my mom, all sorts of ladies moved in and out."

"You mentioned that before," Michelle asked. "An actual boarding house? Everybody had a bedroom and everything else was shared? You don't see those very often."

"It was a big Victorian house. The owner, Evelyn, was a widow and needed income, so she opened up her house."

"That sounds charming," Ivy said.

"It was, but it was also hard because we were really different. At first we fought a lot, but then we discovered that we all had something unique to offer. Evelyn was an empathizer, my mom was good at being an administrator, Mae was the motivator, Tessa was the teacher, and I was—"

"The server," Claire said. It was obvious.

"We didn't realize it right away, but it was like we were living out the spiritual gifts listed in Romans 12." She looked at each one in the room. "I think that's happened here too."

Claire grabbed onto the rope Summer had thrown her. "There's one way to find out." She got out her Bible and turned to the twelfth chapter in the book of Romans.

"I think it's verse four or so," Summer said.

She scanned the verses. "Yup. Here it is." She took a moment to read it silently, then smiled. "This *is* it. Listen. 'Just as each of us has one body with many members, and these members do not all have the same function, so in Christ we, though many, form one body, and each member belongs to all the others. We have different gifts, according to the grace given to each of us. If your gift is prophesying, then prophesy in accordance with your faith; if it is serving, then serve; if it is teaching, then teach; if it is to encourage, then give encouragement; if it is giving, then give generously; if it is to lead, do it diligently; if it is to show mercy, do it cheerfully.'"

"Wow," Ivy said. "Everyone working together, helping in ways that suit their gifts . . . I like that."

"Which gift do each of you have?" Claire asked.

"Which ones are they again?" Ivy asked.

Summer raised a hand. "We pinpointed them this way: you're either a Perceiver, a Server, a Teacher, a Motivator, a Giver, an Administrator, or an Empathizer."

"I like those categories," Michelle said. "I'll go first. I think I'm an Empathizer."

"You do have a kind heart," Claire said.

Michelle turned it back to her. "Claire is an administrator. She likes to be in charge."

"Guilty, *as* charged. And Summer's the Server."

Summer nodded.

Ryan raised a hand. "I'm a Perceiver. I tend to see the reason behind things. I'm always looking for the big picture, the deeper meaning."

"Yeah?" Jered said sarcastically. "You could've fooled me."

Claire glared at him. "So which gift do you have?"

"I'm a performer. It's not on the list."

"That's what you do. That's not your gift."

Ivy touched his arm. "Performing involves sharing. And you used to be a teacher." She nodded. "Jered's a teacher."

"Which brings us back to you, Ivy. Which one are you?"

She looked perplexed, but then Jered answered for her. "She's a Motivator. She's always encouraging me. I wouldn't be where I am today if not for her."

Ivy leaned toward him. Jered surprised Claire by giving his wife a kiss. Jered seemed to be all prickles except where Ivy was concerned.

Summer extended a hand, wanting the Bible. She looked through the verses. "We're missing one. The Giver."

"We're all givers," Michelle said. "That's why we've been brought together. To give something."

"Give to . . .?" Summer asked.

"Someone," she said. "Somewhere."

"That's specific," Jered said.

Silence fell over the room. Then Ryan said, "What's the main task God asks us to do—after loving Him and others?"

Claire knew this one. "The Great Commission: 'Go and make disciples of all nations.'"

Jered shook his head. "You can stop right there. I am not a preacher."

"None of us are," Summer said.

"It's not preaching," Michelle said. "It's living our faith. Acting on it. Sharing it."

"Each one reach one?" Ryan said.

"Exactly," Claire said. Now, they were getting somewhere.

"So we're supposed to reach people?" Summer asked. "Like I said, that's why I have two jobs and am considering a third. I want to reach a lot of people."

"You're already doing it," Claire said.

"But this has got to be about more than what I'm already doing," she said. "Or else why was I brought here?"

Claire felt like they were on the cusp of understanding their mission. "Maybe we need to go back to our lives and see what happens, but make ourselves available to each other. Check in."

"No go," Jered said. "I can't be at your beck and call. I have a life—a very busy life."

Claire froze. *That's it.* "Beck and call," she said. "Maybe we're supposed to be at God's beck and call."

It was quiet as Claire's words sunk in.

"Ooh," Ivy said. "I just got shivers."

"It is cold in here," Jered said.

"Stop it," she said under her breath.

"I think that's it, Claire," Ryan said. "I've been living that way for most of my life."

"Then tell us how to do it," Summer said.

He strolled across the room, put a hand on the mantle, then walked toward the window before facing them. "When I wake up each day, the first thing I say is—"

"Where's the coffee?" Jered said.

Ryan smiled. "That's the second thing. The first thing I say is, 'Yes, Lord.'"

"Yes, Lord *what?*" Jered asked.

Ryan shrugged. "'Yes, Lord, I'm open to whatever You want me to do before You even ask me to do it.'"

"That's nice," Summer said.

"I did that for a while," Claire said. "But I got out of the habit."

"What happens then?" Ivy asked. "After you've said yes."

"It's hard to explain," Ryan said.

"Then we're not going to get very far," Summer said.

He stuffed his hands in his pockets and peered outside. "It's an attitude, a frame of mind. It's being open to Him, to His nudges."

"That doesn't sound very specific," Ivy said.

"It's too *Twilight Zone* for me," Jered said.

Ryan shook his head. "It's not mystical, it's spiritual. I pray a lot. I ask, 'what now?' and 'show me' a lot."

"I could do that," Summer said.

"And God answers and shows you?" Jered snapped his fingers. "Just like that."

"Not just like that, but little by little. It's like steppingstones." He blinked then nodded as if to himself. "Like getting here. I was led here step by step. A week ago I was in Cheyenne, Wyoming. I got the nudge to go east and met two nice college students on the way. Ended up in Lawrence, Kansas, and felt compelled to get this tattoo."

"Which matches the mosaic," Summer said, in awe.

"Then I'm eating on a bench and share my food with a dove who hops up on the arm of the bench, staring at me like it's trying to tell me something."

"It was a magic pigeon," Jered said derisively.

"Not magic at all," Ryan said. "The dove flew east, then came back to the bench. It did this three times. I asked God if He wanted me to go east, and the bird did it again. So . . . I hopped a ride east—to Kansas City. My ride dropped me at the shelter where I met Michelle. She invited me to the fair—where Claire's tent was covered in doves. I met all of you and here I sit."

Claire liked where he was going with his list. "Some steps were tangible—like the rides and the invitation to the fair, but some were more spiritual, like the urge to get the tattoo and following the dove."

"Like clues," Ryan said. "I could have ignored them but I didn't." He was distracted by something outside. He laughed softly. "Well, I'll be."

"What is it?" Ivy asked.

He put a finger to his lips and pointed out the window. "There's a dove outside."

"No way," Summer said.

They all moved to the window—even Jered. A dove pecked at the grass.

"I've never seen doves here," Claire said.

"Until today," Ivy said. "Until God sent one here to tell us we're on the right track."

"Don't be ridiculous," Jered said.

"I'm not." They returned to their seats and Ivy continued. "We saw doves during your entire tour, Jer. You can't deny it. Doves have been following us around city by city." She turned to the others. "A dove landed on the stage more than once."

Jered shrugged.

Claire was impressed. "We need to keep our eyes peeled for other signs."

"More doves?" Summer asked.

She hesitated. "I don't know. Maybe."

"We need to keep our hearts open to inner nudges," Ryan said. "There's a verse—"

"Of course there is," Jered said.

"The apostle Paul wrote a letter to the Ephesians. He says, 'I pray that the eyes of your heart may be enlightened.'"

"You used that phrase earlier," Ivy said.

"It's what I strive for. Seeing what's on God's heart and making it mine."

"That's a commendable goal," Claire said.

"Everything that's happened to bring all of us here… there's no such thing as a coincidence," Michelle said. "Claire and I agree on that one."

Claire nodded. "Everything that happens has a purpose. Every person who crosses our path is there by design."

"Every person?" Ivy asked.

"In a way." Ryan leaned forward, resting his arms on his legs. "Every day, as we go about our lives, certain people are brought to our attention. Take that as God putting them into our path for a purpose."

Jered rolled his eyes. "So the guy pumping gas next to me, and the kid who skins his knee in the park are there for a reason? Get real. You're searching for rainbows."

"You're partially right. I am searching." Ryan clasped his hands together and put them in front of his mouth for a moment. "Being on the road for ten years I've had a lot of time to think about this. It's not that every guy in the gas station or kid in the park has a purpose in *your* life, or you in theirs, but when there *is* a spark or a connection beyond the mundane, it's there for a purpose." He put a fist by his belly. "I get a stirring inside."

"It's called indigestion," Jered said.

"I feel that sometimes," Michelle said.

Ryan continued. "It's just a little flip to make me take notice. I *can* ignore it, but if I don't it usually leads to something meaningful—like being led here to meet all of you."

"We all listened," Summer said. "We're all here."

Ryan leaned back. "Being observant takes practice." He looked at Jered. "As a musician you know all about practice. Same with you, Claire, it takes practice to learn how to create your art."

"Music is tangible," Jered said. "Art is tangible. You're talking about voodoo magic stuff."

Ivy shook her head. "Being observant and open isn't magic at all. It's inspiring."

Jered spoke softly to his wife. "Don't be taken in by all this, Ive."

"I'm not being taken *in,* I'm being *in*spired." She spoke to the group. "I like the idea that life isn't coincidental, that there's purpose to the big stuff *and* the small stuff."

Claire was pleased with the way things were going. Even Jered's skepticism was useful. "Occasionally I see someone in a store or when I'm driving and I feel the urge to pray for them. Just a short prayer, 'Help them, Lord' or 'Bless them.' And then I move on."

"I do that when I hear an ambulance siren or a fire truck," Summer said. "We have no idea if it does any good."

"It certainly doesn't hurt," Michelle said. "If we pray for others, then God will return the blessing to us. Heaven *does* listen."

Jered scoffed. "You think that's so, but you don't know."

"I know," Ryan said. "Because God told me so." He pointed a finger toward heaven. "'Call to me and I will answer you, and tell you great and unsearchable things you do not know.'"

"Oooh," Ivy said. "Is that a verse?"

"Here we go again," Jered said under his breath.

"It is," Ryan said. "Jeremiah 33: 3."

Ivy reached for her purse. "Let me write that one down."

"Traitor," Jered whispered.

She froze. "I am not a traitor for writing down a verse that speaks to me." She finished her task, getting out her phone. After a few taps, she said, "What was it again, Ryan?"

He repeated the reference while Jered shook his head. Claire knew God could use Jered, yet she wondered how. He put a damper on everything.

Michelle started humming something.

"What's that song?" Claire asked.

Michelle looked to the ceiling "It's sung by Babbie Mason." She stood and began to sing, "'I'll be standing in the gap for you. Just remember someone, somewhere is praying for you, calling out your name, praying for your strength. I'll be standing in the gap for you.'"

"You have a nice voice," Summer said.

Michelle bowed and they all applauded—except for Jered. Claire imagined a lot of things in the future would be "except for Jered."

She summed things up. "So we're supposed to go back to our lives and be observant of people around us. Pray for them. Stand in the gap for them. Follow the nudges and see what happens."

Ryan had something to add. "Pray that God opens the eyes of our hearts. That's the first step."

"I'm willing to try," Summer said with a nod.

"So am I," Ivy said. "So are we."

Jered shrugged. "So what happens when we . . ." he made quotation marks by his head. "'follow the nudges'?"

"Whatever God wants to happen."

"That's conveniently vague," he said.

Ryan shook his head. "God is not vague. *We* are vague. He is very specific."

Claire pointed to the Bible. "'Go and make disciples of all nations...'"

"Share your faith," Michelle said. "And be an example of what a Christian is."

"Represent Him well," Ivy said.

"This is exciting," Summer said. "But I want to stay in touch. I want to know what's happening with everyone."

Claire got a pad of paper and sent it around. "Name, phone, and email."

"Maybe we should meet back here and compare notes?" Michelle said.

"When?" Summer asked.

Michelle backed off. "Maybe giving God a timeline isn't a good idea. He has a different plan for each of us."

"Then let Him arrange it," Ivy said. "Or, even not arrange it."

Claire liked this idea. "If we're saying God will lead us here and there, then we need to trust Him."

"Maybe He'll lead us to some other place to gather," Ivy said.

"Make sure it's one of the cities where I'm playing a concert," Jered said.

Ryan scoffed. "I'm sure the Almighty will be happy to abide by your schedule."

"He could if He wanted to," Jered said.

Gracious. Those two. It was good they were all going their separate ways. "That's it then," Claire said.

Michelle piped up. "I'll send the contact list to all of you and we'll take it from there."

"*God* will take it from there," Summer said.

They all stood and Claire held out her hands so they formed a circle. "A prayer seems appropriate."

Although Claire wasn't used to praying out loud, she did so. She prayed for God's guidance, wisdom, and protection and was about to say Amen, when Michelle said. "I offer up a favorite verse: 'Stand firm. Let nothing move you. Always give yourselves fully to the work of the Lord, for you know that your labor in the Lord is in vain.' Amen."

Couldn't have said it better myself.

**

While driving home, Jered noticed that Ivy wasn't talking—which was rare. Ivy was a talker, too much sometimes.

"What's wrong with you?" he asked.

"You."

"What did I do?"

"You tore down everything those people said."

"I didn't tear down anything. They're all going off on their secret missions, aren't they?" He scoffed. "A bunch of salmon swimming upstream."

"Salmon swimming upstream are incredibly strong."

"Strong-willed maybe."

"So you're not going to do it?"

"If by 'it' you mean am I going to go off into the world and preach about Jesus? Not a chance."

"No one is preaching. As Michelle said, we're living our faith, we're *showing* Jesus."

"That's not my strong suit."

"It could be."

He stopped at an intersection so he could look at her. "I don't want to do this, Ive. We have enough on our plates without adding . . . *this.*"

"So you're closing yourself off from God?"

He didn't like the sounds of that. It was too confrontational. "He's got you guys to do His work. I've got nothing to offer Him."

Her voice softened. "He brought you here, Jered. He must think you *do* have something to offer."

He couldn't fathom it. "We've got a few months at home before we have to leave again. Then three months of gigs on the road. I have to write new songs, arrange them, and get them produced. When do I have time to seek out people who need

God? Between two and three in the morning?" He drove through the intersection. "It's not a good time."

"Will it ever be?"

He didn't answer.

**

Claire waved as Summer and Ryan pulled away—Summer had offered to drive him back to the shelter.

She shut the door and leaned against it. "That was fun."

Michelle moved Jered's chair back to the dining room. "Jered kept it interesting." Her hand lingered on the top of his chair. "I'm used to dealing with skeptics, but his attitude was unexpected."

"I agree. I'm not questioning God's choice, and yet—"

"You're questioning God's choice."

Claire fell onto the couch and adjusted a pillow so she could lay on her side. "The other three seemed very willing."

"Maybe this isn't about Jered. Maybe it's about Ivy."

Claire gathered more throw pillows, pulling one to her chest. "I like her a lot."

"Me too." Michelle followed Claire's lead and curled up on the love seat.

Claire felt her eyes grow heavy. "I'm beat."

"Again, me too."

"You're welcome to stay over."

Michelle sat upright. "I was meaning to talk to you about that."

She sounded serious so Claire sat up too. "About what?"

"I need a place to stay. I have a room above the shelter, but we really need the space for an office so we can make the office a bunkroom, and . . ."

"You can move in here. No problem."

"I don't have many things. It's just until I find another place to live."

Claire didn't have to think about it. "You *have* a place to live. Here. With me. I have two guestrooms. My house is yours."

Michelle's face softened with relief. "You don't mind?"

"I'd love the company—*your* company. Besides, it makes sense to live together since we seem to be on a common quest."

"Whatever it is."

Claire laughed. "You sound like Jered."

"Never." Her voice softened. "I promise I won't be a burden. And I'll pay rent and help with expenses."

"You will be a blessing. As far as rent? Forget it."

"But I have to contribute something."

Claire immediately knew what that something would be. "You can contribute lasagna and oatmeal raisin cookies. And your peanut brittle. Keep me supplied with that and I'm a happy camper."

"I discovered an egg and sausage recipe made with stuffing mix that's amazing."

"Bring it on and consider yourself paid in full."

Michelle stood. "This is generous of you, Claire. If it's all right, I'll move my things in after work tomorrow."

"Perfect."

Michelle drew Claire into a hug. "I'm so glad God brought us together those many years ago."

"As am I. Now come choose your bedroom."

**

"It's nice of you to drive me back to the shelter," Ryan told Summer.

"No problem. But you'll have to give me directions. I'm not that familiar with downtown Kansas City." She stopped at an intersection. "Right, yes?"

Don't go there.

There? Meaning downtown? The shelter?

"Ryan? I have to turn."

He needed a moment. "Can you pull over a second?" He pointed to the parking lot of a pizza place.

Summer pulled in. "You hungry?"

"Always, but that's not it. Can you give me a minute?" He put his hands on the dash. *Father? Where do you want me to go?*

"I'll take you anywhere you want," Summer said. "Actually, I'm going home to Carson Creek. You want to come there?"

Go.

Ryan smiled. "That would be nice. Thank you."

"All right then." Summer laughed with surprise. She turned left. "You could stay with me tonight."

Ryan let the invitation settle. *Yes? No? Which one, Lord?*

"You're praying about it, aren't you?"

He smiled. "'I will instruct you and teach you in the way you should go; I will counsel you with my loving eye on you.'"

"All your verses are impressive."

"I haven't learned verses to impress others but to inspire myself. Since I travel around I need them as a constant in my life. *They* never change."

"I like that. I learned quite a few myself growing up with all the ladies in the Sister Circle."

"What's that?"

"That's what they called themselves at the boarding house. They weren't sisters but became just as close. Even though I was only five they let me be a part of it."

"It's sounds wonderful."

"It was—*is.* My aunties and grandma—the Evelyn I mentioned?—they live in the retirement home where I work."

"One of your jobs."

She nodded. "How do you earn money if you're always traveling?"

"Here and there. God provides."

She was quiet.

"He does."

"Sorry," Summer said. "But that sounds like a cliché. Everybody says that."

"Maybe it sounds cliché because it's true. It happens a lot," he said. "It's a huge element of faith to believe that He cares enough to provide what we need."

"Hmm."

"He says as much."

She chuckled. "Go ahead. Lay a verse on me."

Ryan was glad he knew the right one. "'I will do whatever you ask in my name, so that the Father may be glorified in the Son.' John, fourteen-thirteen."

"How do you *know* all that?"

Ryan didn't like that *he* was getting her attention. "I read the Bible until it becomes real to me. But back to the verses . . . God does provide."

"Okay. But I know for a fact He doesn't always say yes."

"You're right. The transaction of asking and getting isn't a Santa Claus transaction. You're missing the stipulation in the verse, asking in Jesus' name for something that glories the Father. If what you're asking for doesn't fit into who He is and what He wants, then He'll say no."

"So I can't be Queen of England?"

He laughed, "Not today."

After they pulled onto a highway heading southwest, Summer asked, "What do you think about our . . . calling?"

Ryan hesitated. "Before I answer . . . what do *you* think it's all about?"

"Being open to what He's doing and joining Him."

He clapped his hands. "Yes! Well said."

"So . . .?"

"I'm excited about it. I'm always excited to get direction. What I don't like are the times when I feel like I'm wandering—I'd say 'aimlessly' but it's more expectant than that. It's like I'm waiting for further instructions."

"I want that," Summer said. "And I *am* searching."

"Want another verse?" he asked, waggling his eyebrows.

"Sure. Blow me away."

He cleared his throat dramatically. "'Ask and it will be given to you; seek and you will find; knock and the door will be opened to you.'"

"In His name."

"In His name."

"That's not so hard," Summer said. "Because deep down I want what He wants."

"So . . .? Do it. Ask."

"While I'm driving?"

"You're talking to me while you're driving. Talk to Him."

She sighed deeply, pointing to the sky. "Father? I want to do what You want me to do. I'm seeking. I'm knocking. Open the door for me. In Jesus' name."

Ryan laughed softly. "Ditto." Then he added, "Amen."

**

Summer pulled into the parking lot of her apartment building. "This is it." She turned off the car. "You never said if you were staying, but since it's late, I'm going to insist."

Ryan didn't argue. "I appreciate the hospitality."

"Want to order a pizza and watch 'Star Wars'?"

He grinned. "I told you God provides."

Chapter 5

Claire

"As for God, his way is perfect:
The Lord's word is flawless;
he shields all who take refuge in him."
2 Samuel 22: 31

As Claire got dressed for the day, she smelled coffee. It threw her for a moment, then she remembered she had a houseguest.

That wasn't the right term. Michelle was moving in. Tenant? That sounded too businesslike.

Friend. She had a friend living with her. And what a friend. Waking up to fresh coffee?

She smelled something else that trumped the aroma of coffee.

Bacon.

She finished buttoning her blouse and went to the kitchen. Michelle had a carton of eggs on the counter.

"How do you like 'em?"

"Wow. I've lived alone for years. Eggs to order? Over medium. Or scrambled."

"We'll do scrambled this morning. And I'll stop at the grocery store and get the supplies for my rent-recipes."

Claire was going to offer to pay for the groceries but didn't—this time. Instead she poured a cup of coffee and freshened Michelle's. Michelle turned the light on in the oven to check the bacon. "Almost done."

"You're making it in the oven?"

"Easier. And less mess."

Claire sat at the breakfast bar. "I learn something new every day."

Michelle cracked eggs into a bowl and whisked in a little milk. "What time does your Sunday service start? I thought I'd join you."

Claire had forgotten it was Sunday. "Ten, and you're welcome to. Do you have to work today?"

"I usually go in for a few hours on Sunday afternoons, but nothing's set in stone. I'm open to any and all plans." She poured the egg mixture into a hot pan where it began to sizzle.

Claire held the coffee mug under her nose and took in the steamy aroma. "I *wish* we had a plan—a real plan. Yesterday we told everyone to go back to their lives and be open to God's nudges. I'm okay with that but—"

"You'd rather He gave you more than a nudge?"

"A push would be nice. Like Summer said, I'm an administrator, I like graphs, pie charts, organization, and projections based on facts."

"Only two facts here."

Really? "Please, tell me what they are."

"God *has* a plan and He wants us to join Him."

The timer on the oven went off. The immediate plan was breakfast.

**

Church was good. Church was nice. Church almost made Claire laugh.

More than once Michelle looked in her direction, her face asking a silent question.

"Later," she whispered, as she scribbled notes on an offering envelope.

Afterward in the car Michelle said, "It's later. What was going on with you in there? You were grinning constantly, and I even heard the occasional chuckle."

Claire delayed turning on the ignition. "Didn't you find it funny that all the quoted verses were ones that talked about God's plan for our lives?"

"I did notice that. But I thought it was wonderful. Not funny."

Maybe Claire *had* overreacted a bit. She got the envelope out of her purse. "I wrote them down."

Michelle read them aloud. "'In their hearts humans plan their course, but the Lord establishes their steps.' That's Proverbs-something."

"Keep going."

"'All a person's ways seem pure to them, but motives are weighed by the Lord. Commit to the Lord whatever you do, and he will' . . . I can't read your writing but I know that one. 'He will establish your plans.'"

"*Our* plans."

"I certainly hope so."

Claire slapped a hand on the steering wheel. "That's all you can say? After you mention God's plans at breakfast and then we come to church and hear about God's plans?"

Michelle was still peering at Claire's notes. "The next is Proverbs 19 . . . ?"

"That's what the sermon was based on. I didn't get it down in time."

"I know that one too. 'Many are the plans in a person's heart, but it is the Lord's purpose that prevails.'"

"That's it! I'm so glad you're a walking verse factory. It's very helpful."

"Glad to be of service. But none of this explains why you were on the verge of laughing."

"Because it's perfect. All the verses say that *we* don't have to stress about it. No matter what plans and motives are in our heart, God will make them good."

"If we trust Him."

"Yes, of course. But I do trust Him, Michelle. Don't you?"

"Unreservedly."

"So we don't have to worry. He's got it."

Michelle spread her hands as if it was a given.

"Sue me if I'm a step behind," Claire said.

Michelle touched her arm. "Sorry. It's not like I have it all figured out either, but as you suggest, maybe that's the point. We don't need to figure it out. He'll do that. We just have to hang tight and do the next thing. And then the next thing."

Claire remembered the group conversation from last evening. "Use the steppingstones."

"One at a time."

**

Since they'd had a huge breakfast, Claire and Michelle skipped lunch. Michelle headed off to gather the possessions from her room at the shelter, and Claire stopped at the studio.

Which was a mess.

Inside the overhead door were tables and tent equipment from the art fair. Last night Darla, Ryan, and Michelle had helped unload but Claire had told everyone to leave it be. She'd clean it up later.

Now was later. Or would be once she put some coffee on.

Coffee in hand, she made quick work of the equipment, moving it to a storeroom. Her art that hadn't sold sat on a table. Luckily they'd sold a lot. Her bills were thankful. *Thank You, God.*

Claire began moving the pieces back into the gallery part of the building, rearranging the displays to fill in the gaps. "I need to create some more. And soon," she said to the walls.

Yet something felt amiss with that idea. If she was supposed to influence people for Christ, how could she do that while she created mosaics—a very solitary task. Her *art* reached people. But for Christ?

The only art left leaning against the wall was the piece that connected them all: the arrow, dove, and rose mosaic.

Then she remembered . . . "I'm giving it away!"

She found the entry box and opened the lid. There were over a hundred slips of paper inside. She was just about to close her eyes and choose one, when she paused. "Father, I assume this is part of Your plan to connect me with someone. So You choose who gets the mosaic."

She reached into the box and pulled out a name. "Billy Cumberson. Very well. Billy, ready or not, you're the lucky guy." As she picked up her phone she realized how strange it might be to tell him, *"Hey, there, stranger. God chose your name out of a box. You may not realize this, but there's a reason He wants us to meet."*

Obviously, she'd save *that* explanation for later.

She dialed his number. The voice that answered didn't sound as young as she expected a "Billy" to sound. "Billy Cumberson?"

"Who wants to know?"

Alrighty then. "This is Claire Adams. Yesterday at the art fair you entered a drawing for one of my mosaics?"

"That arrow thingy?"

Okay . . . "Yes. The mosaic that has arrows, roses, and doves. It's yours. You won."

"Huh."

It wasn't a question but an unenthusiastic comment. Claire looked heavenwards. *This is the guy* You *chose?* "Would you like to pick it up, or would you like me to deliver it?"

"I'll come get it."

"When—?"

"Can I come now?"

She was taken aback but gave him directions. He said he'd be there in a half hour.

Goody.

**

Billy was tall—which also didn't fit Claire's preconception.

And handsome. Which was a nice surprise.

She'd told him to come to the back door as the gallery wasn't open on Sundays. He sauntered in, immediately wandering around, his hands in the pockets of his jeans which caused his untucked plaid shirt to detour up and over. His salt-and-pepper hair kissed his shoulders but was swept back, giving him the aura of a clean-cut rebel.

He paused to pull out a bin of blue glass. Then a bin of green. "You're organized."

"I am."

"You cut all of these into little pieces?"

"Sometimes. Sometimes I buy it already cut up."

"Where's my prize?"

He certainly had an odd way of saying how-de-do. "It's over here." She led him to the mosaic.

He eyed it, then traced his fingers over a dove. "I do like the doves. Seen a lot of 'em lately."

Claire perked up. "You have?"

He shrugged. "Pesky things." His fingers moved to the arrows. "And I like this part. Kind of symbolic."

Now they might be getting somewhere. "How so?"

He shrugged again—obviously his fallback reaction to most subjects.

"I guess I relate to arrows because I'm kind of searching for direction."

Yes!

He traced the arrows with his fingers. "Up, down, left, right. Not quite sure which way to go since . . ." He didn't finish.

"Since?"

"Long story."

Perhaps. But one she needed to hear. "Would you like some coffee? I'd like to hear about your arrows."

He scratched his head behind his ear, then shrugged again. "Why not? I don't have anything better to do than share my woes with a woman I just met."

Claire held in a sigh. Billy Cumberson was a trip. She poured coffee and they sat at a table used for breaks.

"So then, Mr. Cumberson, what happened that's caused you to search for direction?"

He rested an ankle on his knee. "Failure."

"We've all had some of that."

He swept a hand around the room. "Seems like you've licked it pretty good. I've walked by your gallery before. I saw your stuff at the fair. You've found your direction."

She wasn't sure what to say. "Found it and lost it and found it again."

He blew on his coffee then took a sip. "You've got my attention."

Lord, how much should I say? This isn't about me, it's about him.

But he continued. "What happened?"

She smiled. "Long story."

"Touché. You first."

She gave him the condensed version. "So . . . I went from rich and famous to poor and infamous and back again—part way, at least."

He considered this a minute. "I had my own circle-trip. I went from learning carpentry from my dad to being a short-order cook to owning a restaurant to working as a carpenter."

"You owned a restaurant? Which one?"

"Billy Bob's Steak House."

"I used to go there! Great place. But it closed."

"Sure did."

His failure. "I'm so sorry. You had fabulous steaks. And I loved the garlic rolls. Could have *just* eaten them."

"They were my grandma's recipe. She used to make them for every Sunday dinner."

"What happened to close the restaurant?"

He stood and his hands found his pockets again. "I started it with a good friend, Robby, ten years ago."

"You're the Billy. He's the Bob?"

"Robby, but 'Bob' sounded better. It was a fight to get him to agree on the name. Anyway, Robby knew about business and I knew about food. I provided a few of the recipes."

"That's a good fit."

"The bases were covered for a while, until we got some horrible reviews, and a freezer broke and we lost a ton of food—and money—and then the entire kitchen staff quit, including our chef. Nate was a great chef." He sighed.

"It's hard to recover from all that."

"Pretty impossible. I was already in over my head with the cost of redecorating the place, getting new dishes and such. Chose some neat rimmed plates and slanted salad bowls—I usually leave those details to someone else, but not this time. I also did a lot of the remodel myself. I put in beams and a gorgeous burled wood wainscoting. I didn't have much saved beyond those expenses—even splitting them with Robby. So when everything fell apart, we had no choice but to call it quits."

Claire thought about the location. "Isn't there an Italian place there now?"

"Roberto's. It's Robby's place."

Wow. "That's harsh."

"It is what it is. He's thriving without me. Or so I've heard. I haven't been back. The wound is still too raw." He put a fist to his heart. "Failure stabs like a knife."

With that, Claire knew why God had brought Billy into her life. He needed the healing only God could offer. But how could she help?

"I'm so sorry, Mr. Cumberson. We've all failed, and I'm sure there's something better out there for you."

"Because you know me so well?" He looked at his watch. "In the ten minutes I've known you, you can predict my future?"

She hated being put on the spot. "I say that because that's the way God works."

"He completely rips apart a life?"

"To open you up to something better." It was true but came off sounding Pollyannaish.

He pushed the mug of coffee aside. "So working construction is better than owning my own restaurant? Having my savings wiped out is better than being able to pay my bills? Being humiliated as my partner thrives is good for me?"

"It . . . it can be." Now her words sounded lame and she scrambled to think of something to make it better. "When God closes a door—"

"Don't you dare." He looked toward the door. "I need to leave."

Claire stood. "I'm sorry. I didn't mean to sweep your crises into a box."

He glared at her. "But you did, and then tied it with a neat Christian bow." He strode to the mosaic, thanked her for the prize, then left.

Claire stared after him. So much for helping people.

**

Back home, the doorbell awakened Claire from her nap. She rushed to the door hoping it was Billy—which was stupid because he didn't know where she lived.

It was Michelle, holding two suitcases. "Ready or not, here I come," she said happily.

Claire took one of the cases. She led Michelle to her new bedroom.

"I only have two other boxes. I can put them in the closet." Michelle walked toward the front door, but stopped. She faced Claire. "What's wrong? Have you changed your mind about letting me move in?"

Claire felt awful. "No, of course not." She forced a smile, tapping into joy—for she *was* happy about it. "I was napping so my brain isn't fully awake."

"That's why I don't nap. It does me in."

They took the boxes into her room, then Michelle unzipped a suitcase and began to unpack. Claire brought in more hangers. Within twenty minutes Michelle was fully moved into the room and the adjoining bath. She shoved the suitcases under the bed. "Look at that. The room is officially claimed."

"It is officially yours," Claire said. "Want something to drink?" They headed to the kitchen.

"I do but you don't have to serve me. And actually, I should start the lasagna."

Claire poured iced tea and sat at the counter as Michelle started browning some hamburger.

As the meat began to sizzle, Michelle said, "Something happened. You're not yourself."

Maybe she'd feel better if she said it out loud. "I went to the gallery to put the fair-stuff away."

"That's a task. You should have waited. I would have helped."

"It wasn't bad."

"But . . . obviously something was."

Claire sighed. "I chose the winner of the mosaic and called him. Billy Cumberson."

"Was he excited?"

"Not really."

Michelle stopped stirring the meat. "Most people are excited about winning things—anything."

"Billy is not most people."

Her eyebrows rose. "Billy, is it?"

"Actually, no. I called him Mr. Cumberson."

"So he's old?"

"Not that old. Our age."

Michelle grinned. "Handsome?"

"I suppose he is. Was." She shook her head. This was not the direction she wanted the conversation to go. "His looks don't matter because I will never see him again."

Michelle raised her hands. "That's a strong statement. We'd hoped God would choose the winner and there would be some purpose to it."

"I thought there might be when he told me about a string of bad stuff that happened to him, but then I made the mistake of saying the wrong thing."

"Like what?"

She was embarrassed to repeat it. "When God closes—"

"No. You didn't."

Claire nodded. "It was the first thing that came to mind. He's so hurt and bitter I didn't want to throw Bible verses at him—not that one came to mind. I'm not you, Michelle. I don't know a zillion of 'em."

Michelle stirred the meat. "Maybe you weren't supposed to fix it. I know that's your nature, but maybe you were just supposed to listen. And empathize."

"I did. I do. Until I tried to say something that would make it all better."

"That would fix it."

"And it didn't." There was no getting around it. She leaned on the counter and covered her face with her hands. "Argh. I truly hoped there was a reason we'd been brought together."

"Maybe there still is."

She knew there wasn't. Claire wasn't one to cry easily, but she felt like crying now. "I blew it. God brought us together and I blew it."

Michelle set the fork down and went to her, hugging her from behind. "God can work around our missteps. One sentence from you is not going to foil His purposes."

Claire certainly hoped not.

Chapter 6

Ryan

"My eyes stay open through the watches of the night,
that I may meditate on your promises."
Psalm 119: 148

Ryan enjoyed the evening he spent with Summer, and appreciated a good night's sleep on her comfy couch. She made waffles for breakfast. He ate four.

It was nice to talk to someone about God and hope and the future. It was a relief to share questions about their shared quest to be at God's beck and call. Yet with the morning came the knowing that it was time to go out on his own. Again.

He asked her to take him to the edge of town. God would take it from there.

As Summer drove, Ryan noticed the number of buildings in Carson Creek dwindle from many to few. Two blocks ahead the buildings ended and farmland began. His adventure began.

"You can pull in over there," he said, pointing to the row of storage units on the right.

She did so and put the car in park. "Leaving you off like this seems wrong." She pointed to the two-lane highway that led out of town. "I wish we had a bus station. I don't like the idea of you hitchhiking."

"I'm aware of the dangers. Which is why I'm content to walk."

"How far?"

I have no idea.

She let out a huff. "I know, I know, however far God wants you to go."

"You can say it with annoyance or awe. Your choice."

Summer made a face. "Sorry. I'm new to this following-business."

He shook his head vigorously. "No, you're not. You do it all the time. I just happen to do it in miles far away, while you do it in steps close to home."

"You do have a knack for making me feel positive about my life."

"Glad to oblige."

She opened her car door. "I need a proper hug."

They embraced. It was like having a little sister again.

"You have my number, Ryan. Call if you need anything."

He chuckled. "You've already supplied me with two sandwiches, three apples and a banana, a first-aid kit, energy powder to put in my water bottle, a new washcloth, soap, and a dozen oatmeal raisin cookies. What more could I need?"

"I still think you should have taken the extra blanket."

"It's July. My sleeping bag is enough." He kissed her cheek. "God be with you, Summer Peerbaugh. Keep in touch."

She returned to the car and he walked away. He turned to wave at her, then put his thumb out. A few cars drove by without stopping, so he put his thumb away.

**

It took a few hours of walking before someone pulled over and offered Ryan a ride. The truck driver was named Chocko. Ryan offered him one of Summer's sandwiches.

As they chatted he learned Chocko was from Georgia and had six kids. He was a talker, and as the miles flew by Ryan was content to let him chatter about baseball, deer hunting and making his own jerky, and what colleges his daughter wanted to get into versus what he could afford . . . and faith.

But unlike many of Ryan's "rides" over the years, Chocko didn't need saving. He didn't need verses or God-wisdom. He was full to overflowing with faith already. In fact, it was Ryan who was the recipient of Chocko's evangelism.

"You know Jesus?" he asked Ryan after an hour.

"I do. Very well."

"Well, that's that then. It's a good thing, ain't it?"

"A grand thing."

"That's why I pick up hitchhikers once in a while. I figure God set me out on the road to spread His Good News. When I feel an inkling to stop and pick one up, I do."

"So you felt an inkling about me?"

"I did. You don't need saving, but sometimes it's nice to be with like kind, don't you think?"

"I agree."

"I figure it's like this: 'Truly I tell you that if two of you on earth agree about anything they ask for, it will be done for them by my Father in heaven. For where two or three gather in my name, there am I with them.' You and me. We're two."

Ryan smiled. "That, we are."

Chocko took a drink from his enormous insulated cup. "I like that verse because it's easy to remember: it's Matthew eighteen, nineteen, twenty."

"Nice. That will help me remember it too."

"Okay. Your turn. Give me one."

"There are so many."

"Give me *one*."

Ryan forced his mind to clear, hoping God would bring a verse to mind—one that Chocko needed to hear.

When God answered Ryan, Ryan answered Chocko. "Psalm thirty-six, verses five to seven."

"Three for the price of one. Let 'er loose."

"'Your love, Lord, reaches to the heavens, your faithfulness to the skies. Your righteousness is like the highest mountains, your justice like the great deep. You, Lord, preserve both people and animals. How priceless is your unfailing love, O God! People take refuge in the shadow of your wings.'"

"Oooph," Chocko said. "That is a whopper. Write that one down on that notepad there. I'll have to give it the stickum tonight before I sleep."

Ryan wrote it down. He enjoyed Chocko's way with words.

But before he looked up, he felt an inner stirring.

Stop here.

Ryan looked around. They were driving through the Flint Hills of Kansas. Nothing for miles around but grass and sky. Logic said no way. But God?

If you say so. "Please, let me off here."

Chocko took his foot off the accelerator. "You sure? Emporia's not too much farther."

"Here," Ryan said, gathering his backpack. "God just told me to stop here."

"Then we'd better do it." Chocko pulled over to a shoulder and put on his flashers. "You sure about this?"

"As much as I can be."

Chocko smiled. "The Almighty will honor you stepping out on faith."

"And He'll get me back where I need to be if I'm wrong."

"That too. God bless you, Ryan."

"You too, Chocko. Safe travels."

Chocko pulled away with a toot of his horn.

Ryan stood on the side of the road. He looked north, then south. There was no traffic. None. On either side of the road were rolling hills covered with knee-high prairie grasses that swept all the way to the horizon. There were few trees. And no houses.

He was totally alone. And yet, not alone. He took a deep breath and looked to the dome of blue sky overhead. "It's just You and me, Lord. Which way?" He didn't feel a push in either direction. But since he'd felt the urge to stop the truck a half mile back, he backtracked in that direction.

It wasn't the first time he'd been struck by the silence of being alone on a highway, and once again it hit him with the same force. In a world of over seven billion people the only sounds he heard were his feet against the pavement, the scratch of occasional gravel changing the tune. He heard his own breathing and smiled at the proof he was alive in this moment, heading out on the Lord's work. His heart was full, his mind eager, his soul content. And so he began to sing an old hymn from his childhood, "'Praise to the Lord, the Almighty, the King of creation! O my soul, praise Him, for He is thy health and salvation! All ye who hear, now to His temple draw near; sing now in glad adoration.'"

The first verse finished at the same time he noticed a dirt road leading west from the highway. He couldn't see any other breaks in the grasses in either direction, so he turned onto it. It was one lane wide, with well-worn tire ruts. His heartbeat quickened as he realized it might lead to someone God wanted him to meet. And so he paused, got down on one knee, and bowed his head. "Let it all play out according to Your will."

Then he walked on. The road rose up and bent down over rolling hills. He walked toward the sunset where clouds had gathered, promising the colors of pink and purple. Wherever he was going needed to appear quickly or Ryan would end up sleeping on a bed of grass.

Finally a house came into view. It sat in a small clearing. It was a single story with siding that needed a new coat of white paint. The front door and windows were open against the day's heat. There were two wooden chairs outside, and a clay pot sporting three red geraniums. Nearby was a small barn with a decrepit red pickup parked beside it. There were no electrical lines going inside. No telephone wires either.

Who would live out here, totally separate from the world?

Ryan realized whoever they were, they probably didn't get a lot of visitors. When was the last time they'd had someone knock on their door? He didn't want to startle them.

So he began to sing the hymn again, replacing the words with *doo-doo.* As he finished the first-time through a young girl of ten or eleven peeked out the screen door. "Hi."

"Hi," he said. "Sorry to barge in on you like this."

She turned inward and he heard the sound of a man's voice. Then the girl said, "What do you want?"

Good question. Ryan wasn't sure how to phrase it. "I know you've probably been taught not to speak to strangers, but I think we're supposed to meet."

She opened the door so he could see her fully. She had long black hair and was dressed in jean shorts and a tee-shirt that was way too big. It had a picture of a horse on it. "Are you named Ryan?"

He was taken aback. "Yes, I am. How—?"

"I had a dream about a man named Ryan." She cocked her head to look at him. "But I can't really remember what he looked like in the dream."

Thanks for the introduction, Lord. "It's good to meet you," he said. "What's your name?"

"Lisa."

Once again he was taken aback. "My little sister's name was Lisa."

"Cool."

"Hi, Lisa. You don't have to let me in. But I'd appreciate it if I could sleep in your barn tonight?"

She bit her lip.

"Are your parents here? Maybe you should ask them."

"Never had a dad. Mom was here taking care of Grandpa—who's kind of sick—but she ran off. Told me to do it."

"I'm so sorry. Can I speak to your grandpa? Is he well enough to—?"

An elderly man appeared behind her. "What's going on here?"

"Good evening, sir." By the man's expression he would be harder to convince than Lisa. "I saw your road, and . . ." *What can I say?* He glanced at the barn. "I don't want to be a bother, but could I sleep in your barn tonight, please?

Lisa looked up at him, "Can he, Grandpa? His name is Ryan."

The man hesitated. "You and your dreams." He looked at Ryan. "How'd you find us?"

God. "There aren't many roads off the highway. I found myself in between towns."

"I don't abide by towns much." He nodded toward the barn. "Go ahead." He pointed at Ryan. "But no funny stuff. I sleep with my gun close."

"No need for that, sir." Ryan tipped an imaginary hat. "Thanks for the hospitality." He went to the barn. The light was dim and getting dimmer. There was only one stall and it was empty. Most of the space was taken up by old tools and an ancient tractor. He chose a spot under a window and pulled his down sleeping bag out of its bag. It sprang to life and he smoothed it on the ground and adjusted a rolled up pair of jeans as his pillow.

He checked his watch. It was 8:30. Too early to sleep, yet it was too dark to read. So he closed his eyes and prayed.

The barn door rolled open. It was Lisa. "Grandpa says come inside with your stuff. You'll get eaten alive by bugs and varmints out here."

"That's very nice of him." He gathered his belongings and followed her into the house.

The home had electrical lights, meaning they must have a generator. There was a small living room with a lumpy couch and a rocking chair. A wood stove stood in the corner with its black stack cutting through the roof. To the right was a tiny kitchen with a sink, an old fridge and oven, and a table with three chairs. Two interior doors probably led to a bathroom and bedroom. A cot sat along the front wall with a teddy bear on it. A fan rotated left to right nearby.

It was like walking back fifty years—or more.

The grandfather sat in the rocking chair. His age was hard to determine. He looked to be in his 80s, though Ryan knew illness often aged a person, so he might be younger.

"Thanks for letting me come inside, sir."

"Not my doing." He waved at the door. "Close it, girl, before the bugs see the lights and take advantage."

She did so.

"Have a seat."

Ryan sat on one end of the couch.

"Staying inside . . . same rules apply," the man said. "I still have my gun."

Ryan nodded. "Understood. I mean no harm."

"That remains to be seen."

Lisa sat at the other end of the couch.

They were silent for an awkward minute and stared at each other. *Father? What do You want me to say?*

Ryan was spurred to do something that always broke the ice with a stranger. He asked them about themselves. "What brought you to live here?"

"Wasn't my doing," the man said. "My grandparents homesteaded here in the eighties."

Ryan realized he meant the 1880s. "That's a long time ago."

"Near to forever. They eventually sold to a big ranch owner and worked for years with the cattle. Me too. The owners have let me stay on. So now . . ." He rocked up and back. "Never thought I'd be here forever, but so be it. Goin' to die here."

"Grandpa . . ."

"No getting around it, girl. You know that."

Lisa hugged a pillow to her chest. *The poor thing. Left all alone with him.*

Ryan turned to Lisa. "Your mom was here?"

She nodded. "Mom had a job in Emporia. I go to school there. But she left. Said she was done with it." Lisa glanced at her grandpa. "But we know the real reason. She met somebody. Ran off with him."

Leaving you behind.

Grandpa stopped rocking. "Carly never did like being here. She longed for the big city. No big city for miles and miles."

Ryan exchanged a look with Lisa. She shrugged.

With a swipe of his hand, Grandpa moved on. "That's enough of that. What are *you* doing out here?"

Finding you. "I'm traveling."

"Where to?"

He was going to say "nowhere special" when he decided to be bold. "Wherever God wants me to be."

"Pffft. God doesn't care where you are. He's got better things to do."

"He does care. Immensely." Ryan thought of an appropriate verse: *"In your hearts revere Christ as Lord. Always be prepared to give an answer to everyone who asks you to give the reason for the hope that you have. But do this with gentleness and respect."* He let God guide his words for only *He* knew what Grandpa needed to hear. "He is always with us. We're His first priority."

"Maybe *you* are, but us . . ." he glanced at his granddaughter. "Way out here, we're hard to find."

"Not hard for Him to find." Ryan smiled, "'Nothing in all creation is hidden from God's sight.'"

"Says you."

"Says God. It's in the Bible."

"Hmmph."

Ryan wanted to say more, but felt a nudge to leave it there—for now.

Suddenly Grandpa leaned forward in a fit of coughing, making the back runners of the rocker point upward. Lisa ran to get a glass of water. It sounded like he was coughing his lungs out.

During a pause he took a sip. Lisa put a hand on his back. "Breathe in slowly. Now out . . ."

He did so. "Is it time for my medicine?"

She glanced at the clock. "Close enough." She got pills from two prescription bottles. "Let's get you to bed."

He didn't argue. She helped him out of the chair and they disappeared into the bedroom. Ryan heard soft voices and movement. *Show me how to help them, Lord.*

Ten minutes later Lisa returned to her place on the couch. "Sorry about that. I . . ." She covered her face with her hands and suddenly began to cry.

Ryan scooted beside her and put a hand on her back. He was going to say, "It will be okay" but he wasn't sure if that was the truth. "You're a good granddaughter."

She dabbed her eyes with the bottom of her tee-shirt. "I try, but I don't know what to do to make him better."

Will he get better? "Is he under a doctor's care?"

Lisa shook her head. "Kind of. He went once last spring and got some medicine. But he doesn't trust doctors much."

"They might be able to help."

"That's what I said. But he won't go. I can't make him."

"Can you call your mom? Maybe she'd come back to help."

Lisa snickered. "Grandpa being sick is the main reason she left. She hates being around sick people."

Such a gem.

Lisa lit two kerosene lamps and turned out the lights. "Grandpa likes to save the gas in the generator when we can." She looked around the room. "Sorry we don't have TV. Want to play Monopoly?"

He was amazed at how quickly she'd segued from personal pain to pleasure. "Um. Sure."

She took a well-worn box off a shelf. "Since Grandpa isn't playing maybe I can win."

Maybe she could.

Chapter 7

Summer

"Each of you should use whatever gift you have received
to serve others, as faithful stewards
of God's grace in its various forms."
1 Peter 4: 10

Summer missed him already.

She drove home after letting Ryan off at the edge of town. He was off on his God-adventure, open to wherever God would lead.

Summer envied him. He was so sure of himself and his quest, while she was unsure and confused. She'd had an exciting weekend—which was a rarity. Meeting all the mosaic people was the most exhilarating thing that had happened to her since . . . forever. Yet now, with Ryan gone, she was left alone.

Some people feared change, but Summer feared that nothing would ever change. A week from now she'd look back and wonder if any of it really happened.

She parked outside her apartment and walked up two flights to the third floor. Her Shih Tzu greeted her with four yaps. "Yes, yes, Suzu, I'm back."

She tossed her keys and purse on the two-person breakfast bar, replenished Suzu's water bowl, then realized she'd left the coffee pot on. She poured herself a cup, and noticed piles of paperwork on the counter. Two days ago she'd started to go through her toss-box, a bottomless pit of papers, letters, and receipts that hadn't been gone through since before she moved. The tallest pile was a stack of old greeting cards. She took the cards and her coffee out to the tiny balcony that overlooked the Happy Trail Retirement Village.

It was rather pitiful that at age twenty-one she cherished the bond she had with her aunties and grandparents so tightly that she purposely chose an apartment across the street from them. It was also pitiful that she'd given her mom and step-dad grief when they'd dared to move away from Carson Creek to live in Nashville. Everyone's life seemed to change, with Summer running to keep up.

The happiest time of her life had been living at Peerbaugh Place, in the tiny one-bedroom she'd shared with her mom. She was loved by all the ladies who lived there and she loved them. When her mother remarried a few years later, they'd both moved out, but Peerbaugh Place remained the home of her heart from the age of five on.

That all changed during her senior year in high school when Grandma and Grandpa, Aunt Mae and her hubby Collier, and Aunt Tessa decided to move into the retirement home. Peerbaugh Place was sold off. An era was ended.

Mae had said, "We're all moving onto the next chapter of our lives. You too, chickie. Now's your chance to see the world. You're young. You're free. You're single."

Tessa had shown her a scrapbook of exotic places she had visited. Summer had smiled and tried to listen because she loved Tessa, but two hours of travelogue had exhausted her and left her unconvinced she would ever embark on a grand adventure.

Since she didn't want to travel, Grandma and Grandpa said she should go to college—and they would help pay for it. All she'd ever heard about college was that people partied a lot. She was *not* a partier. And the reality of living in a dorm with multiple layers of loud music pounding through the walls made her nerves rattle. It's not that she didn't like people. She just preferred an older crowd.

But when her family became united in their advice to get a degree, Summer succumbed. Somehow she'd held onto her sanity and earned a degree in Social Work—just last May to be exact.

Although her family never said anything negative, Summer knew they were slightly disappointed when she moved back to Carson Creek, across the street from them. They were happily disappointed when she got a job at Happy Trails. Four years of hard work to be a server? It did seem like a waste but she wasn't ready to dive into a real job.

Summer turned her focus back to the greeting cards. There were a dozen birthday cards from her 22nd and 21st birthdays. She chose the prettiest two to keep and set them in the other balcony chair—that no one had ever sat in. An invitation to a distant second-cousin's graduation was put in a toss pile. As were four Christmas cards. Then came the fancy invitation to Sydney Thorpe's wedding. A year ago Summer had been a bridesmaid at Sydney's elaborate, up-scale wedding in Kansas City. Sydney had been a bridezilla, demanding and rude to any who crossed her. The five other bridesmaids had been chosen from their high school's popular clique, and Summer had felt like a pity bridesmaid, Sydney's nod to their childhood friendship. Summer could not afford the $250 bridesmaid dress with matching shoes. If not for her family chipping in, she would have had to decline. It might have been the wiser choice.

Summer let her fingers glide across the embossed flowers at the corners of the invitation. How was Sydney doing? They hadn't stayed in touch—which wasn't surprising. Sydney had been obsessed with Ben since high school and had flaunted the fact they became engaged soon after. Most likely she was living in a 4-bedroom house in KC—with a pool. She probably didn't have kids—hopefully didn't have kids. Sydney was too me-oriented to share herself with a child.

Yet Summer *did* have nice memories of her. They used to play in her mother's bridal shop, draping scraps of fabric to make their own creations. "We wanted to marry brothers and live next to each other."

Summer noticed someone on the sidewalk looking up at her. Had she spoken out loud? One of the quirks of living alone was that she often did that. Perhaps the need to hear the spoken word was a necessity of human existence.

Summer let the invitation sit on her lap. Once again she felt left behind. She'd dated a few times in high school, and even a couple of times in the four years since. But she'd never met any man who sparked her interest in a relationship, much less marriage. *Maybe I'll be single forever.*

She found the notion sad.

Summer shook the sadness away. Ryan was off on his mission to reach people for God. Somehow she had to do the same. But sitting alone on a balcony wasn't the way to do it.

She glanced at her watch. It was time to get ready for work. She grabbed the cards and the now-cold coffee and went inside. Suzu looked up from her place on the couch and started wagging her tail. Summer picked her up and nuzzled her under her chin. "Thank goodness I can always count on you."

**

Summer jotted down a phone order for a birthday bouquet. "We'll have that delivered tomorrow morning, Mr. Greer."

After she hung up, she finished filling out the form and put it in the in-box for the florist to fill. "Got another one, Candy. Lilies and carnations."

Candy came out of the walk-in cooler where the flowers were stored. "Birthday, right?"

"How could you tell?"

"Lilies and carnations are birthday choices. Roses for Valentine's Day."

"And 'I'm sorry' arrangements."

Candy smiled. "That too. And living plants are for—"

"Funerals," Summer said. "Have you ever made a mistake and sent the wrong one to the wrong place?"

Candy peered over her readers. "Never."

"Got it."

Candy looked at her watch. "Where is Andy? There are three arrangements to deliver, ASAP. He's been late four times this month."

"I'll deliver them," Summer said. "I'll be back before you know it."

Candy gave her the keys to the delivery van.

**

Summer drove to her first flower drop-off, feeling hopeful. She'd made a few deliveries before, but today might be different. Better? Today was supposed to be the first day of her mission to change the world for God. In order to do that, she needed to see people. The problem she'd noticed at Flora & Funna was that most people ordered on the phone or online.

She found the first address, just a couple blocks from Peerbaugh Place. She retrieved a vase holding three enormous sunflowers and carried them up the steps to the porch. She rang the bell and checked the name on the envelope. She was ready to greet them by name.

When no one answered she tried to remember what Candy had told her about such times. Leave the flowers on the porch? Leave them with a neighbor?

She couldn't remember. She called the shop, but the line was busy. She tried a few more times, but couldn't get through.

"Okay then. I'll just leave them by the door."

One down, two to go.

She drove to the next stop and brought a smiley-face mug full of yellow and white daisies to an apartment on the second floor. A young woman opened the door with a baby in her arms. Her face lit up at the sight of it.

"For you, Mrs. Conners."

"Miss." The woman's smile faded. She took the mug and closed the door.

Two for two.

Summer checked on the third address. A dentist's office. Surely she'd feel a connection there.

She pulled in the circle drive and put on the flashers. She carried a dozen red roses into a reception area. Three women oohed and ahhed. "These are for Missy Gains?" Summer said. "Are any of you Missy?"

A woman signed for them. "We wish. We'll see she gets them. Thanks."

Three for three.

Summer got in the van, dejected. "What am I doing wrong, Lord? I haven't connected with a single person."

She drove back to the store.

**

During the dinner shift at her second job, Summer looked across the dining room full of the residents of Happy Trails. She knew most of them by name, but usually served the same four tables. There was no one new to meet here. No one new to connect with.

Auntie Mae waved her over. "What's wrong with you, frowny face?"

"Sorry." She forced a smile. "Do you all want the usual appetizers?"

"Of course," Grandma said.

"Speak for yourself, Evelyn," Tessa said. "Tonight I'm going to mix it up and have French dressing on my salad instead of Italian."

"You *are* living dangerously," Mae said.

Summer's mood had to be put on hold as she took their orders and served their meals.

Tomorrow. God would use her tomorrow.

Chapter 8

Jered

"Command those who are rich in this present world
not to be arrogant nor to put their hope in wealth,
which is so uncertain, but to put their hope in God,
who richly provides us with everything for our enjoyment."
1 Timothy 6: 17

Jered ate the last of his toasted English muffin and put his dish on the counter.

"*In* the dishwasher, please." Ivy said.

"I don't do dishwashers." *She knows that.*

"Then maybe I don't make meals. Or dust. Or vacuum."

He poured himself another cup of coffee. "I've told you we can hire a cleaning service."

"We don't need a cleaning service." She freshened her cup, making him feel bad because he hadn't thought of doing it for her. "The house is big but it's just us two. I can handle it."

He slid behind her and pulled her close. "I know you *can* but that doesn't mean you *should.*"

She leaned her head against his. "You know I'd be happy with a two-bedroom house. We don't need all this . . . space."

She always said that. *She* didn't need it. Did *he?*

Ivy reached back and stroked his cheek. "You're a very good provider, Jer. I want for nothing. Except . . ."

He let her go—gently. He knew what she wanted. In the past six months she'd made it crystal clear. "A baby doesn't belong on the road." He jumped directly to what he knew would be her parry. "And we can't take a year off. I've told you, 'out of sight, out of mind'. If I'm not out there the public will forget me."

"Never," she said with that special smile that almost made him believe her. She walked toward the bedroom. "Let's get dressed and go."

"Go where?"

"Out in the world."

He sat on their white sectional and turned on his video game-box that was connected to a 72-inch TV—one of five in the house. "We've been gone for three months. We don't have to go anywhere. I just want to stay in."

"How can you find people to help if you're stuck in here?"

Find people? He gestured around their living room. She had overseen the remodel of their 1920s house in the Mission Hills area of Kansas City perfectly, combining antique furniture with modern. He'd grown up in a house without a mom, which meant it was a house with no style at all. "I'm hardly stuck."

She stared at him a moment. "I wouldn't be so sure."

"Don't give me a hard time." He thought of another reason to stay in. "You know it's hard for me to go out. People recognize me."

She gave him a look. "So you're mobbed like Mick Jagger or Usher?"

Ouch. "You remember the other evening at dinner when that girl came over and wanted an autograph?"

Ivy made a checkmark in the air. "One."

"Don't be mean. Go out if you want. I have things to do here." He turned his attention to the TV and signed on to his Madden football game.

She disappeared in the bedroom and he heard dresser drawers open and close. A short time later she came out, grabbed her purse, phone, and keys. She left without saying goodbye.

He hated when she was mad at him, especially when he deserved it.

He overcame his guilt by playing some football.

**

The trouble with videogames is that they were time-drains. The first time Jered looked up was when Ivy came back.

Oops.

She carried groceries. He rushed to help her put things away.

"So . . . how was your visit into the big wide world?" he asked.

She put a box of Cinnamon Life in the pantry, then leaned back on the counter, tossing an orange back and forth between her hands. "You'll never know."

"Cute."

She tossed him the orange and filled the fridge with a 12-pack of peach tea. "Actually, it was wonderful."

Really? "What happened?"

She stopped with a bottle in her hand. "I had just gone in the grocery store to get a cart, when I saw an old woman with a cane turn toward the carts too. There weren't many of them and the stack was short and far away. So I pulled one out and gave it to her. She said thank you, but when she saw that I was having to go back to get my own she was even more thankful. She said, 'It just proves there are kind people in the world.'"

"That *was* nice of you."

Ivy wasn't finished. "Then, in line I saw a woman with three items and told her to go ahead of me. You would have thought I'd given her a hundred dollars. She was so appreciative." She sighed, beaming from the inside out. "Jered, I felt completely filled up." She pressed her hands against her heart. "I know they were small acts of kindness, but to me they were huge."

He was a little disconcerted by her reaction—her overreaction. "Wow, Ive. You really changed the world."

Her light went out. Her face sagged. She tossed the tea at him and stormed away toward the bedroom. She slammed the door.

By the time he got there it was locked. "Come on, Ive. I didn't mean anything by it."

"Leave me alone. Go play your game. I wouldn't want to be called for interference."

He tried to cajole her a few more times but received only silence.

What could he do?

He slumped onto the couch and took up the game where he'd left off.

And fumbled the ball.

Chapter 9

Claire

"I have not come to call the righteous,
but sinners to repentance."
Luke 5: 32

The day after meeting Billy Cumberson Claire started a new mosaic. Tried to start a new mosaic. Her creativity level was stuck on zero because she couldn't stop thinking of Billy.

She needed to talk to him in person, to apologize for her canned response to his candid story of pain. Even if they never spoke again, she had to at least try to make things right.

Luckily only one Billy Cumberson came up in her online search. She considered calling ahead, but was afraid he'd refuse to see her. And so Claire headed out, hoping he was at home.

His house was in Prairie Village, on the Kansas side of Kansas City. It was a thirties bungalow set among towering trees. It oozed cozy charm. She parked out front and walked up the narrow sidewalk to the front door. She rang the bell. She knocked.

No one was—

A black pickup pulled into the driveway. Billy's face showed surprise at seeing her. He pulled around the side of the house to the garage in the back. She walked around to greet him there.

"You lost?" he said.

"I should have called first. Can we talk?"

He shrugged. "Come on in." He unlocked a side door that led into a tiny kitchen with yellow cupboards and yellow Formica counters. There were flowered tiles dotting the white backsplash, and a valance over the sink window sported daisies spilling out of china teacups. A tiny metal-legged table was flanked by two matching chairs with orange vinyl seats. It was like walking into the sunny past.

He hung up his jacket and washed his hands. "First things first. After working all day my hands are in dire need of soap and water."

"Do you enjoy construction?"

"I do. I like to see something real come out of my work." He dried his hands on a towel embroidered with a dog and the word *Tuesday*. "You didn't come here to ask about my work."

To the point. "I came to apologize."

She expected him to say, "For what?" Instead he said, "Apology accepted."

Again, to the point. "I didn't mean to minimize your pain at losing the restaurant by throwing a trite truism at you."

He leaned against the counter and crossed his arms. "Your words didn't go down well—at first."

"At first?"

"The thing with truisms is that they're often true."

"I appreciate that. But the timing was bad. I probably didn't give you the reaction you hoped for."

He smiled. Slightly. "I don't take you for the kind of woman who says what she thinks people want to hear."

He'd pegged her. "I tend to be more pragmatic than polite."

"You do okay." He stood upright. "Speaking of polite . . . have a seat."

"Thank you, but I shouldn't bother you any longer."

He walked two steps to the tiny fridge. "You like homemade mac and cheese?"

"Well . . . yes. I order it at restaurants sometimes."

He took out some milk and a package of cream cheese, then handed her a brick of sharp cheddar, a bowl, and a grater. "Have at it."

She was surprised, but pleased. The cheese was wrapped in clear plastic. "Knife please?" He handed her one and she slit the package open. "How much should I grate?"

"How hungry are you?"

She hadn't felt like eating lunch because she'd been so upset. "Famished."

"Then go for it. I'll bring leftovers to work tomorrow."

He put a pot of water on to boil and got out a box of macaroni. She loved how at ease the situation felt.

"This kitchen is so homey."

He paused a minute to look at the room as if he hadn't noticed it in a while. "This is my grandma's kitchen. She died last year. She was ninety-nine."

"I'm so sorry."

He looked to the floor. "She was my sunshine."

Claire's throat tightened. Billy continued to surprise her.

He shook his head as though needing to dispel the memory. "I offered to update her kitchen, but she liked it this way. And so . . . I like it this way too."

She knew the next question would sound like she was fishing for information—for the wrong reason. Claire asked it anyway. "Does your wife--?"

"I'm not married anymore. She died."

"Gracious. I'm so sorry."

"Me too." He turned away to check the water on the stove. "We were driving to Chicago for a fun weekend. Hit a patch of ice and . . ."

Claire filled in the rest. "How long ago?"

He turned around to face her. "Nine years. In the years between then and now I thought about remarrying, or rather I thought about thinking about remarrying a few times, but one year flowed into the next. Besides, I was busy bringing up our son."

"You have a boy?"

"He just graduated with his masters." He shrugged. "So that's me. Just turned sixty and living in my grandma's house. Pretty pitiful."

"Not at all," she said. "I just turned sixty too. Last Thursday." She finished grating the cheese.

"Happy birthday to us."

"Happy birthday to us," she repeated. "But did you—are you having trouble accepting it? I was married for twenty years but have been divorced for fifteen. Unlike you, I never had kids. I'm sixty and all alone."

The water started to boil and Billy dropped the macaroni in, placing a wooden spoon across the top of the pan.

"What's the spoon for?"

"It prevents the water from boiling over the top. Grandma taught me." He set a timer shaped like an owl, took out another saucepan, and put the cheese and milk in it. He stood nearby with a spoon, ready to stir. "Do you ever regret not having children?" he asked.

"All the time. Ron and I tried, but it never happened. And he didn't want to adopt and then he informed me that children wouldn't fit into his lifestyle anyway. That just killed me." *I can't believe I'm telling him all this.* "I shut down after that. He had an affair and we decided to go our separate ways. It was for the best." He shook his head and she realized she'd given him another trite answer. "I need to stop saying things that minimize their importance."

"Don't be so hard on yourself. Your 'God closes a door and opens a window' line was right-on. I believe it. I just haven't seen the window yet."

She chuckled. "It's hard to be patient. But I definitely believe it will reveal itself."

"Why?"

Claire was struck dumb a moment, realizing that God had just presented her with an opening to talk about Him. She didn't want to make the same mistake as before. *Please give me the words Billy needs to hear.*

She remembered a verse that had sustained her through the years—and paraphrased it. "God promises He *will* fulfill His purpose in each of us. Not *might.* Will. Closed doors and open windows are a part of that."

He stirred the cheese in silence. "You truly believe that?"

"A thousand percent."

He glanced over his shoulder at her. "But what if I don't have a purpose?"

"Not possible," she said. "God didn't create you and *then* think of something for you to do. There's a reason for each of us being here, in this time. We have control over *where* we live, but time . . . He has control over *when* we live."

"I like the sounds of that, but how do you know it's true?"

"Nothing like being put on the spot."

"Sorry. I just—"

"I know it's true because the Bible says it's true."

"You believe some book?"

"It's not *some* book. It's *the* Book. It's the Word of God, the words *of* God, written down for all time. It's our guidebook for living."

"Hmm." He stirred some more.

She threw the cheese wrappers away. "People spend bazillions of dollars on self-help books, trying to find themselves, become better people, be healthier and smarter. The Bible's been around for two thousand years, and gives timeless answers that help us from the inside out."

"You're a Jesus-freak."

She hated that term. "I'm a Jesus-lover. His follower. His child." She couldn't believe she was saying all this. She wasn't used to being so openly Christian.

But I've called you to be just that. Don't back down now.

And so she said, "Did you know that God brought us together. You and me?"

His eyebrows rose. "He did?"

She nodded. Her throat was dry. "At the art fair my friend Michelle and I prayed about who would win the mosaic, asking God to choose." She hesitated. "You won."

"So I was chosen by God to get your mosaic? It's that important?"

If you put it that way . . . "I'm not sure the mosaic is important, but you and I meeting is important."

He laughed. "You don't say."

Claire felt herself redden. It sounded presumptuous and bizarre.

The timer went off.

Although it was another trite truism, Claire truly felt saved by the bell.

The meal was prepared and they ate together at the tiny kitchen table. It wobbled. There was no more talk of God and purpose. Conversation veered to favorite TV shows and the best places to vacation. To safe subjects that helped them get to know each other.

They even washed dishes side by side. Having his upper arm skim hers. Smelling his musty working-man scent . . .

"Thank you for dinner," she said as she wiped the last plate. "It was fabulous."

"Thanks to Grandma. It's one of her recipes." He dried his hands and opened a cabinet, taking out a file box. "These are her stash. Each time I make one it brings back a memory."

"Are your parents still in town?"

He shook his head. "They moved to Arizona." He picked out a card. "Grits casserole. Yum."

"Grits? We're not in the South." She looked at the card which was written in a lovely cursive.

"Grits and sausage and eggs. It's a favorite. I'll make it for you some time."

"I'd like that."

He put the recipe box away, then faced her. "I'm almost glad you misspoke and made me mad."

"Why?"

"Because if you hadn't . . . Thank you for coming over, Claire. This kitchen was desperate for some lively conversation and homestyle cooking I could share."

She was touched. "Next time, my house?"

His smile was as sunny as the room. "I'll be there."

**

Claire came home to find Michelle eating a plate of leftover lasagna. "Where have you been?"

"Sorry. I should have left a note or called."

"I texted you. You didn't answer."

Claire checked her phone. Sure enough, there were two texts from Michelle. "Sorry again. I didn't hear my phone bing."

"Because . . .?"

She told Michelle about apologizing to Billy and their dinner together.

"Can you get me the recipe?"

"*That's* what you get out of my story?"

"It *is* mac and cheese. Priorities." Michelle rinsed her dish and put it in the dishwasher. "You like him a lot, don't you?"

That's what I *get out of my story.* "I didn't at first—at all. But getting to know him, knowing that God brought us together..."

"You think God got you together for romantic reasons?"

It was complicated. "There can be purpose *and* romance, can't there?"

Michelle closed the dishwasher and filled the lasagna pan with water to soak. "When was the last time you had a beau?"

Claire chuckled. "I'm not sure I've ever had a beau."

"You know what I mean."

"My last 'date' was in December 1869."

"Ha."

"I'm too independent for relationships. I like being single."

Michelle gave her a challenging look.

It was too soon to argue.

Chapter 10

Ryan

"In everything I did,
I showed you that by this kind of hard work
we must help the weak, remembering the words
the Lord Jesus himself said:
'It is more blessed to give than to receive.'"
Acts 20: 35

As usual, Ryan woke up early. It was barely six.

He left the couch where he'd slept, used the bathroom, then went outside and took a stroll. A slight breeze made the grasses dance, but the temperature already hinted of heat in the nineties. He'd grown up dependent on air conditioners yet since living on the road, his body had grown used to the extremes of hot and cold.

He stood in the drive and looked east toward the highway. He couldn't see it, couldn't hear any traffic at all. The only sounds were the soft drone of crickets and the wake-up call of birds flying overhead. The sky in the east showed layers of pink and purple blending into a swath of blue.

He closed his eyes. *This is a day that the Lord has made, let us rejoice and be glad in it.*

On the way back to the house he noticed a pile of cut logs for the heating stove. They had no covering or protection from rain or snow. He imagined Lisa trudging out in bad weather to gather fuel. *I can fix this.*

He went to the barn to find supplies but saw that the slats of the door were deteriorated, the bottom six-inches rotted away. Rusty hinges hung precariously.

I can fix this too.

He spotted some boards piled against a wall. Perfect. On the workbench were coffee cans full of nails and screws, and hand tools. A hand-saw hung from a nail on the wall.

He set to work.

**

A shadow moved across the workbench. Ryan looked up and saw Lisa standing in the doorway of the barn. "'Morning, Lisa."

"Hi," she said. "Where's the door?"

He blew some sawdust off the board he'd just cut. "It's over there on the sawhorses. I'm repairing the bad slats. And then I'm going to make you a surprise."

Her brown eyes lit up. "Really?"

Lisa came to the workbench and looked at what he was doing. "Can I help?"

"Sure. I was just about to replace the old board with a new one." Even though Ryan could have done it himself, he let her help. He fondly remembered his dad letting him help with projects.

He removed the first slat and screwed in the new one while Lisa held it in place.

"That looks nice," she said. "Maybe this will keep the racoons out."

Ryan noticed the hinges. "I know something else you could do to help. If I get these hinges off the door, can you go scrub the rust off of them? There's a wire brush on the workbench."

"I could do that." She began to leave then asked, "You want some coffee and a Pop Tart?"

"That would be great."

A few minutes later she returned with breakfast and a can of paint. "For the door. I told Grandpa what you're doing and he told me this was under the sink. He said there should be some brushes on the bench."

"There are. Thanks."

They heard coughing coming from the house. "I'd better get back. I'll scrub those hinges for you."

Ryan took a break and placed a three-legged stool in the fresh air. He ate the blueberry Pop Tart. His favorite kind. He was already sweating, already tired. His arm muscles objected to the sawing. Yet it was a good kind of tired. There was nothing better than being where he was supposed to be, doing what he was supposed to do.

**

"Time for lunch," Lisa called.

Ryan carried three more boards out of the barn, ready to start his surprise. The barn was too stifling in the noonday heat. If he'd been alone he would have taken off his tee-shirt but that wasn't an option with a little girl around.

Lisa helped Grandpa to a chair on the porch, then went inside and brought out three paper plates and a microwave tray holding a dozen pizza rolls. Grandpa took four. Ryan could have eaten all twelve.

"Careful, they're hot."

Grandpa nodded. "Water, girl."

"Sorry. I forgot." She came back with three glasses of water, then sat on the edge of the porch and let Ryan have the other chair.

Ryan took three of the rolls. "Grandpa can have my extra one."

"Don't mind if I do."

Then Ryan remembered Summer's care package. "I'll be right back." He returned with three apples and a bag of cookies. "Ta da!"

Grandpa took the apple but his eyes were on the cookies. "What kind?"

"Oatmeal raisin."

"I believe I could eat one or two of those."

Thank you, Summer. Ryan passed him the bag. "Take three. You can save one for later."

Grandpa took three. They finished eating and Lisa took the plates to the garbage can by the wood pile.

Grandpa took a deep breath. "Hot as Hades out here, but it's worse inside." He squirmed in the chair. He clearly wasn't comfortable.

Ryan got an idea. "Lisa, hold the door open." He went inside and carried Grandpa's rocker out to the porch. "You might as well be comfortable. I can bring it back inside whenever you want."

Grandpa stared at it a moment, then looked to Ryan. "That's mighty kind of you. Help me sit."

Ryan helped him into his rocker. Grandpa immediately rocked up and back. "Yeah. This hits the spot. Now give me my cookies."

**

Grandpa seemed to enjoy his place on the porch because he could oversee the building of a wood box—the surprise. Lisa helped for a while, but during the final hour she complained about being tired and retreated to the porch steps. "I'm done in. Really done in. Can't work no more."

Ryan was tired too but there was painting left to do. He stirred the paint and began. The color was barn red. "You rest, Lisa. I enjoy painting. In fact, it's the best part."

"Really?" Lisa said.

He immediately thought of *Tom Sawyer*. "I'm not sure you *could* do it. It takes a lot of skill."

She bit a fingernail. "Yeah. It's work. And I'm real tired."

Ryan sighed. "Too bad. You don't get to do this every day." Just like Tom in the novel, Ryan began to meticulously paint a board like an artist creating a masterpiece.

Lisa watched a few minutes, then stood. "I think I could do that."

"I don't think so." Ryan stood up, shaking his head. He caught Grandpa's eye and they shared a grin.

"I think Ryan's right, girl. Painting is meticulous work and since Ryan built it, he deserves the pleasure of painting it."

"But I helped. I helped a lot. You saw me, Grandpa. And I cleaned the hinges for the door too." Lisa strolled close. "When we're done I'll clean the brushes. Just let me have a go at it."

"Well . . . maybe I can teach you. But you have to be real careful and do it right."

"I will. You'll see."

Ryan handed Lisa the brush and gave her a few instructions. Then he went to the porch and took a seat.

"Nice work on that," Grandpa said. "You did a real Tom Sawyer on her."

"Who's Tom Sawyer?" Lisa asked.

"You've never read that book?" Ryan asked.

"Huh-uh."

"He's a boy who got others to do his work by pretending the work was special."

Lisa stopped mid-stroke. "Did you do that to me?"

Ryan smiled. "I believe I did."

"Hey!" Lisa said. "That's not fair."

"Seems fair to me," Grandpa said. "Quit yer bellyaching and finish the job."

She went back to painting, muttering under her breath.

Grandpa winked at Ryan. "I've always loved Mark Twain. Quoted this next one quite a few times over the years." He cleared his throat. "'Work consists of whatever a body is *obliged* to do. Play consists of whatever a body is not obliged to do.'"

"That's a good one," Ryan said. "How about . . . 'It is curious that physical courage should be so common in the world and moral courage so rare.'"

"Now you've gone deep on me."

"Is that a bad thing?"

Grandpa rocked up and back. "Just a rare thing. The trouble with being sick and living out here in the boonies is that I don't see much that's going on. I don't think as much as I should either—not that I ever tired myself with too much thinking in the first place."

Ryan chuckled. "Now *that* sounds like something Twain would say."

Grandpa thought about it a second then added his own chuckle. "Well, I'll be. I'm a wit and didn't even know it."

"Hey, you two." Lisa looked up from her painting. "Don't have fun without me."

"We wouldn't dare. Finish up, girl."

**

Lisa worked hard with the painting and was doing a good job. Which made Ryan want to do something special for her.

When he went inside to use the bathroom, he took a detour to the kitchen. They'd eaten junk food for two meals. If they had a few basic ingredients he might be able to whip up a proper dinner.

The fridge was mostly bare but for ketchup, mustard, dill pickles, and margarine. The freezer portion had frozen waffles, store-brand popsicles, and a few grocery-wrapped portions of hamburger. He took one out. It was just over a pound. He looked in the cupboard and saw some dry cereal, a half loaf of bread, a jar of applesauce, a box of instant pudding, some dry spaghetti, and a bag of white rice. And some soup. He spotted cream of mushroom and knew exactly what he would make.

**

"Whatcha doing in there, Ryan?" Grandpa called from the porch.

"I'm making dinner."

"When will it be done? I'm hungry."

"Hold your horses, it'll be ready soon."

A few minutes later Lisa came in with her dirty paint brush to wash in the sink. "You're cooking?"

"I am. I thought it was the least I could do since you were painting."

She looked at the pot on the stove. "What is it?"

"Patience, kiddo."

She was cleaning out her brush when they heard Grandpa's uneven gait on the porch. Ryan rushed to help him inside.

"I could smell it," he said, eying the kitchen. "My Martha used to say, 'cook it till it smells.'"

"That's a good rule." Ryan led him to the table—which he'd already set for dinner.

Grandpa picked up a paper napkin and touched his plate. "Fancy."

If you can call plastic dishes fancy.

Lisa finished with the brush, setting it upside down to drain. "Can I help?"

"Of course. Butter that bread. Then sprinkle some of that garlic salt on it—not too much."

She eyed the spice jar. "Where did you find this?"

"In the back of the cupboard. You probably couldn't see it. Now, Lawry's garlic salt is best for this 'cuz it has some other spices in it, but plain garlic salt will do."

Ryan set bowls of applesauce near each place. As soon as Lisa was done, he put the cookie sheet of bread in the oven under the broiler.

"You're broiling bread? Why not use the toaster?"

He leaned toward her confidentially. "It's magic. It turns regular bread into garlic bread. Have you ever had broiled peanut butter bread?"

"Nope."

"It's fantastic. Now go sit. I'll get the rest."

In minutes the bread was toasty. He put it on a plate, then on the table. He spooned the main dish into a plastic mixing bowl. "Dinner is served." He set the bowl on the table, sat, then held out his hands to say grace. He was glad when they went along. "We thank you, Lord, for happy hearts, for rain and sunny weather. We thank you, Lord, for this our food, and that we are together. Amen."

They let go of hands. "Hmph," Grandpa said.

"Those words were kind of pretty," Lisa said.

"I grew up saying them." He held the bowl of hamburger and rice casserole for Grandpa. "And this is my mother's recipe. When I was little she was a single mom and we didn't have much money. This was a favorite. I didn't add salt just in case you . . ." He shrugged.

"No one's told me not to use it." Grandpa added salt and took a bite. "That's right tasty. You made this from what we had?"

"Only three ingredients." He passed the bread.

Lisa took a bite. "Broiling the bread does make it special."

Grandpa snarfed down his meal like he hadn't eaten in a week. There were no leftovers. He leaned back and patted his stomach. "That was scrumdiddlyumptious."

"We're not done yet. One more surprise." Ryan got up and took three bowls of chocolate pudding out of the fridge. He loved seeing their eyes widen with pleasure.

"Oh my," Grandpa said. "Such a treat."

"This was up there too?"

"It was," Ryan said, "Behind some stuff. If you want to, we can reorganize the food and move things so you can reach them."

Grandpa savored a spoonful, closing his eyes. "Mmm."

Lisa took a bite and mimicked him. "Mmm."

Ryan did the same. Laughter was the best dessert.

**

After they were done eating, Ryan and Lisa talked about their favorite desserts. Lisa chose Hostess cupcakes and Ryan chose key lime pie—which Lisa had never heard of. "Grandpa, what's your fav—"

Grandpa had his chin down. He was dozing in the kitchen chair.

"I'll go get his rocker," Ryan whispered.

But as the screen door squeaked open, Grandpa woke up.

"I'm getting your chair."

"No need to move it back and forth," Grandpa said. "I'd rather use it outside when it's hot in the daytime. And by evening . . . I go to bed early." He began to cough and held out an arm for Lisa to help him to bed. "'Night, boy. Thanks for the meal."

Lisa spoke over her shoulder. "Wait on the dishes. I'll help."

The respite gave him time to close his own eyes. Being so busy during the day made him feel guilty for ignoring his Bible time that morning. *Sorry about that. But thanks for bringing me here. Show me how I can help beyond chores and a meal. It's no coincidence her name is Lisa.* He thought of his late sister, her troubles, her death.

Lisa came out of Grandpa's room. "He said to tell you he's going to sleep full and happy."

"I'm glad." He began clearing the table and she helped. "Wash or dry?"

"Dry," she said.

Standing side by side at the sink brought back a memory. "What grade are you going into?"

"Sixth."

"What's the capitol of Minnesota?"

"St. Paul. Is this a quiz?"

"Sort of. My mom used to do this when we did dishes. How about . . . Georgia?"

"Atlanta."

"Colorado?"

"Denver. Give me a hard one."

He thought a moment. "Vermont."

She stopped drying. "Uh . . . I didn't mean that hard."

"Montpelier."

"I knew that!"

"Sure you did. . ." Ryan relished their banter. This Lisa would have liked his Lisa.

And vice versa.

Chapter 11

Summer

"The appetite of laborers works for them;
their hunger drives them on."
Proverbs 16: 26

Summer went to work at the floral shop. "I'm here!" she called out.

Candy appeared from the back room. Her face was stormy. She put her hands on her hips.

"Uh-oh. Did I do something wrong?"

"Pretty much."

Summer tried to think of what it might be. Yesterday she got the deliveries to all the right people. She knew she did. "What happened?"

"You delivered the sunflowers to the Rollins' home?"

"I did. They weren't home so I left them by the door. Wasn't that right? I called you a few times to ask what to do but the line was busy."

"Leaving them is fine, but leaving them right in *front* of the door so people can't get them without tipping them over is not fine. Leaving them on the porch floor where their cat ate the flowers and got sick all over their house is not fine."

The scenario was vivid. "I'm so sorry. I should have thought of contingencies."

"You should have put them on a porch table or taken them to a neighbor and left a note . . . not what you did."

If only I could do it over again. "I apologize. You can dock my pay to make them another arrangement."

"Thank you, but not the point." Candy went back to the workroom.

That was a close one.

Andy came out from the back to get the keys to the van. Summer was sure he'd overheard.

"Don't sweat it," he said under his breath. "I've blown a couple deliveries myself."

That did not give her comfort.

**

After Candy's reprimand, Summer didn't feel like eating much for lunch so she bought a latte and a scone at the Coffee Break Cafe. Trying to make herself feel better, she sat with her back to the wall so she could look out over the place to scout for possible connections. "Connections" was an odd term, but it was the word that always came to mind when she thought about her new calling.

There were two people on their laptops, immersed in their work. Three others were on their phones either texting, reading, or talking. The only interaction seemed to be at the counter between the clerks and the customers.

And then she saw it: *Help wanted.*

Within a few seconds Summer went from *why not?* to standing in line.

When it was her turn she asked, "I'd like to apply for a job? Can I fill out an application?"

She was referred to a forty-something man who looked relieved. He led her to a table and sat down with a moan. "Oomph. Sitting feels good." He held out his hand. "The name's Dennis Swanson. I'm the owner. And you are?"

"Summer Peerbaugh. Depending on the hours, I'd like a job."

"Few people like the hours, which is why I find it hard to keep positions filled. I need someone to fill the six to nine slot. You'd have to be here about five-thirty. In the morning."

Yikes.

Dennis lifted up a hand. "I know that's way early, but obviously a coffee shop is a morning place. We don't have a drive-through so people come in. Sometimes the line is out the door."

A line. With lots of people. People she could interact with.

Summer sat up straighter. "The early hours don't bother me, but I can't work past eight because my other job starts at nine, and in between I'd have to zip home to let my dog out."

He cocked his head. "You have another job?"

"Two. I work at Flora & Funna in the daytime, and work the dinner shift at Happy Trails."

"I'm impressed. You're the kind of worker I need, Miss Peerbaugh. Eight it is. Can you come in tomorrow to train and help where you can?"

"Of course."

She went back to the floral shop feeling better.

**

That night Summer couldn't sleep. She was excited about her new job. She glanced at the clock on her bedside table. It was nearly midnight and her alarm was set for 4: 45.

Maybe if she moved around a little she'd be able to relax.

She got out of bed, being careful not to disturb Suzu. She slipped out to the balcony to enjoy the cooler night air—cooler, meaning eighty, not ninety-five. She sat on her chair and put her feet on the railing.

But then she saw movement.

Someone was walking near the building of Happy Trails, next to the bushes. They were sneaking around and wore dark pants and a hooded sweatshirt.

In this heat?

This was no can't-sleep stroll or emergency dog walk. They were clearly up to no good.

Yet she knew the building was locked up tight at night. Even during the day you needed a pass card or had to call the front desk to have someone buzz you in.

The man wasn't walking toward the front or even the side door. He walked toward the back where they got shipments. Where the kitchen door was located.

Summer slipped from her chair to the floor of the balcony to stay hidden. She peered through the railing.

Then she saw the lid to the dumpster open. The man carefully opened it fully without a bit of clanging. Once the lid was out of the way he moved a few crates close, climbed up, dropped one crate and a duffel bag inside, then scrambled over the top.

A dumpster-diver at this time of night?

It was hard to see what was going on as the person was black against the dark green of the dumpster, but a few minutes later, he emerged with the duffel bag. He dropped it to the ground, got out of the dumpster, reached in and retrieved the crate he'd put inside, and put everything back where it belonged. It was quite ingenious, and it was clear this wasn't the first time he'd done it.

Summer watched as the man walked quickly across the street, then away.

He must be really hungry.

Summer took a moment to say a prayer for the man *and* count her own blessings.

Chapter 12

Michelle

"Hear this, all you peoples;
listen, all who live in this world,
both low and high, rich and poor alike:
My mouth will speak words of wisdom;
the meditation of my heart will give you understanding."
Psalm 49: 1-3

Dinner was a cheesy meatball casserole—another hit. Claire was easy to cook for and she complimented Michelle on everything she made. She helped clean up too—an extra bonus as Michelle was a messy cook.

But tonight Michelle told Claire to go read or relax, she'd handle the cleanup. She watched her go out to the patio with a book. Meaning Michelle had the house to herself.

Even after being here a few days it still hit her. She was living in a house. A real house.

A home.

She began washing dishes, enjoying the feel of hot water and suds. Of cleaning. Of rinsing away all that was dirty.

As Christ cleansed me and rinsed away all that was dirty.

She nodded at the thought from Him. Other people might say she was being presumptuous believing these snippets of conversation were from God, but they were wrong. The words *were* from God. She knew it. She felt it.

"It's just You and me, Lord."

It was an oft-repeated statement of fact. Yes, Michelle shared a home with Claire now. Yes, Michelle had jobs at the Nearly New shop and the shelter. Yes, she was around people most of the time. Yet she wasn't close to anybody, not deep down where her soul lived. That spot was reserved for Jesus. He was her

Savior, Christ, Lord, King, and Master. She didn't need or desire anyone else. People would come and go, but Jesus remained.

She finished cleaning up and turned out the light. A lamp was on in the living room and she paused to enjoy its glow, the warm shadows, and the cozy feel of the scene. It reminded her of her childhood home in Denver. Her parents hadn't been wealthy but her mother had liked pretty things and was good at creating homey spaces. Michelle had always felt loved and safe and blessed.

Blessed. Her thoughts moved from her childhood to another chapter in her long-ago life: her husband.

Once grown she'd earned a drama degree and had been hired at the first high school where she'd applied. There, she'd met a teacher named Sergei. They married. They were happy.

He died a hero.

"Penny for your thoughts?"

Michelle saw Claire standing nearby. "My memories caught up with me."

"Memories of . . .?"

"Childhood. And Sergei."

Claire set her book on the coffee table and sat in her usual spot on the couch. "Sergei Leonid Jofsky. Your lovely Ukrainian. Isn't that what you called him?"

"It is." Michelle smiled at the mental image of him: his dark hair that was always tousled no matter how hard he tried to tame it, his chiseled chin with its dimple, his bright smile. And his lovely accent. When he said *Michelle . . .*

She sat on the loveseat. She hadn't thought about him in far too long. "I know it was a lifetime ago, but I still miss him."

"Of course you do. He had a lasting impact on you—and on others."

She nodded. "His students loved him, and he, them." Her memories of Sergei lingered. "He was everything I'm not: patient, generous, kind."

"You're all those things."

"I'm all those things *now*. He made me a better person."

"What a lovely thing to say."

"It's the truth."

Claire tucked her bare feet under a pillow. "I know you don't talk about it much, but I can't imagine the heartache you've been through. I chose to end my marriage. You had it ripped away from you."

The wound flared from its dull slumber.

"Weren't you thirty-something when you lost him?"

Michelle nodded once. "It was a long journey. I was a bitter woman for a long time. I tested God. A lot. But after He got my attention I moved into an efficiency apartment, filled with the minimum. Why did I need two chairs when I was alone? Why did I need four place-settings when I only used one plate at a time?"

Claire looked toward her kitchen. "I have less than I used to but still more than I need. Maybe I should . . ."

Michelle raised a hand. "I will not be responsible for you purging for charity again."

"Fine. I'll restrain myself—for now."

Michelle slumped on the cushions until her head was supported. "One time when I was sick Mom came over and called me a recluse."

"Was she right?"

"Sort of. I didn't take offense because I knew my choices were hard to understand. But I wasn't a recluse. I was a seeker, seeking meaning." She wasn't used to talking about herself so much. "A seeker like you were in Steadfast."

Claire didn't bite. "Not many people would be able to dedicate their lives to helping the same group of people who killed their husband."

She knew it was odd. "When I was in need a shelter gave me a minimum wage job. I felt useful there."

"Feeling useful means a lot, doesn't it?"

"Without purpose we barely exist."

Claire fluffed a decorative pillow. "Aren't you glad God gave us this new calling and purpose?"

"I am." *You have a purpose. You have a calling. I'm not so sure.*

Claire stood. "All emotional discussions need to end with ice cream. Want some?"

Michelle was glad to let the past go. "Two scoops please."

**

Emails.

Michelle awakened with the word on her mind. Emails?

She turned over to go back to sleep.

Encourage them.

She sat up in bed. When the Almighty talked, she listened. "You want me to encourage someone with an email?"

And then she knew it wasn't just some*one* but many: Ryan, Summer, Jered, and even Claire.

But what should she say? *How ya doing?* That wasn't inspiring.

Use My words.

Of course! Michelle threw back the covers, grabbed the paper that had all their contact info on it, and tiptoed into Claire's office off the foyer. Claire had told her she could use the computer whenever she wanted to. So Michelle logged onto her own account and created an email.

Luckily, she knew her way around a computer from creating flyers and posters for the shelter and the shop. She opened up her favorite image-store, found a closeup photo of two pink daisies, and bought it. Within a few minutes she'd added a verse to the image—a meaningful verse for four people just starting to live out their calling. *Mark 10: 27, "Jesus looked at them and said, 'With man this is impossible, but not with God; all things are possible with God.'"*

"How's that, Lord?"

Michelle felt Him smile.

She hit SEND.

Chapter 13

Claire

"No temptation has overtaken you
except what is common to mankind.
And God is faithful; he will not let you be tempted beyond
what you can bear. But when you are tempted,
he will also provide a way out so that you can endure it."
1 Corinthians 10: 13

Claire pushed her bowl of oatmeal aside and checked her phone for the umpteenth time. No emails or missed calls from Billy.

"Did you get an email from me?" Michelle asked.

She found one. "Ooh. Pretty. Nice verse too. You sent this in the middle of the night?"

"God wouldn't let me sleep."

"I hate when He does that."

"I don't, because He always has a good reason."

Claire admired Michelle's constant faith. Her own seemed more variable—especially when it came to Billy.

She turned her phone over so she couldn't see the screen. "Nothing from Billy. I need to stop looking. I'm acting like a teenager."

"You could call him. This isn't the Fifties."

"I could, but I'd rather not." She realized she *was* employing a bit of faith. "I want to leave this out of my hands. If God's truly behind this, we'll be shoved together."

"You're testing the Almighty God, Maker of the Universe?"

So much for that. "Kinda. Isn't that all right?"

Michelle shook her head. "'Do not put the Lord your God to the test.'"

Claire set her keys down. This was getting confusing. "I believe Billy and I were supposed to meet. I just don't want my own will—my hormones—to push our relationship in the wrong direction. Me calling Billy is pushing *my* agenda. Isn't it?"

"I guess." Michelle poured herself another cup of coffee. "You backing away *would* make it more powerful if God continued to bring you together."

"Without me pushing."

"Without you pushing."

Claire didn't want to talk about it anymore. She put her bowl and spoon in the dishwasher, grabbed her purse and phone, and went out to her car—which was full of more donations to the Nearly New Shop. Michelle's previous mention of one chair and one place setting in her old apartment *had* spurred Claire to go through her closet. Again. Odd how she could always find something to donate.

Michelle took her own car and led the way.

They both parked in back—or tried to. A black pickup was parked there with a magnetic sign on its door: The Handy Man. A sawhorse and some lengths of wood were set up nearby, a circular saw sitting on the ground. Claire loved the smell of sawdust.

She opened her trunk but nodded at the truck. "What's being fixed?"

"Not fixed exactly," Michelle said, taking a bag of shoes from the trunk. "We're having more racks installed. We need more shelves for décor and craft items. Kitchenware. We're overflowing right now, can't even put everything out that's been donated."

"That's a nice problem to have." Claire gathered ten hangers and draped the blouses and sweaters over her arm. She shut the trunk. They went in the back way and Claire heard an electric screwdriver out front. They deposited her new arrivals on a rack in the storeroom.

"Let me show you what we're doing," Michelle said.

She led the way out front, said hi to the woman working the counter, then walked toward the wall where shelves were being built.

"Looking nice," she said to the man who was on his knees, getting ready to screw in a lower support.

"Thanks," he said. He looked up. He grinned. He stood. "Claire? What are you doing here?"

Claire's heart skipped a beat. "I could ask the same of you, Billy."

"Billy?" Michelle said. "You're Billy?"

"You've heard of me?"

She glanced at Claire and winked. "In passing."

Claire felt her cheeks redden. "Michelle, aren't there some customers you can help?"

Michelle's eyes darted between them. "I think I can find a few." She bobbed twice on her toes and left them alone.

"I can't believe this," Claire said under her breath.

"Believe what?"

She hadn't meant for him to hear. Instead of explaining she said, "Want to come to dinner tonight? Michelle's a great cook."

"You live together?"

"She just moved in."

He studied her a moment, smiling. "I'd love to come. How about I bring my grandma's apple crisp?"

**

"Are you sure you want me to stay for dinner?" Michelle asked Claire. "Three's a crowd?"

Claire was torn. She wanted to be alone with Billy yet wanted the buffer that Michelle would provide.

The buffer won out. "Please stay. I mean it."

"If you want me to make myself scarce just scratch your nose or something."

"What if I really need to scratch my nose?"

"Look away before you do it?" Michelle stirred the hamburger that was browning on the stove.

When the doorbell rang, Claire's stomach did a backflip. "Here goes nothing."

"Here goes everything," Michelle said.

Billy entered carrying a bouquet of flowers in one hand and an insulated casserole carrier in the other. Hanging from his arm was a plastic grocery sack.

"Here," he said, handing her the flowers. "For you—and the cook."

A mix of pink roses, baby's breath, and white daisies. Did God direct him to buy these particular flowers?

"I figured you liked pink roses and daisies," he said. "You put them in the mosaic."

She laughed. "They're very pretty. Come in."

His eyes swept upward to the beamed ceiling of the great room. "Wow. That's a lot of cubic feet there."

She felt embarrassed for it. Although she'd only seen the kitchen of his house, she could easily guess the living room was small. She led him to the kitchen.

He set his carrier and bag on the counter. "Your island is the size of my kitchen."

She peeked in the bag. "I see ice cream."

"It's a necessity on hot apple crisp." He greeted Michelle then put it in the freezer.

Claire found a vase for the flowers. "Look, Michelle. Pink roses and daisies."

She grinned. "How appropriate."

Claire was amused he was using a casserole carrier—it was so domestic. "It's yellow."

"Grandma's favorite color."

Claire explained to Michelle. "Her kitchen is aglow with sunshine yellow."

"Sounds pretty."

Billy looked toward the stove. "What are we having?"

"Enchilada casserole. I need help putting it together." Michelle poured a big can of enchilada sauce in a bowl and put Mexican cheese in another. She opened a bag of small corn tortillas. "Dip them in the sauce, put them all over the bottom of the baking dish, then layer with meat and cheese multiple times."

"Simple enough," Billy said. "I'll do the messy part. You can do the spooning."

Working beside Billy was completely natural. Almost too perfect.

Lord? I'm supposed to be helping people, not falling for a man.

"Cheese?" Billy asked.

She'd been caught up in her doubts. "Sorry."

"Is something wrong?"

His eyes were a beautiful gray blue. The crinkles at their corners revealed a lifetime of experiences and emotions.

Emotions. That was the trouble. Claire wasn't comfortable feeling this many emotions. "If you'll excuse me a minute?"

She retreated to the master bathroom, sat on the bench at her dressing table, and wrapped her arms around herself. "God? I don't understand what's happening. You've called me to help people, and I thought You sent me to Billy, but the feelings I'm having for him—strong feelings—are going to get in the way of whatever God-thing I'm supposed to do to help him. How can I lead him to You if I'm focused on his gorgeous eyes and irresistible personality?"

Claire caught a glimpse of herself in the mirror. The wrinkle between her eyebrows was pronounced. Her frown lines made her look ten years older.

She knew what to do.

She strode into the kitchen, where Michelle was putting the casserole in the oven.

"Finished it without you," Billy said.

Was that a perfect line or what? She stood at the edge of the island. "I can't do this."

"This?" Michelle asked.

Claire's heart pounded in her chest as she looked at Billy. "I can't do this." She motioned from him to herself. "I can't get involved with you."

"Was anyone asking you to?" he said.

She felt her face redden. "No, but I . . . I can't risk it."

He put his hands in his pockets. "Relationships are always risky."

She couldn't look at him. She grabbed a stack of mail and began to sort it into random piles. "I've been asked to do something special and—"

Michelle stopped her busy hands. "You still can."

Can I?

Billy stepped forward until the island stood between them. "You told me God brought us together. I thought that was a little out-there, but I like the sounds of it. So what are you doing?"

"Yes," Michelle asked. "What *are* you doing?"

What am *I doing? What have I done?*

She imagined a stone being thrown into a lake, causing ripples to radiate outwards. She couldn't undo the toss. She couldn't smooth out the ripples.

He motioned toward the door. "Would you like me to leave?"

Her heart warred with her head. "Not really."

He sighed deeply. "We're just having dinner, Claire. I'm not asking you to elope to Tanzania or anything."

She smiled. He was right, and yet . . .

He studied her a moment, then nodded to himself. "You want to slow things down? We can do that." He glanced at the counter. "Enjoy the dessert."

And he was gone.

The sound of the closing door echoed.

"What in heaven's name did you just do?" Michelle asked.

Claire leaned her elbows on the island, covering her face with her hands. "Argh! I don't know."

"You'd better know. You just offended a really great guy."

She stood up. "I know he's great. That's the problem. I'm falling for him. I can see us as a couple."

"Not anymore." Michelle pointed toward the living room. "Get in there. You have some explaining to do."

Claire sat on the couch and hugged a pillow. "I'm sorry to ruin the evening."

Michelle sat on a chair nearby. "Evening, schmevning. This is about your future, you turkey. God brought an amazing man into your life—a life you have lived alone for over fifteen years. You don't just throw that away."

She wanted to run after Billy, bolt down the street, screaming at his car like they did in the movies. But this wasn't a movie. This was real.

Michelle's tone softened. "You admitted—you told him and me—that God brought you together."

"I must have been wrong."

"Why do you say that?"

"Because God has sent me—sent us—on a journey to be open to His beck and call and help people."

"Getting to know Billy isn't helping him?"

"I'm on a spiritual journey and the feelings I'm having toward Billy are hardly spiritual. And I don't do love."

"Now you're being ridiculous. God *is* love. He created love."

"Yes, but . . . Billy is a distraction from the mission."

"What if he *is* the mission?"

"My love-life is not the mission. It can't be."

"So you're putting limits on God's ways? You're fencing Him into your tiny backyard when he wants to give you twenty acres? Or a thousand?"

The air went out of her. *I blew it! Oh, Father, I blew it!* Claire held the pillow against her face until she had to move it to breathe. She tossed it to the other end of the couch and put her feet on the rug. "I panicked."

"Yup."

"I made a mistake."

"Yup."

"What should I do?"

Michelle moved to the cushion beside her and put an arm around her shoulders. "You're desperate to do God's will, but you just inserted your own will by thinking the Almighty couldn't possibly be giving you something good and amazing in the middle of a mission."

That's exactly what she'd felt. "I thought important missions were hard and serious."

"They can be. But they can also be filled with joy and happy surprises." She pointed toward the door. "Billy Cumberson was a happy surprise."

"Yeah. He was. Do I call him? Apologize?" *Again.*

"Yes. But . . ." Michelle put a hand to her chest. "I suppose there *is* a minute possibility that I'm wrong and you're right."

"I doubt it."

"Maybe you should leave things as they are for a bit? God can fix your mistakes if it's important to Him. Let's see what He does."

Actually, Claire was relieved. She'd already humbled herself to Billy once. Twice might mean there'd be a third time. Three strikes and she'd be out.

Chapter 14

Ryan

"He will not let your foot slip—
he who watches over you will not slumber;
indeed, he who watches over Israel
will neither slumber nor sleep."
Psalm 121: 3-4

Ryan sat on the front porch at dawn, counting his money: $25.26. That would buy some groceries, but it wouldn't leave him much for any other contingencies.

"It will have to do," he said softly. "God provides." He stood to go back inside and saw Grandpa standing at the screen door. "Morning."

"Yes. It is. That your money or mine?"

Ryan was appalled. "It's mine. I wouldn't steal from you. I told you that."

He shrugged and pushed the door open. "Just checking."

Ryan went inside. "I was wondering if I could borrow your truck so I could get some groceries. I was seeing how much money I had."

"I got money."

"You do?"

"What made you think I don't have money?"

The lack of food, a house in need of maintenance . . .

Grandpa sat on a kitchen chair. Lisa was making coffee. "We don't have any food around here because I can't drive anymore. When Carly left, we were kinda stranded."

"When did she leave?"

Lisa had that answer. "June twenty-third."

A month without groceries? "Can't you call a friend to bring you what you need?"

"Phone's dead. Has been since February when an ice storm

brought the wires down."

Five months without a phone?

Lisa turned the coffee pot on. "Grandpa doesn't have a cell phone and he says I'm too young."

"You are." Grandpa coughed, and pointed to the bedroom. "Go get my medicine, girl."

Lisa came back with two prescription bottles. "Only two pills left."

Grandpa peered at the bottles. "You can borrow the truck. When we're in town we can get refills. And I can try to con the pharmacist into giving me some more of that good cough syrup too."

Lisa clapped. "Yay! We're all going?"

"We are. It's time to see the world."

Or Emporia, Kansas.

**

On the way to town Lisa sat in the back of the extended cab which had two seats facing the middle. Because of her location behind him, Ryan got the full effect as she chattered on about nothing and everything, obviously thrilled to get out of the house. Grandpa even cracked a few cow jokes.

"What did the mama cow say to the baby cow?"

"Grandpa, you tell that one all the time."

"I don't know it," Ryan said.

"The mama cow says, 'It's pasture bedtime.' Past-ure. Get it?"

Lisa moaned.

Grandpa had another one. "Why was the cow afraid?"

"Why?" Ryan asked.

"He was a cow-herd." Grandpa cackled. "Off to town, an udder day, an udder dollar."

Ryan wondered about the last time they'd laughed. He remembered a joke his mom had told him. "Knock."

"Who's there?" Grandpa asked.

"Cow's go."

"Cows go who?"

"No, silly, cows go *moo*."

Even Lisa laughed at that one. A few minutes later they reached the edge of town. "Where to now?"

"Turn right at the light. Let's get the medicine first."

Ryan parked at a drugstore and went around the truck to offer Grandpa a hand, but was rejected. "I can do it. I'm not dead yet."

Lisa walked to the pharmacist's counter with her grandpa. She had the near-empty pill bottles with her.

"Hello there, Mr. Pearl. We haven't seen you for a while," the pharmacist said, moving to the computer. "How's Carly?"

"Who knows?" Grandpa said. "She's run off to join the circus."

"What?"

"Might as well have," he said. "She's gone off. Somewhere."

"I'm sorry to hear that. Let me get these filled."

"I need some of that good cough medicine too."

"The one with codeine in it?"

"That's the one."

As if to reinforce that he needed the medicine, Grandpa had an awful fit of coughing. Lisa led him to a chair. When the coughing didn't stop the pharmacist handed Ryan a bottle of water.

Grandpa doubled over, nearly choking.

And then he slumped off the chair.

Onto the floor.

Passed out.

The pharmacist ran around the counter to help, but also pulled out his phone and dialed 911.

"Grandpa!"

The next few minutes were a blur. Grandpa woke up as the paramedics arrived and he was wheeled into an ambulance.

"Which hospital?" Ryan asked.

"There's only one. Follow us."

Ryan and Lisa ran to the truck. "Is he going to die?" she asked.

"He's going to get help." *Please, God. Save him!*

**

Waiting was the hard part. They shared the ER waiting area with a mother and two kids. A TV played *The Price is Right*. Seeing costumed people gleefully jumping up and down seemed wrong. Ryan got up and changed the channel to cartoons. "Is this alright?" he asked the woman.

The cartoons were a magnet, and her kids sat in front of it. "Thank you," she said.

Lisa joined the kids.

Ryan looked at the woman. Her forehead was furrowed, her eyes puffy. "Excuse me?" he said. "I don't mean to pry, but is it a family member who's hurting?"

"My husband. He was using a saw and cut himself." She began to tear up. "His hand . . ."

Ryan sat beside her. "I'm so sorry." He closed his eyes. "Father God? Please help this man's hand recover completely. Give his family comfort."

She looked over at him. "Thank you for that. I've been so worried, but I forgot to pray. Thanks for reminding me." She glanced at Lisa. "Who are you here for?"

"Her grandfather collapsed at the pharmacy. Blacked out."

"Oh dear. I'll pray for him too."

A nurse came out and looked at Ryan. "You two can go in now."

They were shown to a patient area behind a curtain. Grandpa was awake but was hooked up to an IV and an oxygen mask.

"Grandpa? Are you going to be okay?"

He extended his free hand to her. "I'll be all right. They just want to keep me overnight to do some more tests."

"Overnight? In the hospital?" She looked scared.

"That's right, girl. You've got Ryan to take you home and stay with you." He looked at Ryan. "I'm trusting you with my life, boy. Lisa's my life."

"I understand, sir. I won't let you down."

Grandpa nodded once. "By the way, I told them you're my nephew. I was afraid if I told them you were a drifter who we only met a few days ago, they'd take Lisa away."

It was a good possibility. "We'll be fine. You need to do whatever they say to get better."

"Hmm."

Was there something he wasn't telling them?

"I want you two to go now," Grandpa said. "Stop and get some groceries and go home. Ryan, give the nurses your phone number before you leave."

"We'll come back later."

Grandpa shook his head. "Tomorrow is soon enough. I'll call you later from my room."

"No, Grandpa! I want to stay."

"This is no place for you, girl. You come back tomorrow after I'm settled. Now get my wallet. It's in that bag where they put my clothes. In fact, Ryan, take it with you. I don't want it here."

Ryan found it and put it in his back pocket. "Is there anything we can get you?"

"Other than a new set of lungs? Just keep Lisa safe."

So it *was* serious "Don't worry about her. And don't worry about you either. God's got you."

Grandpa snickered. "He's got me all right."

**

"How about a frozen pizza for dinner?" Ryan asked Lisa in the grocery store.

"Okay." Her voice was flat.

What could have been a fun food-excursion had been undertaken in near-silence.

Ryan paid and they took the groceries back to the truck. Lisa rode up front and they put the groceries on the seat between them

He pulled onto the street. "How about some broiled peanut butter bread when we get home?"

"Sure."

"It will be all right, kiddo. The doctors have him. God's got him."

"You said that to Grandpa. But I don't believe it."

"Why not?"

"Why did God let him get sick? I need him."

You need Him. "Sometimes we get tested."

"Like in school?"

"Kind of. Life tests us. If everything was good all the time we wouldn't appreciate it as much."

She scoffed. "Sure we would."

"The Bible says it best. 'Consider it pure joy whenever you face trials of many kinds, because you know that the testing of your faith produces perseverance. Let perseverance finish its work so that you may be mature and complete, not lacking anything.'"

"I'm not joyful right now."

"No, but you'll be stronger for going through this. Just like you've grown stronger for handling things so well after your mom left."

Her head lowered and shook back and forth, tears brimming in her eyes. "I don't want to be tested. I don't want to be strong. I'm tired of being strong."

Ryan wanted to hug her. *Father, help me help her. Help them.*

**

Ryan noticed the blue lights of a police car flashing behind them. He glanced at the speedometer. He wasn't speeding. He was barely out of town. *Are you talking to me?*

The *whoop* of a siren was his answer. He pulled to the shoulder. The police car pulled behind him.

"What's wrong?" Lisa asked.

"I don't know."

Ryan got out his license. The officer stopped just short of his window. "Good afternoon, sir. May I see your license?"

Ryan noticed the nametag on his uniform: Barnes. He handed it over. "Is there something wrong, Officer Barnes?"

"I need to see the registration and proof of insurance, please."

Maybe. "Lisa, look in the glove compartment and see if there are any papers in there."

She pulled out a handful of papers and gave them to Ryan. Did Grandpa have current paperwork? Ryan found the latest papers, which were surprisingly up to date. "Here you go."

"You're not Allen Pearl."

"No, sir. But she's his granddaughter." He looked to Lisa.

"Hi," Lisa said.

Officer Barnes looked at her, scanning the inside of the cab. "You're Mr. Pearl's granddaughter?"

"Yeah."

He looked at Ryan. "Are you related?"

"No, sir."

"A family friend?"

Lisa piped up, "He came to live with us three days ago."

The officer's eyebrows rose. "Three days and you're driving Mr. Pearl's pickup, alone with his granddaughter?"

Ryan nearly panicked. It *did* look odd. And what could he say? That God had led him to their house? "I'm just trying to help them through a hard time," Ryan said.

"Are you sure you aren't causing the hard time?"

"No, sir. Not at all."

"God sent him," Lisa said.

Barnes tilted his head. "Oh really."

She nodded vigorously. "I had a dream about a guy named Ryan and was all worried about Grandpa and what we were going to do since my mom left, and then Ryan shows up and he helped us. He fixed the barn door and made a box for our firewood too, but I painted it. He tricked me into painting it."

"Tricked you?"

Ryan answered. "Tom Sawyer."

The officer nodded knowingly and almost smiled.

Lisa took a deep breath. "Anyway, I think God did it. God sent us Ryan."

Suddenly a dove landed on the hood of the truck. They all remained still, sharing their surprise.

You want proof of God? Look at that.

The officer stared at the bird. "Odd. You don't see doves around here."

You do if God wants you to.

The officer shooed the bird away, yet she fluttered and returned, hopping close to the windshield where she looked in.

"She seems to like this truck," the officer said.

She likes us.

"She's pretty," Lisa said. "Can we try to catch her and take her home, Ryan?"

"I don't think that's up to us," he said.

Ryan wasn't sure if it was the appearance of God's dove, or the fact that Lisa's question showed she wasn't in danger, but whatever the reason Officer Barnes seemed to soften.

"Young lady, where is your grandpa?"

"He's in the hospital. He collapsed at the pharmacy while we were getting some medicine. He's got an awful cough. An ambulance came and everything."

"They just admitted him," Ryan added.

Lisa nodded. "But Grandpa told us to go home and come back in the morning. He wanted to get settled. Ryan just bought us some groceries because we don't have hardly anything at the house. Have you ever had broiled peanut butter bread because that's what we're having for lunch."

The officer's shoulders relaxed. "I've never had the pleasure." He eyed the grocery sacks where the loaf of bread was sticking out the top. He handed the registration and license back to Ryan. "I stopped you because the right taillight is out."

Ryan's nerves quieted. "Thanks for the heads up. I'll make sure it gets fixed."

"Is there anything I can do to help the situation?" Officer Barnes asked.

Ryan was in awe. From nerves to relief in under five minutes. "I think we've got it handled." But then he thought of something. "If you're so inclined, could you pray for Mr. Pearl?"

"I'll do that. Have a good meal."

He pulled away first. Ryan took a deep breath. "Whew."

Lisa looked confused. "Were you scared or something?"

"Not scared, but nervous that I'd done something wrong without knowing it."

"My teacher said police are here to help. We can always go to them if we need something. Kind of like God," Lisa said. "We needed help and God helped."

Ryan was amazed. He'd assumed Lisa had little knowledge of the Almighty, when actually she'd seen His hand before Ryan had acknowledged it.

He put the truck into Drive. "You are so right. Kind of like God."

Chapter 15

Summer

"Humble yourselves, therefore,
under God's mighty hand,
that he may lift you up in due time.
Cast all your anxiety on him because he cares for you.
1 Peter 5: 6-7

The alarm awakened Summer at 4:45. Suzu looked up at her like she was crazy.

Maybe she was.

"You can stay in bed," Summer told the dog. Suzu did as she was told. Good dog.

Summer went to the kitchen and turned on the coffee pot. Then turned it off. She was going to work at a coffee shop. Dennis had told her free coffee was a perk of the job—a yummy perk.

She got dressed, then pulled up the bed covers, forcing Suzu out. She glanced toward her balcony. Summer remembered the man stealing food from the dumpster—"gathering" food. Did he have a family in need? Was he homeless?

Suzu came out of the bedroom, looked up at her, and yawned.

"I know. We'll both get used to it. Come on, I'll take you out then get you some breakfast."

And the day began.

**

The Coffee Break was crazy busy.

Summer was forced to learn fast. Luckily she was familiar with the variations. Whether it was espresso, latte, cappuccino, mocha, Americano, or just plain Joe, it seemed half of Carson Creek wanted some. Now.

Her desire to work at the shop in order to meet a lot of new people was fulfilled but not fulfilling. The ever-present line barred her from chatting beyond asking for a name to write on the cup. She enjoyed working with Dennis and the head barista but again, she never had time to get to know them.

Then Dennis said, "You better get going."

She wasn't sure what he was talking about until she noticed the time. It was a quarter past eight. She needed to get home, let Suzu out, and go to the flower shop.

Summer removed her apron and headed for the door.

"You did good," Dennis said.

Coffee-wise, sure. Connection-wise, she'd bombed.

She was halfway home when she realized she'd never drank any coffee.

**

Since the Coffee Break offered a constant line of customers, the calmer pace of Flora & Funna was a relief. Phone orders came in and there was a wedding that weekend, so there was just enough busyness. Yet what God-good did any of it do? She was always at the counter alone or when she was in back with Candy, her boss was all business.

It was nearly one-thirty when they had their first walk-in customer, a professionally-dressed woman in her fifties. Summer put on her best smile and greeted her. "Good afternoon, how may I help you?"

The woman strode straight to the counter. "I need arrangements for my assistants. Desk-sized. Thirty-dollars each, max."

"What's the occasion?"

"Thank you arrangements."

"How nice. What kind of business do you have?"

The woman made a huff sound but said, "Real estate. Are there some pictures of flowers to choose from?"

"Certainly." Summer took out a 3-ring notebook and turned it to the correct page. "These hydrangea arrangements are lovely. Are your assistants men or women?"

"Two of each."

"So four. How nice. You could choose something unique for each one. Your assistants might think that was special." She noticed the woman's bracelet. "I love your bracelet. Is that Navajo?"

The woman glanced at it as if she'd forgotten she was wearing it. "I have no idea. I'm in kind of a hurry here . . ."

"Certainly, Ms . . .?"

"Carlisle."

"Ms. Carlisle. A good Irish name. I would love to go to Ireland someday. I—"

The woman shoved the notebook away and turned to leave. "Never mind."

She walked out, leaving Summer shocked and silent.

Candy came out of the back room, shaking her head. "I heard. Way to go."

"What did I do wrong? I was trying to be nice and attentive." *I was trying to make a connection.*

"You completely mis-read her. Didn't you notice how she flew in here and stated what she needed in just a few words?"

Assistants. Thank you flowers. $30.

"Then you go asking about her business—which is none of *our* business considering she was in a hurry. And then you mention her bracelet? And Ireland? What was that?"

"I was being polite."

"You pounced. You were fawning."

Summer felt wounded. "I wasn't." *Was I?*

Candy closed the notebook with a slap. "Have you ever been to a restaurant where a waiter gives you too much attention? Talking too much, checking on the table too often. Why do you think they do that?"

"They . . . they want a bigger tip."

Candy touched her nose. "Bingo. They're overly nice because they want something for it. It's not sincere. It's manipulative."

"So being nice is manipulative?"

Candy gazed at Summer over her half-glasses. "You complicated things. You made the transaction difficult. You were forcing a woman who is extremely busy to make more decisions than she felt up to making. You took precious time away from her day when you could have taken orders for four arrangements in a few minutes." Candy took a fresh breath and calmed down. "I'm not telling you to be brusque, but I am asking you to be intuitive. We lost $120 in sales because you weren't."

Although Candy didn't say it, Summer felt like she'd just been given a "Strike two."

One more and she'd be out.

**

While serving dinner at Happy Trails that night, Summer was glad the men of the group were off on a fishing trip. Grandpa Wayne tended to call her out on her moods, and Mae's hubby, Collier, was always quick with advice. She didn't need logic or wisdom tonight. She needed female compassion.

It didn't take long for the ladies to sense something was wrong. Summer hadn't even taken their orders when Grandma asked, "What's going on, sweetie? You seem . . ."

"Discombobulated," Mae said.

"A silly-sounding word," Tessa said. "You seem stressed."

"Same thing," Mae said.

"No, it isn't. Discombobulated means confused and befuddled."

Tessa stirred a sugar in her tea. "Now, there's a silly-sounding word."

So much for compassion. Summer felt like she had her finger in a dike and water was beginning to seep around it.

Grandma must have seen it in her face. "Lay off, ladies. Whatever Summer's feeling, you're not helping."

"Sorry," Tessa said.

"Ditto," Mae said. "How can we help?"

Summer knew if she told them about her new job, or admitted getting in trouble with Candy, or shared her doubts about her God-given mission, the dam would break and all her emotions would flood the room and make a befuddled, discombobulated mess.

Suddenly, there was a huge crash of glasses. Someone had dropped a tray and there was a flurry of activity as it was cleaned up.

The distraction served a purpose, for with all attention diverted, Summer had a free second to collect herself and put a stopper in the dam. She could step away—for now.

"Well then," she said when the ladies turned their attention back to the menu. She even managed a smile. "What can I get for you tonight? The pasta looked really tasty . . ."

**

Despite her stiff upper lip at dinner, Summer felt emotional after she got home. Her anxiety was heightened when she read an email from Michelle. It was innocent enough: "Just checking in." It included a pretty illustration of pink daisies with a verse, Matthew 10: 27: "Jesus looked at them and said, 'With man this is impossible, but not with God; all things are possible with God.'" Summer read it again. "That's a good one," she said aloud.

She was glad no one else had responded to the email. She wasn't up to hearing about the grand conquests that Claire, Jered, or Ryan were having. Maybe not Jered. If anyone was having trouble with their calling besides Summer, it was probably him. But Ryan? He'd probably changed the lives of a dozen people and had told them all about Jesus. She hadn't met *any*one. What was wrong with her?

She sent Michelle a "Thanks" reply, then went to bed.

But her brain wouldn't shut off.

She ended up on the balcony, in the dark.

She looked for the man, but all was quiet. She bowed her head. *I'm trying to help You, Father, but nothing's happening. I got a new job, I tried to make a connection with a customer at the shop. If I'm doing something wrong, let me know. I'll try harder tomorrow. I won't let You down.*

She wished she believed her own words.

Chapter 16

Jered

"Give generously to them
and do so without a grudging heart;
then because of this
the Lord your God will bless you
in all your work and in everything you put your hand to."
Deuteronomy 15: 10

"Hello? Hello?"

Jered barely looked up when Ivy came in the house from her exercise class. "Hi," he said. He was playing defense against another player on Madden. If he wasn't careful they'd get a—

Touchdown!

She hung her purse on a hook by the door. "Sorry to interrupt the important game."

"No problem." He knew it was a snotty answer, but couldn't seem to stop himself.

The next time he noticed her, she was dressed and had gone outside to her beloved garden. She definitely had a green thumb. He knew what daisies, roses, and mums were called, but there were at least a dozen other flowers out there. She'd tried to teach him the names, but he never remembered.

A few minutes later she came in carrying an enormous bouquet. She rarely cut the flowers, preferring to enjoy them while sitting outside.

Jered forced himself to pause the game. "You've cut some?"

"I have."

"Don't cut them all," he said.

"I have more than enough." She smiled and cupped a bloom in her hand. "Pink roses. Don't you think that's appropriate?"

"For what?"

She cocked her head and looked at him. "Pink roses were one of the symbols in the mosaic."

"Oh. Yeah." It didn't mean anything.

"Don't put yourself out," she said.

Which meant he had to put himself out.

She went to the kitchen and got a vase. He sat at the counter and watched as she snipped extra leaves and arranged the stems.

"How do you know how to arrange them to make it pretty?"

She shrugged. "I have to go out again."

"You just got here." *And it's almost lunchtime.*

"I'm bringing these to a woman who works at the gym. She's been out sick the past two days."

"She's a worker?"

"Yes. I see her every time I'm there."

"You know her?"

"Not really. She's a 'hi' and 'have a good day' type of friend."

"Then why bring her flowers?"

"She's feeling bad. I can help." She headed to the door. "You want to come along?"

"No."

"Because . . .?"

"I have things to do."

"Hmm."

She left. Jered went back to the couch and unpaused his game.

**

Where is she?

Jered looked past the TV to the clock. It was nearly one. Ivy had been gone almost two hours. He'd stopped playing the video game and had turned to some reality show about souped-up motorcycles.

The phone rang. He muted the TV and picked it up, eager to talk to--

It wasn't Ivy. It was his publicist. "What do you want, Marv?"

"Nice to talk to you too, Jered. We have a chance for you to be interviewed by a Topeka radio station next week and--"

"The tour is over." *Finally.*

"The traveling is over, but not the marketing. A tour *is* promotion. But after the tour you clinch the sales by keeping yourself in the public eye—or ear in this case. I thought you could . . ."

As Marv droned on, Jered slid down into the cushions, flipping channels.

"Jered? You there?"

"Yeah, I'm here."

"So what do you think?"

"I think--" He heard Ivy at the door. "I think I've already done my job, Marv. Now it's time for you to do yours. Me talking to some nothing-station in Topeka is not the way for you to earn your keep."

"But--"

Jered hung up. "Hey," he said to Ivy.

"Marv wants you to do an interview?"

"I'm not doing it."

"He works hard for you, hon. It wouldn't kill you to be nice to him."

"I pay him big bucks so I don't have to be."

"It's not just how you treat Marv either. You're short with everyone."

Jered didn't want to hear it.

He wanted to ask why she'd been gone so long.

She went into the kitchen. "You didn't eat anything?"

"I was waiting for you." *Waiting for you to make it for me.*

She made a face and got out some ham, cheese, and bread. "Grilled or ungrilled?"

"Grilled."

Ivy got out the griddle and buttered the bread on the outside. "Don't you want to know what happened at Sarah's?"

He caught himself before asking, *Who's Sarah?* "Did she like the flowers?"

"Loved them. Turns out her husband left her last week and she was glad to have someone to talk to. She was feeling rejected and needed someone to listen. I think I really helped."

"I'm sure you did." Ivy always helped people. She had a calming way about her that made everything better.

She put slices of meat and cheese on the sandwiches and added mustard. "You could have come with me. Or gone out on your own. There are a lot of people out there who could use a friendly word."

"I don't feel comfortable doing that. And wouldn't they feel uncomfortable having *me* intrude on their lives?"

She stopped to stare at him, rolling her eyes. "Because you're famous."

"Well, yeah."

She bit her lip and he could tell she was weighing what to say.

"Say whatever it is you're holding in."

She took a fresh breath. "You can rationalize it all you want, Jer, but you're using your fame as a way to distance yourself from responsibility and the world."

"I thought you understood."

"I understand that a lot of famous people help others. A lot. 'From everyone who has been given much, much will be demanded; and from the one who has been entrusted with much, much more will be asked.' You've been given much, Jer. We both have."

"We give money to charity."

"Big whup."

"It is a big whup. We gave fifty-thou last year."

"Out of the ten million we earned? 'God loves a cheerful giver' not one who gives grudgingly."

He left the kitchen and plopped on the couch. She followed him, standing on the other side of the coffee table. "Doing good isn't just about writing a check. You were called to go out into the world and tell people about God."

"That's not my thing." *I'd make a mess of it – make a fool of myself.*

"It needs to become your thing."

She turned off the TV. "You can't do anything from in here." Ivy marched back to the kitchen. "Lunch will be in a minute."

Jered hated guilt trips.

**

Ivy liked to snuggle in bed, so when she lay with her back to him it was a sure indication something was wrong.

Ever since their discussion at lunch she'd been polite but distant. They went through the day encased in their own bubbles, being able to see and hear each other but unwilling to engage.

It wasn't like her to go to bed angry. She was the one who always said she was sorry—even if it was his fault.

Jered didn't like this situation. Not at all.

He turned to face her back and scooted close to spoon her. She inched away. "Not tonight, Jer."

He sat up in bed, purposely taking most of her covers with him. "Enough of this! Tell me what I did that's so bad you have to punish me for it. All day."

"I'm not punishing you. I'm giving you what you want."

He pulled at her shoulder, forcing her to roll onto her back. "What are you talking about?"

She turned on the lamp and sat against the headboard, adjusting a pillow behind her. "You want to be left alone. I'm leaving you alone."

"I never said I wanted to be alone."

"Maybe not in so many words, but you implied that going out into the world, meeting people, interacting with people, and helping people wasn't your thing."

Yeah, he had said that. "That doesn't mean I want to be alone." He touched her leg and was glad she didn't recoil. "I want to be with *you*. There's nothing in the world I love more than being with you."

She sighed deeply. "*We* are great, Jer. But we have a responsibility to look beyond *we*." She put a hand to her chest. "I plan to do that more and more. I'd like to do it with you."

But I don't wanna.

"The world doesn't—and shouldn't—revolve around us. I want to share our lives and our good fortune with others who need help."

"Every time I sing I give something of myself. I make people happy."

Her face softened. "You do. God gave you a talent and you're using it."

"So doesn't that count?"

She pressed her fingers to her forehead. "I . . . I just think there's more. Don't you?"

More? He probably *could* give more. But he had no idea how to go about it.

"It's time, Jer." She reached for his hand.

He took it and drew it to his lips. "I'll try, Ive. For you I'll try."

Her smile almost made him think he could do it.

Chapter 17

Claire

"If any of you lacks wisdom, you should ask God, who gives generously to all without finding fault, and it will be given to you."
James 1: 5

The last thing Claire felt like doing was schmoozing. But that's what was on the agenda.

The Heartland Bank in Kansas City was interested in commissioning a large mosaic for their lobby. She'd prayed for more income? God was opening a door. The commission would pay a lot of bills.

The bank people were taking her to dinner where she would have to be delightful and charming. Normally she could successfully be both, at will. But today it would be a struggle.

Ever since cooling her relationship with Billy, she'd felt dreadful and confused. A relationship was private, between two people. God wanted her to reach many. And if she *was* supposed to break it off with Billy, then why did she feel so horrible?

The bank people were picking her up any minute. She moved her wallet from her tan purse to her black one to match her favorite "little black dress." They hadn't said where they were taking her, but the dress suited most dining experiences.

She heard a car pull up and peeked through the wood blinds. The president of the bank, Al Morton, walked up the front walk. He was dressed in a suit, meaning her black dress was a good choice. She met him outside. This wasn't a date. She didn't need to wait for him to ring the bell.

They exchanged pleasantries and he led her to the car, opening the passenger door for her. Once inside, Claire saw a woman sitting in back.

"Hello," the woman said, extending her hand over the seat. "I'm Al's wife, Beth."

Claire shook her hand. "Nice to meet you, Beth."

Al had said she could bring along a significant-other, but she hadn't realized he was bringing his wife. It would have been nice to bring Billy.

She shut down that train of thought before it left the station. What was done, was done.

They were a nice couple with two kids and four grandkids. Claire hated moments like this when they flipped questions at her and she had to tell them she was divorced and didn't have any children. The usual response was either silence or, "I'm sorry." In this case she got silence from Al and the condolence words from Beth.

They drove downtown and pulled up to the restaurant. Al opened the doors for both of them. "Have you ever been to Roberto's?" Beth asked. "It's one of our favorites."

Claire was struck dumb. God was linking her to Billy again? "I've never had the pleasure," she said.

They were led to a corner booth. Her eyes were drawn upward to the beamed ceiling, and she noticed the burlwood wainscoting—that Billy had put in. They were handed menus and Claire asked the Mortons to name their favorite dishes.

"I'm partial to the mushroom and asparagus tortellini," Beth said. "And wait until they bring the garlic rolls. They're almost as good as the pasta."

Garlic rolls. The recipe from Billy's grandmother.

The women ordered the pasta and Al ordered the chicken parmesan. Caesar salads were served, as well as the garlic rolls—which were rich with butter and had crispy shreds of Romano on top.

Claire tried one and sighed. "These *are* amazing."

"Told you," Beth said.

While they ate some antipasto the conversation was friendly.

Yet she was distracted. When the pasta came she noted the slanted bowls that Billy had picked out. "These are very unique," she said.

"I know," Beth said. "I was hoping to find some for us to buy."

They talked about the mural a bit—and it seemed she all but had the commission—but conversation flowed to others subjects too. Al was a huge fan of the Royals.

When they were nearly through with their meal a man in a suit stopped by the table.

Al introduced them. "Claire, this is Robby Bianchi, the owner."

So you're the man who betrayed Billy. Claire felt the need to bait him. "The garlic rolls were especially delicious. An old family recipe?"

"My grandmother's," he said.

"Really."

He looked uncomfortable. "Nate, our chef, has created another family-inspired dessert for today. Apple-crisp."

With vanilla ice cream? Was it another stolen recipe?

And Nate was the name of the chef who quit Billy's restaurant, and was a big reason it folded. He worked for Robby again? There was something fishy going on.

"Enjoy your meal."

Claire's mind was spinning.

"Are you all right?" Al asked her.

She forced a smile. "This is a very nice place. But there was a restaurant here before, wasn't there?"

"There was," Al said. "Billy Bob's. We loved that place too."

"Actually, a bit more," Beth said.

"What happened to it?" Claire asked.

"I've heard through the grapevine that some bad reviews did it in," Al said. "Beyond that I don't really know."

"Sure you do, honey," Beth said. "When this place opened we asked Robby what happened to Billy Bob's and he said his partner did some shady things with their money."

Claire's heart pounded. Robby had slandered Billy—to an important banker in town. She set her napkin on the table. "I'm sorry to cut this short, but I'm not feeling very well."

Beth's face showed her concern. "Is it something you ate?"

In a way.

Claire told the Mortons to stay. He was a gentleman and called an Uber for her. She headed home with a conundrum. Should she tell Billy what she'd witnessed? It wouldn't change anything. Yet he was wrestling with events that were based on half-truths and lies.

She needed counsel—both physical and spiritual. When she got home she found Michelle in the living room, watching TV.

"How was it?"

"Interesting." Claire tossed her purse on the coffee table and fell onto the couch. She slipped off her shoes, kicking them aside

"Did you get the commission?"

The commission! "I'm not sure. We barely talked about it."

"Isn't that the reason for the dinner?"

Claire couldn't think about that now. "I left early."

Michelle muted the TV. "What's wrong?"

"We went to Roberto's."

"The place that opened where Billy Bob's was located?"

"That's the one. Still a nice place, but some strange things happened." She told Michelle about Robby taking credit for the recipe, the chef, the mention of bad reviews, and the slander about money issues. She ended with, "It's not right. There's something suspicious going on."

"You need to tell Billy."

"I want to. But will it just stir up more conflict and pain?"

Michelle shut the TV off. "It does make me wonder if there's more we don't know about. Billy said everyone quit, and—"

"And they lost a ton of money when a freezer blitzed out."

"I wonder if they got insurance money for their loss," Michelle said.

Claire thought back to Billy's words. "He didn't say anything, or even imply it. In fact, he acted as if the monetary loss was devastating."

"You should talk to the chef. Ask him why he's back."

"That could lead nowhere," Claire said. "People need to work. Robby approached him and hired him back."

"Is the old kitchen crew working there again—the ones who quit?"

"I don't know."

"That would be very suspicious."

Each point seemed to add another block to a precarious tower. "Add the slander and lying about the recipe." She tried to take a deep breath, but her chest felt heavy. "I hate for anyone to think badly of Billy. He would never steal."

"I hate to say this, Claire, but you don't really know him. You met him, were charmed by him, but—"

"But beyond that?" Claire stood. It always came back to this: "God brought us together."

Michelle shook her head. "You say that, you believe that, but then you turned Billy away."

All true. "I turned him away romantically," she said. "Because . . . because romance seemed frivolous compared to my calling."

"Mmm," Michelle said. "God is love but love is frivolous. I didn't know that."

Layers of doubt fell upon her. "You didn't stop me."

"You didn't give me—or Billy—a chance to do much of anything. You made up your mind, and—" She snapped her fingers. "He had no choice but to leave."

The weight of her mistake caused Claire to fall sideways on the couch. "What have I done?"

"The question is, what will you *do?*"

There was only one thing *to* do. She sat up and looked for her phone. "I'm going to call Billy right now."

"Nope."

"Nope?" She found it on the entry table.

"It's time to implement the three-second rule."

"What's that?"

"Since you—and most people, including me—have a tendency to act on impulse, I've found it's wise to wait three seconds before acting. Before calling. Before speaking. Before sending that email that may stir up the world. Try it."

"This is silly."

"You know it's not. You've heard that no-slow-grow-go saying."

"Don't believe I have."

"When the idea is wrong God says, 'No.' When the timing is wrong, God says, 'Slow'. When you are wrong, God says, 'Grow.' But when everything is right, God says, 'Go.'"

"Cute."

Michelle gave her the look she deserved. "It's not cute, it's the truth." She tossed a pillow at her. "Count to three."

This is ridiculous.

"I'm waiting."

"Fine. One, two, three."

"A little fast, but you *have* had time to reconsider calling Billy right this minute. So . . .?"

Claire hated to admit it, but the impulse to call had waned. "Fine. I'll call him tomorrow."

"When your head is clear, your emotions settled, and you've had time to let God have a say."

"I hate when you're right."

"So be it."

Chapter 18

Ryan

"Let the morning bring me word of your unfailing love,
for I have put my trust in you.
Show me the way I should go,
for to you I entrust my life."
Psalm 143: 8

Ryan and Lisa didn't know what to expect when they visited Grandpa at the hospital.

They did not expect to find him sitting on the bed, buttoning his shirt.

He looked up. "Morning, you two. I'm going home."

Lisa gave him a hug. "I'm glad! You scared us."

"Scared me a bit too."

A nurse came in, looked at the visitors, and Ryan saw Grandpa shake his head at her. She seemed to change her mind about what she was going to say. "The doctor wants to speak with you," she said.

"He's done enough speaking with me. I signed the papers. Tell Ryan whatever we need to know." He pointed at a plastic drawstring bag. "Get my shoes outta there, Lisa."

The nurse led Ryan out to the hall and into a small room with two chairs. "Wait here and I'll get the doctor."

Grandpa was trusting Ryan to talk to the doctor?

Soon a woman in a white coat joined them. She shook hands with Ryan. "Hi, I'm Dr. Schubert. You're the nephew?"

"Yes." Something was terribly wrong. "What can you tell me? How is he?"

She sighed deeply. "He has a bad case of bronchitis—which we can treat."

"Good."

"But . . . he has dilated cardiomyopathy." She put up a hand before he could ask a question. "The left ventricle of the heart is enlarged and weakened. Basically, the heart can't pump blood like it should."

Ryan's heart sank. "Should he be leaving the hospital?"

"He can leave. We've given him three new meds, but he—you—have to be aware of what to look for. Fainting is one symptom."

"Should I write these down?"

"I'll give you a sheet about it. He may have shortness of breath, dizziness, fatigue, chest pain, his heart may flutter, and his legs may swell—we've put him on blood thinner to help with blood clots."

That sounded scary. "Should he stay in bed?"

"He needs to listen to his body. Moderate exercise is good. Watch the sodium. Eat healthy."

Ryan needed to ask, "Can he die from this?"

She barely missed a beat indicating she'd had conversations like this before. "It's possible. The coughing from his bronchitis puts a strain on his heart, but once that is controlled, and if we keep an eye on him, he could recover."

Could recover. "Does he need surgery?"

"Perhaps. But not now." She gave him her card. "Call if he gets worse or you have questions."

"So he knows . . . all this?"

"He does." She smiled. "He's an ornery old cuss—which will actually help him beat this. Plus the fact he loves his granddaughter deeply." She stood and shook his hand again. "I'm glad you're around for both of them."

When she began to leave he asked, "I'm just going to sit here a minute and pray about it, if that's all right."

"That's more than all right. I've witnessed the power of prayer many times. I'll add Mr. Pearl to my list."

As soon as he was alone, Ryan bowed his head and asked God the Healer to heal Grandpa.

**

Grandpa was quiet all the way home. And oddly, Lisa followed suit. Ryan hated to hear her worried sighs.

Ryan expected him to go right to bed, but Grandpa took his place on the porch rocker.

Lisa and Ryan stood near the door and shared an awkward moment. Did he want company? Something to eat?

He gave them a disgusted look. "Don't stand there gawking at me. Come sit down. I have something to say."

Lisa sat on the chair nearest him and Ryan took the other. Was he going to tell Lisa how sick he was?

Grandpa looked at each of them in turn. "Gracious. You two are acting like it's my funeral. I ain't dead—yet."

"Oh, Grandpa . . ." Lisa ran to his side, sitting at his feet.

His voice softened as he touched her head. "Come now, girl. Don't make a fuss. I'll be fine."

But would he be?

"Actually, while being bored to tears at the hospital I had an idea. I want to go on a road trip."

"Ryan too?"

Grandpa glanced at Ryan. "We need somebody to drive, don't we? That is, if Ryan can take the time."

The idea took him off guard, but he agreed. "Gladly," he said. "That sounds fun." *Where are You leading us, Lord?*

Once again, Lisa mirrored his thoughts. "Where are we going?"

Grandpa nodded once. "The mountains. The Rockies. I've never seen them. Always wanted to."

"Mountains? Real mountains?" Lisa said.

"Tall ones too. With snow on them—even in the summer." He looked at Ryan. "You been there?"

"I have. And I approve. It's a stunning place." *Where my parents live.* He hadn't seen them in ten years and they hadn't parted on the best of terms.

"Ryan?" Grandpa asked. "We lost you there."

"Sorry. What did you say?"

"I said I want to leave in the morning. First thing. That okay with you?"

"That's fine. But . . ." He had to ask. "Are you up for it? The altitude makes it hard to breathe."

"I got a passel of medicines to help me do that. I'm going." He held Lisa's chin in his hand. "I want you to pack pretty much all you've got. I don't want to need something and have it be here when you want it there."

"How long are we going to be gone?" she asked.

"You got something to do?"

"Not until school starts."

"Then don't worry about it. Go on now. Get to packing. I'll be in soon and you can help me pack my stuff. Use garbage bags when the suitcases fill up. "

She went inside. Ryan stood to go help.

"Hold up a minute."

He sat back down.

"I know you just got here and you don't know us from Adam."

"And you don't know me."

Grandpa shrugged. "Another thing I started thinking about in that hospital was that it was darn good you *were* here. I don't know what would have happened if I'd collapsed at the house with Lisa, all alone." He held out his hand. "I want to thank you for coming into our lives and sticking with us. I never asked how long you were staying, so I'm hoping my little plan doesn't set you back."

Ryan was touched and shook his hand. "The trip sounds great. And *I'm* glad God brought me here. His timing *was* perfect."

Grandpa waved a hand in front of his face like he was shooing away a pesky fly. "Don't know about God doing it, but it's done. And I'm glad for it.

"But God *did*—"

"Go inside and help Lisa pack."

There was one other issue. "Is this trip okay with your doctor?"

"Do they have doctors in Colorado?"

"Yes."

"Well, what do ya know?"

It would be an interesting trip.

Chapter 19

Summer

"Dear friend, you are faithful in what you are doing
for the brothers and sisters,
even though they are strangers to you.
They have told the church about your love.
Please send them on their way
in a manner that honors God."
3 John: 5-6

Today I will do better.

Summer hoped today she'd see a hint of God's plan. She kept praying that He'd let her help Him, and went to work at Coffee Break with her eyes open and her heart eager.

But the line for coffee was just as unrelenting, the social interaction just as brief.

Maybe at the flower shop . . .

She felt on pins and needles there. After her two flub-ups she worked deliberately. Carefully. So much so that when she helped Andy load up the delivery van he said, "What's with you today?"

She should have known her mood would show. "Nothing."

"Wrong answer," he said as he closed the van doors. "You're tense."

She realized her shoulders were tight and tried to relax.

"No go," Andy said, pointing at her shoulders. "It's more than that." He touched his head. "You're tense in here."

He'd never understand, but she didn't feel up to making an excuse. "I just want to do good, do things right."

He walked toward the driver's door. "Stop worrying about the flower-police." He got in and winked at her. "Chill."

Easier said than done.

Perhaps it was good that all the day's orders were online or on the phone.

**

That evening at Happy Trails Summer spotted a new couple at dinner. Perhaps they could be a connection.

She went up to their table and greeted them. "Hi, there. Are you new here?"

"We are," said the man. "Just moved in." He pointed to himself, then his wife. "Vern and Barb Kostner."

"Nice to meet you. I'm Summer Peerbaugh. Where did you move from?"

"Eudora. Not too far away," the woman said.

"I like Eudora. There's an antique shop I like—"

Another server, Bridget, joined them. "Hi, Grandpa. Grandma. All moved in?"

Summer kept smiling, but felt let down. They were taken. She wrapped up the small talk and went back to her regular tables.

When she got there Mae asked, "Newbies?"

"Vern and Barb Kostner from Eudora," Summer said.

Grandma perked up. "There's a great antique store in Eudora."

And that. Was that.

**

The heat and humidity were lower that evening so Summer decided to take Suzu for a longer walk than usual.

Her dog's massive enthusiasm when she realized they weren't immediately going inside made Summer vow to be better about walks. Just because she had three jobs didn't mean Suzu should suffer.

As they walked parallel to Happy Trails, she saw the dumpster. Was the man coming every night for food? She'd only seen him once, but that didn't mean he hadn't been there more often. Getting leftovers was repulsive. Who knew what trash he had to dig through to scrounge up something edible.

Fix it.

She stopped walking, which caused Suzu to look up at her and tilt her head.

Summer turned back toward home. "Come on, girl. We'll walk farther tomorrow."

Once inside, Summer threw open her cupboards and pulled out a dozen cans of food: tuna, chicken, soups, fruits, and vegetables.

She needed something to put them in. She was always a keeper of grocery sacks, but wanted something a bit nicer—after all, it was a gift. She found a handled sack from a bookstore and started to fill it. The cans were heavy. She had no idea how far the man had to walk with it. She hoped he wasn't homeless. She didn't have many foods that didn't need some sort of prep.

She'd have to risk it. She removed some of the cans and replaced them with a box of Ritz crackers, mac & cheese, two granola bars, and two instant oatmeal packets.

It was pretty full. But then she thought of other needs and put in a bar of soap and some purse-packets of Kleenex.

All that was left was a note.

She found a pretty note card with a daisy on it and wrote: *Man in the hoodie? This is for you. I'm praying for you.* After a moment's consideration she wrote down her phone number. But not her name.

Summer glanced outside and saw that it was on the edge of dark. She hurried across the street. Where should she put the bag so he would see it but no one else would? She moved one of the crates he used as a step in front of the dumpster and set the bag beside it. He couldn't miss it. *There, Lord. Thanks for the nudge.*

As she walked back to her apartment, she wondered what would happen if he didn't come? What if someone else took the bag? What if someone from the kitchen saw it first?

She couldn't worry about that. She'd done what God had nudged her to do. The rest was up to Him.

**

Summer sat on the balcony. Her eyelids were heavy and more than once she yanked herself out of a doze.

She was thankful there was some moonlight. She held the camera of her phone toward the dumpster and zoomed in. She could see the handles of the bag peeking over the top of the crate.

But as she put her phone down, she spotted some movement by the bushes.

There he was!

She watched as he approached the dumpster. He stopped when he saw the bag. He glanced right, then left, then looked inside.

Then the man did something that made Summer's heart swell with emotion.

He bowed his head, pressed a hand to his heart, then took the bag and hurried away.

God received two prayers of thanks that night.

Chapter 20

Michelle

"Each person should live as a believer
in whatever situation the Lord has assigned to them,
just as God has called them."
1 Corinthians 7: 17

Michelle sat at a dining table at the Mercy Shelter with three men who frequented the shelter regularly. She appreciated Roscoe who told jokes and always made them laugh. Jamie was a quiet sort and occasionally liked to talk about history. He especially liked the era of Henry VIII. And Seymour was unpredictable. He rocked up and back a lot, and sometimes talked—mostly to himself. She liked all three.

Michelle noticed a young black girl come in the door. Tentative. Looking left and right like a frightened rabbit ready to flee. People came and went all day. It was impossible to greet them all. But this time Michelle felt a little push inside.

Her. Help her.

"Excuse me, gentlemen." She approached the girl, smiling broadly. "Hello there. Welcome."

The girl nodded.

"You hungry? We're serving lunch soon."

She nodded again. "The smell brought me in."

Michelle laughed. "The aroma of fried chicken and mashed potatoes will do that. I'm Michelle. What's your name?"

"Jonette."

"Pretty name." She noticed the girl's shorts and top were nice, if not a little dirty. She was a bitty thing, not five-foot tall. She had nothing with her—which was odd. Most of the people who came in the shelter carried a backpack or trash bags full of their belongings. Yet she was here. She wanted a meal. She needed help.

"Can I use the restroom?"

"Of course. The Ladies is down the hall. You need some toiletries? Toothbrush, comb, that sort of thing?"

Jonette pursed her mouth and nodded. "I had stuff, but everything was stolen. So yeah. Thanks."

"I'll get you taken care of." Michelle grabbed some supplies from a cabinet and was back within a minute. "There are toiletries in there, a few snacks, hand wipes, Chapstick, a bottle of water, a towel . . . that sort of thing. And I found you a backpack to put it in."

The girl's eyes filled with tears. "Wow. Thanks." She left for the restroom. While Jonette was gone, Michelle checked to see if there was a bed free for the night in the women's wing. There was. One. She reserved it for the girl.

By the time Michelle got back to the dining room the kitchen workers were bringing out the food trays for lunch. A line began to form. Michelle took her usual place to help serve. She kept watch for Jonette. Had she slipped out? *Please, Lord. Let her be here.*

Then there she was.

She looked better. Her face was washed and she'd combed her hair so it wasn't so wild.

Before they served the food Michelle raised her hands toward heaven. "Come on, everyone. Let us pause and pray."

After blessing the food Michelle added a silent prayer for Jonette.

When the girl came to Michelle's station and got a roll and butter, she actually smiled. "Thanks for the stuff."

"You're welcome." She wanted to tell her about the place to sleep, but the line was long. She'd tell her later.

As soon as she was able, Michelle left the other servers and sought out Jonette. She was sitting alone at the end of a table. At the other end sat two women who were regulars. Michelle greeted them. "Is the food satisfactory, ladies?"

"As usual."

"Good to hear." Michelle stood between them and Jonette. "Ladies, I'd like you to meet Jonette."

"Hey," they said.

Jonette nodded. Barely. She kept her eyes on her food tray.

"May I sit?" Michelle asked, pointing to a chair

"Sure."

Michelle sat across from her. "Want another piece of chicken?"

"I'm good." Jonette pulled her fork through the mashed potatoes.

"You don't like the potatoes?"

She shrugged. "They're all right, but I make better. I put cream cheese in mine."

Cream cheese was an expensive addition, one the shelter couldn't afford. "Do you cook a lot?"

"I used to."

Michelle waited for her to say more, but that was it. She knew it was best to let people tell their stories in their own time.

"What else do you like to cook?"

There was the slightest glimmer of interest. "Spaghetti."

"Always a favorite."

Jonette ate the last of her dinner roll. "I tried making my own sauce once but it didn't taste any better than the jars, but I like to put other stuff in it like peppers and onions . . ." She stood. "Where do I take the tray?"

"Over there." Michelle stood. "I reserved you a bed for the night—in the women's wing. You'll have to sleep on a bedroll, but—"

"Thanks, but I got it. I'll be all right."

Michelle knew what it was like out *there.* "Stay. Please. It's clean and cool. Much better than—"

Jonette slipped her backpack straps over one shoulder, then lifted her tray. "Thanks for everything, Michelle. I mean it. Bye."

Michelle sat back down, feeling helpless.

"She's new, ain't she?" said Patty, one of the women at the end of the table.

"She is."

Patty shared a chuckle with her friend. "New and naïve. She'll be back."

Michelle hoped so.

**

That night Michelle lay in bed and stared at the ceiling. Where was Jonette sleeping? The thought of her on the street, or in an alley . . . Michelle whispered into the night, "Father, protect her. Keep her safe. Let her come back to the shelter so I can help her."

She turned onto her side, wishing she could shut her brain off. In addition to her worries about Jonette, Michelle was exhausted because of Claire's rollercoaster: Claire offended Billy, liked Billy, pushed Billy away, thought she didn't deserve Billy, liked Billy again . . .

Thank You, Lord, for never putting another man in my life after Sergei.

It's not that Michelle was averse to finding male companionship, but once she'd lost the love of her life she didn't need it anymore. She rationalized her choice to go it alone as being better for *her*. She had chosen the harder—

There was a knock on her door. "Michelle?"

She braced herself for more Claire drama. "Come in."

Claire flipped on the light, then entered wearing a Kansas City Chief's nightshirt. "I hope I didn't wake you."

"You didn't." Michelle sat up, arranging the covers around her. "Is something wrong?"

Claire sat in the chair by the dresser. "I'm wrong."

"Huh?"

"I was stewing in my room about Billy, rereading the same paragraph in my book multiple times, when it hit me that I've been very rude to you."

Michelle wasn't aware of any offense. "How so?"

"Maybe it's because I've been too long on my own, or maybe it's because I'm too pragmatic, or maybe it's just a character flaw."

Michelle smiled. "Self-analysis. Can I be next?"

"That's the point," Claire said. "I have a bad habit of making everything about *me*. I go on and on about Billy and all the problems in my life, completely ignoring what's going on in yours."

This is a refreshing turn. Michelle thought of Jonette. "I did have a girl come in today—newly homeless from the look of it. I offered her a bed but she didn't take it. And—"

"All those homeless people . . . they have big problems. You help them."

"We try to." Michelle wasn't sure what Claire was after. "This girl, she—"

But Claire didn't listen. "I talk about Billy all the time—about *me* all the time—and . . . don't you think it's odd that we both were married but have been single so long?"

So much for Claire listening to Michelle's talk of *her* day. "I was meant to be single."

"God wants you single?"

It could be a touchy subject. "It hasn't always been that way. Sergei was important to my life. But now? Actually, yes."

"Does He want me single?"

"I can't answer that." *And I'm not up to figuring it out for you.*

Claire traced a finger along the arm of the chair. "Surely there's some verse about it."

Although Michelle was tempted to tell her there wasn't, she knew there were many. "There are some verses in Paul's letter to the Corinthians. He told his followers it was all right to be married—that it was a wise choice if they were sexually tempted. But that it was better to stay single so they could focus on God's work." She shrugged. "I chose the latter way."

Claire smoothed her nightshirt over her legs. "I've been single a long time but I didn't do it for God. I'm just too independent and bossy. I like things done my way. Men don't always like that."

Ain't that the truth. "Romance or not, you can be Billy's friend."

Claire nodded but she made a face as if Michelle had told her she could have a carrot stick after she'd said no to a chocolate chip cookie. Then she stood. "I'm so glad you're here. It helps to have someone to bounce things off of." She grinned. "You're my bouncer."

"Glad to help."

Claire moved to the door. "I'll try to be less selfish and ask you about your life more often."

There *was* something Michelle had wanted to talk to her about. "Have you seen my daily emails to the group?"

"I have. They're beautiful visually and spiritually. Have you heard back from anyone?"

"Summer said 'thanks.' I haven't heard from Jered or Ryan."

"It's still good you're doing it. We did tell them to go back to their lives without any concrete instruction . . . I hope they don't feel abandoned."

"It's what the disciples were asked to do after Jesus died. They went into the world to spread the Word."

Claire smiled. "If only *they* could have received an encouraging email from you."

Michelle found the comment presumptuous. "My emails aren't going to change anything. Our friends have God with them. That's enough."

Claire flipped off the light. "The Almighty is lucky to have you on His team, Ms. Jofsky. Good night."

Michelle slipped under her covers. There were no more thoughts of having a man in her life. She was eternally bound to the only Man she needed.

Chapter 21

Claire

"When justice is done,
it brings joy to the righteous but terror to evildoers."
Proverbs 21: 15

It was three o'clock in the morning. Claire couldn't sleep.

Before she had a housemate she would have sat up in bed and prayed out loud. But with Michelle down the hall . . .

So what if she hears? Pray.

She pushed herself to sitting and adjusted some pillows against the tufted headboard. She flipped on the light, hoping it would help her brain see the answer to her confusion.

"Well then," she said softly. "You got me up, Father. What am I supposed to do about Billy?"

She remembered Michelle's words: *God is love.* God created love. Love is good.

Let yourself love.

Claire drew in a breath at the thought. "But won't love interfere with my calling—even if that calling is to help him?"

. . . the greatest of these is love.

It was a snippet from a verse—one that Claire had heard before. She took her phone off the bedside table and did a search for it.

"There you are . . . 'And now these three remain: faith, hope and love. But the greatest of these is love.'" That's the one she knew. And yet . . . in another search result she saw a different translation—*The Message.* It drew her in like a magnet finding its mate. "'We don't yet see things clearly. We're squinting in a fog, peering through a mist. But it won't be long before the weather clears and the sun shines bright! We'll see it all then, see it all as clearly as God sees us, knowing him directly just as he knows us! But for right now, until that completeness, we have three things to do to lead us toward that consummation: Trust steadily in God, hope unswervingly, love extravagantly. And the best of the three is love.'"

Claire gasped and held the phone to her chest. "This is exactly what I feel! Like I'm looking through a fog and can't see where You want me to go. But You're saying the weather will clear and I'll see it all." She glanced back at the phone. "I'm to trust You steadily, hope unswervingly, and love extravagantly. And the best is love." She whispered it again. "The best is love."

She began to cry from the release of it. God had released her to love. "Loving Billy isn't a distraction, it's a part of the journey!" She nearly giggled as she said the next. "I can let myself love him!"

She went to her phone log and tapped his name. Then she looked at the time. 3:16. She laughed again. "Even I know that one. John 3:16, the core of our faith." She looked heavenward and repeated God's promise. "'For God so loved the world that he gave his one and only Son, that whoever believes in him shall not perish but have eternal life.'" She smiled. "That's it. That's You. Help me follow You completely."

Feeling a little foolish, she held the phone up, as if showing God. "Is it okay if I call him now? Michelle said there's a three-second rule."

Count.

She counted. She waited. One. Two. Three.

The need to speak with Billy *now* didn't lessen. She dialed.

He surprised her by answering immediately. His voice wasn't groggy from sleep, but sounded alert and normal. "Claire?"

"Billy, I'm sorry for calling in the middle of the night—"

"I was awake."

"You were?"

"I . . . I'm not giving you up, Claire. You sent me away, but I'm not going to accept that. You said that God brought us together? That means we're supposed to *be* together. Not apart. And—"

"I agree," she said.

"What?"

Her heart swelled with gratitude to the Almighty. "That's why I was calling. I can follow this *thing* God has asked me to do *and* love you at the same time."

"Love me?"

She hadn't meant to say it so blatantly. She was going to hedge but didn't. "Love you. I think I love you."

"Me too."

She put a hand to her mouth. "Really?"

"You hit me like a bombshell, Claire Adams. I wasn't looking for love at all."

"Me neither!"

"It just happened."

He was wrong about that. "It didn't *just* happen, Billy. God arranged it."

"Can you come over?" he asked. "Now?"

She threw back the covers. "I'm on my way."

Claire tried to be quiet as she pulled on some jeans and a shirt, but Michelle showed up when she was about to leave. "Where are you going at this hour?"

"To see the man I love."

Michelle smiled. "Tell him hi."

**

Claire strode up to Billy's front door, realizing—at the last possible second—that she still had two huge claw hairclips on top of her head. She tried—too late—to unclip them.

He opened the door. His eyes traveled to the busyness of her hands on her head.

"Sorry. My hair is—"

He pulled her inside, into his arms, and kissed her. It was just like in the movies. She melted.

When they came up for air, he took a half-step back. "Nice hair."

She removed the clips. "It keeps the waves and gives it body."

He ran his hands through her hair in a most delicious fashion. "You're right."

Although she could have let him continue indefinitely, she had things to say. "Can we talk?"

He led her to a loveseat that was covered with a chintz fabric spotted with yellow and pink roses. Two lamps revealed a room bathed in warmth and welcome. On the opposite wall she saw her mosaic. "You put it up."

"Of course I put it up. It changed my life."

And mine.

She angled her body to face him. "I'm sorry to kick you out. I was wrong."

"Yes, you were."

She chuckled. "So this is how it's going to be? Frank and forthright at all times?"

"Frank and forthright. And fantastic." He leaned against the opposite arm, and drew her legs toward him. "Flip flops? Your feet are freezing." He removed her shoes and tucked her feet in beside him.

It felt totally natural and Claire could imagine many future discussions happening in just such a position.

"What got you up in the middle of the night?" he asked.

"God. And thinking about you and what God's asked me to do. And how those two things fit together."

"What has He asked you to do?"

It was odd she'd never told him about it. She glanced at the wall. "It revolves around the mosaic, but happened before that." She told him about the feeling of anticipation that she and Michelle had shared, the feeling that had opened them to whatever God wanted them to do. The dream, the tiles, the mosaic on the floor, the pin . . ."I met Summer, Ryan, Jered, and you because of all that. We have the mosaic in common."

"They all saw doves?"

"And roses. Daisies. And sometimes arrows," she added.

"So what are the lot of you supposed to do?"

Every time she had to answer this question her answer got more refined and succinct. "We are to look for God at work—and join Him."

"End hunger and bring about world peace?"

She smacked his leg. "That would be nice, but it's more personal. One on one."

"So three people who were drawn to the mosaic are out and about, doing this?"

"I hope so." She sensed a door opening. "As I'm doing this."

"By . . .?"

"Helping you."

His eyebrows rose. "Helping me do what?"

"Find justice."

His eyebrows dipped.

"For what?"

She drew her feet inward and sat cross-legged, facing him. "Justice for the offenses Robby has perpetrated against you." It sounded so formal.

"My ex-partner, Robby?"

She nodded.

"What *are* you talking about?"

Claire hated that her words would hurt him, but hopefully the pain would have a purpose. "I was taken to dinner at Roberto's last night by someone wanting a mosaic."

He looked down. "How was it?"

"The garlic rolls were delicious."

"My grandma's recipe."

She shook her head. "Not according to Robby. He said it was *his* grandma's recipe."

He was silent a moment. "Maybe it's just easier than saying it's the recipe of my ex-partner's grandmother."

"You're being too kind."

"Robby's a good guy."

I hate to burst your bubble but . . . "Nate is the chef again."

Billy blinked and she could see his inner struggle. "He needed a job. I can't blame him."

I can! Claire hoped the next would help Billy realize what was going on. "Robby told my friend that he broke up your partnership because—how did he put it?—you did some hinky things with the money."

Billy sat upright. "I did no such thing."

"I believe you. But that's what he's told people, told my friend who's a banker. I expect he's told others the same thing. Plus, the bad reviews were mentioned."

Billy turned forward on the loveseat, resting his arms on his thighs. "How could he do that to me? It's a lie."

"It's slander."

He looked sideways at her. "I trusted him like a brother."

"It wouldn't be the first time brother betrayed brother."

Billy stood and began to pace. Then he stopped. "What am I supposed to do with this information?"

"I think we're supposed to figure out what he's up to and clear your name."

He put his hands on the fireplace mantel and leaned against it as if he needed it for strength. "How do we do that?"

Claire was glad she'd talked to Michelle about it. "I think we start by speaking with Nate. Find out what happened."

Billy nodded and faced her. "I know where he lives. He's a good guy."

You think everyone is a good guy.

"I'll call him later and go see him. I'd like you to come with me."

She went to him and wrapped her arms around his waist, leaning her head against his shoulder. "We'll get to the bottom of this, Billy. I promise."

Chapter 22

Ryan

"How lovely is your dwelling place, Lord Almighty!
My soul yearns, even faints, for the courts of the Lord;
my heart and my flesh cry out for the living God."
Psalm 84: 1-2

Logistics. It took two days for Ryan, Grandpa, and Lisa to pack for their road trip to the mountains. Grandpa repeatedly answered their questions with, "Just bring it."

When Ryan showed concern that the back of the truck was filling up, Grandpa merely said, "It is what it is" though he did tell Ryan where to find the truck's bed cover, and bungees to hold everything down. At least they wouldn't leave a trail.

Ryan had just returned from a run into town where he'd done some dumpster-diving for empty boxes. Lisa greeted him and helped bring them inside. "You got a lot more than we need. I'm almost packed already."

"Grandpa said to get as many as I could." He looked at Mr. Pearl who was sitting at the kitchen table going through some papers. "You want to tell me why we need all these boxes, sir?"

Grandpa stopped rustling the papers and set his hands flat against them. "We're not coming back."

Lisa's mouth fell open. "What?"

He avoided her eyes. "I didn't plan on it at first, but as we got to packing I realized there was nothing keeping us here. So why not set out and start over?"

"Over?" Lisa sat at the table. "What about my friends? School?"

"Schools are everywhere. And you never see your friends because we're way out here." He scanned the rooms. "This is no place for a young girl, stuck in the boonies with her ailing grandpa."

She reached for his hand. "I don't mind. I really don't. I like it here. And . . . and you've lived here forever."

His nod was strong. "Which means it's time to have an adventure." He smiled and touched her hand. "Getting sick made me think about the future—something I haven't thought of much in years. I think our best future is somewhere else." For the first time he looked at Ryan. "You're a wanderer. Surely you approve."

Ryan struggled to know what he should say. "It's true I've wandered, but . . . I'm by myself. I didn't have a child to worry about."

Grandpa's forehead tightened. "Thanks for the help."

He felt bad. "You're in charge, sir. It's your life. I'll help in whatever way I can. It's just a shock, that's all."

"Change usually is." Grandpa pointed at the mountain of boxes and then the kitchen. "Get back to work, both of you. Take four place settings of dishes and leave the rest. A few pans and mixing bowls—not the chipped ones. You figure it out. What we don't have we can buy when we get settled."

"Settled where?" Lisa asked.

"We'll let God decide, isn't that right, Ryan?" His look was challenging, not necessarily the face of someone who truly believed.

But Ryan *did* truly believe and so he said, "Absolutely."

Challenge accepted.

**

After dinner Lisa fell onto the couch. Ryan did the same. "I've never been so tired," she said.

"Ditto."

Lisa lowered her voice as Grandpa was napping in his room. "Has he told you what he's doing with the house? Are we selling it?"

"He hasn't said. But I assume he will."

Lisa leaned her head against the couch cushion and looked around. "It's not worth much." She pointed to a water spot on the ceiling. "Don't you think that looks like a rabbit?"

He looked up. "I guess it does."

"That's *my* water spot. Every night before I turn out the light I look at it. I'll miss it."

Ryan understood completely. When his family had moved to Weaver, Kansas from Arkansas he'd missed everything about his childhood home. He'd responded by being a sullen, rebellious teen. He hoped this sudden move wouldn't affect Lisa the same way.

He tried to get her to see the bright side of it—not an easy task. "It's kind of exciting to start over."

Lisa surprised him by nodding.

"You're a real trooper, kiddo. You should be proud of yourself."

She shrugged. "I'm not that sad to leave *here*. I didn't have many friends. There was all sorts of gossip when Mom left, and I never wanted to have friends out here because . . ." She spread her hands.

She didn't have to explain.

"I've never been to the mountains," she said.

"They're spectacular. You'll like them."

"I just . . . I just want Grandpa to be okay."

Ryan placed his hand on the cushion between them and she took it. "You are one amazing girl, Lisa Pearl."

She smiled. "Grandpa says I'm *his* pearl."

"I certainly do." Grandpa came out of the bedroom.

How long had he been listening?

"It's time to say goodbye," he said.

Lisa and Ryan exchanged a glance. Goodbye to whom?

He walked to the door. "Come with me."

They followed him outside. He led them around the house to a path between the grasses, so narrow they had to go single file. About fifty yards in, there was a break, a rocky outcropping that overlooked miles and miles of rolling green hills and sky spreading out forever.

"Wow," Ryan said. There was no better word.

"You pegged it," Grandpa said. "Help me sit on the edge there." They both helped him to the rock and he moved a bit back and forth to get comfy. "Your turn. One on each side."

They took their places and shared some silence. Along the far horizon the sun was turning the clouds red and pink.

"Ain't that a sight?" Grandpa said.

"It's beautiful," Ryan said.

"I'm going to miss this," Lisa said.

Grandpa pulled her under his arm. "They've got sunsets and clouds in the mountains. Don't they Ryan?"

"They do." *But not like this.* Not seeing for miles and miles; a rippling expanse of green meeting blue and purple and pink. "I'm glad you showed me this," he said softly.

Grandpa's words caught in his throat and Ryan could tell he was struggling with emotions. "I've had a good life here. But there . . ." He nodded toward the west. "Our future's thataway."

"It's scary," Lisa said.

"Sure is."

"Do you promise it will be good?" she asked.

He kissed the top of her head. "I promise."

Ryan could have talked about God's plans and thought of a dozen Bible verses to cement the moment, but oddly, what he felt most compelled to do was be silent.

And let God take care of the sunset.

Chapter 23

Summer

"Listen to my instruction and be wise; do not disregard it.
Blessed are those who listen to me,
watching daily at my doors, waiting at my doorway.
For those who find me find life
and receive favor from the Lord."
Proverbs 8: 33-35

As the days passed, Summer realized she had four jobs. The three she got paid for, and the one she didn't. Every evening she filled a bag with food and toiletries and left it for the man. And every night he took it, went through his heavenly thank-you ritual, and walked away.

But he didn't call.

Summer wasn't sure whether she was disappointed or relieved. If he *did* call things would get more complicated. Right now, their relationship was good but anonymous. They had a rhythm to it.

Summer had even bought two dozen brightly colored gift-bags to use. Why not add some cheer to the transaction? She'd also gone to the grocery store with the man in mind. But she quickly realized she needed to know whether he was feeding a family or living alone. Or was he homeless?

And so she'd left him the questions in a note and told him to put his answer under the apple crate.

This morning she hoped to get a response.

She took Suzu outside and walked to the dumpster. There were lights on in the Happy Trails' kitchen, so she walked nonchalantly, then quickly, to check for a note.

There it was!

She rushed home to read it: *Thank you for the supplies. Much appreciated. I am alone but not homeless. God bless you.* Summer pumped a fist in the air! "Thank You! Finally. A connection!"

At the flower shop that morning Andy once again noticed her mood—this time for a good reason. "What's with the happy face?"

She felt emboldened by what God was doing with the man. "God's using me."

Andy's bushy eyebrows rose. "Really."

"Yes, really," she said as she carried some mums to the van.

"Sounds like a cocky thing to say."

Oops. "I don't mean it to sound that way. He's doing the good things. I'm just the vehicle."

Andy climbed into the van. "Whatever."

So much for her good mood.

**

At dinner Summer poured refills of tea and Grandma touched her arm. "You seem subdued."

Summer decided it was time to tell them about her jobs—but not about the man. "I got another job," she said.

"Three?" Tessa said. "Now there's a proper work ethic."

"Or craziness," Mae said.

Grandma shook her head. "If you need money, Grandpa and I can help out."

"We all could," Tessa said.

"We don't want you burning the candle at both ends," Mae said.

Summer had never heard that saying and it must have showed on her face.

"Working too hard," Grandma said. "Using yourself up."

Mae pointed at her. "Watch yourself, chickie. Okay?"

**

Summer curled up on the couch and made room for Suzu to jump between the back cushion and the crook of her knees.

She snuggled with a pillow. Her sigh turned into a prayer. "Why can't I reach people at work? I have three jobs. Either no one has time to listen or I offend them. Andy called me cocky when I said You were using me. I can't seem to get it right. What should I do?"

She gave God an entire minute to answer before turning on the TV, where she let the sound of commercials lull her to sleep.

And then the police followed the suspect to their home . . .

Summer's eyes opened to see some crime show on TV.

Follow.

Follow?

She sat up and looked at the clock. It was late. And dark. It was nearly time for the man to collect his food.

Time to follow him?

Summer realized her light pink top and khaki shorts would show up in the dark. She hurried to her bedroom and put on black leggings and a long-sleeved black tee. She pulled her blond hair into a ponytail and put on a black Chiefs' ball cap.

She ran outside and decided to wait behind the sign of her apartment complex, across the street from the dumpster. She hid behind some bushes but was careful not to crouch, lest some late-night walker thought *she* was up to no good.

Summer pressed a hand to her chest. Her heart was beating fast and hard. *Calm yourself down. Take a breath.* She got herself under control just as she spotted the man near Happy Trails. Her heart sped up again.

He picked up the gift bag and walked away. As usual, he crossed to her side of the street and slowed his pace. Other than the hoodie and the odd time of night, he didn't look suspicious—though he did look a bit odd carrying a pink sack. Maybe she needed to rethink the bags.

Summer started walking and regretted not bringing Suzu. At least that would account for her being out so late. But Suzu liked to bark at squirrels, so it was best she was home.

She stayed back until he turned right onto Maple. She quickened her pace so she wouldn't lose him. He stayed the course three more blocks until he turned left.

Summer was out of breath as she turned onto Fifth. She couldn't see him. Had he turned into a house? She nearly panicked.

But then she saw movement in front of a one-story bungalow with a porch. A light was on inside and the man went in and shut the door.

There you are.

Summer made note of the house—it had a huge spreading oak out front and white shutters—though one was hanging cock-eyed, and even in the moonlight she could see the paint was peeling. The grass was full of weeds and the flowers in the pots on the steps were shriveled. The place needed a huge dose of TLC.

One good deed at a time.

She walked home, feeling lighter inside. She knew where he lived.

But now what?

Chapter 24

Jered

"You have shown your people desperate times;
you have given us wine that makes us stagger.
But for those who fear you,
you have raised a banner to be unfurled against the bow."
Psalm 60: 3-4

Ivy made Jered feel guilty about playing video games so he got up earlier than she did to slip in a game. There was usually one other online player up at that time. The player called Boxerdad was good. Jered liked a hard-fought game. At the moment he was up 7-3 and was about to receive the kickoff.

He had a sudden thought about his opponent. Boxerdad . . . the name brought back memories and made Jered wonder. He had known a guy named Kyle Boxer, a musician friend. They'd started out together ten years ago, playing the bar scene downtown. Boxer had a unique voice, kind of like John Denver. Actually, he had a better voice than Jered and blew him away on the guitar. Boxer played a lot of folk-songs. He'd been an old soul and a really nice guy. But as far as Jered knew, his career had never taken off.

What was that old adage? Nice guys finish last?

Jered hadn't thought of him in years. Was he still playing music? Probably not. As far as Boxerdad being *his* Boxer. Kyle a father? Not a chance. Girls swooned over Jered and ignored Boxer completely. What did Boxer think about Jered's success? Was he aware? Jealous?

"You're addicted."

Jered turned around and saw Ivy standing with her arms crossed. "I didn't know you were up."

She tied the belt of her robe. "I am now."

He paused the game. "What's for breakfast?"

She shook her head. "Why don't *you* make us something."

"I don't know how to cook."

"When we were first married you used to make French toast. Do that."

He wasn't sure he remembered how but she wasn't giving him much choice. Reluctantly, he signed out of the game and went to the kitchen.

Ivy got out bread, eggs, and milk. "Here you go."

It was starting to come back to him. "Where's the griddle pan?"

Her left eyebrow rose. "Really?"

"Don't give me a hard time."

She pointed to a lower cabinet.

Luckily, he knew where bowls were, and there was a whisk and flipper in a caddy near the stove. He wasn't sure how much milk to add, but French toast was pretty forgiving.

Hopefully, Ivy would be too.

She made coffee, poured juice, and heated up some syrup.

Fifteen minutes later he put a plate before her. "Voila!"

"Looks yummy."

He sat next to her at the counter. "Hope so."

And it was. But as he was eating he spotted a stamped letter that was ready to mail. He picked it up. "What's this?"

She gave it a cursory glance. "A card."

"To my dad?"

"It's his birthday next week. I thought it would be a nice gesture."

Jered pushed his plate away. "He's not interested in hearing from me."

"That's why *I* wrote him. He and I have always gotten along."

You get along with everyone. "He's never even been to one of my concerts. I tell you, he's not interested."

She got up and poured more coffee. "It's the right thing to do. Now."

Now? "You're talking about the Claire-stuff again?"

She looked incredulous. "Don't act ignorant."

"I told you reaching out like that just isn't me."

"Then who *are* you?" She stood up from the counter and stared down at him. "Who are you, Jered?" Her voice had a tone of disgust in it.

Surely she wasn't waiting for an answer.

Surely she was. "Tell me. Who is the real Jered Manson?"

He dragged a bite of French toast through the syrup. "I'm a musician."

"What else?"

"I'm your husband."

"Keep going."

Going? His memories sped backward, fifteen years. "I *was* a messed up teenager who got in trouble a lot and ran away from home."

"And?"

Really? "And went to jail for stealing."

She shook her head. "Not just stealing."

"Being an accessory to a kidnapping."

"Where a woman got shot."

"*I* didn't shoot her."

"You were there. You were a part of it."

He was done eating. He went to the stove, picked up the pan, and took it to the sink. "The entire world knows my past thanks to the press. What I don't get is why *you* would bring it up. Now, of all times."

"Now that God has called you?"

He thought of a way to use his past to put a stop to this. "There is no reason God would use me—a criminal—to do *good* for anyone. Me saying no is probably a relief to Him."

Her voice softened. "You used to know Him, Jer. You told me you used to pray."

There *was* a corner of his life that held the faith part of him. A hidden corner. "I did pray. But life got busy and—"

"Busy people can't pray? Busy people can't do good?"

"I don't want to discuss this again. Subject closed."

She poured her coffee down the sink. "*You've* closed the subject. God doesn't give up so easily."

"You pray *for* me, Ive. He'll listen to you."

She whipped around to face him. "You can't get to heaven on the coattails of your family."

"Who says I'm going to heaven?"

She sighed deeply. "You believe in Jesus so you *are* going to heaven. You are saved—whether you like it or not. But because of all that, you need to make a little effort to get to know Him."

He took his plate of half-eaten French toast and threw it in the trash. "Doing good deeds, reaching out to my dad . . . are you on a mission to make me feel bad?"

"Is it working?"

"No. So stop it." He stormed off toward the bedroom.

"If it takes you feeling bad to knock you off your butt, I'll take it. God called you, Jer!"

He stopped in the hall and faced her. "That's right. He called *me*, Ive. Not you."

Jered would remember her pained expression as long as he lived.

**

Jered had no idea where Ivy went after breakfast. It was nearly three and she still wasn't back. He'd purposely stayed away from the video games and had only watched one episode of *American Pickers*. He'd even made himself a sandwich using two pieces of French toast he'd rescued from the trash. Not bad.

He'd taken a nap. He'd brought his laundry basket to the laundry room. He'd gone outside to bring the empty trash cans back to the garage. It was then he'd noticed his neighbor's can was turned on its side and some stray trash was in his yard. The guy was pretty old. Jered was ashamed they'd lived there four years and he didn't remember his name. Ivy did. Ivy talked to him a lot.

He hadn't intended to pick up the trash and wheel the man's trash cans back to his garage, he'd just done it.

But afterward . . . He went inside and spotted himself in the mirror in the foyer. He was smiling. "Well, I'll be," he told his reflection. "Now I know how Ivy felt doing something nice."

Feeling good spurred him to pick up his guitar. He usually played it every day. He needed to work on new songs. What *had* gotten into him since the tour ended? It was as though once he'd said no to God he'd also said no to his good habits like swimming laps in their pool or practicing and composing.

He played through one song, then spotted another guitar leaning against the wall. His original guitar. He'd bought it at a garage sale when he was a teenager and had learned to play with a how-to book he'd found. He'd started composing right from the start. Even after he'd run away from home he'd written songs on paper he found in the garbage.

Jered exchanged his expensive Fender guitar for the no-name instrument he'd bought for $6. His dad had never approved of his music. Called it a pipe dream.

He'd shown him.

Hadn't he?

Jered tuned the strings. The guitar felt at home across his thigh. He strummed a few chords and began to sing a song Boxer had taught him, a Peter, Paul & Mary classic. "'Where have all the flowers gone? Long time passing . . .'" Although the sound wasn't as rich and resonant as the Fender, his memories added a richness to the notes. He finished the song. "'When will they ever learn? When will they e-e-ver learn?'"

When will you ever learn?

Jered froze, his hand immobile above the strings. "What?" he whispered. He didn't dare breathe or the inner words might not come back.

But they did. *When will you ever learn, Jered?*

Is that . . . ? He set the guitar aside and stared at nothing. *Is that You, God?*

Although his logical mind immediately jumped in with *of course not,* there was an inner part of him, one hidden in that dark corner, that said, *Of course it is.*

Jered put a hand to his mouth. "What am I supposed to do now?"

And then his eyes fell upon his phone sitting on the rug at his feet. He picked it up. His hands were shaking as he called a number that could never be erased from his mind.

"Hello?"

Hearing the voice, his heart skipped a beat. "Dad?"

**

Jered walked around the outside of his house, not because he wanted the exercise but because his joy was so immense he couldn't be still. His thoughts were a ticker-tape of nothing in particular, yet every possible thing. From *I'm so sorry* to *I'm so happy* to *This is really cool* to *What just happened?*

Added to the mantra was his biggest wish that Ivy would get home. He'd texted her a half-dozen times and she *had* texted him back: *home soon.*

Not soon enough. He was about to burst.

As he walked toward the front of the house for the fourth time, he spotted her car and ran to the driveway to greet her. She slammed on the brakes and put a hand to her chest. She rolled down her window. "You scared me to death. What are you doing outside?"

"Get out." He opened her door.

"Can't I pull in the garage?"

"Please, Ive. Just get out."

She turned off the engine and got out. He took her hands in his. "I talked to my dad."

"Why?"

He chuckled. It was just like her to zip past the trite question and get to the hard one. "God told me to."

Her face flooded with surprise and delight. She wrapped her arms around his neck and held him tight. "I'm so happy for you, hon."

Jered spotted the neighbor coming out of his house to get his trash cans, only to find them sitting by his garage. Jered waved at him. And he waved back. "Hi, Mr. Johnson." *I remembered his name!*

Ivy waved too and whispered. "I didn't think you ever learned his name."

"I've learned a lot of things today."

Jered took her inside and let his heart overflow.

Chapter 25

Claire

"To those who by persistence in doing good seek glory,
honor and immortality, he will give eternal life.
But for those who are self-seeking
and who reject the truth and follow evil,
there will be wrath and anger."
Romans 2: 7-8

The working hours of a chef were long and Nate's free time was limited. But two days after Billy called him, he agreed to meet—at Billy's house.

Claire peeked out the window as they heard a car drive up. A forty-something man who had clearly partaken of his own good cooking walked up to the house. Warily. Without confidence. Like a guilty man meeting his victim?

Or maybe she was over-seeing and over-thinking. It wouldn't be the first time.

He knocked on the door and Billy answered, welcoming him in with a hug. "So nice to see you again," Billy said.

"You too," Nate said without matched enthusiasm.

"This is Claire Adams." Billy drew him into the living room. "She's a local mosaic artist."

Nate nodded a greeting, then saw the mosaic on the wall. "You do that?"

"I did." Claire stepped aside so he could fully see it.

"It's . . . interesting."

So he wasn't a fan. This wasn't about her.

"Have a seat," Billy said, pointing to a chair upholstered with yellow and white stripes.

Billy sat on the couch and Claire sat in a maple glider-rocker. They'd purposely decided to sit apart so it wouldn't appear they were ganging up on him.

"How've you been?" Billy began. "How's Amanda and Ben?"

"We're all good," Nate said. "We're expecting number two."

"Congratulations. Ben will make a great big brother."

"He will." Nate cleared his throat, then asked like an afterthought, "How've you been?"

Billy leaned forward, his arms on his legs, his hands clasped. "Not so good. I miss Billy Bob's. I miss serving customers. Losing it all crushed me."

Nate glanced toward the door. He wanted to leave. "Yeah, I'm sorry about that. All of that. It was a good place."

"Then why did you quit?" Billy asked.

Nate took interest in one of the doilies on the arms of the chair. "It was time. The food in the freezers going bad, the reviews . . ."

Billy shook his head "The bad reviews came after you left and we had to hire someone in a hurry who didn't know what they were doing. The reviews weren't about you or the Billy Bob's that existed a month before."

"I . . . I'm sorry about that, Billy."

"So why did you take the rest of the kitchen staff with you? That was a big part of what killed the restaurant."

Nate shook his head, back and forth, back and forth, looking at the carpet. Finally he looked up and said, "I never meant to hurt *you,* Billy. But we had a ton of bills from Ben's birth, and our roof was leaking and the washer broke, and we really needed a washing machine with the new baby."

Billy and Claire exchanged a look. "You left because of money? You should have told me your problems. I would have loaned you—"

Nate let out a rush of air, like he'd been holding his breath for a year. "Robby paid me to leave—paid me a lot. Paid the others a lot."

Billy and Claire sat back as if Nate's words were physical.

"Sorry, man. I really didn't think it would make that much of a difference, and the money . . . as I said, I needed the money."

"How much did he pay you?" Claire asked.

Nate pressed his back against the chair, gripping the arms. "Ten-K. He paid the help a thousand each." He looked at them, each in turn. "I didn't think it would make you go under. I really didn't."

You had to realize it wouldn't make things better. "Did Robby give you a reason of *why* he wanted you to quit?" she asked.

Nate looked to his lap. "I never believed it . . ."

"What did he say?" Billy asked.

"He said you were stealing from the restaurant and rigged the freezers so we lost all that food."

"I did no such thing!"

Nate shrugged. "It didn't sound like you, but I didn't know. And me and the help figured you might have done the freezer-thing for insurance money or something."

Claire looked at Billy and cocked her head. *He* hadn't gone after the insurance, but had Robby?

Nate stood. "I gotta go, but I want to say that I'm really sorry for everything. The new place is okay but I liked it better when you were running things."

Claire had a question. "How long after Billy Bob's closed did Robby approach you about being the chef at his new place?"

Nate took a step toward the door. "Actually, he might've mentioned it when he paid me the ten-thou." He put his hand on the doorknob. "I never thought it would turn out like this. You're a good guy, Billy. I never had anything against you." He stepped through the doorway and left.

Billy slumped on the couch. "He never had anything against me, but conspired against me?" He ran a hand through his hair. "I had no idea this was going on. I was naïve to think Robby and I were in it together."

Claire sat beside him. "I'm so sorry."

Billy kept shaking his head. "Robby set me up. Set the whole thing up so he could have his own place."

"It seems so." She wanted to bring up the subject of the insurance, but didn't want to add salt to Billy's wounds.

He did it himself. "I never knew of any insurance claim for the food and freezers. Robby told me he got the freezers fixed and asked me for my half of the bill, plus the bill to replace the food we lost."

Claire had a new thought. "What if the food wasn't lost at all?"

"What do you mean?"

She faced him on the couch. "What if Robby moved the food somewhere, staged the broken appliances, showed you fake bills, and pocketed your money?"

The line between this eyebrows deepened. "Money that pretty much wiped out my contingency fund."

It was all coming together. "He gets the kitchen staff to quit, has to hire new people quickly—people who aren't ready for prime time, then purposely asks reviewers to come in, knowing things would go wrong."

"He'd hurt his own reputation?"

"It got you to walk away, didn't it? Then he changes the name, hires back the help, and starts over without you—in the place you designed and put your heart into, using some of your grandma's recipes."

His face was a mask of pain. "How could he do that to me? How could I be so stupid to fall for it?"

Claire ran a hand along his shoulders. "It's not your fault. You trusted him. He's the one who betrayed that trust and moved on with his life as if nothing happened. He should pay for what he's done."

"Pay?"

She second guessed herself. Should she have brought that up? "I just don't want you blaming yourself for *his* sins."

He held his head in his hands. "I'm such a loser. A dupe. An idiot."

"No, you're not." *Father, help me here.* "You're the victim of—at the very least—a con man. At most, a criminal."

He let his hands fall, nodded, and was silent a moment. "What should I do?"

Claire's pragmatic side took over. "I think we need to get more evidence. Do you have access to the bill for the freezer repairs?"

"I do, but only because Robby presented me with one, wanting my half."

"Do you know the name of your insurance agent?"

"Robby handled that, but . . ." he looked to the ceiling. "I think his name was Tommy Tober or Toger, something like that. Both names started with a T."

"That's a start. We talk to the repair guy and the insurance guy." She took his hand again. "It's about the truth, Billy. No matter what, we need to discover the truth."

**

They went into the bedroom in Grandma's house that Billy used as an office so he could go through a box of old papers. Claire sat at the computer doing an agent search for Tommy-something starting with a T.

Claire was successful first. "I found him. Tommy Tobler. Accona Insurance Company. Want me to call him? Ask to meet?"

"Not really, but yes, go ahead. I finished the reno at Nearly New and have today off, but tomorrow I start a new job. A meeting after four-thirty would be best."

She called and got a meeting for the next day.

Within minutes, Billy found the bill. "Here it is: Reliable Appliance Repair."

Claire picked up her phone, but hesitated. "Surely we could stop by. We're just asking about an old invoice—which you have." She set her phone down.

He handed her the bill and put a lid on the box. "Let's go."

She appreciated his decisiveness.

Twenty minutes later, they pulled in front of the business. Billy turned off the car. "What if we find something bad?"

"You'd rather let the lie win?"

He sighed deeply and got out, motioning to her that he would get her door.

Such a gentleman. Such a gentle man.

Inside, a receptionist greeted them. "How may I help you?"

"My name is Billy Cumberson. I have an old bill here and I would like to speak with the person who did the repairs."

The woman's eyebrows met in the middle. "Is there a problem with the work?"

"Not at all. It's fine. I have no complaints."

"It's rather complicated," Claire said with a smile. "We'd really appreciate your help."

The woman took the bill and said, "I'll check the job file to see who did the work."

"Perfect," Claire said.

"If you want to take a seat, I'll be right back."

They sat in the waiting room. Billy fidgeted in his chair. "I hate waiting."

So did she. Luckily, they didn't have to wait long. The receptionist returned with an older woman with pink half-glasses perched on her nose.

"Hello. I'm Agnes. I'm the bookkeeper here." She held two pieces of paper.

"Did you find the name of the worker?" Claire asked.

She sat in a third chair. "We don't have any record of this invoice."

"What do you mean?" Claire asked.

Agnes looked from one to the other. "The bill you brought in is bogus."

"What?" Billy asked.

"It's not real. It's a fake."

Claire was glad she was sitting down. "The logo is the same as you have outside. The address is the same."

It *is* one of our bills—the invoice number is printed on it, and it's real in that sense, but . . ." She sighed. "I need to know where you got it."

"My business partner gave it to me," Billy said.

Agnes glanced at the bill. "For Billy Bob's Steakhouse?"

He nodded. "I'm Billy. Billy Cumberson."

She held out the second sheet of paper. "This is the original Invoice 28503 dated five years ago."

Billy looked at it. "I remember this. Our dishwasher wasn't working right."

Agnes pointed at the newer bill. "This is for freezer repairs. And one replacement freezer."

"Right. Our freezers blew and we lost a ton of food."

She shook her head. "We didn't fix them."

"But there's the bill."

"Someone took an old bill and doctored it."

"But I paid half the bill. Six hundred and fifty-two dollars and twenty-five cents for repairs and two thousand four hundred and fifty dollars for half the new freezer."

"Forty-eight hundred for a freezer?" Agnes shook her head again. "That's way too much."

"Was it a fancy new freezer?" Claire asked him.

"I . . . it looked the same as before."

Was there a new freezer at all?

"Freezer or not," Agnes said. "You didn't pay any of this amount to *us*."

"Did you, Billy?" Claire asked. "Did you write the check to Reliable or—"

Billy's shoulders slumped. "Robby. I wrote it to Robby. He said he would pay the bill."

A fake bill.

Agnes let her glasses hang from a chain around her neck. "You've been had, Mr. Cumberson, and someone has misrepresented our company to perpetrate the fraud."

Fraud. The word resounded with a heavy weight.

"The next question," Agnes said, "Is what do we do about it? On our end I need to talk to the owners. What's the last name of 'Robby'?"

"I'd rather not tell you just yet," he said. "Until I talk to him."

"With a little digging I can find out," she said.

Billy sighed. "Bianchi. But please don't do anything right away."

Agnes stood. "Very well. He hurt you more than us." She retreated to the receptionist's desk and handed Billy a business card. "I'll be waiting to hear from you, Billy. Give Mary your number."

He did so. "I'm sorry to draw you into all this, Agnes."

"It's a sad state of affairs. Good luck," she said.

They returned to the car, but just sat there. "Robby stole from me. He betrayed me. He defrauded me."

"Yes, he did."

"He destroyed our friendship for a few thousand dollars."

"And a restaurant," she said. "You walked away."

"All part of his plan." Billy stared down at the business card. "What I don't get is why God allowed him to hurt me. He allowed Robby to ruin my life. What kind of God does that?"

Hit me with a hard one. "A God whose ways are not our ways?"

"Obviously." He gripped the steering wheel and leaned his head against it. "Why would He make me suffer?"

It was a universal, eternal question. "Maybe it's going to allow Him to showcase how He metes out justice?"

He looked at her. "So I suffer so He can show off? That seems wrong. There wouldn't be a need for justice if God hadn't allowed the sin in the first place."

Claire racked her brain, trying to think of a response. Nothing came to her.

Billy started the car and pulled into traffic. "I'm not sure I want to pursue this."

"Why not?"

"It's too painful. And what good will it do?"

Just then Claire saw a billboard that was bare except for five words: *Want to know the truth?*

"Look at that!"

Billy looked toward it, but only had a moment to see it. "A billboard? I didn't see what it's advertising."

"Neither did I." *I don't know if it was advertising anything.* He was missing the point. "It said, 'Want to know the truth?' It's a message that's perfect for right now, for this situation. For you."

He scoffed. "God sent me a billboard."

"Is the message a valid one?"

"Well, sure."

"Is it something God would say to You?"

"Probably."

"No 'probably' to it. He said 'the truth will set you free.' Do you want to be free of your pain, your uncertainty, your questions, and your feeling of failure?"

He raised his voice in a mocking come-to-Jesus voice, "Preach it, Sister Claire!"

"Don't make fun of me. The questions are valid. And your answer is . . .?"

"There's no way to say no to any of them."

"Exactly." She touched his arm. "Billy, truth is *the* issue right now."

"You're referring to the truth about Robby, which is disturbing, frustrating, and makes me sad."

"You were disturbed, frustrated, and sad anyway."

He chuckled. "Don't take up counseling, Claire."

She knew she wasn't a great empathizer but had to disagree. "I think my counsel is spot on. You're hurting. The truth will give you answers to get past the hurt."

"I've done that. I've moved on. I'm very happy working construction."

"It's not just about moving on *outside*." She put a fist to her gut. "It's about moving on *inside*."

He glanced at her. "You're not going to let this go, are you?"

"Not until *He* tells me to."

"You're ganging up on me."

"That's right," she said. "Don't mess with us. The Almighty God, and the mighty Claire!"

He laughed. "I wouldn't dare."

Chapter 26

Ryan

"The fruit of the Spirit is love, joy, peace, forbearance, kindness, goodness, faithfulness, gentleness and self-control."
Galatians 5: 22-23

Ryan and the Pearls left at sunrise. The pickup was filled to overflowing with belongings, coolers, and one rocking chair. Ryan paused before getting in the truck and prayed a familiar prayer: *Lord, erect a dome of protection around us and keep us safe.*

Lisa sat behind the men in the truck's extended cab. She looked out the back to keep the house in view as they drove down the drive toward the highway. Finally, she looked forward. "What's going to happen to it?"

"I'll call the ranch and tell them they can buy it at a good price," Grandpa said. "They've wanted to buy it for decades."

"What about the stuff we left behind?"

"I told you to bring what you wanted."

"I did. It's just weird."

Ryan remembered something his parents used to say, "We're leaving a house, but taking the *home* with us."

"Good one, boy."

Ryan stopped at the highway. "Left or right? Did you decide you want to go backroads or interstate?" They'd studied a map the day before.

"I think faster is better."

This was not the choice Ryan expected. It being a "road-trip" he'd thought Grandpa would want to wallow in Americana. Was his choice to go the fast way due to his health issues?

"But not too fast," Grandpa said. "I know we can make it in one long day, but let's take our time."

It was a plan. They headed north toward Interstate 70, through the picturesque Flint Hills.

"I am going to miss these hills," Grandpa said.

"We can come back and visit," Lisa said.

Grandpa didn't answer.

An hour in, they stopped for gas at a truck stop and stocked up on Sugar Babies, lemon drops, and orange slices. And a cherry Slurpee, coffee, and a Coke. Junk food city.

As Grandpa paid, Ryan spotted something he had to buy. "I'll be right there," he told them as they headed out to the truck. He made his purchase and climbed into the driver's seat. "Here," he said to Lisa.

"*The Adventures of Tom Sawyer*!"

"I figure you could read it out loud to us."

And so she did.

**

The painting-the-fence part came early on in *Tom Sawyer*. Soon after starting the second chapter Lisa stopped mid-sentence. "This is it—what you did to me."

Grandpa chuckled. "Can't believe you fell for it."

"Read on," Ryan said.

And so she did.

**

"Bison?" Lisa pointed at a sign. "It says there's a bison herd close by."

Subsequent signs announced the bison as well as an historic fort.

"Can we stop?"

"Don't see why not." Grandpa rubbed his thighs. "I need to get out and move anyway. The doctor warned me about blood clots."

Why hadn't he said something? They'd already been on the road three hours.

Ryan followed the signs at Hays, Kansas, south to Fort Hays. It didn't look like a typical fort. There wasn't a fence around it like you always saw in the movies. And there, nearby, was a herd of bison.

They parked and Lisa ran to the fence with Ryan and Grandpa following behind. Grandpa was limping. "You okay?" Ryan asked.

"Shush now. I'll let you know if I'm not."

They joined Lisa at the fence.

"There's so many," Lisa said.

A man who looked to be in his eighties was fixing the barbed wire on the fence nearby and heard her. "This isn't many at all compared to what used to be around here."

"How many was that?"

"Forty million."

"What?"

He took off his cowboy hat and wiped his brow. "When Fort Hays opened in the 1860s men used to hunt them for sport. Killed them off to just a hundred or so."

"That's horrible."

"Sure was. If it weren't for the efforts of a few men who started breeding 'em, you'd never see a single one."

"That's so sad."

He looked at the men. "You going over to the fort museum?"

"Thought we would," Ryan said.

"Enjoy yourself. My great-great-grandpa was a soldier there. He met Custer and Buffalo Bill and Wild Bill Hickock." He glanced at Lisa. "Calamity Jane too. Hays was a rough town back then. Already had over thirty graves in Boot Hill before it even became a town."

"There's boots in a hill?" Lisa asked.

The man chuckled. "In a way. There's men buried there. They died with their boots on."

Suddenly, Grandpa started coughing and Ryan ran and got Lisa's leftover Slurpee from the truck.

"There's a place to sit in the museum," the man said. "Pop and snacks too."

Grandpa shook his head. "We need to move on. Get some lunch and move on."

The man pointed. "You want a good home-cooking meal, go to Rosie's, just a mile north. She's my wife and she'll treat you right. Best chicken-fried chicken in the state. Tell them Sam sent you."

They got in the truck and found Rosie's. It was a nondescript place with a sign that needed a new coat of paint. But the parking area was packed—always a gauge for tasty food.

They went inside and got a booth. The walls were decorated with wallpaper scattered with pink roses.

How appropriate.

A waitress greeted them and brought three waters—which Grandpa downed.

"Thirsty, are you? We're known for our malts."

"Strawberry?" Lisa asked.

"We can do that." She looked at the men. "Three?"

Lisa ordered strawberry and the men ordered chocolate. Plus two chicken-fried chicken dinners with mashed potatoes and green beans, and a hot dog and fries for Lisa.

"Oh," Ryan said as the waitress started to turn away. "We're supposed to tell Rosie Sam sent us."

She smiled. "I'll tell her."

Ryan studied Grandpa. He wanted to ask how he was feeling but remembered being scolded for it.

Lisa did the asking. "You feeling better, Grandpa?"

"Just a cough-spell. That's all it was. Sorry to cut short our visit to the fort."

"It's okay. I wanted to see the bison most anyway."

An old woman approached and introduced herself. "Hey there. I'm Rosie. You spoke to my husband?"

"We did," Ryan said.

"We saw the bison," Lisa said.

"Did he talk your ear off?" Rosie asked.

"He said there used to be forty million of 'em."

"That's a fact. Where you from?"

"Emporia," Grandpa said. "Goin' to see the mountains."

"We're moving there," Lisa added.

"I know the mountains well. What town you settling in?"

They all looked at each other. Grandpa answered. "Haven't picked a place yet."

She chuckled. "Spoken like a true pioneer. Go where the wind blows and settle where the sun shines bright."

"I like that," Ryan said.

"You need to hunt for the Promised Land," she said. "'A land flowing with milk and honey.'"

"Really?" Lisa looked at Grandpa. "You promised it would be good. But milk and honey?"

Rosie touched her arm. "You'll like it there." She glanced back to the counter where a line was forming. "I gotta take some money. But when you're done tell Dorothy to give each of you a piece of my homemade pie—on the house."

Their food was served and heartily consumed. They ordered their pie to-go.

During the meal Ryan noticed an elderly woman sitting with two old men at a booth nearby. They were eating and chatting. Probably locals who came in often.

There was something about the woman that caught his eye. Although she had to be in her eighties she was still pretty. She had a glow that radiated an inner beauty.

Tell her so.

Ryan was startled by the inner nudge and immediately began to argue against it. *I can't go up to a total stranger and tell her how pretty she is. It's just not done.*

His chance was interrupted when a local man stopped beside the woman's table and talked to them. *See? I can't interrupt their conversation.*

Yes, you can.

Ryan rationalized. If the man left before it was time for he and the Pearls to leave, he'd say something. If not, he wouldn't.

"Ready to go?" Grandpa said.

Apparently, that time was now.

They got up to leave. Ryan let the others go first. As he walked by the woman's booth—man standing there or no man standing there—he leaned toward her, and said for her ears alone, "You are one of the prettiest women I've ever seen. I mean it."

Her face lit up and she said, "Why thank you."

After they left the café Grandpa asked, "What was all that about?"

"I got a nudge to tell her she was pretty, so I did." *It was a little more complicated than that, but that's the gist of it.*

"You didn't know her," Lisa said.

"Nope." Ryan put their pies in a cooler.

"Then why did you tell her that?" Grandpa asked.

"God told me to."

"Why?" Lisa climbed in the truck.

"I don't know. And I will never know. Maybe she needed a compliment. Maybe she was feeling down and God wanted me to cheer her up."

"That's just strange," Grandpa said.

"I think it's neat," Lisa said. "I'm going to do that sometime."

"You will not," Grandpa said. "I will not have you telling a stranger they're pretty."

She made a pouty face.

Ryan wasn't going to argue with Grandpa, but he suspected Lisa would take her chance to do something nice when it was offered.

Chapter 27

Summer

"Make a joyful noise to the Lord, all the earth!
Serve the Lord with gladness!"
Psalm 100: 1-2

It was Summer's day off—from *one* of her jobs. After working at the coffee shop, she had the rest of the day off until her dinner shift.

She tried to read. But a story about the plague in the Middle Ages didn't sit well.

She tried to watch TV but the inane chatter and canned laughter made her want to throw the remote.

She turned on some music and decided to deep clean the kitchen. She had no clue how crumbs got in the cupboard holding her glasses, or how an unopened Sweet-n-Lo packet got under her sink.

The food cupboards were out of order from her scrounging for the care packages. She realized that no one—no one—needed lima beans or pickled beets. Why *she* had them was a mystery.

Summer prayed some snippet-prayers as she worked, prayers that were her constant companions lately, though sometimes she didn't even realize she was praying. *Show me how to help…give me a connection…help me, Lord.*

And then a song came on, an oldie-goldie Kenny Loggins song. Summer sang along, rather amazed she knew the words. She sang louder on the chorus: "'Are you gonna wait for a sign, your miracle? Stand up and fight. This is it. Make no mistake where you are. This is it . . .'"

She stopped singing.

She stopped moving.

She looked at the can of chili in her hand and whispered, "This is it."

I've been praying for a connection. The man. He's my connection.

And she knew where he lived.

**

Summer felt awkward going to the man's house unannounced and uninvited. For one thing, he was a man and lived alone. Common sense said she shouldn't go in his house. She had no idea how old he was, though by the way he climbed in and out of the dumpster, she knew he wasn't that old.

Which was one reason she put together another care package for him. If he answered the door and the vibes weren't right, she'd hand him the bag and leave. To give credence to her hand-delivered gift, she'd put in frozen food that she hadn't dared put in the dumpster bags.

Although she could have driven to the house, she decided to walk to give herself time to pray about it—to give God time to stop her if she was traveling down the wrong road.

"Stop being so dramatic," she whispered to herself as she walked the last block. "God sent you here. You wanted a connection, this is it. God will take care of you." She still added a prayer for protection. And for the right words. What should she say to the man?

Enough second-guessing. She walked up the porch steps and ran the doorbell. Her heart pounded in her toes.

Someone cracked open the door without looking out. "Yes?"

It was a woman's voice.

"Hi, I'm Summer Peerbaugh, and I've been—"

The door swiped wide open. "Summer?"

It was hard to see through the screen door because it had patches in it.

But the voice . . . "Sydney?" An old friend.

"Yeah, it's me. Come in."

The small living room was rundown, yet was pure Craftsman with oak pillars and trim, bookcases flanking a fireplace, and squared off spindles on the stairway. Some spindles were missing, and the oak floors were scuffed and worn. There was an overstuffed couch, a floor lamp, and a TV on a stand. As a visitor it would have been normal to compliment the home, but that wasn't possible.

"Sorry," Sydney said. "I know it's gross. Long story. Have a seat."

Summer sat on the couch, still trying to fathom that the hooded man was her friend. Sydney moved some celebrity magazines aside and sat at the other end.

Summer realized she was still holding the sack of frozen food. "I brought you some frozen things."

"What?"

"Food. I've been leaving bags of food?"

Sydney's eyes grew wide. "You're the one?"

Summer nodded. "I live in the apartments across the street. I saw you one night." *Climbing in the dumpster.*

Sydney covered her eyes with a hand. "How embarrassing."

"I thought you were a man."

"So you didn't see *me?"*

The distinction seemed important to her. "Not at all."

She shook her head over and over. "I'm not ready to show myself around town. Too many questions."

Summer had a few of her own.

"I see a car outside," Summer said. "Why did you always walk?"

Sydney chuckled. "My car is a piece of junk. The muffler's shot and it makes a racket. Middle of the night? Racket?"

"Then walking makes sense."

"I have a question of my own," Sydney said. "How did you know where I lived?"

"I followed you home one night. And today . . . I couldn't leave the frozen—"

"Frozen. Yes. Let me put it away. I'll be back in a minute."

Summer used the time alone to study the room. It had potential, but the sparse furnishings weren't Sydney's usually flashy style. The room was rather ordinary. Sydney returned with a glass of water "Sorry I don't have anything else."

"Water is good. Thanks."

They sat in awkward silence a moment. Then Summer asked, "How's Ben?"

Sydney let out a dramatic harrumph. "Gone. We're divorced."

Summer was totally shocked. "I'm so sorry." She didn't know what else to say.

Sydney tucked her feet beneath her. "Yeah. Well. The bubble burst. Bigtime."

"Do you want to tell me what happened?"

"No. But I will." She pulled a pillow to her chest and took a few seconds to collect her thoughts. "Everybody warned me about him, saying he was selfish and all about himself, but I wanted to be married so bad I ignored everything."

Summer had warned her too. She'd even heard Sydney's mom and dad talk negatively about the marriage on the wedding day. Not a good beginning.

Sydney was waiting for her to say something. "You ignored our opinions because you were in love."

"Hmm. Love is definitely blind." She let go of the pillow and angled herself to face Summer. "The trouble with a daddy's girl marrying a mama's boy is that both parties expect to be pampered. Neither one of us knew a thing about real life. Neither one of us could hold a job because we'd never had to."

Summer remembered high school when *she* always had a job and Sydney would brag that her parents said she didn't have to work.

Sydney continued. "Then . . . when I get stressed I eat. I gained a ton of weight. That's when Ben started calling me *fatty* and *pork belly*—and worse."

"That was mean. You look great."

"Now, I do. When I found out he was sleeping around I lost the weight so he'd want me again. But he didn't."

"Nice guy."

"What can I say? He's a creep." She took a sip of water. "I told him to stop with the flings and warned him I would leave. Our parents even talked to him. But he didn't want to fix it. He didn't want to be with me. Period. So, I ended it."

"That must have been hard."

She nodded once, then swiped her dark hair behind her ears. "I couldn't afford the apartment alone, so I decided to move home to be with my parents."

"That's logical."

"But then *they* decided to divorce."

Another shocker. "After all these years?"

"Twenty-five years. You'd think they could have hung on after that long." Sydney sighed. "Looking back I always knew their marriage was rocky. They did a lot of pretending—pretending to love each other, pretending to be important in the community, pretending to have money—Mom told me they're still paying off my wedding. Can you believe it? My marriage is over and the wedding still hasn't been paid off? Anyway, now their marriage is over too. Daddy moved to Florida and Mom got the house here."

Which still didn't explain why Sydney was living in this DIY wannabe. "Why didn't you move in with her?"

"She wouldn't let me."

Summer hesitated, weighing the implications of her reaction. "That's harsh."

Sydney shrugged. "She said it wasn't healthy for two angry, grieving women to live under the same roof." She waved her arms to encompass the room where they sat. "They'd bought this house to flip, so she said I could live here until I got a job and could afford something better." She looked around the quiet room. "It's so embarrassing to come back to town like this. I made a big deal about getting married young and bragged about how great our life would be." She scoffed. "Look at me now, digging food out of a dumpster in the middle of the night. If my friends saw me, they'd have a field day."

Friends. As in other, more important people.

Sydney suddenly raised a hand. "Shoot. That sounded horrible. *You* are my friend, Summer. You've known me longer than anyone."

She was appeased. "I am here for you, Syd."

Sydney nodded. "Isn't it sad how a person's expectations for life can be as phony and worthless as a three-dollar bill?"

Summer understood her pain, but hated her lack of hope. *Father, show me how to help her.*

Sydney pressed her hands against her thighs and stood. "This pity-party is officially over. I'm sure you need to get back to your life." She paused. "Which I know nothing about because all I've done is talk about myself." She sighed deeply, looking like a teenager again. "Old habits are hard to break. I'm sorry I've been such a selfish whiner."

"I'm glad to listen. Always, Syd. Anytime." Then she had an idea. "I work three jobs. Maybe I could help you get—"

"Three jobs?" Sydney shook her head. "Stable, overachiever, Summer. I shouldn't be surprised."

Summer thought of her workplaces and chose one. "How about working in a flower shop?"

She cocked her head. "Maybe." Then she shook her complacency away. "I have to pay the bills. I can't be picky."

It was not the reaction Summer had hoped for. "I'll talk to the owner tomorrow and will arrange a time for you to come in and interview."

"Thanks, Summer. I appreciate it."

"Meanwhile . . . If you'd like to give me a list of things you need, I'd be happy to get them for you. Or I'll go out *with* you to shop. I can spot you the money."

Sydney shook her head. "Go out? Not yet. And I don't need anything at the moment." She smiled. "You've got me well supplied." She nodded at her phone on the couch. "Text me your number and email."

"I will." Summer opened the door. "You'll be okay, Syd. I promise."

"Hmm. Maybe. But I do appreciate your faith in me."

Although Sydney's story was sad and a bit hopeless, Summer left her house feeling as if she could fly home.

She finally had a connection!

**

As she neared her apartment, Summer spotted a mostly-empty pickup backed up to the door of the complex. A sandy-haired man was pulling out boxes, setting them on the ground.

"Need some help?" she asked.

"Wouldn't say no, though I'm down to two." Before she took a box he held out a hand. "Max. Moving into the second floor there."

Summer shook his hand and looked where he was pointing. "I'm Summer. I'm right above you."

He winked. "Truly neighbors then." He moved a box that seemed heavy and gave her a lighter one.

His apartment was already full of furniture. "When did this happen?" she asked.

"Yesterday. I'm surprised you didn't hear me scream when I dropped a dresser on my foot."

"Sorry I missed it. I was probably at work."

"Where do you work?" He offered her a Mountain Dew from the fridge, motioned toward the recliner for her, and moved a box off the end of the couch so he could sit.

"Moving is a pain," he said. "I'm not good at organizing."

"I love to organize." She glanced over her shoulder at the kitchen which had boxes piled two-high on the counters. "Especially kitchens."

"I might take you up on that." He moved another box from the couch that was blocking his view of her. "Your job?"

"Jobs." She told him the details. "And you?"

"I just started at Prairie Construction as an estimator."

"You must be good at math."

"One plus one always equals two. I like that. But *you* have three jobs. What are you saving for?"

She realized it might look like that. "I'm not in it for the money."

His left eyebrow rose. "You love your work that much?"

"Not really. I don't love being a barista, a clerk, and a waitress." She wanted him to think more of her. "I have a degree in social work."

He laughed. "You're helping fill society's need for coffee, flowers, and food."

He made it sound as trivial as it was. She stood. "Nice to meet you, Max. I'll let you get unpacked."

He stopped her before she got to the door. "Don't go. I shouldn't have made light of your work ethic. It's commendable. 'Be strong and do the work' and all that."

She did a double-take. He'd quoted a Bible verse.

"You know that one?" he asked.

"I do."

"How about 'forgive him for he's a stupid fool'?"

She smiled.

"The book of Maxwell, chapter one, verse ten."

She turned toward him. "Verse ten, huh."

"Yup."

"I'd like to hear verses one through nine."

He laughed. "Give me time." He motioned toward the kitchen. "You mentioned organizing? I think there's a package of Oreos in there somewhere."

"Are you bribing me?"

"Maybe. If sweets aren't your thing, I have Bugles."

She laughed. "How about both?"

"It's a deal."

The next hour was spent organizing his kitchen while he finished unpacking office supplies at a desk in the living room. Their banter was easy. He liked reading and movies so they compared favorite titles.

Then suddenly he noticed the time and jumped to his feet. "I have to get the rental truck back by five or pay for another day."

She finished the last of the silverware drawer. "Good timing. All done."

He grabbed his keys and opened the door for her. "Maybe I'll see you tomorrow?"

She thought of her own verse. "'There was evening, and there was morning—the first day.'"

"Of many, I hope."

Talk about flying.

Chapter 28

Michelle

"Whoever is kind to the poor lends to the Lord,
and he will reward them for what they have done."
Proverbs 19: 17

Michelle served breakfast at the shelter, but kept an eye out for Jonette. Although she'd offered the girl a bed for the night, she'd declined. Michelle's own sleep had been fragmented, thinking about her out on the street.

They were nearly out of scrambled eggs so Michelle took the tray back to the kitchen for another one.

As she returned to the front, she saw Jonette come in the front door. She handed the tray to a helper. "Thanks. I'll be right back." She hurried toward the girl—who looked awful. Her hair was mussed and there were dark circles under her eyes.

"Hey. Jonette."

The girl looked up, then looked away as though ashamed. "Hi."

She looked smaller than before, like the streets had diminished her. "Want to eat something?"

Jonette glanced toward the food line. "Can I talk to you?"

"Of course." Michelle led her to an empty table.

Jonette cringed when she sat down, like her body was hurting. "I . . . I made a mistake."

"How so?"

"I shoulda slept here."

Michelle's mind swam with scenarios. "What happened?"

Michelle's face must have revealed her worries for Jonette said, "Not that. Nothing like that."

Michelle sighed with relief. "So where did you sleep?"

"Under some bushes in the park." She began scratching her leg. "It was buggy. I'm bit up."

"I can get you some lotion for that . . . why *under* the bushes?"

"So people couldn't see me." She shook her head. "It's best not to be seen."

Michelle hated to witness her fear. "I'm sorry you had a bad night."

"It's my own fault." She dug into the pocket of her shorts and pulled out a key.

"What's that for?"

"I *thought* it was for my dad's office which is downtown here. I was going to go inside and sleep but the key didn't work." She put it back in her pocket. "I had nowhere to go."

"You could have come back here."

She shook her head. "I felt dumb about it. You'd offered and I'd said no."

Michelle jumped at the mention of her dad. "What's your dad do?"

"He's an accountant. Taxes and stuff."

"Does he know where you are?"

She shook her head, looking like a child who'd been naughty.

"Maybe you should call him. Let him know you're okay."

Jonette hugged herself. "He doesn't need me anymore."

"I'm sure that's not true. I'm sure he's worried."

The girl shook the subject away. "That room you talked about?"

Room? Michelle hoped Jonette didn't expect too much. "It's not a room, it's a bed in a room." *A bedroll in a room.*

"There's just girls in there?" Jonette pressed a hand against her forehead and grimaced.

Was that a bump? "Just girls. The men are on another floor. Did someone hit you?"

"I surprised him, that's all. It's okay."

"It is *not* okay. Let me have our nurse look at it."

"I'm okay!" Jonette said it too loud and people looked her way. She lowered her voice. "Sorry. Really. It's okay. But I would like the bed."

Michelle stood. "Let me check for you. Why don't you get some breakfast. I'll be right back."

As Michelle went to check on the bed-situation, she thanked God for bringing Jonette back safe. She didn't believe her story about the bump on her head, but knew it could have been worse.

The housing manager looked through his lists for the night. "Sorry, Michelle, there's no bed available tonight."

The thought of telling Jonette the news made her cringe. "Can't we squeeze in another bedroll? She's a bitty thing."

"No can do. You know the city only allows so many. It's the law. Sorry. I'll let you know if something opens up."

As she started to walk away, he said, "How are things going for you since you moved out?"

Michelle froze. She answered, "Fine," but her mind was busy with a new idea. "Have they remodeled my room yet?"

"Not yet. They're getting bids."

Michelle thanked him for the information and returned to the dining room with new hope. She found Jonette sitting in the same chair she'd sat in when they'd talked.

She looked up when Michelle approached. "Is there a bed open?"

"Sort of."

"What does that mean?"

Michelle's eagerness nearly overflowed, but she didn't dare say it where others could hear. "Finish eating and I'll show you."

As soon as Jonette was done, Michelle led her upstairs to her old room. It was at the opposite end of the building from the men's dorm and bathroom. Michelle was glad she still had the key. She unlocked the door, swung it open, and flipped on the light. "Voila!"

Jonette looked inside. "It's a room. Not just a bed, a room. But you said . . ."

Michelle opened the blind, letting the small room fill with sunlight. "It was *my* room for years."

"Why did you move out?"

"The shelter needs more office space. But they don't even have bids for the remodel yet, so it's yours if you want it." She turned on the bathroom light. "Small but private."

Jonette ran a hand along the bed's patchwork quilt. "This is so nice of you." She touched the pillow. "You lived here? You don't have family?"

"I had a husband."

"What was his name?"

"Sergei."

"Cool name. Any kids?"

"Unfortunately, no."

"That's too bad. I think you would have made a good mom."

"What a nice thing to say."

Jonette sat on the bed. Her shoulders slumped. Then her eyes misted over. "Why are you doing this for *me*?"

"Two reasons: because I care and I can."

Jonette nodded, but then she began to cry. Michelle sat beside her and tentatively put an arm around her shoulders.

The girl leaned toward her and they both enjoyed the hug they needed.

**

Darkness came late in July—after 9:30. Michelle arrived home long after the streetlights were on.

Claire was in her pjs watching the nightly news. "When you called to say you'd be late, I didn't think you meant this late."

Michelle fell onto the loveseat. "Neither did I."

"Was there an emergency?"

She didn't have enough energy to shake her head. "I lost at Uno. Twice."

"Uno?"

"The card game?"

"Haven't had the pleasure." Claire muted the TV. "How's that girl you mentioned the other night?"

"Jonette. She's good." *For the moment.* She didn't say more. Claire was the type of person who answered questions in great detail. Michelle was not. "How was your day?"

"Extremely interesting. Billy and I talked to the chef who quit Billy Bob's, but then was hired back by Robby. Turns out Robby had paid him $10,000 to quit. And he paid off the kitchen staff too. That man told so many lies it's disgusting. Then we went to the people who supposedly replaced the bad freezer and it turns out they never did any such . . ."

Claire's words faded into an unintelligible hum as Michelle slipped away from the here and now.

She felt Claire nudge her into a reclining position on the loveseat, and was only slightly aware when an afghan was draped over her. The bright light of the nearby lamp was extinguished. The room went quiet.

Michelle slept.

**

Michelle was jarred awake by a sudden thought: *I didn't send a verse!*

She bolted upright. It took her a few moments to remember where she was and why she was in the living room. *I fell asleep while Claire was talking. That wasn't very polite of me.*

She'd apologize in the morning. What couldn't wait for morning was sending the verse.

Yet what did it matter? Claire said they were nice, but no one else seemed to care if she sent them. Who knows if the men even opened the emails? It was a fool's folly. A futile folly.

Michelle stood, folded the afghan, and headed toward her bedroom.

Halfway there she stopped as an inner voice whispered: *Don't give up. Send it.*

She couldn't refuse. Though she was still tired and done-in, she turned around and went to Claire's office computer.

The perfect verse came to her: "Come to me, all you who are weary and burdened, and I will give you rest." She looked it up to get the source: Matthew 11: 28.

Within a half hour, she'd bought a pretty pastel image of pink and blue flowers with a mint green background. It was peaceful. Calm. Perfect for the verse.

Michelle hit SEND then went to bed. To rest.

Chapter 29

Claire

"Not a word from their mouth can be trusted;
their heart is filled with malice.
Their throat is an open grave;
with their tongues they tell lies."
Psalm 5: 9

The Accona Insurance Company was in a strip mall sandwiched between a nail shop and a deli.

Billy parked the car. "I've never heard of this company, have you?"

"Nope," Claire said. "That doesn't necessarily mean anything. I've used the same company for twenty years."

Billy opened the glass door which had Tommy Tobler's name on it, though the second T was missing part of its top. The receptionist had small jewels pasted on her fingernails. "Good morning. May I help you?"

"We're here to see Mr. Tobler. We had an appointment? Billy Cumberson?"

She stood and yanked at her too-tight dress. "Right this way please."

She led them to one of two offices. "Tom-Tom? Your four-thirty is here."

"Thank you, Gina." They all shook hands. "Have a seat and tell me how I can help you on this fine day. Are you in need of auto? Home? I have a juicy umbrella policy you might like." He leaned forward on his desk, his chubby hands sporting two chunky rings.

"I need some information about a past claim," Billy said.

Tommy's smile lessened. "Oh. What was your name again?"

"Not for me," Billy said. "Or not directly for me. It was for Billy Bob's Steakhouse. A year ago. I'm Billy."

"I think I remember that one." He yelled out "Gina? Get me the Billy Bob file."

They heard the sound of a file drawer opening, then closing, and the sound of Gina's heels on the hall floor. "Here you go." She left in a fog of perfume.

He opened the file. "I thought I remembered it right. Three-thou for spoiled meat and five for repairs and a new freezer. Total paid out, eighty-three hundred."

Claire and Billy exchanged a look.

"Who was the check made out to?" Billy asked.

"Robby. Got a copy right here." He closed the file. "Me and Robby go way back." He raised a fist. "Go Spartans!"

Billy let out a burst of air. Claire could tell he'd had more than enough.

"Can we get a copy of that check and the claim?" she asked. "For Billy's records. Please?"

Tommy's smile left him. "Is there a problem?"

Billy recovered. "I'm not good at keeping files. Just playing catch up."

Tommy seemed unconvinced, but bellowed Gina's name.

They left a few minutes later, copies in hand. Billy sat in the truck and stared at them. "He took money for something that never happened."

"And charged *you* for half the repair costs and a freezer that wasn't replaced."

"He charged me for food too. Said the insurance wouldn't pay."

"I'm so sorry." She sensed he needed to work through this privately. "Would you like some time alone?"

He nodded. His face was drawn, his eyes heavy with the grief of betrayal. "I'll take you home."

A few minutes later he pulled into her driveway and opened the door, helping her out. He drew her close for a quick kiss. "Thank you for helping me with this fiasco."

"I'm here to talk, anytime."

"I know."

Claire waved at him as he pulled away.

When she went inside she found Michelle stirring something at the stove. "Where's Billy? I'm making enough for three."

Claire sank onto a stool. "He needed to be alone."

Michelle turned around, catching the drips of the spoon in her palm. "Did you have a fight?"

"No. We're good. But I *was* instrumental in blowing his past apart."

Michelle shut off the burner. "Tell me everything."

Claire did just that, ending with a question: "Do you think it was wrong to pursue it?"

"Painful, yes. Wrong, no. Besides betraying Billy, slandering, and defrauding him, Robby defrauded an insurance company and falsely represented a repair company. That's criminal."

Claire agreed. "It's much more serious than rehiring old staff and misrepresenting a recipe. I encouraged him to pursue the truth. There was even a billboard about truth. . ." Claire shared that story too.

"I love when God does stuff like that," Michelle said.

"*I* thought it was God, but you do too?"

Michelle shrugged. "I always like to give Him credit, just in case. What is Billy going to do now?"

"He doesn't know. That's why he needed to be alone."

Michelle went back to the stove. "It's good he has you to help him through it."

"That's one reason God put us together," Claire said. "I think."

"Again, I like to give the Almighty credit, just in case. Set the table. Dinner will be ready shortly."

Chapter 30

Ryan

"If you say, 'The Lord is my refuge,'
and you make the Most High your dwelling,
no harm will overtake you,
no disaster will come near your tent.
For he will command his angels concerning you
to guard you in all your ways."
Psalm 91: 9-11

After their big lunch at Rosie's Café, Grandpa napped in the truck, leaning his head on a pillow against the window as they drove. Ryan taught Lisa the license plate game.

"Illinois!" she whispered from her place behind him.

"I thought we had Illinois," he said.

"We had Iowa. I'm the list-keeper. I know."

They reached a patch where traffic was scarce. "Do you have any games on your phone?" she asked.

He handed it to her. "The Blendoku is fun. You arrange colors in order."

"Good one. Mom had it on her phone too."

Since she'd brought it up . . . "Do you miss her?"

"Sure. But actually things are better without her. She liked to argue."

"With Grandpa?"

"With everybody. She wasn't happy."

So she made you unhappy.

"I was wondering how she'll find us, since we left without telling her."

"You can call her if you want."

Silence. Then, "Maybe later."

Lisa started playing the game, giving Ryan a play by play of how many she got right. It was nice not to talk for a while. He was used to being on his own. Silence was important to him. Silence fueled him.

But then he saw something that made him slow down. He veered to the right, into a small parking lot. The change in momentum awakened Grandpa.

"What? What's going on?"

"Sorry." Ryan put the truck in park. "Look."

There was a big *Welcome to Colorado!* sign. People were taking pictures in front of it.

"Can we do that?" Lisa asked.

"That's why we're here."

They got out and waited their turn. Ryan offered to take a few pictures for other travelers, and someone reciprocated and took their picture.

As he was checking to make sure they had a good one, a rough-looking man came close.

"Hey," he said.

In spite of the fact that *he* often approached strangers, Ryan's wary-bells chimed. "Hey."

The man was short, fortyish, and scruffy. Ryan did a quick scan of the parking lot and matched the other travelers with their vehicles. This man had to be a hitchhiker. He nudged Lisa toward the truck, telling the man, "Have a nice day."

The man held out an old flip-phone. "Would you take my picture?"

How could he say no? "Sure."

The man ran a hand through his hair and smiled for the photo. "Thanks."

Lisa hadn't gotten in the truck so Ryan took her hand and walked in that direction. But she pulled them to a stop and spoke to the man. "You need a ride?"

No!

The man smiled. "Sure do. Thanks."

Lisa beamed and looked to Ryan. "It's the nice thing to do."

She was too young to be able to differentiate *nice* and *wise.*

"You need to ask Grandpa first." *Grandpa will say no.*

Lisa ran ahead and asked him. Grandpa gave the man a keen once-over, but surprised Ryan by saying to the man, "We got nothing to steal but clothes and an old rocker. So if that's what you're after . . ."

The man held up a backpack with a sleeping bag tied to the bottom. "I have everything I need right here."

"Then come on. But behave yourself."

"Yes, sir."

The man got in the back behind Grandpa, facing Lisa. Ryan could only imagine how awkward it was for her. "We'll take you as far as the next town."

"I appreciate it."

They pulled away. "What's your name?" Lisa asked.

"Arlo. Like Arlo Guthrie, the folk singer."

Grandpa glanced over his shoulder. "I love his music."

"Me too. What's your name, sir?"

"Allen Pearl. This is my granddaughter, Lisa."

"Hi," Lisa said. "And that's—"

Arlo didn't wait for her to introduce Ryan. "Where you headed?"

"The mountains," Grandpa said. "Don't ask more cuz that's all we know."

"You're keeping your options open. I like that. Sounds like my journey. Wherever the wind blows."

"We're going to the promised land," Lisa said.

"Now *that* sounds like a nice place. And you, young man," he said, touching Ryan's shoulder. "Care to explain that interesting tattoo on your hand? You following the arrows? You in a cult or something?"

"Of course not."

Arlo persisted. "Arrows . . . what's it mean?"

The truth was vague. "I'm not sure."

"Then why did you get it?" Arlo asked.

He'd never see this man again. Might as well be plain about things—as plain as he could be. "I was directed to do it."

"By who?" Arlo asked.

Just say it. "By God."

The man didn't respond. Ryan assumed the answer had turned him off.

But then Arlo said, "'I have put my trust in you. Show me the way I should go, for to you I entrust my life.'"

Ryan felt a stitch in his innards. "Well, yeah. That's it."

"Thought so. You're willing to go wherever He sends you, right?"

"I am. Thanks for that. What verse is it?"

"Psalm 143: 8."

"Great," Grandpa said derisively. "Another Bible-nut."

"I take no offense at the title," Arlo said. "Here's one for you, Mr. Pearl: 'Gracious words are a honeycomb, sweet to the soul and healing to the bones.'"

Ryan heard Lisa suck in a breath. "Grandpa needs healing. He's sick."

"Shush, girl."

"But you are. That's why we're going to a place of milk and honey—and now he said honeycomb!"

"It seems I did. You are a wise girl, Miss Lisa. You want a verse?"

"Yes. Please."

"How about this one: 'Jesus said, "Let the little children come to me, and do not hinder them, for the kingdom of heaven belongs to such as these."'

"Oooh. I like that."

"Thought you would."

Grandpa waved his hands in front of his face. "Enough of this babble. You're not along to give a sermon."

"Didn't mean to offend. Just offering up some goodness."

"You've offered enough. Be qui—"

A siren whelped, and Ryan saw the lights of a police car behind him. He glanced at his speedometer. He hadn't been speeding. He pulled onto the shoulder and the police car pulled behind him.

"What did you do?" Grandpa asked.

"Nothing that I know of."

"I bet it's the taillight," Lisa said. "We never got it fixed."

"What taillight?" Grandpa asked.

"It's broken. We got stopped back home too."

"Why didn't someone tell—?"

The officer was at the window. The exchange was very similar to before. Yes, it was the taillight. But there was more.

"We had a call about someone picking up a hitchhiker at the state sign? Hitchhiking is against the law on the interstate." He peeked in the window.

Grandpa cocked a thumb toward the back. "He's the one."

"Will you get out, sir?"

Arlo got out and talked to the officer. They couldn't hear what was said, but Ryan saw Arlo give him some ID.

"We need to take him to the next town," Ryan said to Grandpa. "I don't want him left here."

"I've had enough of him," Grandpa said. "Let the officer take him."

Ryan got out and walked to the pair. "Sir? If it's all right, we'll drop him off at the next town. He's not caused us any harm."

He thought a moment then said, "I can't do that. But I'll take him."

Suddenly Lisa shimmied out Arlo's side of the truck. "Wait! I want to give him something." She rummaged in the back of the truck and removed her pie from the cooler. "Here," she said. "It's cherry."

Arlo smiled. "My favorite." He put a hand on her head. "Bless you, Lisa. And you, Ryan. For you did not forget to show hospitality to strangers." He grinned. "Hebrews thirteen-two. Take a look." He gave them a two-fingered salute and left in the police car.

Lisa and Ryan waved after him.

"That was nice of you to give up your pie," Ryan said as he helped her back in the truck.

"I didn't want him to be hungry."

"I'm glad he's gone," Grandpa said.

"He seemed nice," Lisa said.

Grandpa shook his head. "Thought he might be normal, but he wasn't."

"Sharing a few verses doesn't make him abnormal," Ryan said.

"It makes him pushy."

"He wasn't pushy, Grandpa. The verses were nice."

Ryan remembered Arlo's parting words. "Just a minute." He got out his phone. "He told us to look at Hebrews thirteen-two." He read it and felt a shiver. "Oh my."

"What's it say?"

"'Do not forget to show hospitality to strangers, for by so doing some people have shown hospitality to angels without knowing it.'"

Lisa looked over his shoulder. "Let me see." He handed her his phone. "Was he an angel?"

"Don't be ridiculous," Grandpa said.

"There's no way to be sure," Ryan said. "But I think he just might have been."

"That's so cool," Lisa said. "And I believe it, because he called Ryan by his name when he left."

"So what?" Grandpa said.

"We never introduced him to Ryan. You said your name and mine, Grandpa, but we never said Ryan's name. And Arlo said 'Ryan.' Isn't that cool?"

Very.

**

As they drove into Colorado, Lisa kept talking about the "angel-Arlo". Ryan was happy for her enthusiasm, but felt the need to add a life lesson into the mix.

"It's great we could help Arlo," Ryan said, "but we have to be careful about strangers. Wise about it. Not all people are nice like him."

"But you hitchhike, right?" she asked. "That's how you found us."

He had no idea what to say.

But Grandpa did. He turned around to look at her. "You, girl, will never pick up a hitchhiker. Ever. You promise me that right now."

Ryan couldn't see her face but imagined a pout. "I can't even drive."

"When you can drive, you won't do it." Grandpa pointed a finger at her. "You hear me, girl?"

"I hear you."

They stopped in Limon, Colorado for gas and restrooms. As Ryan was filling the truck he saw Lisa talking to a woman who was sitting on a brick wall in front of the station. She held a sign that said, *Help me please. Homeless.*

He saw Lisa pull some money out of her pocket and give it to her.

No!

The woman smiled and thanked her profusely. Lisa was beaming when she came back to the truck.

"What did you just do?"

She looked over her shoulder and waved at the woman—who waved back. "I gave her all the money in my pocket. She needed it more than me."

Ryan thought of the story of the poor widow in the Bible, who gave everything she had. Christ commended her for her sacrificial giving compared to the rich who gave a pittance of their money.

"It was only seven dollars." Lisa frowned. "I'm not supposed to do that either?"

Encourage one another and build each other up.

Ryan nodded. He smiled at her. "You did a very good thing, Lisa. God is pleased."

"Good."

What an amazing child.

**

"I see them!" Lisa yelled.

Grandpa put a hand to his chest. "Gracious, girl! Don't yell like that! I have a bad heart."

She pointed out the windshield. "There! Aren't those mountains? Those shadows in the distance?"

"They sure are," Ryan said. He felt a calm wash over him. "I will never get over the thrill of seeing them."

"They're still so far away," Lisa said.

"Not that far. A few hours." He glanced at Grandpa. "Do you want to stop for the night?"

"Nah. Not if we're this close."

They'd bought a map of Colorado in Limon. "Here, Lisa," Ryan said. "Pick us a destination."

He heard the rustle of the map as she found Limon and figured out where they were at that moment. "Pick a town where the map shows a swath of green—that's the mountains."

"Not too far. I do need to be done traveling pretty soon," Grandpa said.

"I know you do. I know it's tiring."

"Your cough seems better, Grandpa," Lisa said. "The medicine's working."

"We'll see."

It wasn't the cough that worried Ryan, it was Grandpa's heart and the risk of blood clots.

Suddenly, "I found it!"

"Again, girl, stop the yelling."

"Sorry, but I found the place we're supposed to go."

"How so?" Grandpa asked.

"There's a town named after you, Grandpa. Look." She handed him the map. "Right there, left of Lyons. Allenspark!"

"Well, I'll be," Grandpa said.

"Ryan? How's Allenspark sound? You go through Lyons and turn onto Highway 7."

I know how to get there. "It's a plan."

An interesting one.

**

Ryan drove up the mountain and rolled down the windows. "Smell."

"Fresh," Grandpa said.

"Pine," Lisa said. "Like a Christmas tree."

They were both right. Despite his personal misgivings over their destination, Ryan couldn't help but smile. The Rockies always had that effect on him. The first time his family had vacationed here, he and his little sister, Lisa, had stretched out in the car's backseat so they could look up at the mountains that towered over the road. His mom had teased them, saying they should have a contest to see who could count the most trees. Ryan had given up the contest at 312, declaring Lisa the winner.

He had often let her win because he loved her, and because it made life easier for everyone.

At the enormous boulder that separated the highway from the business loop of Allenspark, Ryan turned onto the road that led into town. The narrow road led them around log cabins and aspen groves, past a spring where you could get ice-cold water, a few art studios and shops, a pizza place, and a charming stone church. He pulled into a parking lot. "From here to there, that's the extent of it."

"Hmph," Grandpa said. "My town is tiny."

"Around five hundred, last I knew," Ryan said.

Grandpa waved a hand. "Find me a motel. I need to sleep."

"I'm afraid there aren't any," Ryan said. "But there are cabins to rent."

"Get us one of those then. Pronto."

Ryan turned onto a gravel road near the church. Interspersed between vacation cabins were a few tiny resorts. But which one?

"There!" Lisa said. "Honeycomb Cabins! Honey, Grandpa!"

They pulled in but Grandpa stayed in the truck, giving Ryan a credit card. "Set us up. I trust you."

Lisa went inside with Ryan. An elderly woman with snow-white hair and a ready smile set down her knitting and greeted them. "Evening. How can I help you?"

"We need a cabin with two bedrooms. And a couch. Three of us."

"Grandpa's real tired," Lisa said, pointing to the truck.

"Then we'll find you a comfy cabin so he can rest. The Columbine cabin has a meadow view and the Mountain Rose has—"

Ryan smiled inside and out. "We'll take the Mountain Rose."

As soon as they were checked in, the woman—Bertha—led them to the cabin. "My parents opened this place a hundred years ago. The cabins ain't fancy, but you get the full mountain experience."

She gripped the railing in order to climb the three steps to a small porch.

"Look, there's three chairs," Lisa said. "Just enough for us."

"Just enough, little lady. Come to the office tomorrow morning and I'll get you a bag of peanuts. You can sit right there and the chipmunks will skitter up onto your leg to grab one." She unlocked the door and led them inside. The ceiling had open beams, the walls were scraped logs, and the furniture was hewn from pine.

It was perfect.

Grandpa sat on the couch by the fireplace while Ryan and Lisa finished the tour. "There's actually a cot you can set up in that corner, if you want," Bertha said. "Got a rolled up piece of foam that works pretty nifty as a cushion. Sheets and such in the cupboard."

"I want that!" Lisa said.

Ryan argued that she should have the tiny second bedroom, but she was adamant.

"There's a small general store at Meeker Park, four miles up. They closed at five so I'll bring you over some chili if you like."

"You don't have to do that," Ryan said. "We have some food in the coolers."

"Save it for another time. Even though I've been a widow for seven years I still cook for two. I'll be glad not to have leftovers tomorrow." She handed Ryan the key. "Settle in and I'll bring the chili over."

Lisa and Ryan figured out what to bring in from the truck to get by, just as Bertha brought over the chili and some dinner rolls with butter. "There you go," she said. "Let me know if you need anything. By the by, you might need a fire tonight as it's supposed to get down in the forties. Plenty of firewood 'round the back."

They had to wake Grandpa from a nap to eat, and his heart wasn't in it. "My body knows what it knows. Sleep is what I need."

Lisa helped him get to bed and came back to finish the meal. The kitchen had two-feet of counters, a skinny stove, a microwave, and a tiny fridge and sink. Yet it was enough.

Besides the couch there was an armchair so Lisa and Ryan got comfortable.

"Isn't it weird to think we were back home this morning?" Lisa asked.

"Very."

"This day seemed so long yet other days go by in a flash. Why is that?"

"Busyness, I guess."

She looked around the room. "There's not even a TV."

"Nope."

"Do you have cell service?"

Ryan checked his phone though he knew the answer. "Nope." He braced himself for her complaints.

"That's okay." She explored a bookshelf. "Puzzles! Want to do one?"

**

They turned over all 1000 puzzle pieces and got most of the edge pieces put together, but that was it for Ryan. Driving eight hours had wiped him out. Plus, there was the time change. The clock on the mantel said ten but his body was at eleven—though it felt like midnight.

He offered Lisa the bedroom again, but she declined. She was excited about sleeping on a cot, saying she wanted to watch the fire and listen to its crackle.

His bedroom was tiny, just wide enough for a full bed with less than a foot to spare. The bedside table was big enough for a clock that glowed the time in neon green. There was a pull-chain lamp within arm's reach from the bed and hooks on the logs for his clothes.

And yet, he was content. He got under the covers and pulled the light's chain, changing the day into night. He couldn't remember the last time he'd slept in a bedroom. He slept on the ground a lot, in shelters, or on the occasional park bench—which were all fine, all part of the life he'd chosen. The Pearl's couch had been a luxury. And now, to have his own bedroom where he could be alone . . . it was a precious haven.

He found it ironic that his mission was to help people yet God had created him as an introvert who needed silence and solitude to recharge. Although he was good at small talk and making conversation, the process drained him as though he had a hole where his energy leaked out. The only way to fill himself back up was to be alone and quiet. Silence was his friend, as vital to his well-being as air and water.

He whispered a verse that always comforted him: "'The Lord will fight for you; you need only to be still. 'Be still, and know that I am God.'"

With that, he slipped into the refuge of God's peace.

Chapter 31

Summer

"Let us not become weary in doing good,
for at the proper time we will reap a harvest
if we do not give up."
Galatians 6: 9

Summer stood outside Flora and Funna, ready to meet Sydney for her job interview. Candy wasn't gung-ho about it, but agreed that she *could* use some additional help with the fall weddings they had coming up. Summer did her part and talked Sydney up, saying she had exquisite taste.

"Is she a hard worker?" Candy had asked.

Summer had dodged the question. "She loves flowers and she really needs the job."

Candy was unimpressed but agreed to the interview—which was this morning. The friends were meeting out front a few minutes before ten o'clock so Summer could make the introductions.

She checked the time. Sydney had one minute to go . . . *Come on, Syd. Don't be late.*

Summer heard Sydney's car before she saw it, like a grouchy dragon preparing to attack. It pulled into the parking space beside her. When it was shut off the world went silent.

Sydney got out. "Hey."

"Hey, yourself." *You're nearly late.* "Candy's waiting."

There was no apology for being late—which was classic Sydney.

They found Candy at the counter. She gave Sydney a once over, peering over her half-glasses.

"Candy, this is my friend, Sydney Thorpe—"

"Canon now. Sydney Canon."

Summer felt stupid. Of course. "Sydney, this is Candy, the owner of the shop."

"Hi," Sydney said.

Candy didn't speak. A crease had formed between her eyes. There was something wrong. The silence grew awkward.

Then Sydney pointed at the flowers in the display case. "These are really pretty. I like mums."

"No you don't," Candy said.

"Yes, I do."

Candy removed her glasses completely. "Cut the act, girlie. I remember you. The Thorpe-Canon wedding a few years ago."

"Eighteen-months."

Candy shook her head. "I remember you well. You complained about the flowers—loudly and long. And then you bashed the shop on social media. You gave us a horrible review."

Sydney looked around the shop, as if putting two and two together. "I . . . I'm sorry about that. It's just that I thought the arrangements should have been bigger."

"They were as big as you ordered—as big as you paid for."

Summer's stomach tied itself in knots. As a bridesmaid she remembered some brouhaha over the flowers but hadn't known they were from Candy's shop. "It was a long time ago," she said weakly.

"Not long enough," Candy said. She waved a hand toward the door. "Move along, Miss Thorpe, Canon, whatever your name is. Your help is not needed here."

Sydney stood still for a moment, stunned. Then with a flip of her hair, she stormed out. Summer gave Candy a plaintive look. "I'm so sorry. I didn't know."

"Now you do. You might consider the wisdom of backing that girl in any job ventures. She's a demanding, spoiled brat."

"She's changed."

"Hmm. Go on with you. Console her or whatever it is you're going to do, then come back to work."

Summer found Sydney pacing between their cars, seething. "How dare that woman dismiss me like that! I wouldn't take a job here if she paid me double."

There's no chance of that. "Didn't you remember the shop did your wedding flowers?"

"I had a few other things on my mind." She opened her car door. "I'm going home."

"But . . ."

The beast started up, spurting out black smoke as Sydney drove away, leaving Summer stunned and speechless. There'd been no *thank you for trying,* no repentance for her past actions. Summer leaned against her car. *Lord, why did You lead me to her? She doesn't want to be helped. She's difficult and demanding. I don't know what I can do for her. I don't* want *to help her.*

God didn't answer so Summer went back to work.

**

That evening, as Summer carried a tray of entrees to the dining table, she suddenly realized she couldn't remember who got what. Such details were usually clear. Sometimes she didn't even write orders down.

She reached her family's table and asked, "Who had the tenderloin again?"

They all stared at her.

"That would be me," Grandma said.

"Of course. Sorry." But then she started putting the chicken breast with gravy at Tessa's place.

"You know I hate gravy. That's Mae's."

She felt her face redden and managed to set Tessa's plate right, though she nearly spilled it in her lap.

She started to walk away, but Grandma touched her arm. "What's wrong, sweetie? You're not yourself."

Tessa harrumphed. "I mean, me? Gravy?"

"I'm just tired."

"You're usually a powerhouse," Mae said. "What's different? You've seemed out of it all week."

Summer held the tray as a shield. Her defenses were definitely down. The fiasco with Sydney and a busy day at the flower shop had left her near empty.

Then the words came out, "The truth is, I'm tired because I have three jobs." She quickly told them the details—*not* mentioning her fourth job of helping Sydney. "God gave me the jobs so I can meet people for Him." She looked to her other tables. Mrs. Crenshaw was holding up her coffee cup. "I need to go."

Mae flashed Mrs. Crenshaw a look and held up a finger indicating Summer would be there in a minute. "You will do no one any good if you collapse from trying."

"You are not a robot," Tessa said.

"Something has to give," Grandma said. "You need money? Come to me."

"Come to us," Tessa said.

"It's perfectly plain: you need to quit one job," Mae said. "Your choice."

"But not this job," Tessa said. "We need to see you here."

"That's a selfish thing to say," Mae said.

Tessa bobbed her head back and forth. "*You* don't want to see her every day?"

"Of course, I do," Mae said.

They started discussing her jobs and what she should do.

Mrs. Crenshaw held up her cup again.

Summer left her family to figure out her life without her.

Chapter 32

Michelle

"'What should we do then?' the crowd asked.
John answered, 'Anyone who has two shirts
should share with the one who has none,
and anyone who has food should do the same.'"
Luke 3:10-11

Before leaving home for the shelter, Michelle checked her email. As usual, there was no response from her four comrades in Christ.

She sighed and signed out of her account. It took time to find, pay for, and adapt pretty floral backgrounds, and careful thought to choose verses of encouragement. She sent the emails daily without fail. Summer occasionally replied with "Thanks" and Claire had told her they were nice, but Michelle hadn't heard from the men at all. Crickets. Did they even read them? Was she speaking to an empty room?

She hadn't said anything to Claire about her disappointment and fears, but she truly wondered if the other three had forgotten about their calling, if everyday life had usurped their initial enthusiasm.

Maybe it wasn't her place to prod them. Maybe they were turned off by the emails, like they might tune out a nagging parent or boss.

She left the house and drove to the shelter and tried to think positive thoughts. Maybe her friends were too busy to reply to her emails because they had already made special God-ordained connections. Their lives had changed as *they* changed the lives of others, each one a perfect example of the Great Commission. That would be nice, but . . . she was doubtful.

She parked in the back lot, turned off the car, and bowed her head. "I hope the rest are doing good things for You, Father, but personally I feel like I'm in a maze, lost and getting nowhere." She sighed deeply. "Not much has changed for me, Lord. I'm slow and steady Michelle, plugging along. It doesn't seem . . . enough."

A kitchen worker pulled up beside her. Michelle waved, got out, and waited for him. "Morning, Julio."

"Morning, Michelle. How you doing?"

"Slow and steady."

He chuckled.

Yeah, it was kind of funny. Or pitiful.

**

Michelle was happy to see Jonette come into the dining area. Although others arrived and sat in small groups, she was still alone. It wasn't surprising. Newbies were wary. Their eyes were skittish and watchful.

Michelle made a point of greeting her as she served pancakes. "How did you sleep?"

"Good. Thanks for arranging it. I haven't slept good for a few nights, so it was a big relief."

"I'm glad." The food line was backing up behind Jonette. "One pancake or two?"

As soon as the serving was finished, Michelle made the rounds, greeting people as they ate. When she noticed Jonette was almost done eating, she sat across from her. "Did you get enough to eat?"

She nodded, covering her mouth with a hand while she chewed. "Mama used to make flap-jacks on Saturdays. She put cinnamon in 'em."

Used to? "Is she still around?"

Jonette shrugged. "She died when I was twelve. It's just been Daddy and me. Until . . ." She shrugged and made a face.

Michelle had heard it before. "Did your dad remarry?"

"Bet—that's her name. Isn't that a stupid name? Go by Betty or Elizabeth or Beth. Not Bet." She shuddered.

"You don't like her." It was not a question.

"She's okay and she tries, but . . . it was time for me to leave."

"Did you leave a note? Have you called him?"

She shook her head and looked down. "I just left. And I don't have a phone. It was in my backpack when it was stolen."

Michelle pulled out hers. "You can use mine."

Jonette stared at it, then said, "No thanks."

Michelle would have liked to push it, but knew it was best to let Jonette's problems—and their solutions—get handled at *her* speed. Asking too many questions too fast made walls go up.

As Jonette drank her juice she pulled at the too-wide neck of her t-shirt. Her ill-fitting clothes dovetailed Michelle's latest idea. "I work part-time at the Nearly New Shop that has donated clothes and such. They have some really nice things there. I was going over this morning. Want to come with me and get yourself something that fits?"

Her face changed and lost some of its worry. She looked like a teenager again. "That'd be cool. Thanks."

Michelle stood. "Hang around for a bit while I finish up and we'll go."

Jonette looked toward the kitchen. "I could help. I'm used to being in a kitchen."

"It's a deal."

**

Michelle was impressed with Jonette's willingness to work hard. She cleared and wiped off tables, and she helped with the dish-washing. As she worked her eyes lost some of their wariness, and she actually laughed with the other helpers.

She's a good one, Lord. I can tell.

Finally it was time to go to the shop. "Ready?"

On the ride over Michelle asked the one question that usually opened a floodgate of conversation. "If you could spend a day in any way you wanted, what would you do?"

"Any way?"

"Sky's the limit."

Jonette answered immediately, as if she'd thought about it. "I would spend the day with Daddy, binge-watching some TV show. I like mysteries but he likes comedies, so we'd watch some of each. He'd work on a puzzle and I'd crochet. Mama taught me how to crochet when I was eight. She was always making afghans, stuffed animals, and baby blankets for friends."

"That's a nice skill to have."

Jonette nodded, and returned to her special-day wishes. "For dinner Daddy and I would make chicken-fried chicken with mashed potatoes and gravy. And brownie sundaes for dessert. "

"Sounds lovely—and yummy."

Jonette nodded once. "That would be a perfect day. What about you?"

Michelle was surprised by the question. "No one has ever asked me that."

"Have you thought about it?"

Not really. But the answer wasn't hard. "I'd do what I do every day. I'd hang around people and talk."

"There?" she asked, pointing in the direction of the shelter. "Really?"

"Well, yeah. I like meeting new people, finding out about their lives. And helping them."

"Like you're doing with me."

She smiled. Michelle pulled into a parking lot. "We're here."

She introduced Jonette to Mary, the volunteer on duty. "Look around. Find some things you like. There's a fitting room near the back."

Jonette tentatively looked through the racks. Then she returned to the counter and motioned Michelle aside. Her voice was low. "I thought these were donations. They cost money. I don't have any of that."

Oh, sweet girl. "They *are* donations. We sell them and give the money to the shelter. But since you're staying at the shelter you don't have to pay."

Her eyes widened. "I don't?"

"Merry Christmas."

Jonette's face lit up. As the girl went back to shopping Mary spoke softly to Michelle. "Is it really okay to give stuff away free?"

"In special situations. Jonette fits that special situation. She ran away from home. Her backpack was stolen."

"Poor thing." Mary bit her lip.

"What's wrong?"

"I'm all for giving her what she needs, but . . . won't she take advantage and be greedy?"

Michelle watched Jonette drape a fifth shirt over her arm. "Are we putting a limit on our charity?"

Mary shifted to the other foot. "Well, no, but . . ."

"She'll do fine." *It will be what it will be.*

Jonette's arms were full when she asked, "Back there?"

"Yup. Let me know if you need anything."

While she was waiting Michelle looked through the shoes. Jonette had to be a size five or so. She found some barely worn tennies, then went to the underwear section where they had brand new packages of underwear and socks. Might as well start completely fresh.

"I'm almost done," Jonette called from the fitting room. "Can I wear it now?"

"Of course."

A few minutes later Jonette came out wearing a pair of jeans and a pink button-up shirt. "You look very pretty."

She shook her head and smoothed the blouse over her hips. "I like pink."

"You look good in it. Bring what you want up to the counter."

Jonette looked confused. "I'm wearing it."

And they'd been concerned about greed? "Ah, hon. You can get more than one set of clothes."

"I can?"

"Of course." Michelle could have cried.

Jonette went back into the dressing room and came out carrying a pair of khakis, a baby-blue shirt, a peach tee-shirt with a yellow star on it, and a very familiar hand-knit sweater. "For when it gets cool out," she said.

Claire's pink sweater. Michelle grinned at the ways of the Lord. Then she showed Jonette the underwear, socks, and shoes. "Try the shoes on."

They fit. *Of course they fit.* "Do you like them?"

She bounced on her toes. "They're great. My other ones were wearing out."

Michelle crooked a finger at her. "One more thing . . . come with me." She led Jonette back to the craft section. "Yarn. Crochet needles. Instruction books."

"Oooh." Jonette fell on the supplies like a kid in a toy store. She paged through a book. "Look! Beanies. I used to crochet some like this with my mom." She turned the page. "And scarves. I could crochet a scarf for winter."

Michelle pointed at the skeins of yarn. "Any color strike your fancy?" Then she laughed. "Let me guess. Pink."

Jonette nodded. There were two matching skeins. "I could make one for you too."

"I'd love that."

"In fact . . . that girl you introduced me to? Patty? She might like one."

Michelle got an idea. She went to the counter and got a shopping bag. "Fill 'er up. You can be the crochet expert of Mercy Shelter."

On the way back to the shelter, Jonette leafed through an instruction book—one of three. Then she closed it. "Why do you help people you don't even know?"

Michelle's answer easily came to mind. "First off, there's the Golden Rule. Do unto others as you would have them do unto you."

"I've heard that one."

"The other reason comes from the Bible. 'We love because he first loved us.'"

"He?"

"Jesus."

"I've heard of Him too. Haven't thought about Him in a while."

"He's thought about you."

"Really?"

"Yup. 'He will never leave you nor forsake you.' He promised."

"Cool."

"You'd better believe it."

I hope you believe it.

Chapter 33

Jered

"Do not withhold good from those to whom it is due,
when it is in your power to act."
Proverbs 3: 27

Jered was shocked that the euphoric feeling he'd gotten for being nice to Mr. Johnson lasted a few days. Wanting it to last longer, he'd kept the good attitude alive.

He was polite in an online chat with the utility company when they'd messed up their bill. He was patient with his assistant when she asked him the same question for the tenth time. And he put his own dishes *in* the dishwasher.

Jered wasn't dumb. He knew in the scope of the world his small actions didn't change anything, but somehow he felt they were changing *him.*

During the middle of the night he thought of two more ways to be nice. He got up before Ivy—but not to play video games. First on the agenda was breakfast. He started the coffee pot and wished he knew how to make something besides French toast.

He walked in the pantry to look at his selections, moving around boxes and jars. And there, behind the Coco-Wheats, he saw them. He smiled and grabbed a box of cherry Pop Tarts. Ivy loved them—so much so, that she often hid them from herself.

He put two in the toaster then took an apple from the fridge and quartered it. He poured some coffee and arranged the apples and Pop Tarts prettily on a plate. He placed everything on a footed bed-tray, added a napkin, and quietly slipped outside where he cut off a single pink rose. He didn't know where Ivy kept the vases, so he put it in a water glass. "There," he said as he surveyed the offering.

When he approached the bedroom he heard Ivy let out her usual morning groan as she stretched her arms overhead. He hurried into the room and caught her with her legs dangling over the side of the bed. "Breakfast is served!"

Her surprise was genuine. "What are you doing?"

He motioned her back into bed. "Making my wife breakfast in bed."

"What's the occasion?"

Because I feel guilty? Because I'm sorry for being such a jerk for too long? "Because I love you."

"Ahh, Jer." She adjusted a pillow against the headboard and smoothed the covers across her lap. He placed the breakfast tray before her. "Sorry I sacrificed one of your roses for the cause."

"It's lovely." She reached toward him to draw his face forward. They kissed. "And Pop Tarts. Where did you find them?"

"Where you hid them in the pantry."

She bit off a corner and moaned with delight. "I forgot they were in there." She picked up a slice of apple. "And fruit. I am impressed."

"I seem to remember someone telling me that a person always needs something healthy on their plate."

She ate the slice and handed one to him. He climbed onto the bed from his side, being careful not to jiggle it too much. It was time for part two of his plan for the day. "I thought we could go down to the Plaza and walk around. Maybe . . . see *people.*"

She pretended to gasp. "People? Real people?"

"I'll give it a shot." He touched her arm. "For you."

She pointed upward. "And Him?"

"You're easier to please."

"Not really." She took a sip of coffee. "God is compassionate and gracious, slow to anger, brimming with love and truth. And all-forgiving."

"Are you? I've been horrible to you for a long time, horrible to pretty much everyone. I've made so many mistakes. Do you forgive me?"

She drew his hand to her lips. "Always, m'love. Always."

**

Jered couldn't remember the last time they'd walked around the Plaza in Kansas City. He loved the old-world feel of it. The area *was* old. It was created in the early 1920s, and many of the quaint streets, small shops, and plentiful restaurants were in the original Seville-style buildings.

He wore sunglasses and a Royals ballcap as a disguise, but quickly realized he wouldn't have needed to. People weren't out and about looking for anyone famous—or kind of famous—they were enjoying their time together.

"Oooh." Ivy stopped at a bakery window. "Look at those strawberry tarts." She grabbed his hand. "Let's go in."

The pastry case was full of tarts, pies, cupcakes, and macarons. There was a line.

"Forget the tart," Ivy said. "I've changed my mind. I adore macarons."

The woman in front of them turned around with a smile. "Me too. Try the lime and strawberry ones. They're to die—" She looked at Jered, then did a double-take. "Are you . . . are you Jered Manson?"

He shouldn't have taken off his sunglasses. "I am."

Soon the other three people in line surrounded him, wanting autographs. The clerk had some napkins to write on and Ivy had a pen.

Surprisingly, Jered was okay with it In a way, being recognized made him feel . . . real.

The ladies were satisfied and went back to buying pastries.

"Sorry," Ivy whispered.

"It's all right. No biggie." But then he noticed a bald man sitting by the window with his laptop open. The man was staring at him. He smiled. And then he stood up.

As the man walked toward them, Jered recognized him. He was the owner of the Red Rim Bar where Jered used to play. "Christopher Tarler?"

He drew Jered into a man's embrace with a quick pat on the back. "Jered, my boy. So nice to see you." He looked at Ivy. "Hi there, Ivy. You're looking lovely, as usual. Pick your poison and come sit with me. Let's catch up."

They bought a tart, four macarons, and coffee and sat down at Christopher's table. His laptop was closed. "Well then," he said. "Congratulations on making it to the bigtime."

"Thanks." Jered took a bite of a macaron, feeling oddly awkward. Christopher had been a big supporter. He shouldn't feel awkward around him. "Is the Red Rim still going strong?"

"Yup." He wiped some latte froth off his mustache. "Same-o, same-o. We still pack 'em in."

Jered's memories were many and vivid. "I loved playing there, having people so close."

"Yeah, I'm sure things have changed for you. In those big venues you certainly have more distance between you and your audience."

Jered realized another difference. "I may have the big numbers, but there was something special about seeing the people's faces, right there." He held a hand in front of his face.

"Up close and personal. That's the Red Rim." Christopher sat forward. "By the way, Boxer still plays there. He's playing tomorrow night."

"Boxer?" It was so odd that Jered had recently thought of him.

"Kyle Boxer?" Ivy asked.

"That's the one. You should come hear him play. He's better than ever."

Jered looked at Ivy. Usually he'd say no without considering it, but this time . . . "You want to go?"

She nodded. "We'll be there."

Christopher put his laptop in a bag. "We'll talk more then." He stood. "I'm still in awe that Boxer giving up his spot for you gave you your first big break."

Spot? "What are you talking about?"

He cocked his head. "That night at the Red Rim? The night the record producer from Realtone was there?"

Ivy raised a hand. "Wait. Are you talking about the night he approached Jered and offered him a contract?"

"That's the one."

The night that changed his life. "What about it?"

Christopher looked incredulous. "You're kidding me, right?"

Jered scanned the café, feeling foolish. He lowered his voice. "I have no idea what you're talking about."

Christopher sat down and leaned toward them. "Remember how the acts took turns on the weekends?"

"Yeah."

"Remember how it *wasn't* your turn to play that particular Saturday night?"

He wasn't sure.

"I remember," Ivy said. "You called at the last minute and said Boxer couldn't play. You needed Jered to fill in."

"Oh yeah," Jered said.

Christopher sat back and nodded. He looked smug. "Boxer wasn't sick. He specifically asked me to call you in."

"Why would he do that?"

"Because he knew Realtone was going to be there and he wanted *you* to have the chance at a contract."

Ivy put a hand to her chest. "Why would he do that?"

"Because he knew you wanted it more than he did." Christopher picked up his cup and finished the sip he'd left behind. "He sacrificed his future for *you,* Jered."

Jered's thoughts swirled and intertwined with memories of that night when he'd sung one of his best sets ever. He hadn't known the record-rep Corey York was going to be there, and was completely shocked when Corey came up afterward wanting to talk about a deal. "I don't get it."

Christopher chuckled. "I guess not. I thought you knew."

"How would I know? I didn't see Boxer much after that."

"Because you got the contract and were on your way to fame and fortune."

Ivy took Jered's hand. "I'm speechless."

Ditto.

"I'm surprised Corey didn't say something to you about it. He was coming to hear Boxer, not you."

The shine of the moment tarnished. "He wanted Boxer?"

"I'd bragged him up."

What he didn't say was huge. *You didn't brag about me.*

"When he found out Boxer wasn't playing he almost didn't stay," Christopher said, wiping a drip of coffee on the table. "I convinced him to hang around."

"Because you thought Jered was good," Ivy said.

"Because Boxer thought Jered was good." He shrugged. "Not that I didn't think you had talent, but . . ." He got up to go for real this time. "Anyway. See you tomorrow night."

"We'll be there," Ivy said—because Jered couldn't find any more words.

Too many words. Not enough words. Not the right words.

"You okay?" she asked him when they were alone.

"No."

She nodded. "You want to go home?"

He shook his head. "I need to walk. Just walk."

Jered was aware of Ivy getting a to-go box and lids for their coffee. And he vaguely heard the autograph-getters tell him good-bye. He *thought* he said goodbye back. As they walked around the Plaza there might have been a few whispers and extra looks as people recognized him. But none of it mattered because *he* wasn't supposed to be famous. Boxer was.

Somehow they ended up back at the car. Jered let Ivy drive home. Once there, she led him outside to the two Adirondack chairs in her flower garden. "Tell me what you're thinking."

"I shouldn't be here." He waved a hand toward the house. "I shouldn't live in a house like this or travel the world and have tens of thousands of people cheering and singing along with me."

"Hold up, Jer. Yes, the initial contract came about oddly, but since then, it's been your talent that's carried you from there to here."

That made him feel a little better. But . . . "What about Boxer? He's still playing the bars. I know he wanted the same thing I did. Why did I get it and he didn't?"

Ivy didn't answer right away. Then she said, "I guess it's how God wanted it to turn out."

Another thought rammed its way into Jered's mind. "Why did God call me to go out and find people for Him? Why didn't he call Boxer? He's a far-better person than I can ever be."

"I don't know the answer to that either, but . . . maybe you can ask him about it tomorrow night."

Yes. Yes. Boxer would have the answers Jered needed.

Chapter 34

Claire

"Therefore, as God's chosen people, holy and dearly loved, clothe yourselves with compassion, kindness, humility, gentleness and patience."
Colossians 3: 12

Claire hadn't slept. She'd left multiple messages with Billy, wanting to know his thoughts about Robby's deceptions and crimes, and what he wanted to do moving forward.

Did he want to move forward? She couldn't imagine not. Why had God led them onto this path if not to follow it to the end?

More than once Claire had to admonish herself for taking charge, and for wanting to continue to take charge. This was not her fight or her life. She knew she had a tendency to be a buttinski, which sometimes was welcomed but often was not. She was a do-er to a fault.

So as she sat at her worktable at the studio, checking her phone for the twentieth time, she prayed for patience. *Help me wait gracefully.* Over the years she'd fine-tuned this mantra from *Don't make me wait* to *Hurry up, please* to *Help me wait* to adding *gracefully* to her plea. She knew that waiting, though not enviable, was inevitable. So why not strive to do it better, with more acceptance and less stress? The results varied according to the importance of the situation. *Help me wait gracefully* in a grocery store line was implemented with far more success than now, waiting gracefully for the new man in her life to call back and tell her what God was telling *him.*

Darla came over to the worktable, eyeing the containers of glass Claire in the middle of the workspace. A bare pottery bowl waited to be prettified.

"Artist's block?" Darla asked.

"Maybe."

"A bowl is fine, but shouldn't you be finetuning the mural design for the bank?"

"I should. But that needs full concentration, which is why I took up this bowl. I thought if I did something easy . . ."

Darla moved the pot of glue and its brush close. "I've heard you need to place *one* tile and the rest will follow."

"You're using my own words against me."

"Not against you, to help you." She pointed to a pretty orange tile that had sparkles. "That one. Start with that one."

Claire glued the orange piece in the middle of the bottom. "Happy now?"

Darla gave her a disgusted face. "What's wrong with you today?"

It was hard to explain. "Billy's going through some issues and I want to help but don't know how. I've called but he won't answer."

"Are you two . . . okay?"

"It's not about *us*. It's other things going on in his life."

"Then he's in charge. You have to wait."

Waiting. There it was again.

**

Lunch time. During the morning at the studio Claire had received fourteen phone calls. Every Tom Dick and Sally had called, selling a better interest rate on her credit cards, wanting money for some iffy charity, or announcing she had been chosen to get a free weekend at a very special timeshare in Orlando. Her waiting gracefully had been tested to its limit.

The microwave dinged and Claire removed her cup-o-soup. She grabbed some saltines from a jar and sat down to eat.

Her phone rang again. She nearly let it go to voicemail but couldn't do that—was glad she *didn't* do that when she saw the name she had been waiting for, appear on her screen. "Billy! I've been dying to hear from you."

"Sorry," he said. "I had something to do early, then got busy at work and . . . honestly, I didn't know what to say to you."

Didn't know. "You know now?"

"I need to talk to Robby. In person."

"Excellent. It's time he was confronted. Are you going to arrange a meeting?"

"*If* I go, I think it's best I show up unannounced."

"At the restaurant?"

"I don't want to bother him at home. His wife and kids will be there."

"But he always has people around him at Robby's."

"Not early. That's where I was first thing this morning. I went there at seven and he was just getting there. That's his way. Beyond all he's done wrong he's a hard worker. He always went in at seven to make sure everything was ready for lunch."

Claire was confused. "You went there this morning but you didn't talk to him?"

"I didn't. I parked on the street near the alley. I don't know if I will go through with it either. I . . . I don't usually admit this, but I was thinking about God's place in all this, and since I'm not that familiar I'm calling an expert. You seem to know what He's doing."

The pressure made her heart skip a beat. "I try to know what He's doing."

"*How* do you try?"

"I pray. And watch for what He might be doing around me."

"Good. Then do it. Pray."

"Me? How about you? You need to do it too."

There was silence on the line. "Billy?"

"I get it. I'll pray. And watch."

She pressed a hand to her chest, letting out a breath.

He changed the subject. "Want to go to a movie tonight?"

It took her a second to change gears. "Go on a real, old-fashioned date?"

"You like popcorn, don't you?"

"I adore popcorn. With butter dripping from every kernel. I've been known to eat popcorn for dinner."

"That's what I was thinking. I'll pick you up at six-thirty."

Maybe God's answers would show up at the movies.

**

Claire opened the door and was thrilled to see Billy. She gave him a peck on the cheek. "How was your day?"

"Thankfully, I was busy on the new reno. Yours?"

"I tiled a bowl," she said. "Half a bowl." She hadn't been busy enough to fully distract her from the Robby business.

They left the house and drove off. As they neared the multiplex Claire asked, "What are we going to see? You can choose."

"I don't particularly like romances or comedies."

"Me either! I like complicated plots with lots of twists and turns."

"We'll choose one of those."

They got their tickets and Billy gave Claire free rein on the butter for the huge tub of popcorn. She even filled some small plastic containers with more butter to add as they ate.

"I usually go for four extra ones," Billy said.

Claire had gotten three. "Want another—?"

"Three is plenty." He carried a massive cup of Diet Orange Fanta. They found their seats just in time for the previews.

Billy raised the armrest that divided them and set the popcorn in the middle. This was just what they needed.

The movie had an intricate plot about good versus evil. Claire loved stories where justice won out. She kept glancing at Billy. Was he applying the movie's quest for justice to his current situation?

At the pinnacle of the story, a character gave a quote attributed to Gandhi: "Truth never damages a cause that is just."

Claire looked at Billy. Billy looked at Claire. He took her hand. Message received.

The movie ended and they headed back to the car. "We made a good choice with that one," he said.

God used it. "I liked that quote about the truth," she said.

"So did I. Is my cause just?"

Claire slipped her hand around his arm. "You lost your business and your dream because of someone's lies. Robby and Nate and your other employees conspired to keep the truth from you. Bringing the truth into the open will make things right."

"And stir things up—which isn't my style."

"Being a victim isn't a choice. But staying a victim is." When he stopped walking she wondered if she'd gone too far. "I didn't mean to offend."

"You didn't." He faced her. "I don't want to be a victim anymore. I don't."

"Good."

"I have to finish this and discover the truth. I have to talk to Robby. Will you come with me? Tomorrow?"

"Of course."

Chapter 35

Ryan

"Religion that God our Father accepts
as pure and faultless is this:
to look after orphans and widows in their distress
and to keep oneself from being polluted by the world."
James 1: 27

Ryan woke up in the Mountain Rose cabin when he heard someone in the bathroom. It was light outside. The clock read seven-thirty. He couldn't remember the last time he'd slept so late.

As soon as he peeled the covers off he felt the chill of the day and knew shorts and a tee-shirt wouldn't do—even if it was July. He got his jeans and a long-sleeved shirt from his backpack and added a sweatshirt. Socks too.

He made his bed and went out to the living room. Lisa was just coming out of the bathroom. "Look what I found!" She held some bills in her hand. "Seven dollars in the pocket of my jeans! I didn't know I'd left it there. It's exactly the amount I gave that lady." She ran to Grandpa who sat on the couch with a blanket over his legs. "Look, Grandpa. Isn't this amazing?"

He looked at the money. "Well I'll be." He raised the blanket to let her in. She snuggled up next to him. "A fire would be nice, Ryan."

Yes, sir.

**

They ate from the coolers.

"What's on the agenda today?" Ryan asked.

"I don't do agendas anymore," Grandpa said. "Never did abide by them much."

"I want to go exploring," Lisa said. "Let's walk up the road."

"You two go," Grandpa said. "I don't feel up to it."

Lisa's face grew worried. "Do you need anything?"

"Just sitting on the porch in the sun will be enough for me."

And so they left him bundled up like a cocoon and walked up the dirt road toward the mountains. Wildflowers were scattered among the grasses, with aspen groves and towering pines interspersed between the occasional log cabin so seamlessly, it was hard to know which had come first.

Lisa had to stop to get her breath. "We're not climbing but my heart is racing."

"The air is thinner up here. Kansas has an elevation of about a thousand feet. Up here, we're at 8500."

"Big difference."

"Your body will adapt. Take it slow. Drink lots of water."

She kicked a pebble up the road. "What about Grandpa and the altitude?"

"He's not walking much, but we should watch him." He saw a narrow path veering to the right. "Let's follow it."

As they walked Lisa had a question. "My seven dollars . . . Did God do that?"

"How else do you explain it?"

"Coincidence, I guess."

"Coincidences are how a non-believing person explains God's ways. There's a reason for everything."

"Everything?"

"Sometimes we can't see it, but it's there."

They walked a few steps in silence. Then Lisa turned to face him. "I want to see it. See everything."

"Then you will." She'd caught him off-guard, but Ryan's heart sang a *Halleluiah!*

The path was only a foot wide, most likely a deer path, but it eventually led to an outcropping of rocks. They both stopped and stared—had no choice but to stop and stare.

"Wow," Lisa said.

"Wow," Ryan said. They sat on the rocks and gazed out over the snowy mountains stretched before them. The horizontal line of trees was distinct, marking an altitude where trees couldn't grow in the thin air.

"There's snow up there and it's July."

"There's always snow up there." He pointed toward the tallest mountains. "That's Mt. Meeker at nearly 14,000 feet, and just beyond it is the highest in the park, Long's Peak at 14,256."

"You know these mountains?"

"I've climbed them."

"When?"

"A few years ago. Before I started traveling."

She looked out over the peaks. "Was it hard to climb them?"

"Very. Long's Peak is fourteen miles up—one way. At the top you can see for miles and miles in every direction." He touched his tattoo.

"Did you touch heaven?"

A childish question, but a good one just the same. "I believe I did. I was deeply moved by the majesty of it all. It's like God was showing me something special that only a few ever get to see. I prayed." He put a hand to his heart. "It filled me up. It was hard to leave."

She drew her knees to her chest. "Could God hear you better up there since you were closer to Him?"

He glanced at her and saw her question was real. *Help me say the right thing.*

And then it came to him. He didn't know the passage word for word, but knew it came from the book of Jeremiah. "God told a prophet named Jeremiah that if he prayed God would listen. If he sought God, he would find Him—if he sought Him with all his heart." Then a song came to him, one from his childhood, and he sang, "'Seek and ye shall find, knock-knock, and the door will be opened. Ask, and it shall be given, and the love come a'tumbling down.'" He smiled. "I haven't thought of that song in years."

"I like it," Lisa said. "Teach it to me."

And so they served the Lord with gladness and came into His presence with singing.

**

On the way back to the cabin they had a contest to see who could find the biggest pinecone. One after another were discarded as a larger one was found.

"I win!" Lisa said. "There's no way you can find one bigger than this." It was six inches long.

Ryan happily conceded and tossed his aside.

"I want to show Grandpa." Lisa began to run, but stopped at the crook in the road. She motioned Ryan closer, putting a finger to her lips.

Ryan expected to see Grandpa sleeping on the porch. Instead they found him on a ladder, helping Bertha hang the Honeycomb Cabins sign from some hooks along the roof's edge.

"I haven't seen Grandpa do much of anything for a long time."

The power of a pretty smile? Whatever the reason, Ryan was glad for it.

They approached the duo carefully, not wanting to surprise Grandpa while he was in a precarious position.

Bertha didn't see them as she held the ladder. "I knew that hook was set in a rotted piece of soffit. I think we need to move the entire thing over a few inches. Reset both hooks."

"You need a new soffit is what you need."

"Oh dear."

Grandpa examined the board that edged the roof line. "I could probably do it. There a lumber yard near here?"

"A couple in Estes Park, sixteen miles north of here."

"You got a tape measure? Let me get—" He saw Lisa and Ryan. "How was your walk?"

He acted like nothing was unusual. Ryan played along, "It was gorgeous."

Lisa wasn't so easy on him. "You shouldn't be up on a ladder, Grandpa. Not with your—"

"Stop right there, girl. Bertha's place needs some repairs and I intend to help."

"You are such a godsend," she said. "I'll get that tape measure."

Lisa rushed to hold the ladder. "What are you doing up there?"

"Something. That's what I'm doing." He nodded to the porch of their cabin. "I was sitting there—just sitting, doing not-a-thing—all bundled up like an invalid, when Bertha came out and started fixing the sign. She's as old as me. I didn't plan on helping, but suddenly I found myself out of the chair, and here I am. Honestly, it feels kinda good."

"But—"

Ryan shook his head at her, stopping her words. He knew how important it was to feel a sense of purpose. That Grandpa's came about because of a widowed woman was a nice surprise.

**

Ryan was nervous driving into the town of Estes Park to get the lumber and supplies. He'd offered to go alone, but Lisa and Grandpa wanted to go too.

The Pearls were in a grand mood, exclaiming at the views of Meeker Mountain, Twin Sisters, and Lily Lake.

"People are walking around it," Lisa said as they stopped at a highway crosswalk. "Can we go?"

"Not today," Grandpa said. "Bertha's waiting for us."

Ryan had walked around Lily Lake a hundred times. Plus, he could give a commentary about what was around each bend in the road leading to Estes. He should be excited to be home.

But he wasn't.

Luckily, the lumber yard was on the edge of town. Hopefully, they could get what they needed and leave before anyone recognized him.

Grandpa and Lisa left the store first, letting Ryan pay.

The clerk—Bob Milton—said, "I know you. You're Ryan Bauer, yes?"

"Yeah. Hi. Nice to see you, Mr. Milton."

"Been ages and ages. You visiting your parents?"

"Yup." He got the receipt and headed toward the door. "Have a nice day."

He wondered how long it would take before the Estes grapevine got back to his mom and dad.

He knew the answer.

**

Ryan was glad his cellphone didn't work up at the cabin—not that his parents had his number anyway. That was the way he'd planned it when he'd run away from his life. He'd cut all ties. Not because he didn't love his parents—he did. Immensely. But because they wouldn't understand what he was doing.

Do I know what I'm doing?

"Ryan?" Grandpa said. "You need more nails or what?"

Ryan was up on the ladder, fixing the soffit. His daydreams must have made him stop working.

He went back to nailing, but the inner question kept returning: *Do I know what I'm doing?*

He liked the short answer best. He did know what he was going: he was spending time with three people who needed him.

**

Bertha invited them to dinner. She was a good cook. A great cook. She made a bierock casserole, fresh corn on the cob, and blueberry streusel cake.

"It's so nice to cook for guests again," she said. "Ever since Arnold died I've lived on soups, eggs, bread, and tuna. I just don't have the heart to cook the meals he loved." She smiled. "Until now." She lifted her glass of lemonade. "To new friends—and hard workers!"

They clinked glasses. Lisa made sure she tapped each one.

"How many cabins do you have here?" Ryan asked.

"Five."

He hadn't seen any guests. "Has it been a busy year?"

Her plump face clouded. "Off and on. Repeat guests mostly. Once they come here they love it. They actually like being away from phones and TV."

Ryan liked it, but wasn't so sure about most people. It sounded idyllic and nostalgic, but businesswise it might not have been a wise choice. "Do you advertise?"

"In the newspaper here, and in Estes once in a while." She shrugged and poured Grandpa some more lemonade. "But it's a Catch-22."

"What's that?" Lisa asked.

Bertha looked at the log ceiling for the answer. "It's a situation where you can't win. I need money to advertise and get guests, but I don't have money to advertise without guests."

"It's like the chicken," Lisa said.

"What?" Grandpa asked.

"Which came first, the chicken or the egg?"

They all laughed. "That's a good one, girl."

Grandpa's laughter was like a soothing balm. Coming here was the right choice for him.

But was it the right choice for Ryan?

Chapter 36

Summer

"Fools make fun of guilt,
but the godly acknowledge it
and seek reconciliation."
Proverbs 14: 9

Summer hadn't heard from Sydney since the Candy confrontation—two days ago. She knew she should call her, but didn't feel up to it. She felt a cold coming on.

At the Coffee Break she was careful to wear gloves and wash up more than normal, but when it was time to go to the flower shop she knew she needed to stop home and take some medicine.

There was a sticky note on her door: *"Let's taco about how awesome you are." Maxwell Chapter 1: 2. "Mexican food, my place, tonight at 6?"*

She chuckled. What a good guy. After helping Max move in they'd walked Suzu together a few times, and she'd made him brownies. Their interactions had been short but meaningful, like they were both wading in the shallow end of an inviting pool.

Right now she just wanted to dive into bed. Unfortunately that wasn't possible.

She was greeted by Suzu, wanting to play. Summer wasn't up to it, and took the puppy outside in a quick minute, then took some Dayquil, and was off to job number two.

As she drove she remembered her family urging her to slow down and quit a job—as long as it wasn't at Happy Trails. The idea *was* enticing, but she wasn't ready to let go.

Not yet.

**

Candy stepped out of the workroom and stared at Summer. "You sick?"

Summer stuffed a tissue in the pocket of her apron. "Just a cold. I'm fine."

Before returning to the back Candy gave her a skeptical look—a look that Summer had seen far too often of late.

Summer sat on a stool. She felt like a truck hit her. She hoped today would be another phone and internet type of day.

But then . . . the front door opened and a middle-aged man came in.

She stood to greet him. "Good morning, sir. How can I help you?"

He glanced in the cooler at some arrangements.

"What's the occasion?" she asked.

He turned toward her. "Guilt."

Okay then. "I'm sure flowers will make things better."

"They'd *better.*" He pointed at a vase of purple asters and yellow daisies. "That one."

"Very good. Would you like to include a card?"

He hesitated. "Sure."

She handed him one and after a few moments he wrote some words on it, sealed it in an envelope, and wrote *Hannah* on the front. "Here."

"I need a full name and address."

He gave her the recipient's information and his own. She wrote up the bill. "It's good you're doing this, Mr. Horowitz." She suddenly realized she was having an actual conversation with a person. Could he be a connection? She thought of a verse about being sorry for something—or part of a verse. "'Repent and be baptized,'" she said.

He stared at her. "Repent? Baptized? I'm Jewish."

Uh…

He took a step back. "I resent you attacking me with your Christian malarkey."

What? "I'm sorry. I didn't mean anything by it."

He put his credit card away. "I feel bad enough without you condemning me."

"I'm not con—"

He walked out.

Summer stared at the door. What just happened?

She was on the verge of tears so slipped the order sheet under the counter and headed to the restroom in the back, asking Candy to watch the counter for a minute.

She stared at herself in the mirror. "Lord? I shared a verse. How can that be wrong?"

Her reflection looked back at her in pain.

That was the key. Mr. Horowitz was in pain. He was trying to make things right with his wife, but Summer made it worse.

She turned away from the mirror, unable to look at herself a moment longer. "I'm so sorry. I meant well but I blew it. Help me! Please."

Make it right.

She blinked, letting the thought sink in. And then she knew what she had to do.

She splashed water on her face and nodded at the resolute woman in the mirror. "Let's fix this." She went to Candy and said, "There's a rush delivery for a customer I have to make."

"Rush? What are you talking about?"

"He just came in. I'll take my own car. It won't take long."

Before Candy could argue she went to the front, retrieved the address, the note, and the arrangement, and left.

**

The Horowitz home was four blocks from Flora & Funna Summer parked out front. *Let this work, Lord.*

She walked to the front door and took a deep breath before ringing the bell.

A very old woman opened the door. She leaned on a cane. "I'm looking for Hannah Horowitz?"

"That's me."

It's not his wife, it's his mother. "These are for you."

Her face brightened. "Oh my. How lovely. Can you bring them in for me?"

"Of course." Summer brought the flowers inside.

Mrs. Horowitz pointed to a coffee table in the small living room. "Put them there so I can see them all day."

Summer placed them in the center of the table, then handed her the card. She read it and put a hand to her heart. "My son, my son. You dear boy." She looked at Summer with bittersweet eyes. "He is such a good man." Her smile took years off her face. "I love him so very much."

Summer was touched. "'Love covers over all wrongs.'"

Mrs. Horowitz smiled. "A proverb for the ages."

It was from the Bible? Summer hadn't planned to share a verse, the words had just come out.

The woman touched Summer's arm. "Thank you for bringing these to me."

"You're welcome." She went out to the stoop. "If you could do me a favor?"

"Of course, dear."

"Would you tell your son that *I'm* sorry."

She looked confused.

"He'll understand." *I hope.*

Driving back to the shop, Summer was confused. She'd quoted the Bible the first time and had received a negative response. Then she'd unknowingly quoted it a second time and had received affirmation.

"So it is," she sighed.

There was no predicting which response she would get. Perhaps that wasn't important. It was her responsibility to share—to the best of her abilities. The rest was between the hearer and God.

Summer pulled into the parking lot behind the shop and got out just as a dove swooped down and landed on the hood of her car.

She laughed out loud, then went inside. "Candy, I'm back."

Candy was on the phone in the workroom. Summer used the moment when she was distracted to pay for Mr. Horowitz's flowers out of her own money. It was the least she could do.

She had just closed the cash register and was blowing her nose when Candy came out front. "That didn't take long."

"Nope."

"I was on the phone with a Mr. Horowitz. He said he began to order some flowers for his mother and she just called and said they'd been delivered?"

Summer's insides tightened. "Yes, they have." *What else did he say?*

"He told me he didn't pay." She held a slip of paper. "Here's his info."

"Thanks." Summer took the credit card information but had no intention of charging him.

"This all seems strange. Want to tell me what's going on?"

I learned something. "The flowers made an old woman very happy."

Candy studied her, and Summer could tell she wasn't convinced that was all there was to it.

Summer suddenly had a sneezing fit. "Ugh. I'm so sorry."

"Gracious. Go home."

"I'll be okay."

"No, Summer. Go home. I insist."

Candy didn't have to tell her again.

**

Summer was in her pjs, in bed, within five minutes of getting home. She pulled a pillow close, then remembered three things she had to do before she slept.

She retrieved her phone and called her boss at Happy Trails, telling her she wouldn't be in. There was no argument. Retirement homes did *not* want contagious people around.

Second, she texted Grandma to tell her she wouldn't be there for the dinner service, but she was fine. She just had a cold.

Then she texted Max, asking for a Mexican food rain check. He immediately texted back, telling her to rest and get well.

Her business done, she grabbed the pillow and tried to do just that.

**

Summer opened her eyes. It took her a moment to realize she was in bed, and only a half a moment to remember why she was there as she grabbed a tissue and sneezed three times.

The clock read seven, which explained why she was hungry. She hadn't had lunch, and must have slept through the afternoon and dinner.

Suzu ran into the bedroom and did a little dance.

"Oh dear! I never let you out!"

Suzu whined once.

"And I haven't fed you. Hang on." She got out of bed and tied on a robe. She slipped on flip-flops and grabbed the leash.

But as she opened the door she nearly ran into Grandma and Mae.

"You're alive," Mae said.

"Barely." Suzu ran between them, whining. "She needs to go out."

"I'll take her," Grandma said.

"And look," Mae said, holding up a lunch cooler. "We brought you some soup."

"That's so nice of you. But I'm okay."

"Nonsense." Mae barged in, in that way she had of convincing people they were better off with her *in* rather than *out*. "Turn on some lights in here." She flipped on a lamp by the couch and the kitchen light. She opened the fridge. "Good. You have milk. We forgot milk." She nodded toward the breakfast bar. "Sit."

Grandma and Suzu returned and Summer told Grandma how much food to give her.

"Forgetting about your dog?" Grandma said. "You must be sick."

She didn't want to tell them she'd slept seven hours. "You really don't have to do this. I have food here."

Mae put her hands on her hips. "Stop it. I know you have a servant's heart for others, but did you ever think that maybe others like to do nice things too?"

"I don't want to be a bother."

Mae rolled her eyes and took out a Tupperware container of soup. Chicken noodle. "Why do you serve others?"

It sounded like a trick question. "It's the right thing to do."

"Pish-posh," Mae said.

Grandma softened the words. "That's very true," she said. "But . . ."

Mae raised a finger. "If you're completely honest you help so you feel like you're doing something useful, like you have a purpose."

Grandma nodded. "It makes you feel good." She took over the serving, putting a ham and cheese sandwich on a plate and peeling a banana.

"Thank you. Yes, I suppose it does."

"So . . ." Mae spread her hands. "The conclusion?"

Summer wasn't sure her mind was up to working so hard, but she did get what they were saying. "I need to let you help me because it gives *you* pleasure and a purpose."

"Bingo!" Mae yelled. "You are serving others by letting them serve you. Give the girl a sparkle star."

"Mae . . ." Grandma said. "Enough of the life lesson. We need to leave Summer alone to eat and rest."

Mae pushed the cooler into a corner on the counter. "Can we do anything else for you?"

Summer smiled. "Am I supposed to say yes?"

"Telling us the truth is fine. But do tell us. Do call us if you need anything."

Grandma kissed her fingers and blew a kiss to Summer. Mae did the same and they left. The air in the room took a moment to settle.

Summer tore off a piece of ham and held it for Suzu. "Here, puppy. Eat this. It will make me feel good."

And it did.

Chapter 37

Michelle

"One person pretends to be rich, yet has nothing;
another pretends to be poor, yet has great wealth."
Proverbs 13: 7

Michelle's phone woke her up. She fumbled for it on the bedside table. "Hello?"

"Michelle, Barb here."

She sat up. Barb was the night supervisor at the shelter. "What's wrong?"

"We had a death."

Michelle flipped on the light. "Who?"

"Roscoe. Overdose."

Michelle's heart sank. Roscoe, the man who always made people laugh. What happened? He'd been clean for a long time. *Lord, oh dear Lord.* "I'll be right there."

**

By the time Michelle got to the shelter, things had calmed down—as much as could be expected. It's not that they'd never had anyone die, but Roscoe had been visibly healthy and had seemed happy. Michelle wasn't aware of anyone who knew he was using again. His death was a shock. He would be missed.

She checked in with the staff and did what she could to get people calmed down and back to the dorms. But then she heard an argument and spotted Patty and Jonette in the dining room—yelling at each other. Michelle hurried in that direction.

Patty was inches away from Jonette. "Don't give me that crap. You are a spoiled, ungrateful brat! You have a place to go. You have a mom and dad."

"She's not my mom!"

Patty shook her head derisively. "Go home, little girl."

"Fine, I—"

Michelle waved a hand as she approached. "Stop it! Both of you."

Patty pushed Jonette with two fingers. "You don't belong here."

Jonette attempted to get in her face, but being so short . . . "You think I want to be around dirty homeless people who use drugs and—"

"Stop it!" Michelle stepped between them, facing Jonette. She lowered her voice. "You need to calm down."

"What about her?" She tried to reach around Michelle.

Michelle addressed Patty. "You too. Go back to the dorm. We've endured enough drama for one night."

"Fine," Patty said. "I'm fed up with this snot-nose kid who doesn't have sense enough to appreciate what she has."

"You don't know what I have!" Jonette yelled.

With a nod to Patty, Michelle nudged Jonette away. Patty was a good person. This outburst wasn't like her. "I'll talk to you tomorrow."

"Okay, Mama Michelle. But only because it's you." She pointed a finger at Jonette, then walked away.

"I don't like her."

Michelle hesitated. *God, give me the right words.* "You should. She's an amazing woman who's turned her life around." She pointed to the stairs. "Let's go talk in my room."

She let Jonette lead the way. Once inside, Jonette sank onto the bed. Michelle sat in the only chair. "What's going on?" Michelle asked. "I know Roscoe's death is upsetting but—"

"He was nice. He told jokes."

"It's hard when bad things happen to nice people."

Jonette crossed her arms. "Patty was mean to me."

"It sounded like you were giving as much as getting."

"She called me spoiled and told me to go home. She has no idea what I've been through. Nobody does."

Neither do I. "So tell me."

Jonette shook her head. Once. Adamantly. "I hate these people."

"Then go home."

The girl hesitated a split second, but shook her head again.

"The thing is, if you're here, you have to treat people with respect."

"But they're awful people who have done awful things."

"That's not true at all. Have you taken the time to get to know them, and find out why they're here?"

Jonette didn't answer.

"Did you know Patty's mom was a junkie and she was put in foster care when she was eight? She lived in six different foster homes—some good and some not. She didn't have parents who loved her."

"*My* mom died."

"I know she did, hon. I hate that you went through that kind of loss. But you still had your dad—have your dad." Michelle chose *not* to mention her step-mom. "When she aged out, Patty was on her own—for over a year. That's when she ended up here."

"Why's she still here?"

"I got her a job doing laundry for the shelter. We thought it was temporary but she liked it and she's good with people. She gets paid and is saving up for her own apartment. She's working on her GED—her high school diploma."

"I'm pretty good at school. I like math."

"Not everyone has a chance to go to school like you do."

She shook her head as though discarding everything Michelle had said.

It was time to be more forceful. "It's not just about you, Jonette. These people have stories to tell, some tragic and some inspiring. But the one common denominator is they don't want to be here and would go home if they could."

"That's them. They're not me." Jonette pouted and turned away, staring at the wall.

How could Michelle get through to her? *Maybe it would help if I tell her* my *story.* "I used to hate homeless people."

Jonette glanced over her shoulder. "Did they steal from you too?"

"In a way. They stole my husband's life."

Jonette did a double take, then turned back around. "Serge?"

"Sergei."

"What did they do to him?"

Michelle raised a hand to give herself a moment. She sat in the chair. She needed to properly set up the most horrific experience of her life. "He and I were out on a date night, walking hand in hand after going to the theater. We were talking about a trip we wanted to take that summer. Suddenly we heard a woman scream. We ran toward the sound and saw a woman being attacked. Sergei tried to stop it but the man turned on him and stabbed him." She took a fresh breath. "He died in my arms."

Jonette's forehead crumpled. "Wow. I'm so sorry."

Michelle closed her eyes a moment, pushing the memory aside. She opened her eyes and continued. "The man who killed him was homeless and hungry. He was stealing to get money for food." She looked Jonette straight in the eye. "I wanted him dead." Michelle braced herself against the flood of emotions. "I let hatred rule me for years. I didn't just hate the man, or homeless people in general, I hated anyone who had a spouse and was happy."

"I can't imagine you hating anyone," Jonette said. "How did you get from hating the homeless to helping them?"

"God."

Jonette slipped off the bed to the floor, leaning against the mattress. "What'd He do? Send a bolt of lightning?"

"Not quite but almost. After Sergei died I was destroyed. My faith was in shambles. If God was love, why had He taken *my* love away? I went through that whole downward spiral thing. I quit teaching and got a job that paid me just enough to get by. I spent my weekends bar-hopping with friends. I pretended I was fine—what an awful word. I was independent and arrogant. I didn't need God."

"Until . . . ?" Jonette asked.

"Until one night in a bar I got into a shouting match with my friends and stormed off—not a great choice for a woman at night."

Jonette bit her fingernail. "What happened?"

"I knew it was stupid to be walking alone. I was about to turn back when I had this feeling . . ." She put a fist to her midsection. "It's like I was supposed to go down a specific street. That's when I stumbled upon an old man sprawled unconscious on a train track." Michelle cringed, still hearing the train whistle echo in her mind. "A train was coming. Fast. I pulled him off the track just in time."

"Wow," Jonette said. "You saved somebody."

"Yes, I did. And in a way, he saved me back."

"How'd he do that?"

"The whole experience stirred my soul and made me question my priorities. My life wasn't just about me. Maybe I was supposed to help people." Michelle wasn't sure Jonette would understand this next part but she'd shared too much to turn back. "Then I had a vision and saw Jesus. He told me to give up everything and follow Him. I fought it for a while, but God was persistent and didn't give up on me."

"Everything?" Jonette said.

Michelle nodded once. "I left behind my job, my apartment, my friends, and my lifestyle. My parents tried to talk me out of it, but the Heavenly Father had more clout." She shrugged. "I ended up working at a shelter in Denver, and eventually ended up here in Kansas City."

Jonette looked around the tiny room. "This room is all you had in the whole world?"

"It was. And it's all I needed. I'm staying with a friend now." With a groan, Michelle got down on the floor, facing Jonette. "I lost a husband and everything I had, yet if I was asked to do it again I wouldn't change a thing. We're given choices—some of them hard. You have a choice too." She peered into Jonette's dark eyes. "You *can* stay here at the shelter—but you need to do some heavy thinking about what's wise." Jonette squirmed but Michelle wasn't done with her yet. "Did you know that wisdom is something God always gives us if we ask?"

Jonette shook her head.

"James one, five: 'If any of you lacks wisdom, you should ask God, who gives generously to all without finding fault, and it will be given to you.' *Will* be given. Not *might* be given."

Yet instead of making Jonette feel better, the verse seemed to make her feel worse. She hung her head and looked to the floor. "I don't know what to do."

Michelle took one of her hands.

"Ask," Michelle said. "Ask for wisdom."

Jonette hesitated. Then she took a fresh breath and looked at the ceiling. "God? Give me wisdom. Let me know what to do."

Michelle repeated the prayer for her own sake.

Chapter 38

Claire

"But if you do not forgive others their sins,
your Father will not forgive your sins."
Matthew 6:15

It was early. Way early. Claire and Billy sat in his truck near the back alley leading to Robby's Steakhouse.

He kept tapping his fingers on the steering wheel.

"You nervous?"

He stopped. "Very. I haven't talked to Robby since the business folded."

"How long ago was that?"

"One year, September tenth."

He knew the exact date?

"I have no idea what to say to him." Billy stared down the street.

"How do you want me to help?"

He sighed. "Maybe fill in details when I falter—which *will* happen."

"I'll do my best. How do you think he'll react? I mean, what can he say?"

Billy rubbed his eyes. His hands dropped. "What can he say?"

"Want to pray?" she asked.

"Anything to help."

Claire put a hand on his shoulder and bowed her head. "Lord, we need Your guidance and Your words. You are the God of justice. Let everything happen according to Your will."

A car drove toward them, turning into the alley. A white Range Rover.

"That's him," Billy whispered. He pressed a hand against his chest. "I'm going to have a heart attack."

"No, you won't." *At least I hope you won't.* "Think of it this way. In less than an hour you will have the truth, you will have confronted the man who sinned against you, and you will . . ." She wasn't sure how to finish the sentence. They'd never discussed how they wanted this to end. A payout? A trip to the police?

"I'll have closure," he said.

They didn't have time to discuss it more because Billy opened his door and got out. Claire was glad she didn't have to prod him. They walked down the alley to the back door and after a moment's hesitation, Billy went inside.

They entered a storeroom attached to a large kitchen. To the right were the freezers, the non-new, never defective freezers.

The light was on in a small office and Claire could hear Robby toss his keys on the desk.

Billy moved to the doorway. "'Morning."

Robby spun around, his eyes large. "Well now. Hiya, Billy." He glance at Claire. "Hello."

"Can we talk to you?" Billy asked. His voice cracked and he cleared his throat.

"Of course," he said, though he didn't sound at all sure. He motioned toward the two chairs in front of his desk and took a seat behind it. "Nice seeing you, Billy."

"You too."

He looked directly at Claire. "And you are?"

"Claire Adams. Billy's friend."

He nodded once. "How've you been, Billy?"

Billy leaned his elbows on the arms of the chair and sat up straighter. "Not good. It's been hard."

Robby didn't say anything.

"You're doing well," Billy said.

"I'm doing okay. You never know with these things, do you?"

"We could have done well too," Billy said.

Thatta boy. Great opening.

"We gave it a good go," Robby said. "But sometimes things go sour."

"By design," Billy said.

"Excuse me?"

Billy took a deep breath and Claire could tell he was ready. "I talked with Nate. He told me everything."

Robby blinked too often. "I'm not sure what 'everything' you're talking about."

"He said you paid him and the other kitchen workers to quit, which put us in a bind, which led to bad reviews."

Robby lifted his hands in the air. "They quit. It did us in. That's not my—our—fault."

"Are you calling Nate a liar?" Robby asked.

"He *is* lying. That's all I can tell you."

Claire thought of something to add. "If he's such a liar, and his leaving was partly to blame for Billy Bob's going under, why did you hire him back? Why hire a liar and a troublemaker?"

Robby pressed a hand on the seat of his chair, making himself bob upward an inch before settling down again. "I resent you speaking with him. You have no business—"

"You have no business filing an insurance claim for freezers and food spoilage that never happened."

There was the slightest pause before he spoke. "It did happen. You were here."

Billy shook his head. "I spoke with Reliable Appliance and Repair and they said they never replaced a freezer or even fixed one even though you charged me half."

Claire piped in, "Even though the insurance company reimbursed you for them and the supposedly ruined food. That's insurance fraud."

Robby's hands waved again, as if he wanted to shoo them away. "Hold on there. You can't accuse me of something that I—"

"We can prove it," Billy said. "We have the paperwork for the freezers and food replacement that never happened, and we can get testimony from the business owner."

"Tommy Tobler was very interested to hear that the whole thing was an insurance scam." Claire took out her phone. "Let's give him a call right now."

Billy put a hand on hers, stopping her. "Why did you do it, Robby? Why did you go to all this trouble to get rid of me? We were partners. I thought we were friends."

Robby leaned forward on his desk, looking down at

nothing. He didn't move for a long while. Billy and Claire exchanged glances. Should they say something?

Finally he looked up. "It all comes down to this: I had money problems. You know Manda. She has expensive tastes and—"

"Don't blame it on your wife," Billy said.

Robby sat there a minute, the muscles in his cheeks tensing. "I wanted to go in a different direction. Italian."

"Why didn't you say so?"

"I mentioned it when we were thinking about a place, but you wanted to use some of your family recipes. Billy Bob's was your vision, not mine."

Billy shook his head, incredulous. "It wasn't *my* vision either. Neither one of us got the restaurant we wanted."

"Yeah. Maybe not."

"If you were done with it, why not let me buy you out? I would have found a way."

Robby shrugged. "I thought about it. But when I looked at other locations, this one was too good to leave."

"Which brings up another question. We owed back rent and were evicted—at least that's what you told me. But here you are."

Robby rubbed the back of his neck. "I negotiated with the landlord."

This was a new development. Claire turned to Billy. "We'll have to talk to him next."

"No!" Robby said. "Don't do that. Please."

It was Claire's turn to ask a question. "What about all the tables and chairs and kitchen equipment inside? Why wasn't Billy paid his portion?"

"That's right." Billy leaned forward. "I was supposed to get half after all of it was sold. What happened with that?"

"You took the equipment," Claire said. "Virtually stole it for your own use."

"I planned to pay you," Robby said. "I would have come through."

"When?" Billy said. "Billy Bob's folded a year ago. Roberto's has been open . . . how long?"

"I was going to pay you your half." He raised a hand as if taking an oath.

Billy sighed. "I'm supposed to believe you? After all the deception and betrayal and fraud?"

Claire loved how he stated it plain. All Billy had to say now was, *"My lawyer will be contacting you."*

Suddenly, Robby cupped his face in his hands. "I'm so sorry. It was wrong. I knew it was wrong, but once it started I couldn't stop." He began to sob. "I'm so sorry."

Contrition is a good first step. It will make prosecution easier.

Robby continued to mumble apologizes and Claire believed he felt bad, but that didn't change any—

Suddenly Billy stood and put a hand on Robby's back. "I forgive you."

What?

Robby looked up at him, swiping the tears from his face. "You do?"

Billy nodded. In a few awkward moments Robby stood and the two partners embraced.

What is happening? This isn't how it's supposed to go!

The two men moved apart. "You want a stake in Roberto's, I'll give it to you, Billy. We can start over."

At least that would be something.

Billy thought about this for a brief moment, then said, "No thanks. I think it's best to move on." He turned to Claire. "I've got what I need here. It's time to go."

But . . . but . . .

Billy stood at the doorway, waiting for Claire to exit. They walked out the back door. Robby appeared at the exit and yelled after them, "I'm sorry, Billy! I'm really sorry!"

When they got in his truck Claire asked, "What was all that—?"

He put a finger to his lips. Then he drove away. She had a hundred questions, but with difficulty, stayed silent.

He didn't talk until he'd pulled into her driveway. He shut off the truck and angled to face her. "I know you're disappointed."

"You bet I am. He broke the law of the land. He broke the law of decency and friendship and right and wrong."

Billy nodded. "He did. And I was on the cusp of going to the cops, getting a lawyer, and making him pay for what he did to me."

"Well, yeah."

"But when he apologized. And sobbed . . ."

"Because he got caught."

Billy shrugged. "It was more than that. I've never seen him so upset. He *was* sorry. He *was* ashamed."

"He should be."

Billy looked out the window as if searching for words. "While we were sitting there I had an image of me and him in a courtroom with Manda and his kids sitting in the audience. I thought of all the newspaper articles and the gossip and . . ." Billy looked at her. "What good would that do anyone? He'd have to pay me back or even go to jail. Roberto's would go under and Nate and all the rest would be without jobs and . . . I still wouldn't have a restaurant."

Everything he said was correct and yet, "Didn't you want revenge for the pain he caused you?"

"I got revenge. He knows I know. He knows others know. He knows what he did was wrong. Me forgiving him puts the burden on him. I for one, am free of *my* burden."

He was a walking talking saint. Claire felt her eyes grow hot with tears.

He touched her cheek. "What's wrong?"

"You . . . you shame me. I was hellbent on revenge, I wanted to make him pay—and it wasn't even my fight. But you, the man who was so utterly wronged, you forgave him. I never even considered doing that."

"You would have. Eventually."

She shook her head adamantly. "I'm not sure. And that's more than embarrassing, it's convicting."

"You're too hard on yourself."

"Not hard enough." Her insides burned with spiritual pain. "I thought God brought you and I together for me to help *you*. But now you've helped me."

His eyes were kind—which convicted her again, for she knew her limitations in that regard were also immense.

"Aren't we here to help each other? Isn't this a part of *our* journey?" he asked.

The logical answer was yes, but she wasn't ready to let herself off the hook. She opened her door and got out. He immediately opened his door, but she spoke across the seats, "No, Billy. Don't come in. I'm extremely happy for you and unbelievably proud of you, but I need a little time to deal with . . . me."

"Claire . . ."

She walked toward her house, then paused to offer him a bittersweet smile and a wave. She went inside and heard him drive away.

Claire leaned against the front door, incapable of standing on her own. She gasped and let the tears come. "I'm so sorry, so sorry, so sorry . . ."

She sank to the floor and drew her knees to her chest, repeating her apologies.

She remembered Robby saying he was sorry amid his own sobs.

And then, just as Billy had offered Robert forgiveness, she felt the Almighty offer her the same.

**

The phone awakened her. Claire was on the couch, an afghan pulled over her shoulder. "Hello?"

"Claire." It was Billy. "How are you?"

She turned onto her back, adjusting a pillow under her head. "Better. I'm sorry for bailing on you like that. You'd done a marvelous thing but I felt guilty about my attitude, felt shamed for it, and—"

"I don't want you to feel ashamed. I felt like you did. I wanted revenge too. I wanted him to suffer like I had. Worse—if possible."

"You didn't seem vindictive."

They shared a moment of silence. Then he spoke. "It was the oddest thing. The time between thinking about forgiving him and doing it was a split-second. I heard myself saying the words and almost couldn't believe it was me saying them. It was like a—"

"A God thing." They said it at the same time.
Wow, Lord.
"Two great minds mean it's true?" Billy said.
It seemed true. It seemed right. It seemed good.
As was God.

Chapter 39

Ryan

"'Truly I tell you,' Jesus said to them,
'no one who has left home or wife or brothers or sisters
or parents or children for the sake of the kingdom of God
will fail to receive many times as much in this age,
and in the age to come eternal life.'"
Luke 18: 29

The days at the Honeycomb Cabins were filled with work and sore muscles, laughter and stories. They'd fixed broken steps, painted the floors of three porches, replaced two kitchen faucets, re-stretched the screen in a door, and even patched the shingles on all five roofs. That wasn't all there was to do, but it was a good start.

Ryan silently noted that no one mentioned leaving. Bertha didn't ask and Grandpa didn't say. The fact he'd asked Ryan to get his rocker off the truck and put it on the porch was a big indicator Grandpa planned to stay a while. It made Ryan a little nervous to stick around, not because he didn't like it here, but because of the proximity to his parents.

He'd made so many mistakes with them, caused them so much grief. Every time he went into Estes he worried he'd run into them. And then what? Conflict was something he avoided at all costs. He wished he were more courageous, but it just wasn't his way. Even the thought of conflict made him want to hide.

Luckily, the Honeycomb was a good place to do just that.

Every day the three of them ate their meals at Bertha's. In the evening they gathered in front of the fireplace and played

Mexican Train and Phase 10. Once Lisa had her first s'mores, it was added to the ritual.

Then one night Lisa pointed at a guitar that leaned against the wall. "Do you play?" she asked Bertha.

"Goodness no. I used to sing and Arnold would play. We'd gather outside, sit by the fire ring, and sing camp songs with the guests. When the fire got low we'd look at the stars and name the constellations."

"We could see a lot of stars at our house in Kansas too. But I never knew the names of them."

"You'll have to learn." She looked at Ryan. "There's a library in Estes. Get Lisa a book."

"I'll do that."

Lisa stared at the guitar. "Do they have music books?"

"I'm sure they do." Bertha retrieved the guitar and handed it to her. "Here. It's yours."

"Wow. But . . . I couldn't."

"It's doing nobody no good sitting there silent," Bertha said. "Try it."

Lisa held it reverently and strummed the strings.

"Let me have that," Grandpa said. He took it and expertly tuned the strings. Then he began to play. "'Oh give me a home, where the buffalo roam . . .'"

Everyone was stunned. Bertha and Ryan joined in. After a few tries, Lisa learned the words too.

What a lovely sound.

**

The next day Lisa and Ryan drove to the library. "Can I get other books too?" she asked.

"Of course. You know Mark Twain wrote a bunch of books besides *Tom Sawyer*."

"I want to look at all the books."

Point taken. "I know you'll find something." He decided to share his other idea. "Actually, I wanted to spend a little time in the library to use the Wi-fi."

"What for?"

"I want to find out how to create a website for Bertha so she can get more customers."

"You know how to do that?"

He knew nothing about it. "I'll get a book on it."

Lisa went off to her section and Ryan found a computer nearby. He checked his email for the first time in a week. There were seven emails from Michelle—beautiful verses of encouragement. And a plea to please share what they were doing.

Being asked to put his adventure into words made Ryan wonder what he *was* doing. He imagined it would sound very strange to the others, yet he gave it a shot. *I met a man and his granddaughter in Kansas and the three of us have moved to Allenspark, Colorado where we're helping a woman fix up her resort. Not sure where it will lead but I do think God brought us together. Hope you are all doing well. Thanks for the verses, Michelle.*

He sent the email, and was about to sign off, when he heard his name.

"Ryan?"

His stomach did a flip. He looked up. "Mom."

She was pushing a cart filled with books. She stared at him as though seeing a ghost. She abandoned the cart and came over to him, but stopped short. Hesitant. Then with a shake of her head, she pulled him to standing and drew him into her arms. "I can't believe it's you! I'm so glad it's you. Finally you!"

A hug. When was the last time he'd hugged anyone? He enjoyed the familiar scent of her perfume. Her warm welcome wasn't what he'd expected. He felt tears threaten but willed them away.

She let go and led him back to the bench. "What brings you here? How long are you staying? Where have you been?" She touched his cheek, her eyes full of emotion. “Sorry. It's just that we've missed you so very, very much. Did you . . . ?”

Miss us?

Ryan chose to ask his own questions rather than answer hers. “How are you? How's Dad?”

“We're good. Older but good.” She touched her chin-length hair which was streaked with gray. “Dad's working at the hospital and I'm working here.” She nodded at him. “You're all grown, completely grown. “

Ten years will do that.

She got back to her questions. “Where are you staying?”

The choice to tell or not to tell was determined when he heard himself answer. “Up in Allenspark.”

She sucked in a breath. “Not far, not far at all. Where in Allenspark?”

“At the Honeycomb Cabins.”

“I didn't know that place was still there. What's it been? Fifteen? Eighteen years since we stayed there?”

He sucked in a breath. “We stayed there?”

“You don't remember? We stayed in a little cabin. You and Lisa used to hike up the road and come back with pinecones.”

His memories flashed in short snippets. Why hadn't he remembered?

She took his hands, staring at him as though still unbelieving. “My boy. My son. You're here. Thank God you're really here.”

Her joy made his guilt deepen.

She slapped a hand on her thigh. “Come to dinner tonight. Dad will be thrilled to see you.”

Thrilled. Not angry?

“You have to come, Ryan.” A line formed between her brows. “You can't appear, then disappear, without spending some time with us.”

There's no such thing as a coincidence. “All right, I'll come.”

“Is anyone traveling with you?”

Actually . . . "If it's all right I'd like to bring a friend and his granddaughter along, and Bertha, the owner of the cabins."

"Bertha. I remember her. Great laugh, big smile. Her husband still around?"

"He passed away."

"To think of her running that place alone . . . Yes, absolutely. You're all welcome. We're where we always were, on Fish Creek Road. Six-thirty all right?" She kissed his cheek. "This is God, Ryan. You know it is."

**

"You're quiet," Lisa said on the way up the mountain.

"Sorry," Ryan said.

"I saw you talking with a lady. She kissed your cheek."

"She's my mother."

Lisa gasped. "No way. She lives here?"

"My dad too. She asked us to dinner tonight. Grandpa and Bertha too. Does that sound okay?"

"It sounds nice. How long has it been since you've seen them?"

"Ten years."

"Whoa!" Lisa said. "That's a long time. Like as old as I am. Like forever."

But was it long enough? The jury was still out on that one.

**

At 6:28 they parked the truck in front of his parents' home.

"Nice place. You lived here?" Grandpa asked.

"For a year. Until I went to college." *A lifetime ago.*

"Which college?"

"University of Colorado."

"What did you major in?" Bertha asked.

It was but one of the many sore subjects that might plague the evening. "I dropped out."

"That was dumb," Grandpa said.

At least he didn't ask *why*.

Ryan put an end to the subject by getting out and opening the door to the extended cab.

Grandpa had surrendered the front to Bertha, but getting him out of the back took a bit of doing. "It's official. I am not a pretzel."

"I told you I'd fit back there better than you," Bertha said. "On the way home, you ride shotgun."

Normally, Ryan would have enjoyed their easy banter—as if they'd known each other forever—but this evening his thoughts were occupied with worries about seeing his parents again.

The front door opened before they reached it. "Welcome!" Ryan's mom stepped back to let everyone inside.

She kissed his cheek and gave his arms a squeeze. "It's *so* nice to see you, honey." Her face radiated sincerity and love. *She* wasn't the problem. The problem was . . .

His father stood nearby. He looked different because his hair was completely gray. He didn't smile. Ryan wasn't sure if he should hug him or shake his hand or get back in the truck and drive away. "Hi, Dad."

Nothing happened for a full count of three, but then Dad stepped forward and drew Ryan into a hug. "Son." Ryan heard a catch in his throat. "Words can't express how happy I am to see you."

They lingered in the embrace as if making up for years of missed hugs. "Me too, Dad," he said softly. *Thank You for Your mercy, Lord.*

When his dad stepped back, Ryan saw him brush his eyes with a hand. Ryan sniffed, dealing with his own emotions. *They're genuinely happy to see me!* And with that revelation came another: he was genuinely happy to see them.

Grandpa broke through the moment by extending his hand to Ryan's dad. "Allen Pearl. And this is my granddaughter, Lisa."

Dad shook his hand. "We had a daughter named Lisa."

"I know," Lisa said. "Ryan told me."

Mom put a hand to her chest. "My name is Kathy."

"And I'm Roy," Dad said.

Mom smiled at Bertha. "Bertha? Do you remember us?"

"It's been sixteen years, Kath," Dad said.

But Bertha grinned. "Ryan told me he'd been at the Honeycomb before. I didn't remember him but I do remember you. You're an artist, right?"

His mother glowed. "I try to be. I paint."

"I remember you walking around with a sketchpad. There's a lot of inspiration in the mountains."

"There is. But I don't generally paint landscapes. I prefer people."

"Plenty of those around too."

"Would you like to see one of her paintings?" Dad asked.

It was a good segue and they were led into the living room where Ryan saw a familiar painting of his mother with a toddler's arms around her neck. You couldn't see either face.

"Is that your daughter hugging you?" Bertha asked.

Mom nodded. "That was our Lisa." She glanced at Ryan. "She died in a car accident when she was fourteen."

Grandpa let out a *hmm,* then said, "We knew she was gone but didn't know how. We're mighty sorry about that. I don't know what I'd do without *my* Lisa."

Lisa found a place under his arm. "Ah, Grandpa . . ."

With a nod to her memories, Mom moved the situation along. "Please come in and have a seat."

"What can I get anyone to drink?" Dad said. "We have iced tea, lemonade, and Dr. Pepper."

People made their choices and Dad poured the drinks. Mom brought in a plate of pinwheel appetizers and cheese-wrapped olives. Always the hostess.

"My, my," Bertha said as she placed some food on her plate. "How fancy."

Mom sat in a chair with a needlepoint cushion. Ryan remembered her working on it when he was young.

"So. How did you all meet our Ryan?" Mom asked.

Ryan looked at Grandpa, then Lisa, trying to wrap his mind around what he should tell them.

He didn't have to.

Lisa raised her hand. "I dreamt about a man named Ryan and then he showed up at our door. Just in time too because Grandpa needed to go to the hospital and couldn't drive, so Ryan took us." She looked to Grandpa for verification.

He shrugged.

"Hospital?" Bertha asked. "You've never mentioned any hospital. Are you okay?"

"Got some meds. I'm fine."

Ryan's dad spoke up. "I'm a doctor. If you need to see one while you're here, call me."

"Thanks, but I'm doing okay."

Bertha reached over and touched his arm.

They chatted about Estes: the tourists that flocked in during the summer and the elk and moose sightings. Ryan was glad for the small talk. Maybe having the others around as a buffer would keep the conversation off himself. Yet even as he thought the thought, his mind replied, *Fat chance.*

When dinner was ready they moved into the dining room. The centerpiece was a vase of pink roses. Ryan was moved at the sight of them for they proved this wasn't some random dinner, this was a part of God's plan.

His mother served roast, mashed potatoes, corn, dinner rolls, and a green salad—the whole of which made Grandpa grin with pleasure.

"My kind of food," he said, taking a huge helping of potatoes which he flooded with brown gravy.

"Glad you like it." She smiled at Ryan. "This is one of Ryan's favorite meals."

He'd guessed her choice was purposeful. "I've missed home cooking."

"Excuse me?" Bertha said with a smile.

He felt himself redden. "Until we came to the Honeycomb, that is. Bertha is trying to fatten me up."

"Not going to happen," she said. "You work it off doing chores for me."

"I don't remember you serving meals," Dad said.

"I didn't. Don't. Usually. But since business is slow... I love having people to cook for."

"So do I." His mother passed the butter around. "Most weekends we'd have a family dinner when Ryan came home from college."

His stomach tightened.

"But then you didn't come home." Dad set his fork down.

And here we go . . .

His dad continued. "Excuse me. But Ryan, I think you owe us an explanation. You were in your last semester and everything was fine, then suddenly you went silent and we heard you dropped out. Your roommate called to tell us to come pick up the car we gave you. *He* called. Not you."

"You disappeared." His mother's brows dipped. "Without a trace. Without a word."

Ryan tried to think of some defense. "I sent you a letter after I left—and birthday cards every year." It sounded as feeble as it was.

Dad tossed his napkin on the table. "Cards where you wrote nothing and only signed your name."

Mom pressed a hand against her chest. "The postmarks told us where you were. *You* didn't offer any information. We had no way of contacting you either. We suffered ten birthdays alone, Ryan. Ten Christmases. Ten Easters . . ."

Ryan felt everyone's eyes and wanted to run outside. Guilty, as charged.

"You need to explain yourself," Dad said. "Going off on your own was bad enough, but why no contact?"

It was hard to explain and Ryan risked sounding arrogant if he tried. "I wasn't on my own. I wasn't traveling of my own volition. God was leading me, bringing me into certain people's lives, letting me help them. I had to concentrate on what He was saying. I guess I didn't have the ability to divide my loyalties between Him and . . . and . . ."

"Us?" Mom said.

He nodded. "I'm really sorry it was so hard on you."

"That's it?" Mom's cheeks had reddened. "You run away and expect it to be made right with one 'I'm sorry'?"

"One 'I'm *really* sorry'," Dad said derisively. He waved the apology away. "Fine. You're out on a road-trip for God. Don't you think you could have finished your degree first?"

Ryan hesitated, remembering how difficult the decision to leave college had been. "Actually, no, I couldn't have. 'God's gifts and his call are irrevocable.'"

Dad threw his hands in the air. "A verse for every occasion."

"He spouts Bible-junk to us all the time too," Grandpa said.

Lisa came to his defense. "I like it."

Mom gave her husband a look. "So do we. Or we used to."

Dad shrugged. "You left your life and became a wanderer. How's that worked out for ya?"

Ryan knew they wanted a quantifiable answer but he couldn't give them one. "It's gone pretty well."

Lisa nodded vigorously and came to his defense. "When Grandpa decided he wanted to see the mountains we packed up most everything in our house and headed west. We saw some bison and had pie, and Ryan told an old lady she was pretty, which made me give some money to another lady at a gas station. But later I found the same amount in my pocket, and..." She took a quick breath. "We also picked up a hitchhiker named Arlo."

"What? That's not safe," Dad said.

Lisa shook her head, making her dark hair swing. "Arlo was nice and told us verses about honeycomb and milk and honey and then we found the Honeycomb in a place called Allenspark—Grandpa's name is Allen—so we knew we were at the right place. And Arlo called Ryan by name even though nobody had told him his name." She nodded and smushed a crumb with a finger. "We think he was an angel."

His mother put a hand to her mouth. "God is giving you signs like He did when you were little."

Suddenly, Ryan felt an inner stirring and knew the Almighty *had* brought him home, to this dinner, at this time.

He walked through God's opened door. "As a kid, God gave me signs without me seeking them, but now I actively look." He pushed his empty plate toward the middle of the table. "I was brought to the Pearls in time to help Allen, we were led to the Honeycomb, and I was led back to you. God did that. All of it. He has a purpose to it. To everything."

"Let's say that's true," Dad said. "Why now?"

Ryan had no easy answer.

His father's face battled with emotions, but with a fresh breath it softened. "You left us but now you're back. The prodigal son, returned."

But am I really back? Or just passing through?

"We've always known you were unique," Mom said. "We knew you were called by God to do special things. And we don't necessarily disagree with your choice. But . . ."

Dad took over. "But the way you did it was hurtful. A slap in the face."

"I didn't mean it like that."

Dad continued. "We had a dream for you—as most parents do. I know kids grow up to have their own dreams, but the way you walked out was like thumbing your nose at everything we'd given you: college, support, a car . . ."

Bertha pushed herself away from the table. "I think you three could use a little time alone. Lisa? Allen? Let's clear these dishes."

Mom objected, but Bertha prevailed and they were left alone. Ryan and his parents shared an uncomfortable minute in the dining room.

Mom spoke first. "The big issue is love," she said. "You deprived us of the chance to show our love for ten years. We wanted to be a part of your life and now you're grown." She began to cry. "We've missed so much."

Ryan's heart broke, but quickly found comfort. "God said, 'I will repay you for the years the locusts have eaten.'"

Mom dabbed at her eyes and nodded. "I haven't heard that verse in ages." She took a breath in and out. "I guess we *can* start over."

After some hesitation Dad said, "I'm game."

"How about you, Ryan?" Mom asked.

His heart swelled with emotion. He'd avoided his past for ten years, but God had brought them back together for a yet-to-be-discovered purpose. "Thank you for being so gracious to me," he told them. "I don't deserve it."

"You've always heard the beat of a different drummer." Mom smiled. "The Almighty drummer. It's true we all could have done things differently. Should have. And I can speak for your father and I by admitting that we were guilty of trying to hem you into our model of a life. That wasn't right either."

"You loved me well."

"Tried to."

Dad nodded. "Tried to."

Mom reached across the table. "You, my dear Ryan, are a free spirit." She raised a finger. "That's not exactly correct. You've freely chosen to have *His* Spirit, the Holy Spirit, work within you."

"We can all do that, Mom. You and Dad did it when I was little. You accepted God's invitation and changed our lives."

Her sigh was wistful. "I was brave then. I'm less brave now. I think . . ." She looked to her husband. "I think we've fallen into a rut. I think we've stopped listening like we used to. Don't you think that's true, Roy? We do the same thing day after day and nothing changes. *We* don't change and we don't help others change either. We're not living our faith, we're coasting."

Dad fidgeted in his chair, then folded his napkin. Once. Twice. Then set it aside. "I hate to admit it, but we *have* been coasting. And it's not because we got busy. It's because . . . at least on my part, I suddenly realize it's because I was jealous of your relationship with God." His words came faster. "And when you left to spend more time with Him? Gave up everything to follow Him? I was mad at both of you—I turned my back on both of you." He pressed his fingers between his eyebrows. "I can't believe I never saw it before now but I was jealous of my own son and mad at God for blessing him!" He covered his face with his hands and bowed his head. "I'm so sorry, so sorry, so sorry . . ."

Mom and Ryan rushed to his side. Their emotions culminated in a family hug.

Ryan knew with full certainty that God smiled.

**

Ryan drove back to the Honeycomb, happy and greatly relieved about the time he'd spent with his parents. For years he'd imagined it would be an angry, bitter exchange. That they had bared their hearts *to* him and showed their love *for* him . . . God was good.

Grandpa sat in the front seat. He glanced at Ryan, then away. "What's got you smiling like a crazy man?"

Ryan gave the short answer. "God."

"Pffft."

"Don't say that, Allen," Bertha said from the back. She touched Ryan's shoulder. "While we were in the kitchen we couldn't help but overhear some of your conversation. It's a good thing you came back to them."

"God brought you back," Lisa said. "He sent you away then He brought you back."

Grandpa shook his head. "Again, I say *pffft*. You were a rebellious, ungrateful teenager who broke your parents' hearts. Yeah, you're back. Big deal."

"It was more than teenage rebellion," Ryan said. "I heard God tell—"

Grandpa hit the dashboard with a hand. "Stop it! Cut the 'listening' malarkey. All you listened to were your own selfish desires."

"But—"

He crossed his arms. "I have a headache. No more talking."

So much for happiness and relief.

Chapter 40

Summer

"Bear with each other and forgive one another
if any of you has a grievance against someone.
Forgive as the Lord forgave you."
Colossians 3:13

Summer knew she was bored when she watched *The Holiday* for the 444th time. It was comforting to play a familiar movie while dozing and still know what was going on when she opened her eyes. But it was also an indication that she didn't have the energy to think fresh thoughts.

While the movie played on, she checked her email and saw the daily verse from Michelle. But this time—for the first time—someone had replied. Ryan had met two people and they'd all moved to Colorado. There, he was helping someone fix up their resort. Above all, it was clear God was at work in Ryan's life.

Summer shook her head, newly in awe of him. It was not surprising he'd found a way to reach people.

Maybe it was time for her to share something too. She hit the Reply-All button and poised her fingers over the keyboard. What could she tell them?

She typed: *I got a third job so I could meet more people . . .*

"But it's not working the way I planned."

She added, *I tried to connect with a customer at the flower shop and shared a verse. . .*

"But I offended him and he stormed off."

She typed some more. *I saw a person getting food out of a dumpster and started leaving food for them . . .*

"But then I got sick and can't help her anymore. Or go to work at any of my jobs. So I'm in limbo."

Summer stared at the screen. Her "success" was marginal. Ryan had traveled to a different state and was deeply involved in the lives of multiple strangers.

"I shouldn't compare myself with him." She looked at Suzu and finished her thought. "At least Jered hasn't answered. He probably hasn't done anything." It seemed wrong to feel good about that.

She was pulled from the moment when she heard a text ping. She sent the email, then checked the text. It was from Max: *How you feeling? I'll bring you lunch. Burgers or Chinese food?*

She texted back: *Chinese. Thanks.* He'd been so kind. Their friendship was fairly new, but he hadn't abandoned her. His texts and notes always made her smile.

About noon he knocked. She cracked the door, mainly because she was wearing pink Hello Kitty pajama bottoms and a red Kansas City Chiefs' tee-shirt. And fuzzy slippers with a puppy head on them.

"For you, Miss Peerbaugh." He offered her a bag from the local Chinese place. "I got you orange chicken, an egg roll, fried rice, and three crab rangoon."

"I couldn't have ordered better." She turned her head to sneeze. "Sorry."

"Bon appétit," he said. "I hope you feel better." He grinned and pointed toward the floor. "Love the slippers."

She jiggled one of her feet so the puppy's ears wagged. "Aunt Mae gave them to me."

Suzu came to the door and Max bent down to pet her. "Heya Suzu. You taking good care of your mama?" Suzu wagged her tail. "Do you want me to take her out for you?" Max asked.

Yes, but . . . "Surely you have to get back to work."

"A couple more minutes won't matter. I told them I was bringing lunch to a sick friend. Get me her leash."

Summer heard Mae's voice in her head. *You are serving others by letting them serve you.* "Thanks. I'll get it."

She heard Max and Suzu scramble down the stairs. Summer went to the balcony and watched them in the grass. "Good Suzu. Good puppy." He was very good with her. Summer had the feeling Max was good with every living thing.

He brought the puppy back to her door. "I'll stop by after work and take her out again. You want me to bring you anything else?"

She was a bit overwhelmed with his constant kindness. "Taking her outside is great. But I'm okay for dinner. You've been wonderful. Thank you."

"Verse three," he said. "Whenever possible be helpful to sick friends by offering Chinese food and potty breaks."

She laughed, and he left with a smile and a wave. She made herself a plate of food, sat on the couch, and indulged.

But then one of Max's words came to mind. He'd called her his sick "friend." They *were* friends but each day made her want to be more. Which was ridiculous. They'd only seen each other a few times. Their busy lives and her illness had sent their relationship into phone and text mode. That wasn't the stuff of a real relationship.

Was it?

Not that she would know. Summer had little to no experience with romance. In high school she'd found the boys too obsessed with cars, sports, partying, and sex. In college it was much the same. Add to that the statistical fact that there were very few men getting degrees in social work, and the result was a natural lack of dating opportunities.

In truth, Summer didn't have many female friends either—females under sixty-five. She knew the main reason she bonded so easily with older women was her upbringing. And her mother's single-mom status and pragmatic nature had made *their* relationship swing on the side of a partnership more than a mother-daughter bond.

Summer was okay with that. She never felt her social life was lacking, which was one reason she was so willing to work three jobs. Her schedule allowed her enough interaction to keep her from earning a hermit designation. She knew the first names of the four tenants on her floor but wasn't one to stand out in the hall to talk. Chit-chat drained her.

She liked her own company. Yet just because she enjoyed being alone didn't mean she didn't like people. She did. In small, controlled doses. She didn't need a gang of friends, just a few good ones. Close ones.

Did that include Sydney? Their friendship *had* been close, then wasn't, then involved a wedding, then faded, and now . . . it was odd and up in the air.

And what about Max?

She smiled at the thought of him.

**

There was a knock on the door. Summer glanced in a mirror and combed her fingers through her pillow-head hair.

She expected Max, but found Tessa at the door.

Aunt Tessa put a hand to her chest. "You couldn't have an apartment on the first floor?"

Summer moved a blanket from the couch. "Sit. Catch your breath."

Tessa leaned heavily on her cane but took a seat. At ninety, she was proud she didn't use a walker. But three flights? That often took Summer's breath away.

"You should have called to talk to me," Summer said. "You didn't have to come over."

"I'm not bedbound, you know."

But she was over-exerted. Her dark skin took on a deeper tone. Her nose was a bright red.

Summer got her a glass of water.

"Thank you, dear. That's kind of you considering you're the one who's sick." Tessa looked around the living room and her eyes lingered on the used tissues on the coffee table as well as the carry-out container from lunch. "At least you're eating."

Summer cut a quick swath through the room to gather her trash. "A neighbor brought me take-out."

"I'm glad you're taking care of yourself. It's the reason I'm here." She waved a bony hand at her. "Sit down. You're making me nervous."

Summer sat at the far end of the couch. Tessa had always been bossy and they hadn't always gotten along. At first, Tessa had resented having to deal with a five-year-old at Peerbaugh Place.

Suddenly a memory surfaced. "You helped me once before when I was sick," Summer said. "I was little and Mom was away for some reason. You took care of me." It had been the beginning of Tessa's softening to the idea of being friends with a child.

Tessa took another sip of water. Her coloring was returning to normal. "I remember that. You were a pretty child."

"Thank you."

"A pretty woman too if you come down to it."

Summer smiled. "Thank you again." *Why are you here?*

Tessa set the glass down and placed her cane across her lap. "There's been a lot of talk about you having a servant's heart and all that, and I don't discount it. I agree. But with that gift comes a few flaws."

Now this *sounded like Tessa.* "Which are?"

"You're pushy."

Summer chuckled. "Really."

"Yes, you are. You've always been too eager to help out. I remember you incessantly bothered your grandmother by asking how you could help cook or clean. It was exhausting."

Summer laughed again. "I just wanted to be useful." *Still want to be useful.*

"Yet you find it hard to accept help from others."

Ahhh. Summer knew where this was going. "Mae and Grandma already talked to me about this. I need to let others help so *they* feel the satisfaction of it."

"True. But there's another level to it."

Leave it to Tessa to dig deeper.

"Remember that big car of mine, my husband's Caddy?"

Vaguely. But she said, "I do."

"That car was Alfred's pride and joy. He washed that thing at least twice a week, kept the gas tank above three-quarters, and if I so much as left a tissue on the seat, he'd make me go out and throw it away."

"He took care of it."

Tessa raised a finger. "Yes, he did. But . . . what if Alfred had let the car stay dirty after a rain or snow? What if he'd let the tires go flat, tossed hamburger wrappers in the back, and spilled coffee on the upholstery? What would you say to him?"

Was she talking about the messy tissues? "I'd tell him he needed to take care of his car."

"Exactly. Alfred always used to say "A clean car is a healthy car."

A healthy car?

"You, my dear girl, are not a healthy car."

"I'm feeling better."

Tessa shook her head. "I'm not talking about this cold you have at the moment. I'm talking about you not keeping your body fueled, letting yourself get run down, and . . . messy."

"I'm sorry about the tissues."

Tessa tossed her hands in the air. "You are missing the point, child. How can you help anybody else when you aren't taking care of your car?"

Summer put her feet up on the couch and hugged her knees. "Okay. I get it."

"Do you?"

"I do. I let myself get run down."

"You ran out of gas, that's what you did."

"I did. And it was wrong to do so because it *has* set me back."

"If you don't slow down, God's gonna step in and do it for you."

"I can see that now." *I get it. I really do.*

"Your body is a temple, young lady. The Holy Spirit lives in there. You want to mess up that arrangement? I don't think so."

Tessa did have a way with words.

"One more thing and I'll get out of your hair. Remember in airplanes how the stewardess talks about what to do if the oxygen masks fall down from the ceiling in an emergency?"

"I've only flown a few times, but yes. I remember that talk."

"She always tells you to put on your own mask first, *then* help your kids get theirs on. I always thought that seemed selfish, but there's a reason for it. If you don't take care of you, you won't be fit to help others."

Summer liked the plane analogy better than the car one. "I understand everything you're saying, Aunt Tessa."

"You'd better, because—"

There was another knock at the door. Summer answered it, again thinking it might be Max.

It was Sydney. "Hey," she said. "Can I talk to you?"

"Sure." She stepped aside and let her in. "Sydney, you remember Mrs. Kraus, don't you?"

Sydney suddenly hung back, wary. "Hi."

Tessa gave her a once over. "Hi yourself. You just got divorced, didn't you?"

Summer nearly gasped, and Sydney took a step backward, running into the door. "How did you know that?"

"Your mother and I are in the same book club. Heard too much about all your troubles."

"Mom is telling people?"

"That's what friends do. She's having issues of her own, you know." Tessa waved a hand. "Move over here so I can see you. This old body of mine doesn't abide twisting."

Sydney came into the living room and stood by the coffee table.

"You don't look well at all. Are you eating right?"

Sydney glanced at Summer. "I'm doing okay."

"Your mother said you're renting a place in town?"

"Well. Yeah."

"How are you settling in after your personal . . . drama?"

"Okay, I guess."

"You guess?" Tessa leaned on her cane and shook her head. "We all suffer, Sydney. The trick is to find comfort in Jesus."

"Well . . . okay."

Tessa's eyebrows rose. "Trusting Jesus deserves more than a *well . . . okay.*"

"Yes, ma'am?"

"That's better."

Ma'am? Summer had never heard Sydney be so polite. Obviously Tessa intimidated her—like she did most people.

Tessa eyed her. "Do you have a job?"

"Not yet, ma'am."

Tessa looked at Summer. "Don't we need another server in the dining room?"

She'd heard that, but wasn't sure Sydney would be willing—or would be good at it. "They *are* looking for help."

"There," Tessa said with a wave of her hand. "Go get yourself a job at Happy Trails."

"Doing what?"

"Being a waitress. You too good to serve old people?"

"No . . ."

"It's settled then. When I get back there, I'll tell them you're coming over to speak with them about it." Tessa held out a hand, wanting Summer to help her to standing. "My job is done here."

"Thanks for coming over, Aunt Tessa," Summer said. "I appreciate everything you've said."

Tessa smiled and had Summer hold her cane while she opened her purse. She pulled out a napkin wrapped around two cookies. "I saved these for you from lunch."

Summer was touched. "You're very sweet. Thank you."

"Now be polite and share one with Sydney."

"I will."

Summer moved to hug her but Tessa motioned her away. "Love you or not, I don't want your cold. I'll be going now. We're starting a new puzzle today and I want to help organize the pieces into puzzle trays. Your grandmother's too haphazard about it."

Summer opened the door. "I'll help you downstairs."

Tessa gave her a once-over. "You will not go outside wearing pajamas. It's not proper. Slow and steady. I'll be all right. Remember the oxygen mask."

"I will." Summer closed the door and faced Sydney. "Want a cookie?"

"No thanks." She pointed at the rumpled blanket and pillow on the couch, and the box of tissues. "You really are sick."

You doubted me? "I'm nearly better, but I do need to sit."

"Sure."

"You can sit too," Summer said, though she really hoped Sydney wouldn't stay. "Did you need something?"

Sydney remained standing. "I was going to take you up on the loan and a trip to the grocery store. But it can wait."

Summer felt bad. "It's good you want to go out."

Sydney turned toward the door, then looked back. "Mrs. Kraus still scares me."

Summer smiled. "Me too. But she's right about the server-job."

Sydney made a face. "I'm not sure about that. Waiting on tables . . .?"

"You have something better in mind?"

She shrugged. "Not really."

"It's a good job. The people are nice and the hours aren't long. They give bonuses at the end of the year, and sometimes you get tips for Christmas."

Sydney hesitated, playing with a button on her shirt. "Tempting, but I think I'll pass."

Summer's head was throbbing—from her cold, but also from dealing with her friend. She was *done.*

She lay back on the couch and pulled the blanket over her shoulder. "Whatever. Close the door on your way out."

Sydney returned to her place by the table. "Don't be snarky with me. I don't *have* to take the job, you know."

"No, you don't. So find your own job."

"Now you're being mean."

Summer threw back the blanket and sat up. "Then stop acting spoiled, self-absorbed, and . . . and helpless!"

Sydney's eyes grew large. "Whoa. Excu-use me."

Summer stood. "You know what? You aren't excused. I've bent over backward to help you. You refuse Tessa's offer, I got you an interview with Candy, and—"

"Candy kicked me out of the shop."

"Because of your past attitude! Don't you see, Syd? You can't always make it all about you. You can't treat people like gum on your shoe. And you can't use people and then tell them they're not helping you in the right way. It's rude. It's frustrating. And it makes people not want to help at all."

"Then don't!" She rushed out, slamming the door behind her.

Summer's legs wobbled and she sank onto the couch, letting her head fall back onto the cushion. Her breathing was heavy. Her heart pounded. Yet honestly, it felt great to have let it out.

But . . .

Regret fell on her like dark rain. "I blew it, didn't I, Lord?"

Summer could imagine the Almighty with His arms crossed, nodding.

She needed to fix it.

She picked up her phone and dialed Sydney's number. Not surprisingly, it went to voicemail. She left a heart-felt apology anyway. Hopefully, Sydney would forgive her.

Forgive . . . Summer tossed her phone on the coffee table, leaned forward, and bowed her head. "Sorry about that, Father. But she's making me crazy. I wanted a connection, but . . . why didn't you send me someone who's easier to help?"

"It is not the healthy who need a doctor, but the sick. I have not come to call the righteous, but sinners."

Remembering the verse, Summer sighed. Grandma had made her memorize it when she was eleven or twelve, when she'd complained that people didn't appreciate her help like she thought they should. She'd declared she only wanted to help people who said thank you. Grandma disagreed, and had told her helping difficult people was a test of the heart.

"A heart that helps without a thank-you is a heart that loves like the Lord.'"

Summer nodded. "Forgive me, Lord. Help me help Sydney in whatever way she needs help—even without a thank-you."

With that, she lay down and fell asleep under the blanket of God's forgiveness.

Chapter 41

Jered

"Were not our hearts burning within us
while he talked with us on the road
and opened the Scriptures to us?"
Luke 24: 32

Jered and Ivy walked toward the Red Rim. They could hear music from a block away.

There were a lot of people mingling outside, some grabbing a smoke, some taking in the night air. Jered braced himself to be recognized. He couldn't wear sunglasses at night and had accidentally left the ball cap at home.

The people stirred as he walked past, as if he was a pebble tossed into a lake.

"Hey!"

"Jered Manson!"

"Hey, dude!"

He said hi and smiled, but he and Ivy hurried inside. Jered received more greetings, but hated that his entrance might distract people from the musician on stage. As a performer he remembered the annoying distractions from noisy patrons, broken glasses, or a drunk falling over a table.

He smiled and nodded at people, but put a finger to his lips and pointed toward the music. Toward Kyle Boxer.

The owner, Christopher, spotted them and came over. "Glad you came," he said beneath the music. "Got a table reserved for you." He led them through the crowd to a place near the stage.

They were there for mere moments before Boxer saw him, stopped singing, and stopped his band. "Hey! Look who we have here! It's Jered Manson!"

The crowd clapped and hooted. Jered acknowledged them but quickly sat down.

"Come on up here, man."

This was *not* what he wanted to happen. But Boxer persisted and the audience egged him on.

"Go on, hon," Ivy said.

He climbed on stage and hugged Boxer. "So nice to see you, Jer," the man said in his ear. "Christopher said you might stop by." Boxer let go and asked the audience, "How'd you like to hear a song from Jered?"

The next five minutes were a blur, as Boxer gave Jered a guitar and he sang for the crowd. Thankfully he sounded okay—especially since he hadn't warmed up. The experience brought back bittersweet memories of his early days. There was something special about playing to a crowd of a few hundred where he could see their faces, when it was just him and a guitar without all the trappings of a production.

It was made perfect when Boxer started singing with him. Their voices blended and were made better, like adding chocolate syrup to a glass of milk. They finished the song and the crowd roared and whooped. Ivy beamed and was on her feet.

Every cell vibrated with energy. An intricate—yet basic—transaction had taken place, an eager give and take between Jered and the audience and back again, each feeding off each other, bringing out the best of them both.

Jered could have stayed up there all night—and Boxer graciously asked him to stay—but with a nod to an inner voice reminding him this was *not* his gig, he deferred. As they hugged one more time in parting, Boxer said, "Come over to the house afterward."

Jered didn't hesitate. "We'd love to."

**

After the evening drew to a close Jered and Ivy followed Boxer back to his house in the Prairie Village area of Kansas City. The streets were canopied by large trees, and porch lights revealed bright splashes of floral color in window boxes. Most driveways had at least one car or truck parked in them as the houses only had one garage.

"These houses are so cute," Ivy said.

"They're small." Jered noted.

"Charming."

"Old."

She slapped his leg. "No matter what it's like inside, be gracious."

On the outside he'd be gracious, but inside . . . he struggled with a lot of what-if questions.

Boxer parked in the drive and Jered parked on the street. Boxer waited for them at the front door. "I texted Polly. She's excited to see you again. But the kids are asleep so . . ." He put a finger to his lips. "We can go sit on the patio."

Kids? He had kids?

Polly opened the door for them. Her hair was shorter but she still had fabulous laughing eyes. Her smiles and hugs were heartfelt. "Come on back."

They walked into a tiny living room that was spotted with toy trucks, stuffed animals, and picture books. To the side was a U-shaped kitchen with white cupboards and kids' paintings on the fridge.

Ivy detoured to a photo held there with a magnet. "Are these your children?"

"They are," Polly said. "Joshua is six and Rachel just turned two."

"They're lovely. You're very blessed."

"Indeed we are." Polly handed Ivy a tray of crackers, sliced cheese, and a bowl of cashews. "I'll bring the drinks."

"I'll get them," Boxer said, taking the tray from his wife. "We just found out she's expecting number three."

"Congratulations!" Ivy said.

Jered knew the subject of babies would come up again. Soon.

They went through the sliding glass door to a small patio strung with white Christmas lights. They sat at a round table. Jered could see a swing-set in the shadows of the backyard.

Polly poured four glasses. "Mango iced tea."

"Sorry we don't have beer," Boxer said. "Gave it up."

"Was for your own good," Polly said—but her voice was kind.

"Yes, it was." He passed around the snacks.

Ivy asked, "We loved your set tonight. It brought back memories. Do you perform full-time?"

Boxer chuckled. "Wish I could. I teach high school music."

Ivy perked up. "That's wonderful! I was a teacher. Third grade."

"Do you still teach?"

She shook her head. "With the touring and all . . ." She looked to Polly. "Do you have an outside job?"

"Beyond the kids I make quilts for charities to auction off."

"I used to sew," Ivy said. "I'd love to see your quilts sometime. Love to see the kids too."

"I'm sure we can arrange it."

It was hard for Jered to ignore how happy both women looked. Ivy didn't have many friends anymore.

Boxer slapped his hands on his thighs. "Enough about us. You've got the stories to tell. We're so proud of you, Jer."

Polly nodded. And so did Ivy.

They were proud of him. Yet it didn't seem right. Not now, knowing what he knew, knowing how much Boxer had given up. He felt his emotions threaten and pressed a hand against his forehead.

"Did we say something wrong?" Boxer asked.

Please give me strength not to fall apart. Jered shook his head and took a few deep breaths. Then a sip of tea. "Sorry. It's just that Ivy and I heard something about you, Box. About what you did."

"What I did?"

"At the Red Rim. For me. The night Corey York was in the audience."

Boxer hesitated a moment, then nodded. "I'm glad it worked out like it did."

Jered leaned forward, his arms on the table. "Why did you do it—for me? Why did you give up *your* big chance?"

"Yeah. It wasn't easy."

"Then why did you do it?"

"Well . . ." Boxer looked at Polly, who gave him a loving look. "Because God told me to." He lifted a hand. "I know that sounds weird or maybe even trite, but it's true. You remember Polly and me were dating back then."

He remembered seeing Polly hanging around. He nodded.

"She was worried about my drinking. Playing in bars all the time caused me to overindulge." He smiled a wry smile.

"He used to drive drunk," Polly said.

"It was only a matter of time that I'd have an accident." He looked up at the strands of light. "Joshua calls these our 'family stars.'"

"How sweet," Ivy said.

"I never got into drinking much," Jered said. "Never liked the taste."

Boxer chuckled. "Taste didn't have much to do with it, Jer. I liked the buzz."

"Until . . ." Polly prodded.

Boxer sighed and once again looked up at Joshua's family stars. "One night after a gig I totaled the car."

"And . . .?" Polly said.

"And nearly killed a man." He wiped the condensation off his glass with a hand. "I wasn't hurt that bad and he survived, but it was a wake-up call from God." Polly reached for his hand and squeezed it. "I got help but it wasn't easy. I wasn't instantly cured. Far from it." He took a sip of his tea.

Jered dug into long-forgotten memories. "I remember you talking about the accident. But I didn't know about the drinking part."

"Yeah. Well. I wasn't proud of it. A couple months later I heard Corey York was coming to the Red Rim. To see me."

This last bit . . . "So you gave up a sure thing?" Jered asked.

"Far from that, but . . ."

"Yes," Polly said. "They had talked once before but Corey said he had to hear Kyle one more time to be sure. He had one slot to fill in their recording lineup. Kyle would have been famous. I know it."

Jered was incredulous. He stood and paced up and back. He wanted to scream the next words but remembered the kids. "If you knew it would mean big things for you . . . why give it up for me?"

Boxer touched Polly's hand. "She knew—I knew—that going on the road and dealing with fame would put me smack dab in the middle of temptation. I wasn't strong enough to deal with it."

"Then," Polly said. "You weren't strong enough *then.*"

He nodded once. "Besides, we wanted to get married and have kids, and . . ." Boxer's sigh started in the depths of his being. "I had to make a choice between a healthy normal life with a family, and fortune and fame."

Polly tugged him in her direction and gave him a kiss. "You chose well, grasshopper."

"Yeah," Boxer said. "A hard choice. But I wouldn't change any of—" He cocked his head in order to see something toward the house.

Jered turned when they heard the sound of the sliding door.

"Hey, bud," Boxer said. "What are you doing up?"

A little boy came out of the house wearing Spiderman pajamas. His hair was tousled, his chin a bit pointed. Definitely his father's son. Boxer motioned him over and took him onto his lap. Joshua immediately pulled his knees up, letting Boxer's ample arms encase him.

"I heard voices," Joshua said.

"Some friends came to visit. This is Jered and Ivy."

"Hi."

Jered sat back down and caught Ivy's look. He had to admit he was touched by the scene of Boxer as a dad. Then he thought of something. "Do you play Madden?"

"I enjoy a game from time to time, when I have the chance."

"You're Boxerdad, aren't you?"

"I am. Who are you?"

"Musicman."

Boxer held out his hand to high-five. "You're a formidable opponent."

"As are you."

Polly brought the conversation back to the night at the Red Rim. "It was a really hard decision for Kyle, but once he made it—"

"We made it," he said.

"Once *we* made it—after much praying about it—we had to follow through."

"I hated to lie and say I was sick, yet in a way I was." He shook his head slowly. "That was a hard night for us. Even though I knew I was making the right choice, a large part of me wanted to burst in at the last minute, take over the stage, and let fame find me."

"And possibly harm you," Polly said.

"We'll never know about that," he said. "When I heard you got the contract I suffered a huge attack of the green monster. And the first time I saw you on the charts and saw you in the news . . . Man. Envy-city. But by then we were married and we had this one on the way." He kissed the boy's head. "I knew God had me where He wanted me. 'The Lord *will* fulfill his purpose for me.'"

For you maybe. But then Jered remembered the past few days. "Your name has come up quite a few times lately."

"Interesting," Boxer said.

"Is that . . .?" Jered didn't want to sound presumptuous.

"Is that God?" Boxer asked.

"Well, yeah. It makes me wonder."

Boxer smiled. "We wonder about the wonders . . ." He looked to his wife and together they recited, "Many are the wonders you have done, the things you planned for us. None can compare with you; were I to speak and tell of your deeds, they would be too many to declare.'"

"Psalm forty, verse five. It's our verse," Polly said. "God saved us then and continues to bless us now. He performs His wonders and frankly, is quite wonder*ful*."

"Amen," Boxer said.

"It's a great verse," Ivy said. "Personally, I hold onto Matthew seventeen-twenty: 'If you have faith as small as a mustard seed, you can say to this mountain, "Move from here to there," and it *will* move. Nothing will be impossible for you.'"

"You have a verse?" Jered asked.

"Many, actually," Ivy said.

Everyone knew verses but him. Jered waved his hands in front of his face. "All those verses are great, but how do you *know* stuff is coming from Him, that it's God doing it?"

The three of them exchanged a look, making him envious of their bond. Boxer spoke for all of them. "It's a feeling in your gut more than your head."

"A peace," Polly said.

"A *knowing,*" Ivy said.

Now he *really* felt left out. "I don't know such things. He doesn't give me gut feel—"

Then he remembered the inner nudge to help Mr. Johnson. And seeing his old guitar—which he always ignored—and hearing the words of the folksong, *When will they ever learn* and feeling something deep inside. Not in his head. In his gut.

A peace. And dare he say it, a *knowing?*

"You've felt it too," Boxer said softly. "I can tell."

For the first time in his life, Jered hated having people look at him. "Maybe."

Joshua stirred. Polly stood and held out her hand. "Let's get you back to bed, Joshie." She took him inside.

Boxer leaned forward on the table like a salesman closing a deal. "If it *is* God doing it, we need to give Him credit. And if it isn't? What have we got to lose by giving Him an extra atta-boy?"

Ivy chuckled. "It's best to err on His side rather than miss acknowledging something He's done."

"Exactly," Boxer said. "Want a verse to scare the daylights out of you?"

Jered's mind was about to explode. "Not really."

"Listen anyway. Psalm seventy-eight, thirty-two: "In spite of all this, they kept on sinning; in spite of his wonders, they did not believe.'"

"In spite of all *what?"* Jered asked.

"Blessings. God was talking about the Hebrews. He rescued them from slavery, fed them, gave them everything. Gave them Himself. Repeatedly they said the right words, but they didn't live them. They defied Him and denied Him. And because they did, 'he ended their days in futility and their years in terror.'"

"Yikes," Ivy said.

Jered didn't know what to say. Futility and terror from God? It scared him to death.

Boxer chuckled. "Now that I've thoroughly petrified you, let me say that despite their rebellious hearts and their defiant actions, God forgave them. Over and over."

Jered felt a small wave of relief. "Why would He do that?"

"Because He's the God of love."

"And forgiveness." Ivy gave Jered a pointed look.

"What's that look for?"

She shrugged, then looked at her watch. "We should get home." She stood. Jered had no choice but to stand too.

Polly came out of the house. "You're leaving?"

Ivy drew her into a hug. "It's so nice seeing you after all these years. Thank you for your hospitality." She looked at Boxer. "Thank you for sharing your faith. And for . . ." She eyed Jered.

He obliged. "And for giving up your chance for me."

Boxer wrapped his arms around him. "I'd do it again, a hundred times again. You've done great, Jer. The chance wasn't wasted." At the front door Boxer said, "We need to do this again. Keep in touch."

"I agree," Ivy said. "Next time at our house."

They got in their car, offered one last wave, then drove away. "I know they seem happy here," Jered said. "And I'm glad you asked them over. But what will they think of our house? Won't they feel bad seeing our house as compared to theirs?"

"Don't act like their house is a shack in the swamp. It's lovely. It's a home. I'm not sure our house is a home yet."

Here it comes.

"I want a family, Jer. It's time."

"I have another tour coming up."

"We shouldn't wait. We'll deal with it. We'll make it work."

He *had* been softening to the idea.

"You're not saying no?"

"I'm just tired."

She grabbed his arm. "You're not saying no!"

"We'll talk in the morning."

She faced forward. "They are such good people. Godly people."

"I knew Box drank, but I never knew he had a drinking problem. I'm glad I don't drink. I don't do drugs. I don't sleep around. I'm not the stereotypical musician."

"But you are."

"What?"

"You *do* fit part of the stereotype. You're arrogant and proud."

He was silent a moment. "So you're perfect?"

"Of course not."

He felt anger seethe inside him. "I made it big because I took advantage of the breaks and worked hard—I work hard."

"Yes you did and you do. It's all about you."

It sounded like a trick. "I didn't say that."

"Didn't you?" She crossed her arms. "You are where you are because of hard work, but also because of the break Boxer handed you. The break God handed you."

"I'm not negating any of that. It's just that *I* had something to do with my success."

"'Pride goes before destruction, a haughty spirit before a fall.' Watch it, Jer. Or you'll fall."

How could she make him feel so big, and then so small? "Boxer said they were proud of me."

"You're proud of yourself."

He swerved onto a side street and stopped the car. "Don't I have a right to be?"

"Sure. But . . ." She looked out the windshield. "'Commit to the Lord whatever you do, and your plans will succeed.' You're missing the first part."

"That's not my fault. If God chose to give me success then I'm not going to stop Him."

"'A man's ways seem innocent to him, but motives are weighed by the Lord.'"

"Sheesh, Ive. You memorized the whole Bible?"

"Just the parts I need. We need."

He grabbed onto the we-part. "So *our* motives are weighed by God?"

"They are. I admit I've enjoyed the ride. The perks of fame."

"You make it sound like the ride's over."

She shook her head. "That depends."

"On what?"

"I . . . I don't want to change the subject."

He tossed his hands in the air. "Hey, why not? It's dump on Jered time."

"Stop it."

"No. Tell me. What makes you think the ride's nearly over?"

"Because you don't take any responsibility for the ride. You take credit, but no responsibility."

She was confusing him. "I work my butt off—"

"Again with the *you!*" She angled in her seat toward him. "Jer, you have dozens of people working for you, sometimes hundreds."

"I know that."

"Without the roadies going ahead and setting up the stage and lights and sound, without the ticket sellers, the ticket takers, the custodians cleaning up before and after, the concessions workers, the ushers, the security—"

"Okay, okay, I get it. I appreciate all of them."

"Then show it."

He didn't know what she meant. "They're paid well."

"They're paid okay. But beyond that, would it kill you to be nice to them? To stop being demanding and arrogant and—here's that word again—proud."

He remembered many times on the tour where he'd lost his cool, yelling at people. "I'm under a lot of pressure."

"And they aren't? You have no idea what's going on in their lives." She took a fresh breath. "Did you know that the wife of Barry from the lighting crew just found out she has breast cancer? And Mary from wardrobe had to move her mother into a nursing home?"

"They don't talk to me about that stuff, Ive. They talk to you. I can't be expected to know every detail of a hundred people's lives."

She reached over and touched his arm. "I don't expect you to, but I do expect you to be kind and realize you are not their king and they are not your subjects."

He remembered various stagehands muttering, "Yes, your highness" more than once.

Ivy must have sensed his inner turmoil for she took his hand in hers. "I'm sorry it seems like dump-on-Jered night but maybe this is *your* wake-up call."

He pulled his hand away and drove home in silence.

**

"You coming to bed, hon?" Ivy asked.

"I'm going to check my email first. Go ahead."

Jered knew the right thing to do would have been to be with his wife, but he just couldn't. She'd ripped him good tonight and his world had been shifted off its foundation.

What he needed was to read some fawning fan mail.

Which will feed your pride.

Whatever.

He opened his laptop. A screensaver greeted him—an eagle soaring over mountains. He liked getting a new image every time he opened it up, usually a photo of exotic places he'd like to visit someday. He liked the variety.

He read a few fan emails and immediately felt better. *So there.* He forwarded them on to his assistant to answer.

But then he saw an email from Michelle Jofsky. He'd seen a few others from her but had ignored them when he'd seen they were Bible verses. He was sure the others thrived on them. But he opened the email, just in case it was important. Maybe there were details about where they might meet—not that he really wanted to get together again.

He was surprised to see a response from Ryan. And Summer. A bunch of do-gooder junk. He'd done good too. He'd put Mr. Johnson's garbage cans away, hadn't he? Yet Jered didn't think it was enough to share.

He saw the newest Bible verse, and read it out loud, mockingly. "'Those who hope in the Lord will renew their strength. They will soar on wings like eagles; they will run and not grow weary, they will walk and not be faint.'"

Eagles. Soaring.

He clicked back to his opening page, just sure the background would be gone. But it wasn't. There, before him, was the eagle. It was a perfect illustration of the verse. And then he saw it: in the corner was some writing: *"Those who hope in the Lord will renew their strength. They will soar on wings like eagles; they will run and not grow weary, they will walk and not be faint." Isaiah 40: 31.*

Jered shivered.

One verse shown to him two times in two minutes.

Hope. Strength. Soaring, Running. An end to weariness and feeling faint-hearted.

Jered looked at the eagle who soared with an inner strength.

Given to him by God.

Soar, Jered. Soar.

He immediately felt something shift inside.

It wasn't physical. It was deeper than that. Something that always *was.*

And always will be.

"My soul." He whispered the words, letting them hang in the air. "Oh bless the Lord, my soul." He smiled at the words and said them again. And again.

He didn't know if they were a verse, but if they weren't, they should have been.

**

Jered slipped into bed and scooted toward Ivy, drawing her close. She nestled under his arm, resting her head on his chest.

"Love you," she said sleepily.

"Love *you.*"

And You, God. I . . . I love You too.

Chapter 42

Claire

"There is a time for everything,
and a season for every activity under the heavens."
Ecclesiastes 3: 1

The days passed with Billy and Claire finding a lovely rhythm. The Robby-issue had been set aside and they spent every evening together, basking in their joy that God had brought them together for another important reason: love.

Claire was surprised at this growing emotion. Yes, she was pragmatic. Yes, she'd set aside any thought of remarrying or even pursuing male companionship. She'd sailed that ship for twenty years with her husband and had ended up with pain and betrayal. Yet being with Billy was like taking a cruise on a fifty-foot yacht, standing arm in arm with the warm wind filling the sails, leading them on an adventure.

A thought which was the opposite of pragmatic.

Part of their rhythm was being content with *home.* Neither of them felt the need to go out on dates. They'd been to one concert but both agreed the traffic and the crowds weren't their thing. They'd gone to church together, gone on long walks in their neighborhoods, and had gone out to eat a little and had cooked together a lot. They'd watched a ton of movies, binge-watched a series on Netflix, and had spent many happy hours on Claire's patio, just *being.*

Today they were heading to the Mercy Shelter to help cook dinner. Not serve, cook, because the usual cook was recovering from surgery for a few days. This was Billy's chance to show off Grandma's recipes.

The shelter was downtown and they had to park a block away. "What are you going to make?" Claire asked.

"Grandma's hamburger and rice casserole, corn with green chilies, peach fluff, rosemary rolls, and fruit cocktail cake."

"I have no idea what any of those are, but I'm sure they're yummy. Are they hard to make?"

"Not hard. But I had to come out last night after I left your place to make the peach fluff. It needs to set."

"I could have come with you."

He tweaked her nose. "You need some time alone once in a while."

Not anymore.

Michelle was already there, browning enormous amounts of hamburger on a huge commercial stove. "Hail, hail. The chef is here."

"Cook," Billy said. "I'm no chef."

She tapped her fork on the pan. "This is ready. And I have the dinner roll dough rising. What next?"

With help the dinner was prepared, served, and enjoyed. People got in line for seconds. There were no leftovers.

One elderly woman who came back for a second piece of cake told them, "My mama used to make this cake for us. She let me pick the cherries out of the fruit cocktail first."

"That's my favorite part too," Billy said. "This is my grandma's recipe."

The woman smiled. "I knew it! I can always tell a grandma recipe. Everybody loves grandma-cooking."

Claire was in awe of the whole evening. Billy cooked like a pro, served the needy with grace and humor, and even started scrubbing pots.

"Oh no you don't. There will be none of that," Michelle said, tossing him a towel to dry his hands. "You've done your good deed for the day. Off with the two of you. Enjoy the rest of your evening."

Billy removed his apron and slipped his arm around Claire's shoulders. "Don't mind if we do."

They slipped out the back and walked to his truck, relishing the successful dinner—and the whole experience.

"I love cooking like that," he said.

"Everyone loved it."

"As the woman said, 'everybody loves grandma-cook—" He stopped walking in front of a small storefront. He pointed to the painted sign on the windows.

It said *Grandma's Cookin'.*

Claire put a hand to her chest. "Whoa."

"Grandma's Cookin'," he whispered. "I used to come here a lot."

"You came way down here, to downtown?"

"I was a waiter at a restaurant nearby yet I preferred the cooking at this place. I can't believe I didn't notice it when we walked by before."

Claire felt a shiver course up and down her arms. The place had a CLOSED sign in the window. "When were you here last?"

Billy kept staring at the sign. "At least ten years ago. Before Robby and I started Billy Bob's. Since I wasn't working downtown . . . and then I got busy."

They both cupped their hands against the glass.

"Everything's still in there, but it's a mess," she said. "It's permanently closed."

He let out a long breath. He took a step back. "Maybe not."

"What?"

He put a hand to his mouth, his eyes flitting back and forth as though he was watching a movie in his mind. "Everybody loves grandma-cooking."

The shivers continued. "What are you thinking? You want to open your own restaurant?"

He nodded, staring at the words on the glass. "And cook Grandma's recipes."

She touched his arm. "In Grandma's Cookin'."

"Oh Claire . . ."

She put a hand to her heart, overwhelmed. "I know. I know."

He walked from one end of the storefront to the other, his energy needing release. Then he stopped and pointed. "Look."

There was another sign in the corner of the window that said FOR LEASE.

She laughed. "What are you waiting for?"

**

The leasing agent was eager to show them the place.

It was like stepping into the past.

While Billy and the real estate agent talked back in the kitchen, Claire spent her time out front. There were five booths covered in aqua vinyl, six other tables with Formica tops edged in metal, and matching aqua vinyl chairs. Some seats were ripped, but they could be easily recovered. The floor was a black and white checkerboard. Some tiles needed to be replaced. The walls were white and in need of paint. The acoustical ceiling had to be completely ripped out and done up fresh.

The pictures on the wall were faded and mundane, but Claire immediately thought of framing poster-sized photographs of other diners from the 50s and 60s. *And the waitresses can wear vintage-style uniforms . . . pink with black trim.*

The counter and cash register were old but fabulous. They could easily add a credit card machine. Claire stood behind the counter and looked out over the café, imagining it filled with happy people and bustling servers. They'd play old rock 'n roll—but not too loud. People needed to be able to talk to each other.

She smiled and felt full inside. This was completely and utterly right. *Thank You, God. It's perfect.*

Then she looked at the server-station, at the classic white pottery dishes. Most were in great shape. There were cups and saucers . . . maybe they should get some mugs? The silverware was iffy. Some of the glasses were scratched and chipped but being so classic in design, Claire was sure they would be able to get replacements, or if not that, find some dishes that would fit the cozy, down-home decor.

Speaking of . . . She was drawn to a photograph on the wall near the counter. It was a black and white photo of a family standing in front of a brand new "Grandma's Cookin'." There was a couple with four children, and an older woman holding a bouquet of roses.

"Nice to meet you, Grandma."

Billy and the agent came out from the kitchen, still talking. "So you think the landlord will allow some money toward repairs?"

"I think the landlord will do most anything within reason to get someone in here. It's been empty for six years."

"That's a long time," Billy said.

"Actually, the whole block was bought back then. There was going to be a huge development with condos and retail, but it got blowback from the city and it fell through. Grandma's has been sitting like this for nearly a year."

Just waiting for you, Billy.

"I'll give the landlord a call." The agent looked at his watch. "Actually, I have to get to another appointment . . ."

"We really need some time here, looking things over," Billy said. "Can you leave us here and come back to lock up?"

"I can do that. An hour okay?"

As soon as he left, Billy and Claire both took deep breaths, letting them out with a laugh. "Well then," he said.

"How's the kitchen?"

"Salvageable." He turned around full circle in the dining room. "This isn't bad."

"Let me tell you my ideas." Claire filled him in, then realized she'd said *a lot.* "I don't mean to take over like this."

He pulled her close. "I'm happy you are." He kissed her once, then looked at her eye to eye. "I want this to be our project, Claire. I know you're an artist and have obligations, and the big mural project, but—"

"I'd love to help." She smiled. "A lot."

His smile was like sunlight. "Really?"

"In any way I can."

They sealed the deal with a kiss.

Chapter 43

Ryan

"For God so loved the world
that he gave his one and only Son,
that whoever believes in him
shall not perish but have eternal life.
For God did not send his Son into the world
to condemn the world,
but to save the world through him."
John 3:16-17

"What's on the agenda for today?" Bertha asked.

Ryan sipped his coffee. "Lisa and I are heading into the woods to drag some downed trees back to cut into firewood."

Bertha slipped another pancake onto his plate. "Then you'll need more fuel."

Lisa held out her plate. "I'll need more fuel too."

"That's four pancakes, girl," Grandpa said.

Bertha settled it by putting another pancake on *his* plate. "Now you *all* have four. Quit yer belly-aching."

Lisa poured more syrup, though her plate was already a pond of maple. "I had a dream last night—a God dream."

"Hmph," Grandpa said.

"It *is* from Him," she said. "I know it is."

Bertha pressed a hand to calm the moment. "What was in this God-dream?"

Lisa set her fork down. "I was playing guitar at the firepit and there were people all around, rows and rows of people. But then I forgot the words but somebody else knew them and . . ." She took a fresh breath. "It made me feel all warm inside."

"Fires will do that." Grandpa shrugged. "So you had a dream about the firepit and the guitar. What's so special about that? What's so God about that?"

Ryan could tell she was flustered. "Is it because of how it made you feel?"

She grabbed onto that. "Yeah. That's it. It was different from how we sit around the fire now. There were lots of people there, sitting on long logs. I wasn't a visitor. I was . . ." she glanced at Bertha. "Home."

Bertha came around and kissed the top of her head. "You sweet thing. You *are* home as far as I'm concerned."

Really?

For the first time since they'd come to the Honeycomb, Ryan felt a shift in his thinking.

"Well that's ridiculous," Grandpa said. "God isn't telling you this is home because it's not. And He's not telling you anything in a dream. Get real, girl."

"Don't tell her it's not real," Ryan said. "'For God does speak—now one way, now another—though no one perceives it.'"

Grandpa wiggled his hands by his eyes. "Oooh. Magic voodoo stuff."

"Allen!" Bertha said.

He set his fork down. "It's just plain weird. Talking about *God* talking? I'm seventy-two years old and He's never talked to me."

"I think you're wrong," Ryan said.

"You know me and my life better than I do?"

"Of course not. But God does speak. He does. You just might not be listening."

"So it's my fault?"

"Well . . . yeah, pretty much."

Grandpa's mouth gaped open. He tossed his napkin on the table and stood. "God's never taken no never-mind to me so why should I give Him the time of day? I'll leave that to you holy ones." He walked out the front door, slamming it behind him.

"Oh dear," Bertha said.

Lisa began to cry. "I didn't want him to feel bad. It was a good dream."

"It was," Bertha said, motioning her to come close for a hug. "A lovely dream."

Lisa rested in the woman's arms. "Wasn't it God, Ryan?" she asked plaintively. "I had a dream about you and you came true."

"In the Bible God often used dreams. It's not up to me to say it wasn't Him. Not at all."

"But Grandpa said—"

"Shh, shh, child," Bertha said. "My daddy used to tell me, 'to have faith, have faith.' You hang onto yours long and hard. It will get you through everything."

Lisa nodded against her chest. "But Grandpa . . ."

"We'll say some prayers for him, but God needs to do the melting of Allen's heart. That's not for mere mortals like us."

"I shouldn't have said what I did about him not listening," Ryan said. *It's a bad habit.* He remembered another man who had walked out when he'd said something similar—Jered Manson.

"Nonsense." Bertha let Lisa stand on her own. "Truth is strength—but it *is* hard to take sometimes."

Ryan looked toward the door. "Should I go after him?"

Bertha peered out the window. "He's walking up the road and I say, let him. You are not Allen's Holy Spirit, Ryan. None of us are."

"What does that mean?" Lisa asked.

Bertha stayed at the window. "God loves your grandpa and wants him to follow Him. But it's not for us to push them together but for God to draw Grandpa close."

"What if Grandpa says no?"

"God doesn't give up on us," Ryan said. "He'll keep trying."

Lisa joined Bertha at the window. "How do you know?"

The memories were dark, but Ryan knew that the lessons learned from such times were supposed to be shared in the light. "He never gave up on *me*. When my sister died, I turned my back on God."

"Really?"

"I'm not proud of it, but I was mad at Him for taking her."

"I would be too," Lisa said.

"It's understandable," Bertha said. "I wasn't too keen on God after He took my Arnold either."

"But you both turned back to Him?" Lisa's eyes were hopeful.

"I did," Bertha said.

"I did too," Ryan said. "Though I didn't make it easy on the Almighty. I fought it a long time."

"But He won," Lisa said.

Ryan smiled. "He always wins in the end. It's a question of whether we surrender to Him now and live a life being blessed by the relationship, or wait years and years, living confused and alone, without Him."

"Like Grandpa."

They couldn't see Grandpa anymore as he'd passed over the ridge.

Bertha held out her hands. "Let's pray that God is more stubborn than that old coot."

**

Ryan didn't want to leave the resort to get firewood until Grandpa returned. He'd been gone an hour. What if he'd fallen or his lungs gave out, or—

He glanced out the window and was relieved to see him walking toward them.

"Grandpa!" Lisa ran to him and gave him a hug. "We were worried."

He didn't say anything but ruffled her hair. He walked past Ryan without a word and went to the porch to sit in his rocker.

Ryan's stomach was in knots. "Hey, Allen. I'm sorry. It wasn't my place to act like I knew what's going on between you and God."

Grandpa rocked up and back. "Don't you have some firewood to fetch?"

Ryan knew that was all he would get from him. He gathered an ax and some rope, and he and Lisa walked up the road.

As soon as they were out of earshot, Lisa asked, "Is he still mad?"

"You know him better than I do. Is he?"

"I don't know. He kinda always acts like that. But you're right. I don't think Grandpa listens for God." Lisa kicked a pinecone up the road. "I don't think he's ever mentioned God to me at all. Mom didn't talk about Him either."

How sad. Ryan had spent most of his childhood—at least since the age of four—in a God-believing home. He took a turn with the pinecone. "So you never learned about Jesus?"

"My friend Becky told me he was born on Christmas and died on Easter."

"That's partially true. He was born on Christmas but died three days before Easter."

She kicked the pinecone farther. "Then what's Easter?"

"It celebrates the day He rose from the dead and went to heaven, signaling what will happen to us when we die—if we believe He is who He says He is."

"He's Jesus."

"He's Jesus, the Son of God. He's God on earth."

"That sounds creepy."

It did. They turned into the forest and Ryan started hacking off the branches of a fallen tree. "The Old Testament of the Bible predicted that a Savior, a Messiah was coming to save the Jews. They expected a man to come with an army and chariots, someone who would conquer their enemies. But God surprised them by having Jesus be born as a baby."

Lisa took the branches and put them in a pile. "Babies don't have any power."

"Babies grow up. Jesus grew up and taught thousands of people about His Heavenly Father. He taught them about love and hope and faith. But that didn't go over very well with the Jews who wanted a conqueror. So they had Him arrested and brought to trial before a Roman ruler named Pilate. Pilate wanted to spare him, but the crowd demanded Jesus be crucified."

"That's the cross, right?"

"It's a horrible way to die. Jesus was nailed to the cross and experienced horrific pain."

Lisa stopped working and faced him. Her eleven-year-old face was drawn in pain. "Why would God let His Son die like that?"

"For us. Because our sins needed to be dealt with. We all deserve to die for our sins, but Jesus took the rap for us. He died so we can be saved. So we can go to heaven forever and ever."

Lisa was on the verge of tears. "But why would God do that to His own Son? Why didn't God save Him?"

Ryan set the ax aside and leaned down to be on her level. He took her hand. "Because He loves us and wanted to create a way for us to be with Him forever. Heaven is a perfect place that doesn't allow sin. So someone had to pay the price for the bad things we've done. God sent Jesus to do that—Jesus who had no sin at all."

Lisa flew into Ryan's arms, sobbing. "It's not fair! Why would He do that for us?"

Ryan held her close. "Because he loves us as His children. He loves us unconditionally. It was His perfect plan so we all can be saved."

She pushed back. "So I'm saved?"

Ryan realized the immensity of the moment. "Do you believe what I just told you?"

She nodded.

He lifted her off the ground and spun her around. "Then you are saved, Lisa Pearl! You are saved." He set her down. "Do you realize there are angels singing in heaven right now, celebrating you saying yes to Him?"

She giggled. "Really?"

"An angel chorus."

"That's so cool."

He laughed. Only a kid would call an angel chorus *cool*.

She picked up a branch and held the pine needles under her nose. She inhaled. Then exhaled. "I'm so sorry God had to do that to Jesus. For us. For me."

"I know it's hard to fathom, but yes, for you. And me."

"For Grandpa?"

"Him too."

"I want him to believe."

"I do too."

"Will you talk to him like you talked to me?"

Ryan glanced back toward the resort. "I'm not sure he'd be open to talking to me right now."

"Maybe not right now, but will you?"

"You could talk to him too, Lisa."

She stared down the road. "I don't know. . ."

"Why don't we let God open the door? God wants Grandpa to believe even more than you and I do."

Lisa looked toward heaven. "God? Reach Grandpa. Please?"

It was the perfect prayer.

**

Grandpa was quiet all day. He talked but wasn't his usual self. Though Ryan thanked God for Lisa's newfound faith, he kept praying about Grandpa, and that *he* wouldn't say anything that God didn't want him to say.

Trouble was, God seemed to tell Ryan not to say anything.

And so, he didn't. God knew Grandpa. God wanted him to believe. So Ryan trusted God's timing.

Chapter 44

Summer

"But in your hearts revere Christ as Lord.
Always be prepared to give an answer
to everyone who asks you to give the reason
for the hope that you have.
But do this with gentleness and respect."
1 Peter 3: 15

Summer got sicker.

She felt like a truck hit her. Around midnight the cold-truck that had side-swiped Summer did a U-turn and ran her over again. The idea of getting up at 4:45 was akin to asking her to run a marathon. It wasn't going to happen.

Despite the late hour she texted Dennis at Coffee Break: *Still sick. So sorry.* She texted Candy the same message. She dozed, then heard a couple *bings* on her phone. Both bosses told her to get better. *I'm trying.*

Her body's need for sleep overshadowed her guilt. She woke up to Suzu pouncing on her shoulder. It was almost nine o'clock.

"Yes, yes, sorry. I'm coming." She got up and put on her robe. Hopefully, most of her neighbors had already gone to work. As Tessa said, she didn't look very proper right now.

When she opened her door she spotted a sack on the floor. Inside was a bagel and cream cheese and a note from Max. "Hope you're feeling better. Call me later."

What a guy.

She called Happy Trails, then Grandma, Mae, and Tessa to say she was still under the weather. Mae said she'd bring over lunch.

Then there was the Sydney situation. Summer checked her phone for the umpteenth time to see if there was a response to her apology.

Nada.

Maybe by evening she'd feel better and she could call Sydney and talk things through.

She looked in a mirror and realized she looked as horrible as she felt. A shower might work wonders. It certainly couldn't hurt.

**

As usual, Mae entered like a whirlwind. "I come with a goodie bag." She set the shopping bag on the counter, then studied Summer a short moment. "Wet hair. At least you're clean." She attacked the bag like it was a treasure chest. "First off, totally worthless but fun-to-read celebrity magazines. Did you know they buy groceries and take out their trash, just like us peons?"

"I'd read that somewhere."

"Next, a book of sudoku and crossword puzzles." She flipped open the latter. "Ten across: edible rod."

"Licorice?"

"Hmm. Maybe. How about twenty-down: court accessory."

"Net?"

She made a face. "I was thinking *gavel.*"

"Different court."

"Anyway . . . I brought you a pencil with a good eraser." Next came the food. "Red grapes, my fav—a Little Debbie oatmeal cream pie, a tuna sandwich, and Fritos. Feel free to sprinkle chips *on* the sandwich if that's the way you roll."

"I've never tried that."

"You must." Mae arranged the food on a plate. As soon as Summer sat at the counter her phone rang. It was her boss, Dennis. "Hi, Dennis. Sorry I couldn't come in but—"

He spoke but Summer couldn't believe what she was hearing. He'd hired someone else who'd worked there before. She wasn't sure whether it was in *addition* to herself, or to replace her. "I hope to be back tomorrow."

He was very nice about it, but the truth became clear. "Okay then. Thanks for giving me a chance." She hung up. "My services are no longer needed at Coffee Break."

"That hardly seems fair. You've only been sick a couple of days."

"An old employee moved back to town, and came in, wanting a job. They're fully trained. Dennis said I could come back in the fall after school starts. They might need me then."

"I'm so sorry," Mae said. "But you were already planning to quit, weren't you?"

"Maybe. But I don't like having the decision taken from me." At all. "Excuse me if I want to scream right now. It's obvious I need to be well ASAP."

"You're not *that* sick."

"Apparently sick enough. All I'm trying to do is help God but He keeps taking me out of the picture. Instead of reaching people in three jobs, now I can't reach anybody. How can I help while I'm stuck here?" *Where I can't help Sydney either.*

Mae looked in the cupboard and got out a packet of Crystal Light. "May I?"

"Of course. Pitcher's on the right."

She mixed the drink. "It's not about you, chickie—not all about you. Stop trying to force God into giving you a purpose. Let it flow. Let it play out His way, not yours."

"I thought I was doing that. But then . . . *this.*"

"Maybe you were on the wrong road and this is His way of stopping you. The flip side of wanting Him to hear *us* is that we need to wait patiently until we hear *Him.*"

Summer lifted up the top piece of bread and sprinkled Fritos on the tuna. "I thought I *was* being patient."

Mae pointed a finger upward, which was always a sign she was about to recite a verse. "'With the Lord a day is like a thousand years, and a thousand years are like a day.'"

"That's not encouraging."

Mae put ice in a glass and poured some lemonade.

"Aren't you having any?"

"Sorry. Tessa and I are playing in a bridge tourney at one. In fact . . ." She folded up the bag, grabbed the cooler from the night before, and headed to the door. "I hate to have *you* eat and run, but I gotta go."

"But what am I supposed to do? I feel so worthless."

"Don't think of the situation as a mistake. Think of it as an opportunity. Maybe it's time for a little He and me time." Mae paused with a hand on the doorknob. "You *have* been crazy busy lately. God probably couldn't get a word in edgewise so He had to slow you down."

"That's what Tessa said."

"Zounds. I hate when she says something first. Ta-ta, girl."

Summer took a bite of the sandwich. The Fritos *were* a good addition.

When she was through she brought the magazines out to the balcony. It was hot, but she had the afternoon shade.

She ruffled through the pages. She looked at the clothes the celebrities wore: gowns and designer this and that, sleek hair—those *had* to be extensions—and perfect manicures on nails that were scary long. Everything seemed fake, like they weren't living real lives with real problems.

Oddly, the pictures made her think of Sydney. Her friend was living a life that was very real, but was a far cry from the happily-ever-after life she'd hoped for. She'd mentioned that her parents were great pretenders. Was Sydney?

Am I? She closed the magazine. Was she pretending to be helpful, pretending she had a servant's heart? Was it all a ruse? Maybe she wasn't being driven by compassion and love but by duty, and a fear of failure.

Summer saw an older man walking on the sidewalk across the street. He carried the white cane of someone who couldn't see well.

But then a memory came flooding back. A memory that haunted Summer. A memory rife with failure.

She'd been sixteen, taking an evening walk. She'd been going through some emotional teen-stuff and had desperately wanted to feel useful. During the walk she'd prayed that God would use her. Some way. Some how. After three blocks she'd neared an intersection at the bottom of a hill. There, she'd seen a man on the corner across the street, reading a piece of paper. It was dusk and his features were hazy, but she noted he was wearing white tennis shorts and a white polo shirt. He looked at her. Had he said something?

Summer had ignored her plan to turn right and turned left to cross the street toward him. She nudged her headphones off her ears so she could hear him if he spoke. "Hello," she'd said.

"Is this Hayes Street?" He'd pointed up the street from where he'd come.

He had wanted directions.

Knowing what happened next made Summer feel sick to her stomach. *I'm so sorry. So sorry.*

Suddenly, her phone rang, jolting her out of her memory.

"Hey there," Max said. "How you doing?"

She began to cry.

"Summer? What's wrong?"

In spite of her shame, no matter what Max might think about her, Summer knew she needed to finally tell someone about the incident with the man. "Can you come over?"

"I'll be right there."

A minute later she heard his feet on the stairs. Then a knock. She opened the door for him. She longed to fall into his arms, but didn't want to add getting him sick to her guilt.

"Let's sit outside." She grabbed a box of tissues.

Max followed her out to the balcony, sitting in the spare chair.

"How can I help?"

"Have you ever done something so wrong that the guilt lingers long after you did it?"

"Sure."

"A few minutes ago something came back to me like a punch to my jaw."

"You want to tell me?"

"I've never told anyone."

His eyebrows rose. "Maybe you'd feel better if you did?" He shrugged. "It's up to you."

Summer hesitated. But then she heard herself say, "If I could?"

"Okay then. What happened?"

She looked across the street. The blind man had moved on. But the one in her memories remained. *Help me share this.*

Summer told Max about her walk and coming upon the man who asked directions. "He asked if a certain street was Hayes. I told him it was and walked on." The tears started again. "Here's the good part. The man mumbled that he was legally blind and was trying to find his son. But he couldn't see the street signs."

"Poor guy. It's good you were there to help him."

The guilt pressed down on her. "Yes, it was. But what did I do? I repeated that yes, the street was Hays, and continued on my walk."

Max blinked. "Oh."

"I know." She felt the shame anew. "It took me a good half block to realize what I'd done. A man who was legally blind asked for my help and I pointed him in the right direction and left him to it. At dusk."

"Wow."

"Big wow. The biggest wow. I backtracked, hoping to catch up with him. With my half-block diversion, he should have been a block ahead of me. The sunset was past its prime and the shadows were closing in." Her chest felt heavy.

"Did you find him?"

She shook her head. "Why didn't I help him? Why did I keep walking?" She looked at Max, hating that he was witnessing her disgrace, yet needing him to do so. "I looked everywhere for him. I begged God for another chance. I begged for His forgiveness."

"You didn't find him so he must have found his son's house."

"That's not the point. Once I got home I sat on the front steps until it was dark, watching for the man. Praying for the man. And praying for myself. An hour earlier I'd asked God to use me. Within minutes, He'd answered my prayer. And within minutes, I'd let Him down. I asked Him for another chance. But another chance didn't come."

He leaned forward and touched her leg. "I'm sure He's given you more chances since then."

She nodded. "He has. Many times. Recently, He gave me Sydney, an old friend who's back in town."

"She needs help?"

"She does." Summer told Max about Sydney and the dumpster. Sydney, who she'd scolded and yelled at. "She's a complicated person in a complicated situation. My compassion had limits, which was very, very wrong." She sighed. "I want to understand her better."

"You mentioned her mom was in town? Maybe you could talk to *her*."

The guilt lifted the smallest bit. "That's a marvelous idea. I'll go as soon as I'm well." She looked at this handsome neighbor she'd happened to meet when she was walking home from—

"I never would have met you if it weren't for Sydney."

"How's that?"

She hesitated, hating that he was discovering so many of her flaws. "I like to help people but I also tend to hole up and . . . and . . ."

"Hide out?"

She chuckled. "You're the first neighbor I've ever had over." She pointed at his chair. "You are the first person to ever sit in that chair." It was embarrassing.

He gripped the armrests. "I am honored. And I'm glad God brought us together. We do seem to have a connection."

He'd used two words that spurred her thinking forward: *God* and *connection*. "Can I tell you something really strange—more strange than my blind man incident or helping a friend who was dumpster diving?"

His face grew serious. "You can tell me anything."

Somehow she knew it was true. But how best to tell the story of meeting Claire and the others, and their mission?

At the beginning.

"It all started with pink roses."

Summer told the entire story. And Max? He didn't scoff. He didn't leave. He listened. "So that's the gist of it. I took a third job to try to meet more people, hoping for a connection." *A job I just lost.*

"You found Sydney."

"And you." She said it boldly.

His smile was lovely. "And me."

"Have you heard of the Great Commission?" she asked.

He sat up straighter in his chair. "Actually, I have a story to tell you."

"About . . .?"

"*My* search for connections. My journey of being at God's beck and call."

It was her turn to gawk. "You're doing it too?"

He laughed, "Yes, I'm *doing* it. God got my attention and..." He took a cleansing breath. "'Each person should live as a believer in whatever situation the Lord has assigned to them.'"

She grinned. "Not from the book of Maxwell?"

"One of the letters to the Corinthians, I believe."

"How did God get your attention?"

"I almost died."

"Oh my." Summer jerked back. "That would do it. What happened?"

"College. Drinking. Drugs. Partying."

All the college things Summer had hated—and avoided.

Max pressed his hands against his thighs. "I'd been to dozens of parties over the years, but at this one I had an overdose. Fell down a flight of stairs. Didn't break any bones, but there were internal injuries. I woke up in a hospital to find my dad sleeping in a chair beside my bed. I'd been there three days. It was seeing him that made something click inside."

"God?"

"Not God yet, but it was His doing. It was like a light switch had been flipped on in my brain and everything seemed clear."

"I know that one: 'I was blind but now I see.'"

"Exactly. I realized I'd spoiled my college years by being reckless. I got an education. I got a degree, but my behavior wasn't honoring God or my poor dad who slept beside my bed, not knowing if I would even live."

"Do we ever outgrow the need for our parents' care? Their approval?"

He shrugged. "I'd kept all my partying a secret from him. I'd go home and visit and tell him about classes, spewing out details of a made-up life I knew he wanted to hear." He sighed. "Did you ever lie to your parents like that?"

She tried to think back. "Not about that. I didn't party. I'm too much of an introvert for that." Then she remembered something. "But I have lied to them, saying I have lots of friends when I don't."

"Sounds lonely."

She chuckled. "You are obviously *not* an introvert. I'm not lonely at all, but I know they won't understand that." Summer wanted to get back to his story. "Your switch was flipped. You obviously recovered. How did you know what to do next to follow Him?"

"I chose a job."

"The job you have here."

"Right. Although I was a partier, I somehow did well in school and graduated. After I recovered I spent a few months working with my dad until my head cleared. Then this spring I applied for some construction jobs and interviewed with two companies. They both made me offers for an estimating position."

"Good for you." At least he was using his degree. "How did you choose?"

"I prayed about it and made a list of pros and cons."

"I do that!"

"And then I let a TV show do the choosing for me."

She laughed. "How did it do that?"

He gave her a sheepish look. "The jobs were from Cougar Construction and McKinley Contracting. I turned on the TV to a show about cougars playing."

"No way."

He held up a hand. "Totally true. I don't remember ever watching an animal station, yet when I turned on my TV it was there. I laughed out loud."

"And called them."

"And called them." He spread his hands. "And here I am in Carson Creek, enjoying the job, and sitting in the chair of honor on your balcony."

"We're both on the same journey," she said.

"Not just our journey. Everybody's."

She was ashamed she'd never thought of that.

"What's wrong?"

Summer couldn't say it. It was the epitome of pride.

"You *were* chosen," he said quietly. "We both were. God wants everyone to know Him. It's the *Great* Commission not a small one. It's going to take a lot of connections."

Her pride faded and was replaced by a different feeling. "We're in this together. One God. Many workers."

He stood. "Do you have a Bible handy?"

"Of course." They went inside and she got it from the coffee table.

Max looked through the pages, muttering to himself. "Romans? No, Hebrews I think . . ." Then, "Here it is." He read it aloud. "'Therefore, since we are surrounded by such a great cloud of witnesses, let us throw off everything that hinders and the sin that so easily entangles. And let us run with perseverance the race marked out for us, fixing our eyes on Jesus, the pioneer and perfecter of faith.'" He snapped the Bible shut. "We're in this together."

She nodded, feeling comforted. She wasn't on her journey alone. It wasn't just up to her. She had a role in the task, but others were working toward the same goal.

She began to sneeze, then cough. "Sorry."

Max went to the kitchen and brought her a glass of water. "Lie down. The world needs you healthy again."

She did as she was told and he tucked an afghan around her legs. Suzu jumped into her place in the crook of her knees. "I'm so glad I met you," she said.

He bent down and kissed her forehead. "Speaking of meeting . . . I'd like to call my dad and arrange for him to meet you—when you feel up to it. Are you game?"

She was honored.

**

As soon as she opened her eyes, Summer knew she was better. The fog of her cold had lifted. Her sniffles were gone. The aches had left her head and body.

She looked at the clock. 3:16.

She laughed. This wasn't the first time God had awakened her at that special time. She always took it as a special message from Him. So now, as before, she repeated the verse, John 3:16.

"'For God so loved the world that he gave his one and only Son, that whoever believes in him shall not perish but have eternal life.'"

With God's promise reaffirmed, she went back to sleep knowing that tomorrow would be a glorious day.

Chapter 45

Michelle

"There are different kinds of gifts,
but the same Spirit distributes them."
1 Corinthians 12: 4

"Sure, I'll make you a beanie, George."

Michelle smiled when she looked over at Jonette who'd set up shop in the corner of the shelter's dining hall.

"My head's kinda big," George said.

"Don't worry. I'll make it fit. Let me measure."

Jonette had changed a lot since the night Roscoe died, the night she and Michelle had talked about choices and getting to know people at the shelter. Although Michelle still thought Jonette should go home, the girl had made a real effort to be friendly. People gravitated to her now. There was no more sitting alone.

Crocheting had been Jonette's ice breaker. Michelle had brought her a measuring tape, a pad of paper, and a pen to take orders. Plus some scissors. She'd lost track of how many beanies Jonette had made. Mealtime revealed a scattering of beanie-covered heads.

Michelle approached. "All hail the crochet queen." She bowed like a gallant. "Your highness."

The people around Jonette chuckled. "Crochet queen . . . you're not going to live that one down," George said. He walked away, chatting with another customer.

"Thanks a lot," Jonette said, pretending to be mad.

"It's the least I can do." Michelle looked in the shopping bag. "You're getting low on yarn already?"

"Uh-huh." She let her latest beanie rest in her lap. "It's not right for you give it to me free. I was wondering if I could exchange some work in the kitchen for more yarn. Barter."

Michelle was going to say she'd buy the yarn, but recognized the importance of earning it. "It's a deal."

**

Jonette carried a huge can of green beans out of the pantry. She stopped mid-stride and looked back.

"What do you need?" Michelle asked.

"You got any cream of mushroom soup and corn flakes?"

Michelle looked to Julio who handled the ordering. "Do we?"

"I think so. Why?"

"Green bean casserole. It's one of my dad's favorites. The corn flakes go on top and make it crispy. It's real yummy."

Michelle was familiar with the old standard, but hadn't made it in a while. She exchanged a glance with Julio. He shrugged. "Go for it," she said.

The soup and cereal were found and the casserole made. While it was in the oven, Jonette strolled back into the pantry.

Michelle followed her in. "I see your thoughts swirling."

She put a hand on a big can of tomatoes. "I know a yummy recipe for taco soup. It has corn in it. It goes great with green chilies cornbread."

"You're making my mouth water."

"My dad liked this recipe too." Her face looked wistful.

Michelle put an arm around her shoulders. "He'd be very proud of you. You are using your many talents."

"I can think of more recipes."

"Our stomachs are yours. Write them down."

As Michelle walked away, she high-fived Julio. "You have yourself an assistant."

**

Back home Michelle got the verse of the day ready to send. She was shocked to see that Summer had responded to Ryan's response. Two out of four!

Claire walked by the office and Michelle called her in. "Come see!" She pointed at the screen.

Claire read over her shoulder. "Nice. See? You didn't have to worry. People are reading the verses and now they're responding—and they're having success."

"*Some* people are responding."

"Did you really expect Jered to share?"

"No. But I did expect someone else to share."

Claire feigned surprise. "Me?"

"You." Michelle spun the office chair around to face her. "You and I started this thing, Claire. We need to set an example."

Claire took a step back. "I don't see that you have shared about what you're doing."

Oops. "Me? You mean Jonette?"

"Yes, I mean Jonette."

Why haven't I shared? "I guess I was waiting to see how it turns out."

Claire pointed at the computer. "Do you think Ryan or Summer knows how their ventures are going to turn out? It sounds like they're in the midst of them. Seems like I've heard someone tell me that the journey is as important as the destination."

Michelle *had* said that a time or two. "Very well. I'll post if you'll post."

Claire waved a hand toward the screen. "You first."

Michelle turned back to the computer and created a blank email for a response. She began to type:

So good to hear from both of you! It sounds like God has placed you in the paths of people who need your help. I've been working with a runaway girl, hoping to get her home to her father. We had a death at the shelter the other night, so that's a heartbreak, but our successes far outweigh our sorrows. Keep responding! It's important we keep in touch. And don't just share your successes. Share your struggles too. We are here to help each other. King Solomon said, "Though one may be overpowered, two can defend themselves. A cord of three strands is not quickly broken." Let's take strength in each other.

Michelle stopped typing. "How's that?"

Claire shook her head. "Brilliant. As usual."

Michelle relinquished the chair. "Next!"

Claire logged onto her email server. She found the conversation and created a new email. "What should I say?"

"Billy? Betrayal? Grandma's Cookin'?"

Claire told a condensed version of these very important developments, ending with, "So I've found love, justice, and a new business venture—none of which I was looking for. Stay tuned!"

"That's good," Michelle said. "I like you mentioning that God surprised you."

"Since it meets your approval can I send it?"

"Send away." Michelle looked at the screen. "I wish Jered would respond."

"Maybe he's not an email type of guy."

"Then I'll call him." She retrieved her phone and the contact list.

"Do you think he'll answer? He might have people do that for him."

"I guess we'll see." The phone was ringing.

"Speaker phone," Claire said.

Michelle turned her speaker on just as Jered answered.

"Hello?"

"Jered! This is Michelle Jofsky?" How could she explain who she was? "From the mosaic meeting?"

"Oh. Hi, Michelle. How you doing?"

"I'm doing fine. I'm calling to find out how *you're* doing."

"I'm okay."

"Just okay?"

"Well . . . I guess some things have happened."

Michelle and Claire exchanged a look. "What kind of things?"

"I've had a few . . . maybe *you* would call them God-moments."

"Excellent!" Michelle said while Claire silently clapped.

"You guys talked about listening to God and I thought it was dumb and never ever thought it would happen to me, but…" The phone got quiet. "I think I'm finally hearing Him."

Michelle put a hand to her chest. "That's marvelous, Jered."

Claire mouthed, *Ask what God's telling him.*

Michelle nodded. "What is God saying to you—if you want to share."

"I'm not completely sure, but I *have* reconnected with an old musician buddy and . . . there's something there. Something important. I'm not sure what yet, but . . ."

"You're seeking. You're open," Michelle said. "That's a huge part of it. Please keep us in the loop."

"Maybe I will. I mean, I've seen some of the emails. The verses are nice. And I read what Ryan and Summer said."

"Claire and I just posted too. Will you write and tell the others your good news? We need to stay in touch."

He hesitated. "I suppose I could do that. We'll see."

They said their goodbyes and Michelle hung up.

"Well I'll be," Claire said. "Never in a million years did I expect God to . . . expect Jered to . . ."

"Get to know each other?"

"Exactly." She looked upward. "Sorry, Father. I don't mean to offend." She turned back to Michelle. "If I could give the Almighty a high-five, I would."

Michelle chuckled.

Claire put her hands on Michelle's shoulders. "See how you're helping people? See how your verses aren't sent in vain?"

"I do. I won't ever complain again."

"Good. Want some ice cream?"

Claire's ability to switch subjects always amazed her. "No thanks. I have a bit more work to do on the computer."

Claire left the office and Michelle turned back to the screen. Her other task concerned Jonette. The other day Jonette had let slip her last name: Wilkins. Which gave Michelle just enough information to search for accountants with the last name of Wilkins who had an office in downtown Kansas City.

Yet before she hit the *Search* button she hesitated. Although she wanted Jonette to go home, maybe forcing the issue wasn't the way to do it. Especially not now, when Jonette was gaining confidence in her own abilities.

But her dad's got to be worried sick about her.

Michelle was torn between easing a father's pain or helping his daughter gain some important life skills.

She smiled at the memories of Jonette crocheting beanies and working in the kitchen. She was coming into her own.

Michelle had earned her trust. To force the reunion would be a betrayal of that trust. Jonette wasn't in danger. In a way she was thriving. It would mean so much more if *she* was the one who reached out to her dad.

Michelle stared at the screen. *Father?*

Wait.

Michelle logged out.

Chapter 46

Claire

"But these things I plan won't happen right away.
Slowly, steadily, surely,
the time approaches when the vision will be fulfilled.
If it seems slow, wait patiently, for it will surely take place.
It will not be delayed."
Habakkuk 2: 3

The microwave in Billy's kitchen dinged. Claire carefully removed the melted butter. "Now what?"

Billy poured a thick batter into a glass pan. "Now you mix in the brown sugar, cinnamon, raisins, and a little flour."

"Flour in a crunchy topping?"

"It helps bind it together in little clumps."

She did as she was told. "This is a lot of topping."

"I double the amount my Aunt Betty used to put on her coffee cake. Personal preference."

"Which I agree with completely. Is this one of Max's favorites?"

"It is. When I invited them to brunch, he asked for it specifically."

"Meeting the girlfriend is a big step," Claire said, then realized it was times two. "Her *and* me."

"I'm so glad he called. It's been just the two of us for so many years . . . " He gave her a smile. "I'm glad we both have a woman in our lives."

She touched his cheek. "Aww. So we make your lives complete?"

"Pretty close." He turned his head and kissed her hand.

"The feeling's mutual, dear man." Claire hadn't felt so complete in . . . in ever. She would have liked to set the cake aside and cuddle, but they had guests coming. "Do I just pour the topping on?"

"Drop dabs on top and I'll cut it into the batter."

Soon it was ready for the oven. "Now we wait," he said.

"That's the hard part." Claire took the bowls to the sink. "Your menu at Grandma's should have a little line about the recipes, like 'I've doubled the crunchies from Aunt Betty's recipe.'"

"You think so?"

"Customers would love it. People love stories. You're making their experience personal."

They washed and dried the dishes together. Claire had no desire to use the dishwasher when she had this alternative.

Then they moved to the dinette table where a myriad of recipes were scattered. "So," she said. "This will go on the breakfast menu . . . how many items do we have so far?"

He went through his grandma's recipe cards. "Five for breakfast, six for lunch, four for dinner." He sighed. "We have a ways to go."

"Are you sure we have to kitchen test all of them? You know they're good."

"I'm sure. I'm putting Grandma's reputation on the line. I can't wing it."

The doorbell rang and they stood in unison. "Are we ready?" Her stomach endured a zillion butterflies

He winked at her. "I'm eager." Then he opened the door. "Welcome!"

Billy's son hugged his father, but Claire's eyes immediately went to the girlfriend.

"Summer?"

"Claire?"

The men looked confused. "You know each other?" Billy asked.

"She's one of the people who met at my house, the people God brought together."

"No way," Billy said.

"You're Summer's Claire?" Max asked.

"That, I am." They all laughed and Claire drew Summer into a hug. "Oh, my goodness. This is incredible."

Summer stepped back, grinning. "I just got chills."

Claire hugged Max too. "I can't believe how I ended up meeting your father and Summer met you."

"What a cool coincidence."

Claire and Summer exchanged a look and said, "There's no such thing" which elicited another laugh.

As they moved to the living room Summer passed the mosaic. "You have the mosaic. How . . . ?"

"I was the winner of the drawing," Billy said, taking a seat in a wing chair. "That's how Claire and I met. How did you two meet?"

The next half-hour was spent catching up and marveling at God's amazing ways.

"When does your new restaurant open?" Max asked.

Billy stood. "We're finalizing the recipes now. Come into the kitchen and give us your opinion."

Max showed Billy the recipes they'd chosen and the two exchanged memories of family meals shared in this very house.

Claire stood by Summer, watching the scene. "You should have emailed the group to say you met someone."

"You mentioned a man," Summer said, "but never said his name." She shook her head. "I'm still in awe."

"And shock," Claire said. "Happy shock."

The timer on the oven rang and Billy took Betty's Coffee Cake out of the oven.

"I thought that's what I smelled," Max exclaimed. "I'll get some butter out."

"Coffee anyone?" Claire asked, pointing at the pot.

They all nodded. "Let's sit in the dining room," Billy said.

The four made quick work of setting the table and serving the cake.

"Ummm," Summer said as she took her first bite. "Is this going to be served at Grandma's?"

"It is." Billy glanced at Max. "I couldn't open a place without it."

Summer stirred sweetener in her coffee. "If you have all these recipes . . . why didn't you start a restaurant like this the first time?"

Billy dabbed his mouth with a napkin. "I've been thinking about that a lot. The influence was *always* there. When I was a waiter downtown, I went to the original Grandma's often enough she called me by name."

"She worked there?"

"Harder than anyone. She was always talking to people, helping serve if they needed help. She even cleaned tables." He nodded once. "That's the kind of owner I want to be."

"What was her name?"

He thought for a moment. "Grandma. That's what everyone called her."

Claire spread some more butter on the cake and watched it melt over the crumbs. "Even then you had a connection with this type of food."

"So when you got the idea to venture out on your own, why did you choose a steakhouse?" Summer asked.

Billy considered this a moment. "Sometimes circumstances force dreams to adapt."

"Or cave?" Claire asked. "Sorry. That was harsh."

He shrugged. "You may be right. I wanted to offer homey foods, a diner-type place, and Robby wanted a restaurant with Italian food."

"With a name like Roberto Bianchi, that's not surprising," Max said.

"Neither one of you got what you wanted," Claire said.

"Robby did. Now," Max said. "I can't believe he cheated you like he did."

Billy waved his hand as though consigning those acts into the past. "We both made mistakes."

"But now your dream is becoming reality," Claire said.

Billy looked to the floor. "It's . . ." His voice cracked and he cleared his throat. "It's almost like God was holding the dream safe for me until I found it again."

"That's beautiful," Summer said.

Claire extended her hand to him, then reached for Max on the other side. The four of them held hands. "God is good," she said.

"All the time," Billy said.

Chapter 47

Ryan

"Command them to do good,
to be rich in good works,
to be generous and ready to share."
1 Timothy 6: 18

Chopping wood was hard work, yet Ryan found satisfaction in it. His frustration at himself came out through each chop, each spray of sweat from his brow. He found a rhythm to it. With each chop he mentally prayed three words over and over: *Let. Grandpa. Believe.*

Bertha was busy showing a new guests around the Pinecone cabin. They'd just arrived and had a girl Lisa's age. Ryan marveled how easily the two girls bonded. He'd never made friends easily, yet Lisa had already asked permission to show the girl the stream and they'd run up the road.

He was glad Bertha had some business. He'd been reading the how-to book on websites but hadn't had time to go down to the library to implement it yet—*if* he could even handle it. While being on the road Ryan had virtually missed everything . . . virtual.

Bertha said there was no hurry because there were still a lot of repairs to do. It did no good to book guests if they'd be unhappy because a window was broken or a toilet seat kept coming off. Add to the list rotting window boxes, dangling shutters, a broken stove, light switches that didn't work, and so on. The work never seemed to end.

He heard a car drive up the gravel road. Bertha was occupied so he put the ax down, wiped his face with a towel, and went to greet the visitor.

He was surprised to see his parents. "Morning, Ryan," Mom said. "We've come to help."

Dad got a toolbelt out of the back of the SUV—it looked brand new. "I haven't swung a hammer in a while, but I'll do my best."

"How did . . .? Why . . .?"

"At dinner Bertha mentioned the place needed some fixing. I called her and asked if she needed help—if *you* needed help. So . . . here we are."

Dad looked around the area. "I have good memories of this place. There's a fire pit over there, yes?"

"There is."

Mom looked at the cabin where Ryan was staying. "It's still here. The Mountain Rose."

Ryan looked at it with new eyes. "It was our cabin?"

"Don't you remember? You slept on a cot in the main room. Lisa insisted on having the second bedroom."

"She didn't insist," Dad said. "Ryan offered it to her."

"Always the gentleman," Mom said with a proud smile.

Ryan marveled how God brought things full-circle.

Bertha finished up with the family and walked toward them, waving. "You came! Welcome."

Dad held his hammer up. "Ready for service! Point me toward a nail."

She laughed. "Come with me." She led them to the Columbine cabin.

"I'll be there in a minute," Ryan said. "Let me finish up the wood."

He finished the log-splitting and gathered his tools to join them. The entire situation was surreal: his parents were at the resort they'd all visited when he was a kid, a resort he was led to while traveling with two strangers who'd become more than just friends. A few weeks ago he'd been alone. Now he was fully where he belonged. And all of it had happened in ways beyond his control, even in spite of his control.

Before going inside the Columbine Ryan paused and bowed his head. *You are amazing, Lord. I am in awe of Your ways.*

Inside, Bertha was showing his parents how the flooring was peeling in the kitchen and bathroom. "If it were me, I'd just glue it down and add another layer on top, but Arnold did that too many times already. It really needs to be taken down to the floorboards." She pointed at utility knives and a floor scraper. "At least Ryan bought the right tools."

He picked up the scraper. "I'll start by seeing what comes up with this, but we might have to cut it into smaller sections."

Mom exposed the blade of a utility knife. "I'm ready."

Bertha chuckled. "Please don't hurt yourself." She turned when the door of the cabin opened.

"Phone call," Grandpa said.

"Coming."

"Morning, Allen," Dad said. "Nice to see you."

Grandpa just nodded and left with Bertha.

"Is something wrong?" Mom asked.

"Yeah. Pretty much."

"What?"

Ryan hated to admit his mistake. At the moment his parents thought he was simpatico with God. That opinion might change if they knew how he'd blown it with Grandpa. "It's okay. I can handle it."

Mom shook her head. "I know you're used to handling everything on your own, but we're here now. We're together again. We'd like to help—if we can."

Maybe they *could* help. "Allen's not too open about God-stuff."

"I noticed that at dinner," Dad said.

"I'm afraid what he overheard between the three of us when they were in the kitchen made it worse. Plus . . ." Ryan told them about the "hearing God" discussion. "I implied his attitude might be the reason he wasn't hearing anything, and he got mad and stormed off in a huff. He's been pretty quiet ever since."

Mom put a hand on Ryan's back. "It's hard to know what to say. Some people are walking on a balance beam. We can't predict what will make them topple off."

"I've apologized, but he won't listen."

Dad leaned on the floor scraper. "One time I yelled at a friend, 'You need Jesus!'"

Ryan smiled. "I'm sure that did the trick."

"Yeah. Well . . ."

"Did he come around?"

"He did—no thanks to me."

Ryan appreciated his dad sharing his own botched attempt to share Jesus. "I wondered if I should try to talk to him more about God or just let him be."

Dad shook his head. "I think the best thing to do is respect his silence. Trust that God is working on him in ways we can't fathom."

"But what if He isn't?"

Dad gave him a look. "You are not Allen's Holy Spirit."

"That's what Bertha said."

"I knew I liked that woman. Now, let's get to work to help *that* woman."

**

After they removed the flooring, Ryan and his parents took a break and sat on the front porch, enjoying the mountain breeze. Bertha had brought over some sandwiches and iced tea before she and Grandpa drove off to show the guests where they could ride horses at nearby Meeker Park. Lisa went along.

"I'm glad she's having some fun," Ryan said. "She's been in some tough spots, forced to handle responsibilities beyond her years."

Dad pointed to the pickup that was still full of belongings. "Are they moving here?"

"I don't know about *here,*" Ryan said. "But yes, they left everything behind—pretty much on a whim. Grandpa's family homesteaded in the middle of the Flint Hills. Acres and acres of grassland, way out in the boonies. He's lived in the same house his whole life."

"Leaving must have been hard for him."

"I don't know that it was." Ryan thought back to the circumstances. "He had a bad cough and ended up in the hospital. He has dilated cardio-something."

"Dilated cardiomyopathy?" Dad asked.

"What do you know about it?"

"The left ventricle is enlarged and weak. The heart doesn't pump as well as it should. How's he doing with the altitude?"

"I think he's doing okay. He hasn't said anything."

"Are they going to do surgery?"

Surgery? "Not that I know of, but he has medicines. And actually, his cough has gone away."

"That's excellent."

Mom poured more tea. "Health issues . . . that's one reason to start over. Especially if their house was isolated."

That *was* part of it.

Dad sipped his tea. "As I told Allen, if he needs a doctor I'm here."

"Thanks. I'm watching him close, trying to be aware."

Mom touched his knee. "That's our Ryan. Always aware of others. Always the perceiver."

Ryan thought back to Claire's house when she'd assigned them spiritual gifts. Claire had also called him a perceiver.

Dad took a bite out of his ham sandwich. "The big question I have is what are *you* going to do? You're here. Your life is intertwined with the Pearls. Are *you* staying?"

Mom shook her head. "Add my question . . . where have you been for ten years and what brought you to the Pearls in the first place?"

"And where—and why—did you get that awful tattoo on your hand?" Dad asked.

Three questions that deserved answers. Ryan considered telling them about Claire and the mosaic, the Mercy Shelter, meeting the others, and the pinks roses, doves, and arrows . . . but he felt much of it was extraneous. Did it really matter?

And then he thought of two words that would explain everything. "What have I been doing? Where am I heading? Why the tattoo?" He spread his hands. "One answer: the Great Commission."

They studied him. Would them commend him or condemn him?

His father was the first to speak. "You've been preaching?"

"No, no. Not preaching. I'm no preacher."

"Then what?"

How could he explain it? "I make myself open to God. I try to listen and be aware, and follow His nudges."

"Nudges," Dad said. "That sounds vague."

"Not at all." Mom brushed crumbs off her lap. "Nudges led me and the kids toward God when they were little And they led us to you."

Dad sighed. "Of course. You're right. As I said last night I've gotten in the bad habit of setting God aside and not giving Him His due."

She smiled at him. "You're back in His fold now. We're both back thanks to Ryan. But we're getting off topic," Mom said. "So you've been going where God sends you? And he led you to Allen and Lisa?"

"He did."

"You're very fond of them."

"I am." *More than I'd like to be.* "Lisa is a great kid. She's smart, caring, and approaches God with an innocent enthusiasm—in spite of Allen." He set his drink on the porch beside his chair.

"Hang in there," Mom said. "God won't give up on him and neither should you."

Ryan nodded. "To sum up the last ten years? I know where I've been but I don't know where I'm going." He pointed to his tattoo. "Wherever God sends me."

Mom eyed the arrows. "Maybe He'll let you stay put and plant some roots."

"Maybe."

"Would you be interested if He did?" she asked.

Ryan knew what his mom wanted him to say, but he shrugged. He honestly didn't know.

Mom collected their plates and stacked them on a table. She stood at the top of the porch and took a deep breath. "I love it up here. It's a shame it's gotten so run down. Bertha needs more customers."

"I was going to create a website for her because she has nothing online. I've been reading a how-to book and—"

Mom whipped around. "I can do that."

"You can?"

"I built a website for my paintings. I'd be happy to build one for her."

Ryan was completely relieved. He stood and gave her a peck on the cheek. "Thanks, Mom. That would be awesome."

She walked off the porch and seemed to look at the grounds with new eyes. "Once we get it fixed up I'll take photos of each cabin." When she turned back to them she was smiling. "This will be fun."

I'm glad she thought so.

Chapter 48

Summer

"I am not ashamed of the gospel,
for it is the power of God for salvation
to everyone who believes."
Romans 1: 16

When Summer got to the shop, Candy was behind the counter, putting the cash tray into the register. "Why are you grinning so much lately? You win a million bucks or something?"

"I'm just happy."

"Obviously, you have reason to be."

What?

Andy came out of the back. "Candy, here's the first delivery." He stopped when he saw Summer. He gave Candy a questioning look.

She waved a hand at him. "Save yourself a trip."

Andy handed Summer an arrangement of bright summer flowers. "These are for you."

"Me?"

"The order was put in online, last night," Candy said. "Who's Max?"

Max? Summer took out the card and read it. *You brighten my life. Max.*

"You have a boyfriend?" Andy asked—far too bluntly.

For once in her life she could say it. "I do."

Candy smiled. "Good for you." That was the extent of Candy's interest in her personal life as she turned to Andy. "Since your delivery is finished I'd like you to clean the flower cooler. It needs a good dusting and some Windex." To Summer she said, "Enjoy your joy. I relinquish the helm."

Summer admired her bouquet. Max had been so kind. He was such a good man. And meeting his father and finding out *his* girlfriend was Claire reinforced her certainty that God was behind all of it. They were meant to be.

A customer walked in. Summer's stomach did a flip when she saw who it was. "Good morning, Mr. Horowitz." He'd already complained about her to Candy. What now?

"Morning." He glanced at Andy, then back at her. "Can I have a word with you—in private?"

This did not bode well. "Of course. Andy? Would you go help Candy for a few minutes, please?"

Andy slipped into the back room. "How can I help you today?" she asked him.

"The arrangement you took to my mother . . ."

"Is she enjoying it?"

"She is. But . . . I've been checking my account and it was never charged to me. I came in to pay for it."

She glanced toward the back. She didn't want Candy to overhear. "You don't owe anything."

He shook his head. "I don't want the shop to eat a sale. I know I stormed off, and I'm willing to pay."

Summer kept her voice low. "The shop didn't eat it. I . . . I paid for it."

His brown eyes stared at her. He blinked "Why would you do that?"

"Because I offended you. I had no right to spout a Bible verse at you—and mention baptism. I didn't think about it at the time, but I know that's not a Jewish sacrament."

"It's not. And yes, I was offended—at the time. I was in a mood because I'd argued with my mother, so I took my guilty anger out on you. I'm sorry."

She was shocked by his apology. "It's all right. I'm sorry too. I overstepped."

He nodded, but looked like he had more to say. He shifted his weight from right to left. "Speaking of that baptism thing? I'd never thought about the word, much less what it was. So I asked a good golfing buddy of mine—he's a pastor—and he told me about baptism, and Jesus, and how He is the Messiah that Jews have been waiting for, and . . ." His forehead furrowed. "He and I are going to talk again. He gave me the New Testament to read."

Summer sucked in a breath and put a hand to her chest. "That's wonderful. I'm so happy for you."

"We'll see where it goes. My friend says God opened some narrow gate and I've walked through it." He shrugged. "We'll see where it leads."

Summer was aware of a verse about walking through a narrow gate to Jesus. And she knew where this could lead. Her heart did a happy dance.

"Thank you for coming in to tell me, Mr. Horowitz. I'm excited about your journey."

For the first time, he smiled. "Actually, I am too. Have a good one, Summer. Shalom."

As soon as he left, Summer let her happy-dance move to her body. She boogied behind the counter and let out a, "Yay, God!"

Andy returned from the back. She stopped dancing. "Did you overhear?" she asked.

"Uh. Yeah." He came close, his voice low. "You talked to that customer about God?"

"He came in the other day, upset. I quoted a verse but it offended him and he walked out."

"But he came back."

"He did."

"The verse stuck with him."

"It did."

"What was the verse?"

Summer felt a little flip in her chest. "'Repent and be baptized.'"

Andy bit his lip. "What does that mean?"

She sucked in a breath. This was serious. *Father! Help me say the right words!*

But suddenly she felt calm about it. God *wanted* Andy to understand. He would help Summer with the words.

She straightened a pile of brochures on the counter. "The repent part? You know all that stuff you feel bad about, stuff you wish you hadn't done or said? Repent means you tell God you're sorry for it. You say you don't want to do it again.

Repenting is all about turning around. You make a one-eighty and go the other way."

He bit a fingernail, which made him look very young.

"Do you have things you're sorry about?"

He let his hand drop. "Well . . . sure."

"Then tell God you're sorry and don't do it again. Try to live the way God wants you to live."

He nodded once. "When I came in here you were yelling, 'Yay, God.' God heard that?"

She chuckled. "He did. He hears us if we yell, cry, whisper, stand up, sit down, even if we hide away. He hears 24/7. All the time, no matter where we are."

"That's cool."

Yes, it is.

Andy fiddled with the Windex bottle. "And the baptized part? What's that?"

Round two, Lord. She thought of a great analogy, one her mother had shared with her years ago. "Do your parents wear wedding rings?"

"Yeah."

"If they took their rings off does that mean they're not married anymore?"

"Mom takes hers off when she washes dishes but she's still married."

"We wear rings because we love our spouse and we want the world to know who we belong to."

"Okay."

"It's the same with getting baptized. It's a way to show God we love Him and show the world Who we belong to."

"It's just a ceremony."

"It's not *just* anything. Same as a marriage isn't *just* a ceremony. It's a public commitment."

"But babies get baptized and they can't commit. They can't even talk."

"But their parents, families, and even the congregation do it for them. You can get baptized at any age. Repentance is your decision. Baptism is your pledge."

He thought about this a moment. "I wonder if I'm baptized."

"Ask your parents."

He turned the Windex around in a full circle. "My friend Jason goes to church a *lot*."

"Maybe you could go with him."

"He's asked me."

"Then say yes."

"Okay. I think I will." He took up the bottle and cleaned the cooler.

Summer held in another *Yay, God!* but celebrated bigtime inside.

**

Summer knew exactly where Sydney's mother lived because it was the same house the Thorpes had lived in since the girls were little. Summer had played there and had enjoyed many sleepovers. She'd always been envious of Sydney's canopy bed with its pink ruffled bed skirt. Secrets and childhood dreams had been shared in that house.

She'd called ahead to reconnect with Sydney's mom, and asked if it was okay to come by. Donna seemed thrilled to hear from her and said to come right over.

Donna looked ten years older than last time Summer had seen her—which had probably been at the wedding. She'd let her hair go gray and had cut it boyishly short. She wore no makeup. She didn't look bad, but she wasn't the perfectly groomed Mrs. Thorpe Summer had known.

Donna led her into the kitchen. "I hope you don't mind talking back here. I don't use the living room much anymore. Too many memories." She nodded to the dinette. "Have a seat. Lemonade?"

"That would be nice."

Donna poured two glasses and sat across from her. She let out a breath and smiled. "I was surprised to hear from you. I've kept tabs on your life through Tessa, but I'm probably behind as I've missed a few book club meetings." She ran a finger around the rim of her glass. "I've been a bit . . . preoccupied."

Summer wasn't sure how much she should admit to knowing. "I'm sorry you're going through hard . . . stuff."

Donna snickered. "Stuff. Yup. That's the gist of it."

Summer looked around the kitchen. There were dirty dishes on the counter, a package of Oreos, and an open box of frosted flakes.

Donna followed her gaze. "I used to forbid Sydney from eating sugary foods but . . ." She sighed, then changed the subject. "Actually, I can thank Sydney for my current situation."

She was blaming her daughter? "How's that?"

Donna lifted a hand. "It's not a bad thing, it's good. Sydney is the bravest person I know."

It took Summer a moment to transition from blame to praise. "How so?"

Donna leaned her forearms on the table. "We all knew Ben wasn't a great guy, but we didn't know how bad he was until after the wedding. Sydney tried to hide it from us: the emotional abuse, the yelling, the threats, and the affairs. She was embarrassed and tried to handle it herself."

"She didn't tell anyone?"

Donna shook her head. "You know Syd is hard on friends. She thought Ben would be enough for her and let her female friendships slide. It took a lot of guts to finally say *she'd* had enough."

Summer had never thought of Sydney's divorce taking courage.

Donna sat back. "I know the church and the Bible are against divorce except when infidelity is involved because that breaks the marriage vows. So Sydney *was* justified. But even then some people gave Syd a hard time and told her it was her duty to stay. Buck it up. Be a good wife." She shook her head. "For twenty-five years *I* bucked it up and tried to be a good wife—in spite of Jay's abuse, his drinking, and his women."

The transition from daughter to mother was jarring. Summer didn't try to conceal her shock. "I'm so sorry. I didn't know."

"Nobody did. Like daughter, like mother, we both kept our secrets. Both played the good wife. But we were also alike in finally standing up for ourselves and, shall we say, cleaning house?" She glanced at the dishes and chuckled. "I admit I've gotten a bit lax without Jay being a taskmaster. He always insisted on everything being perfect." She shook her head. "Perfection is a myth."

"Are . . . are you happy now?"

Donna scoffed. "That's a toughie. I'm glad to be rid of the tension, and I'm relieved to not be a victim anymore. But I miss him. I still love him. Yet his kind of love was destructive. I don't miss that." She took a fresh breath. "I wish I could have offered Syd a place to stay, but things are still too raw for me. I can't be of much help to her until I help myself."

It was Tessa's oxygen mask analogy played out in real life.

Donna smiled. "I'm glad she called you. She needs a friend right now."

"She didn't call me, but . . ." Summer hesitated before deciding to tell the full truth. "We met because Sydney was getting food out of a dumpster in the middle of the night."

Donna's head jerked back. "A dumpster? My Sydney? Why would she do that?"

"She doesn't have any money."

Donna stood, shoving her chair aside. "That's ridiculous. Jay said he was sending her $1000 to tide her over."

"She never said anything about money, and from how she's living, I don't think she got it."

"I know she doesn't have much furniture, but she was supposed to use that money to paint and fix up the place. And food? Yes. Use it to buy food."

"That hasn't happened."

"This is ridiculous." Donna dug her phone out of her purse and dialed a number. "Jay? What's going on? You promised to send Syd a thousand dollars. Why haven't you done it?"

She listened, then made a face. "Oh. Okay. Sorry. Bye."

Donna held the phone to her chest. "He said he *did* send her a check but she sent it back. She said she didn't want his money."

"Talk about brave," Summer said.

Donna pursed her lips, deep in thought. Tears came to her eyes. "She gave up the money in support of me." She put a hand to her mouth. "*I've* taken Jay's money—I'm asking for more. Yet Sydney rejects it on principle." She looked at Summer, her face a mask of awe. "My own daughter humbles me."

Summer's throat grew tight. Sydney wasn't just complicated, she was inspiring.

Donna burst into action, suddenly on a mission. She strode to the cupboards and pulled down a pig-shaped cookie jar. She brought it to the table, stuck her hand inside, and pulled out money. Soon there was a messy pile of fives, twenties, and ones.

"Even when Jay and I were together I always had a secret stash in case I needed it. I need it now. Sydney needs it now. How much is there?"

They took a few minutes to sort and count the bills. "There's $854," Summer said.

"I had no idea there was that much. Let's use it to fix up her house and buy Syd some groceries. Get her settled in right." She beamed. "It's nice to be able to say it's not her father's money. I earned that money by baking pies for Banyon's Bakery."

"Those pies come from you?"

"Yup."

"I love the French Silk."

"It's a best-seller."

Summer's mind sped ahead. "I have some friends who could help with simple repairs and painting."

"Perfect." Donna sighed deeply. "My oh my, Summer Peerbaugh. You certainly have a way of lifting me out of my funk and bringing out the best in me. I'm glad you came over."

The feeling was mutual.

**

After work that evening—after asking Grandma, Mae, and Max to help fix Sydney's house—Summer went back to her apartment and searched through her music playlist for a very specific song.

"Found it!"

She turned on the Pointer Sisters. The strains of "I'm So Excited" filled the room. Summer danced with wild abandon.

A few minutes later there was a knock on the door. She paused the music to answer it. It was Max. "I heard pounding on my ceiling. What's up?"

"I'm dancing because I'm happy."

He grinned. "Why are you happy?"

She shook her head. "I'll tell you later." She held out a hand. "Care to join me?"

They danced together as Suzu pranced around them.

Chapter 49

Jered

"The Holy Spirit, whom the Father will send in my name,
will teach you all things and will remind you
of everything I have said to you.
Peace I leave with you; my peace I give you.
I do not give to you as the world gives.
Do not let your hearts be troubled and do not be afraid."
John 14: 26-27

For the second day in a row Jered awakened with his new motto on his mind. Ivy was already up, working in the garden.

He poured himself a cup of coffee and repeated the words out loud, "Oh bless the Lord my soul. Oh bless—"

"The Lord my soul." Ivy sang the words.

"I didn't hear you come in."

She was smiling ear to ear. "I didn't know you knew that song."

"Song?"

She began to sing—bouncing to the beat and using hand movements. "'Oh, bless the Lord, my soul, His praise to thee proclaim. And all that is within me join to bless his holy name, oh yeah.'"

He was clueless

"*Godspell?* Written in the seventies? A Broadway musical? Nominated for a Tony?"

He felt stupid.

She poured herself some coffee. "I was in a *Godspell* production when I was sixteen. I sang that 'Bless the Lord' song."

"I didn't know you were in musicals."

"I'll have you know I also was in *Fiddler on the Roof, My Fair Lady, Brigadoon…*"

He felt even more stupid.

"I did have a life before you." She poured some Life cereal in a bowl. "Want some?"

"Sure." He got out the milk, poured, then sat beside her.

"Obviously I know the lyrics of the song, but where did you learn it?" she asked. "It's a good thing, but . . . it's not like you."

How could he explain it? "I don't know the song but . . . a couple nights ago at the computer . . . Michelle's been emailing verses and—"

"She has? Can I see them?"

"Sure . . ."

"Why haven't you told me about them? You know I love verses."

Why hadn't he told her? Actually, he knew the truth of it, and he couldn't tell her about his God-experience without fessing up. "I knew you'd like them. But I thought you'd get too excited and make me feel bad about *not* caring about them, and so I kept them to myself. It was wrong."

"Jer. We're a team. Don't leave me out."

"Sorry about that." There was more to tell. "Some of the people have posted about what's happened to them."

Her eyes brightened. "I want to see!"

He nodded. "I'll show you later. Michelle actually called me, to check in."

"What did you tell her? And have you posted anything?"

"Not yet. But now . . . I want to tell you about one of the verses Michelle sent the other night."

She set her spoon down. "I'd love to hear it."

He pushed his cereal away. He felt awkward because they'd never talked much about faith stuff.

"Come on, hon. Tell me."

He took a fresh breath. "There was this verse about soaring on the wings like eagles. And then my screen saver had the same verse on it." He made a fist in front of his midsection. "Somehow I knew it wasn't a coincidence. And I felt something stir in me, Ive. Something shifted. Changed. I felt . . . the Lord bless my soul."

She pushed back her chair and flung her arms around him. "I'm so happy for you!"

"For what?"

Ivy sat down again. "That stirring was the Holy Spirit doing His work in you."

"I don't know if I like the sounds of that."

She leaned close and pressed her hand against his heart. "The Trinity? You've heard of that, haven't you? Father, Son, and Holy Spirit."

"I suppose."

"What you felt was *Him.*" She patted his chest. "When Jesus left this earth He sent His Spirit *to* us to be *in* us."

"God's in us?" *Yeah. Right.*

She nodded. "God is in us. Right now. All the time."

"Why?"

"To guide and comfort us. Teach us. Intercede and advocate for us. He moved in you, Jer. He made Himself known to you."

A week ago Jered would have deemed the whole experience creepy. But now—because something *had* changed in him—he embraced it. "Will I feel it again?"

"You will. Over and over. Stay open to Him and He will rush right in." She pulled him to his feet and hugged him hard. "It's a day to celebrate!"

Jered felt a seed of joy planted in his soul.

**

Jered rummaged through the desk.

"What are you looking for?" Ivy asked.

"Stationery? Note cards, maybe?"

"I've got some with an *M* on them. Would that work?"

Perfect.

She had a box of them. Jered sat at the desk and took up a pen.

"What are you doing?" she asked.

He hesitated telling her because he didn't want her to jump on it.

"Jer?"

"I'm writing an apology to my publicist."

"About the radio interview you turned down?"

"Yeah. That." *And other stuff.*

She ran a hand over the back of his neck. "Oh bless the Lord, my soul. I'll leave you to it."

Jered opened the notecard and was immediately stuck by the blank page. The last time he'd written any kind of note was when his dad had made him write a thank you note to his grandma when she gave him a cool model airplane kit. *Dear Grandma . . .*

He didn't want to say *Dear Marv*. Maybe if he just wrote his name?

He shook his doubts away. "Sheesh, Jered. Just do it."

He wrote Marv's name and then his apology. Apologies. Unfortunately, there were many more instances when he'd been mean, impatient, arrogant, snappish . . .

After filling two sides of the note and ending with a vow to be better, he exhaled a long breath. "There. Done."

Only he wasn't done. His memories grew heavy with other times, other places, other people he'd hurt in one way or another.

One note became three, became ten.

Ivy came in to check on him and noticed the pile. "Wow."

"I know. Once I got started I couldn't stop. Do we have addresses for everyone?"

"I can get them." She stood behind his chair and hugged him. "You're a good man, Jered Manson."

Trying to be. Trying to be.

**

That evening they sat outside in Ivy's garden. Dusk settled over the flowers, making their colors fade. "We should put Christmas lights out here like Boxer has," Jered said.

"Family stars. You'd like that?"

"Wouldn't you?"

"I'd love it. I'll dig some lights out tomorrow."

Jered leaned his head against the back of the chair and looked up at the night sky. The moon was a crescent. He sighed.

"Is that a sigh of contentment?" Ivy asked.

"Oddly, it is. I feel filled up. Overflowing. Like I'm going to burst with it."

She laughed softly. "God-given joy does that. You want everybody to feel like you do. You want to share."

Share.

Deep inside, Jered heard Ivy's word repeated. Then again.

Share, Jered, share.

It was a nudge. Like an inner directive.

Share what?

Suddenly an idea surfaced. It wasn't like a seed being planted, it came to him backward, with the image of the end result flashing in his mind.

He saw himself in a studio. But he wasn't alone.

And then he knew *what* and *how* he was supposed to share his joy.

Unable to remain seated he stood.

"What's wrong?" Ivy asked.

He shook his head. "Actually, something cool just happened, and . . . I'd like to run something by you."

"Sure. Always."

"When you said the word 'share' I got an idea. Actually, it was more concrete than that. I saw myself in the studio with Boxer. Singing together."

She sat forward. "You want to record an album with Boxer?"

Yes, yes. That's it! "That's exactly what I want to do. We sound good together, don't we?"

"You do. Your voices blend like—"

He remembered the image that had come to mind. "Like pouring chocolate syrup in a glass of milk?"

She laughed. "Exactly like that. Do you think he'll do it?"

"I do. It's like it's a done deal. In fact . . ." He wasn't sure he was ready to say the next.

"In fact what?"

"In fact I have a feeling—actually, it's more like a knowing—that singing together is why we reconnected."

"There's that Holy Spirit working on you again."

Jered and Ivy sat outside a long time, immersed in something new and wonderful.

Chapter 50

Ryan

"What do you think? If a man owns a hundred sheep,
and one of them wanders away,
will he not leave the ninety-nine on the hills
and go to look for the one that wandered off?"
Matthew 18: 12

It was Bertha's idea. After days and days of working on the cabins, and with the guests gone, Bertha declared a day of vacation.

She made the announcement at breakfast. "We're going to hike to Copeland Falls."

"Falls?" Lisa asked. "Like a waterfall?"

"Powerful falls on a rushing stream, deep in the forest."

"I'm not going on any hike," Grandpa said. "Too strenuous."

"It's three-tenths of a mile, much of it paved. Toddlers walk it." She cocked her head. "You're stronger than a toddler, aren't you, Allen?"

"Don't be mean."

She began clearing the dishes. "Let's get going."

"Now?" Lisa said. "It's not even seven-thirty."

"To properly hike in the mountains, you go early and get back early, to avoid the afternoon showers." She took Grandpa's coffee mug out of his hand. "Besides, sometimes early birds see a moose or two."

Lisa's eyes grew large. "Let's go!"

It didn't take long to get ready, though Allen grumbled the entire time.

As they got in Bertha's car she shook a small backpack. "I brought cookies and juice."

Allen eyed her. "Chocolate chip?"

"Yup."

His grumbling lessened and Ryan knew a lot of it was for show. Or out of habit. Unfortunately, the rift between the two men remained. Although Grandpa spoke normally with Lisa and Bertha, he still answered Ryan with one or two words. Maybe some time in the forest would make him forgive and forget.

The road to the trailhead was one-lane and winding. Lisa opened her window, letting in the smell of pine and fresh air. The parking lot was half-full—which was surprising at this early hour. Obviously, Bertha wasn't the only one who lived the early-bird life.

Bertha handed out walking sticks. "It's not a proper hike without a stick."

"I don't need a cane," Allen said.

"It's not a cane, it's a walking stick. Take it. It's fun. Remember fun?"

He took one. Ryan offered to wear the backpack. And they were off.

Lisa ran ahead, but stopped often to exclaim about the wildflowers or the enormous trees or the chipmunks that scampered across the trail.

Bertha called after her, "Don't get too far ahead, in case you see a moose."

Lisa stopped in her tracks. "What do I do if I see one?"

Allen harrumphed. "Run like—"

"You stop and be very still and quiet. You back away." Bertha looked at Allen. "You don't run."

They walked on, though Lisa stayed close. "I don't remember seeing moose when I came here as a kid."

"That's because there weren't any—that I ever saw." Bertha pointed to a pine tree that had orangey bark. "See that? Bark beetles killed it—killed millions of trees in the mountains. It was worse on the west side of the Divide, and I think moose over there, moved over here. At least that's my reasoning."

It didn't take long to get to Copeland Falls where Lisa gasped with delight. The wall of water sprayed mist in the air. The scene was mesmerizing and the sound of water was soothing and magnificent.

Lisa teased the edge of the stream by putting a leaf in the current and tracking where it went. Ryan remembered doing the same thing with *his* Lisa. They sat on boulders and enjoyed their cookies and juice.

Then Lisa saw a sign, "It says 'Upper Falls'. Can I go up there?"

"I'll go with you," Bertha said. "You coming, Allen?"

He shook his head and remained seated on a boulder. "This is far enough."

Bertha looked at Ryan. He didn't want to be left alone with Grandpa, and yet . . . "I'll stay here too." They sat on their rocks and watched the falls and the stream. *Father, please use this time we have alone.*

Grandpa finally talked. "Gosh darn it."

"What?"

He swept a hand toward the falls. "That."

"It's gorgeous, isn't it?"

He shook his head.

"It's not gorgeous?"

Grandpa said, "It's not *just* that. It's perfect." He looked annoyed.

"So what's the problem?"

"God made it."

Ryan's ears perked up. "Yeah, He did."

"Just like He made that other place."

"What place?"

Grandpa kept his eyes on the falls. "That overlook I found when I walked up the road the other day."

"Where you can see for miles?"

"That's the one."

"Lisa and I found that place too."

They sat without talking a few minutes, letting the white-noise of the water provide the background.

"I heard Him."

Ryan's heart quickened. He realized what he said next would be important. "What did He say?"

Grandpa shrugged. "More like a feeling that He was there with me, letting me know that He created everything I was seeing." He looked down. "And me. He created me."

Ryan wanted to jump up and shout. Instead he said, "It's a good feeling, a good knowing, isn't it?"

"It is." His gaze returned to the water. "Actually, I knew that. I'd felt it back home looking out over the hills and watching the sun set. Man, He does a bang up job with sunsets."

Ryan chuckled. "Yes, He does."

Grandpa repositioned himself on the boulder so he was facing Ryan. "The other day when you said I wasn't listening? You were right. I felt God talking to me back home, but I ignored Him. Too concerned with my problems and life in general, I guess. I made a lot of mistakes I'm sorry for. I wasn't a great dad, or husband neither. Wasn't too proud of myself for much of anything, so I figured God had better things to do than bother with the likes of me."

Ryan realized the immensity of his confession. "Everyone has fallen short of who God wants them to be."

"Even you?"

"Especially me. Everyone, Allen. I know the word 'sinner' isn't popular, but it's true. We're all sinners and don't deserve God's care and love."

"That's encouraging."

"We don't deserve it, but He gives it anyway. That's why He sent His Son to us, to cleanse us of our sins so we can draw closer to Him."

"That's heavy stuff."

"The heaviest. Yet Jesus and His forgiveness lightens our burdens. Lifts them clean away."

Allen leaned his head back, closed his eyes a moment, then looked back at Ryan. "The big thing I want to say is this: I'm sure He exists because of you." He looked at Ryan. "God brought you to us, boy, sure as He gave you a map and said, 'Go up that road.'"

He pretty much did just that. "I agree with you, Allen. I'm where I'm supposed to be."

Grandpa chuckled. "Bet you never imagined traveling seven hundred miles with two strangers."

Ryan chuckled. "We're not strangers anymore."

"Guess you might say . . . could say . . . we're almost family."

Ryan's heart swelled with joy. "I'm honored."

With a nod Grandpa said, "I'd probably be dead if it weren't for you."

Ryan paused to take a fresh breath. "I don't know about that."

"I do know. I was the one living it. Sooner or later I would have died in that house, leaving Lisa alone to figure out what to do next." He shivered. "You saved me. You saved Lisa too. It was wrong of me to keep her stuck in that old house like that. She's thriving here. She's happy. When she laughs . . ." He shook his head with the awe of it.

"She's a wonderful girl."

He nodded again. "You couldn't save your Lisa, but you saved mine."

Ryan sucked in a breath, feeling the sting of tears. All he could do was nod.

They heard Lisa's voice coming down the trail.

As usual, God's timing was perfect.

**

They were driving the winding road from the trailhead back to the highway when Lisa yelled, "Stop!"

Bertha stopped the car.

"Up there," Lisa whispered. "That black thing back in the trees. Is that a—?"

"Moose!" Bertha said softly. "Yes! That's a moose."

The legs of the moose were four-feet tall. It was a male with a wide rack of antlers and a beard. It pulled on the leaves of an aspen, making the branches bow and quiver.

"Wow," she whispered. "Grandpa, that's a moose!"

"I know, girl. It's perfect." He glanced back at Ryan when he said it.

**

After lunch—and a nap—Bertha and Lisa sat at a picnic table with watercolor paints and paper. Bertha was painting an aspen grove and Lisa was trying to paint a picture of their cabin.

Ryan played a beanbag game of corn-hole with Grandpa. Allen was winning—bigtime.

"Apparently I have zero hand-eye coordination," Ryan said as his beanbag missed the board entirely.

"Practice, boy, practice." Grandpa hit another hole with a *plop* and a *whoosh.*

"I need practice painting too," Lisa said. She peered at Bertha's trees. "Your painting is better than mine."

"You'll get the hang of it." She inspected Lisa's paper. "You forgot the chimney."

"Oh!" Lisa dipped her brush in paint.

It was Grandpa's turn to throw, but he held the bag still and faced them. "I want to make an announcement."

The other three exchanged glances.

Grandpa must have noticed their worried looks. "Sheesh. Lose the frowny-faces. It's a good announcement."

"You scared me," Lisa said.

His face softened and he sat across from her at the picnic table. Ryan followed, sitting across from Bertha. "I wanted to announce that ever since coming here I've felt a lot better."

"Really, Grandpa?" Lisa's face glowed with relief. "I thought so, but . . . really?"

"I haven't been to a doctor to have them confirm anything, but from what I can *feel* . . . I *am* better."

She ran around the table and hugged him then went back to her place.

Grandpa extended a hand across the table toward Bertha. She took it. "You, dear lady, have something to do with that."

She blushed. "Oh my goodness. You can be a sweet old coot."

He looked at Ryan. "And you, boy . . . none of us would be sitting here in this amazing place, feeling these amazing things, if you hadn't wandered up our road."

"He was sent up our road, Grandpa," Lisa said. "God sent him."

"Yes, He did."

Ryan's chest was tight with emotion. "I'm so glad you're feeling better. And since it's confession time . . . I have to say I love you guys. Truly. I feel blessed to be here with all of you."

Grandpa's eyes grew misty, but the man looked down and recovered before tears fell. "Because of all this lovey-dovey stuff, I have a thought. Why don't we stay here permanently?"

Lisa's eyes lit up. "Like really live here? Go to school here?"

"That would be the plan."

Lisa nodded enthusiastically. "I say yes! Yes!"

Bertha grabbed Grandpa's hand and pulled him toward her, halfway. She gave him a kiss. "Nothing would make me happier. You three could move into the Pinecone. It has three bedrooms and—"

"That's not what I was thinking," Grandpa said.

She pulled her hand away. "What were you thinking?"

His cheeks reddened. "I was thinking I could move into the main cabin with you. As your husband. How would you like that?"

With a squeal Bertha scurried around the table, slid onto the bench beside him, and kissed him. And kissed him again while Lisa and Ryan cheered them on.

Chapter 51

Summer

"You, Lord, hear the desire of the afflicted;
you encourage them, and you listen to their cry."
Psalm 10: 17

Summer's stomach was in knots as she and Max sat in her car a half-block away from Sydney's, waiting to surprise her with a house fix-up.

"I've never seen someone give a steering wheel a massage before," he said.

She realized she'd been running her hands over the wheel, gripping it, holding on for dear life.

"Why are you so nervous?" he asked.

She forced her hands in her lap. "Last time Syd and I talked I yelled at her. I called her spoiled, self-absorbed, and helpless."

"Low blows. But you apologized."

"But she hasn't accepted. I left a message. I've texted and emailed but she doesn't respond."

"There's only so much you can do."

Summer didn't like the sounds of that. "God doesn't give up on us so I don't want to give up on Sydney."

"Summer the server strikes again."

She was trying.

He studied her a moment. "You're worried about something else too, aren't you?"

He was far too intuitive. "My aunties and grandma are meeting you for the first time."

"Which are you more nervous about?"

If she said "him" he'd question their relationship. If she said "Sydney" she'd be lying.

She had hesitated too long. "Me," he said. "You're most nervous about them meeting me?"

She sought his hand. "I know they'll love you and approve of you."

"But?"

"But I don't want their eager enthusiasm to ruin what we have." *What's just starting to blossom.*

He stroked her hair behind an ear. "How could their enthusiasm ruin anything?"

Let me count the ways. "They'll be pushy. They haven't even met you and they think we're getting married."

He laughed.

"Don't laugh. Mae will push for a summer wedding because she'll want to preside over a big outside shindig. Tessa will prefer a Christmas wedding because she likes things to be elegant and formal."

"And your grandma?"

Summer sighed. "She'll just want me to be happy."

"Me too." He took her hand and pulled her toward the center console for a kiss.

She felt tears threaten.

He sat back. "Why are you crying?"

She dug a McDonald's napkin out of the console and wiped her eyes. "Why is God doing this to us?"

"*This* being a good thing?"

"*This* being wonderful."

He kissed her again.

"I wasn't looking for a boyfriend," she said.

"We were both looking for connections. And got them."

The moment was broken when an unfamiliar car pulled up behind them.

It was Donna. They all got out and Summer introduced her to Max. She carried an open pan of brownies and an eight-pack of Dr. Pepper. "Fuel for everyone—and Sydney's favorites."

Just then Summer's family pulled up behind Donna's car.

"And here we go," Summer said.

Donna went to say hi to Tessa.

Max leaned toward Summer, confidentially. "If they ask, are we agreed on an outdoor, summer wedding? Maybe yellow would be a good color for the bridesmaids?"

She swatted his arm.

Mae drove and Grandma helped Tessa out of the car and onto the sidewalk. Donna gave Tessa a hug before greeting the others. It was nice they all knew each other.

When Summer and Max approached, the ladies' eyes zeroed in on him.

"Zounds," Mae said. "You're a looker."

"Behave yourself," Tessa said. Then she smiled. "Yet I agree with you. You're a handsome buck, young man. That you are."

Max wisely approached Tessa first. "You must be Mrs. Kraus."

"Oooh," Tessa said. "Look at the gentleman using my proper name." She peered up at him through thick glasses. "I can tell your daddy brought you up right."

"He'll be happy you approve."

"My turn." Mae extended her hand. "Mae Ames. We look forward to finding out *everything* about you. Are you from around here? What do you do? What—?"

Grandma intervened. "Hi, I'm Summer's grandma, Evelyn. I'm very glad to meet you. But what's your last name? I must have missed it."

"I never gave it, ma'am. It's Cumberson."

"Cumbersome?" Tessa asked.

He smiled. "Cumber*son*."

Mae raised a hand. "Is your father Billy Cumberson?"

"Do you know him?"

She turned to the other ladies. "Billy Bob's Steakhouse."

"Billy is your father?" Evelyn asked.

"He is."

"We love the garlic bread there," Tessa said. "We'll have to all go to dinner sometime."

"Unfortunately," Max said, "Billy Bob's closed about a year ago. My dad is doing handy-man work. But he called last week to tell me he's opening a new diner downtown. Grandma's Cookin'."

"Sounds like my kind of food," Mae said.

"And what do you do, Max?" Grandma asked.

"I'm an estimator for a contractor in Carson Creek."

"You're good with numbers," Tessa said with a nod, as though she'd checked off a box. "That's always an asset."

"Yes, it is, ma'am." Tessa wobbled and Max took her arm.

Tessa beamed. "Like I said. Such a gentleman."

Summer was pleased the first meeting had gone well.

Grandma added, "You make a very handsome couple."

"Very," Mae said.

"Two peas in a pod," Tessa said.

"That makes no sense, Tessie," Mae said. "Max and Summer are not the *same*, they *complement* each other. Like peas and carrots."

"Or peanut butter and jelly," Grandma added.

Max leaned toward Tessa, "I love peanut butter."

"Me too."

Mae looked past the group toward the row of houses. "Which one is Sydney's?"

"The one with the questionable shutters." Summer opened the trunk of her car. "Come get the supplies, but be quiet about it. This is a surprise." She grabbed a bag of drop-cloths and brushes, and let Max take the paint. "Donna, do you want to go first and tell her what's happening?"

"Absolutely not," she said. "Let's storm the porch, just like they do on those remodel shows on TV."

"I do not *storm,*" Tessa said.

They found a happy medium, as they all walked to Sydney's house and congregated at the bottom of the porch steps. Donna tiptoed to the door and took a deep breath. "You ready?" she whispered.

They all nodded. She knocked.

Sydney opened the door and stared out. "Mom? What's going on?"

"Surprise!" Summer said. "We've come to fix things and paint and . . . happy housewarming!"

Summer got worried when Sydney's forehead furrowed, but then she saw her eyes fill with tears. "I'm . . . this is really nice of you. But . . . Mom?"

Donna handed her the pan of brownies. "I should have fixed it up before I let you move in here. Better late than never. So say thank you, and let us get to work."

Summer realized Sydney hadn't met Max and hadn't seen Mae and Grandma in years. She made the introductions.

"Nice to see you again, girl," Tessa said, scanning the living room. "You have a hard back chair for me to sit on? Your couch would swallow me whole. I'm here to supervise." As Tessa got herself settled, she asked, "So. What needs to be done?"

Sydney looked to her mom.

"Paint," Donna said. "Let's start with paint."

Max and Mae began taping off the trim in the living room. Grandma spread drop-cloths on the floor. Summer started to patch the drywall. But as she took up the spackle and putty knife Sydney joined her.

"I can help."

"Do you want to spread the spackle or sand it when it dries?" Summer asked.

"I'll spackle." Sydney took the small tub and the knife. But then her head hung low. "I . . . I'm sorry I didn't respond to your apology."

Summer appreciated her words. "I meant it. I was hard on you. Are things okay between us, then?"

"They are. But . . . I didn't respond because all the stuff you said about me? It was true. I have been acting spoiled, self-absorbed, and ungrateful."

"I didn't say ungrateful," Summer said.

"What was it then?"

Summer hated to say it. "Helpless?"

Sydney smiled. "That too. Or I *was*. Yesterday I got a job as a receptionist."

"That's wonderful! Congratulations."

"It's thanks to you."

"Why me?"

"Because you pushed me to shut down my pity party. The thing is, I'm not sure how long I would have sat here in limbo if you hadn't yelled at me."

Summer chuckled. "God works in mysterious ways."

**

After spending the day working at Sydney's, Summer's back hurt. Her legs hurt. Her shoulders hurt. Yet it was a hurt steeped in satisfaction. The repairs and the paint turned

Sydney's house into a home. Spending time together was frosting on the cake. It was a Saturday they would never forget.

She and Max walked toward their apartments. "Thanks for helping," she told him.

"I wouldn't have missed it." He put an arm around her shoulders. "You did good, Summer. I can hear God shout out a hearty, 'Well done, good and faithful servant.'"

"You too."

"You want a back rub?"

"Yes, but no. I'm going to take Suzu out, then soak in a steaming tub."

"See you tomorrow then?"

"Yes, please." They kissed good night and parted.

While the tub was filling up, Summer checked her email. There was another message from Michelle.

There was always a message from Michelle. Today's verse was Hebrews 3:1: *"Therefore, holy brothers and sisters, who share in the heavenly calling, fix your thoughts on Jesus, whom we acknowledge as our apostle and high priest."*

A heavenly calling. That's what they'd experienced today by helping Sydney. Everyone had worked together doing God's work. Even Tessa, by just being there, encouraged them on.

Summer caught up with the email replies of the others. Ryan had reconnected with his parents and was staying in Colorado after ten years on the road. Michelle was helping a runaway find purpose and confidence. Claire and Billy were opening a restaurant. And Jered . . . even the skeptic Jered had posted, saying he'd had some God-moments.

She sat back and looked at the screen. *So have I.*

She sat upright. "So have I!"

She'd wanted connections? God had given her connections! Sydney, Donna, Mr. Horowitz, Andy, and especially Max. Plus, the four strangers who'd been led to meet each other by a God who had a plan for them.

"Wow," Summer whispered. "Wow, God. Just wow."

She put her hands on the keyboard and shared her joy with her new brothers and sisters in Christ.

Chapter 52

Claire

"My chosen ones will long enjoy
the work of their hands.
They will not labor in vain."
Isaiah 65: 22-23

Grandma's Cookin' was ready. The menus had been carefully crafted with reasonable prices for any budget. The staff had been prayerfully hired. For the front staff Claire had won out, getting them pink uniforms with black piping, though she'd compromised by settling for shirts and black pants instead of dresses. The repairs and updates looked fresh and bright with vintage photos of happy diners. The sign on the window had been repainted with their new tagline added across the bottom in a grandma-cursive: *Everybody loves grandma-cooking!* And a bouquet of pink roses crowned the pay counter—a gift from Michelle. Today was it: opening day.

The mosaic that had started the whole thing, hung in a place of honor, its aqua and pink colors finally making sense.

There was a line outside, waiting for the doors to open.

Billy polished the top of the counter for the umpteenth time.

Claire stopped his busyness with a hand. "It will be wonderful. You know it will."

He sighed deeply. "I know it will." He grasped her hand. "Thank you for everything, dear woman." He kissed her cheek. Then he called out to the staff. "If you would gather round a minute, please?"

Three waitresses, two cooks, and two kitchen helpers came close. Billy held out his hands and they formed a circle. He bowed his head. "God? You did this. Please help us do our best and bless all who come through the doors. Amen."

"Amen."

"Ready?" he asked the staff.

"Ready!"

Billy unlocked the door, stepping outside with Claire. He hugged the first three people in line: Max, Summer, and Michelle. "Thanks so much for coming."

"How could we miss it?"

Claire hugged them. After mere moments, someone in line shouted playfully, "Hug later! We're hungry!"

Billy raised his hands. "Thank you all for coming today. It means a lot to me and Claire, and everyone who has worked so hard to bring Grandma's back to Kansas City." There was applause and some hoots of approval. "I present to you the grandma-cooking we all love. Welcome!"

The tables were quickly filled, with more people waiting outside. The exterior benches Claire had suggested for customers were much needed.

Billy and Claire served water all around and chatted with the customers. They both visited one special guest—the elderly woman from the shelter who'd given them the tag line. "Glad you could make it, Mabel."

"Me too, Billy. I can't wait to try the sausage and grits casserole. Never had that one."

They helped serve drinks, and in fast order, the food started coming out.

Billy and Claire tried to greet everyone personally. They eventually stopped at a table where an elderly woman with very thick glasses sat with a younger woman. "Good morning," Billy said. "Welcome to Grandma's."

The older woman studied him. "You don't look like I thought you would."

"Excuse me?"

The younger woman explained. "This is the original Grandma. *My* grandma."

Claire gasped. "I have a picture of your family—it's still hanging up, right where you left it."

The women looked where Claire pointed. "Meant to take that with me," Grandma said. "Hmm. Someone brought you pink roses. That's what I got that day too."

Claire wasn't surprised. "You said that Billy doesn't look like you thought he would?"

Grandma patted the chair next to her. "You got a minute 'cause I got a story you need to hear."

Billy and Claire looked around the café. Everyone had their food. The waitresses were making the rounds of refills. They *had* the time.

As soon as they were seated, Billy said, "I used to come here a lot. You probably don't remember me, but—"

"Oh, I remember you. You always ordered fried chicken. You were a waiter, right? You wanted to start your own restaurant?"

"You remember that?"

"That's the thing. When the developer bought up the block six years ago it broke me. I didn't feel up to starting over. My health wasn't that great either. That's when I thought of you. Maybe you'd like to take this place to another location and keep it going for me. But then you stopped coming in."

"I got busy opening a steakhouse."

"Steakhouse. Mmm. Fancy. I wanted to get a hold of you, but I didn't know your last name."

"If only I had told you sooner. It's Cumberson."

She held out her hand. "Nice to meet you, Billy Cumberson."

"And what's your name?" he asked.

"Bethesda Reynolds."

It suited her. Down home and unique. Claire introduced herself, as did Bethesda's granddaughter.

"Truth be, I gave up on you—you in particular anyway. I just prayed that God would send somebody to save this place, especially when the corporate-deal fell apart last October and it wasn't going to be torn down."

October?

Billy blinked more than once. "I closed up the steakhouse in September."

Bethesda pat his hand. "There you go. You were free, the café was free. And here we are. Praise the Lord."

Absolutely.

She took his hand and squeezed it. "God knew what He was doing."

Claire flashed a smile she couldn't have held in if she'd tried. "He certainly did."

"Funny how I was praying for someone to come take it over, never knowing it would be you. I'm glad it was you."

"Me too."

Bethesda looked toward the main wall—at the mosaic that hung above her table. "That's different."

"Claire made it," Billy said.

"Made it? A lot of mighty tiny pieces there. You've got talent, Miss Claire." She studied it a minute. "You can just see Jesus pouring out of that piece."

"You can?"

"Sure. The roses of purity , the dove of the Holy Spirit, and the arrows pointing outward, so we spread His good news."

Billy and Claire laughed. "You pegged it. "

"Of course I did." She leaned forward confidentially. "God answered my prayers and brought us together, Mr. Billy Cumberson. And He *will* bless what you're doing."

Bless the Lord!

Chapter 53

Michelle

"Guard my life, for I am faithful to you;
save your servant who trusts in you.
You are my God; have mercy on me, Lord,
for I call to you all day long.
Bring joy to your servant, Lord,
for I put my trust in you."
Psalm 86: 2-4

It was one of those moments—those rare moments—when Michelle sat in the dining room at the shelter by herself, looking over the room as if she was invisible. She closed her eyes and let the murmur of conversation, dishes, doors, and chairs wrap around her.

Suddenly, she felt very alone. Very unneeded. She recognized a wave of self-pity coming on and knew what she had to do to stop it.

She got her purse then made her way to the front door, nodding and chatting with people along the way. Then she went outside and turned left. Within two blocks she reached her destination. A park.

It wasn't a big park—though it probably *had* been at one time before buildings and parking lots encroached. It consisted of three benches scattered among trees and flowers like a tiny urban oasis.

Michelle sat on a bench. No one else was around. She looked up at the lush branches and leaves overhead and the patches of blue that danced between them. To combat loneliness and self-pity, Michelle bowed her head and mentally recited one of her favorites: *"Your love, Lord, reaches to the heavens, your faithfulness to the skies. Your righteousness is like the highest mountains, your justice like the great deep. You, Lord, preserve both people and animals. How priceless is your unfailing love, O God! People take refuge in the shadow of your wings."*

She opened her eyes and saw a dove perched at the other end of the bench. "Sorry I don't have anything to give you."

But you do.

Michelle blinked. She looked at the dove again. Ahh. "Yes, Lord. I see You. I see *You." You say I have something to give You. What? Show me what it is. The others . . .*

She thought of her friends. Since God had called the mosaic-people together Claire had found renewed faith and had helped bring Billy to a place of forgiveness and faith. Summer had found purpose by helping an old friend and had found a godly man to share time with. Ryan was reunited with his parents and was starting a new life in Colorado. And Jered had opened himself up to God. She was pleased her daily verses had found good soil. Though her emails had started out falling on rocks and shallow ground God's persistence was bearing fruit.

You are bearing fruit, Michelle. You are the seed on good soil.

She shivered. "I try to be," she said softly.

An old man came into the park and began digging through the trash receptacles, muttering to himself. "Morning," she said.

He glanced up, then held a discarded sack from Starbucks against his chest. "I ain't doin' nothin'."

"If you want a tasty hot meal walk two blocks north. The Mercy Shelter will be happy to serve you. You can sleep there too, and wash up."

He eyed her warily, "Don't want no God-stuff."

"Serving food and helping *is* God-stuff."

He smiled. "You's tricky."

Tricky for the Lord. "Give it a try. Remember, we're always there for you."

He tossed the bag in the trash. "Don't mind if I do." He gave her a one-finger salute and shuffled off. She heard him whisper something, barely discernible.

"What did you say?" she asked.

He looked over his shoulder and smiled, "Remember, I am always there for *you*."

Michelle watched him cross the street and disappear around a building. She smiled with full contentment. "Yes, Lord. I hear You."

**

Michelle returned to the shelter, feeling rejuvenated. There was no reason to feel lonely or down. Many lives were bearing good fruit.

She looked for the homeless man from the park in the dining room, but didn't see him. She'd keep a look out. She waved at Jonette who was in her corner, crocheting. Maybe the man would like a beanie.

Then she noticed a forty-ish couple come in the front door. They were well-dressed. They didn't look homeless. They scanned the room as though searching for—

"Daddy!"

Jonette ran across the room into the man's arms. They cried and laughed at the same time.

Jonette's parents? *God be praised!*

Jonette led the couple over to Michelle. "Daddy, Bet, this is Michelle, the lady who saved me. She's my friend."

Michelle could think of no better title. "You have a lovely daughter—a talented one too."

Jonette's father put his arm around his daughter. "We know that and we've missed her terribly. You'd never believe the relief we felt with Jonny called a week ago."

"A week ago?"

Jonette nodded. "I didn't want them to worry."

"Why didn't you go home?" Michelle asked.

"Because there's work to do here."

"That's very kind of you," Michelle said. "But you don't have to stay here anymore. You can go home."

Her father nodded. "We want you home, sweetie. We need you home."

"We do," Bet said. "We're a family. We'll work everything out. I promise." She looked at her husband. "Your father—we both—miss your cooking."

Jonette looked from one to the other. Then she turned to Michelle. "If I go live at home can I still crochet beanies for people?"

"Of course you can,"

"Beanies?" her father asked.

Jonette took him by the hand and led them to her corner.

For a moment Michelle was left alone again. But unlike the hopeless feelings she'd suffered earlier, she found her heart teeming with joy. She was not alone. Never alone.

She remembered the words God had sent her in the park. *I am always there for you.* She drew in a cleansing breath, letting His assurance fill her up to overflowing.

Chapter 54

Ryan

"Give, and it will be given to you.
A good measure, pressed down, shaken together
and running over, will be poured into your lap.
For with the measure you use,
it will be measured to you."
Luke 6: 38

Bertha carried a pink-frosted cake to the table, the thirteen candles blazing. "Happy birthday to you . . ."

They all sang together and finished the song.

"Make a wish!" Ryan said.

Lisa's youthful face glowed in the candlelight as she looked at each one of them in turn. "I wish we could be like this forever."

"You're not supposed to say it out loud," Ryan's mom said.

"It's okay," Grandpa said. "We all agree with you."

She blew out the candles and Bertha cut the cake while Mom scooped out strawberry ice cream.

"I can't believe you're a teenager." Grandpa looked wistful.

Lisa must have noticed the look too. "I'm still your 'girl.' I'll always be your girl."

"Stop it. Don't make an old man cry." He nodded to Ryan. "Get that thing for me, will you?"

Ryan knew about the special gift and retrieved it from a shelf where he'd seen Grandpa hide it.

Grandpa held the present a moment. "Since you are officially a teenager, I thought it was time to give you a special gift." He handed her a box that was wrapped in paper with pink roses on it.

Lisa delayed opening it, basking in the special moment. "Thank you, Grandpa."

"You don't even know what it is."

"It doesn't matter. I know I'll love it."

She was such a good girl.

She untied the white ribbon and carefully peeled back the paper. Inside was a vintage-looking, gold velvet jewelry box. She opened the lid and gasped. "Pearls!"

"Those are your great-grandma's pearls that she got as a wedding present when she became a Pearl. My mother wore them at her wedding, and I was going to give them to your mother for her wedding, but . . ." He let his words trail off. "I decided I didn't want to wait for yours. I want to give them to you now, at another milestone. " Grandpa pushed away from the table. "Let me help you put them on."

Lisa stood and held up her hair so he could fasten them. She turned around to face him, her fingers touching the white gems. "Wow, Grandpa. I mean . . . thank you."

He hugged her. "You deserve them, girl. You have always been my precious pearl."

There wasn't a dry eye in the house.

**

After the cake and ice cream had been eaten and the dishes cleared, Bertha, Ryan, and his parents remained at the table to go over resort business. Grandpa and Lisa sat near the fireplace with the guitar. Lisa was a quick learner.

"Now then," Bertha said, after bringing Grandpa a mug of coffee. "What's the plan?"

Mom had brought her laptop and moved to a seat beside Bertha so she could show off the new website. On the home page was a wide-angle picture of the cabins from the drive, showing the woods up the road and the mountain range bumping against a bright blue sky.

"It's lovely," Bertha said. "You really captured it."

Dad agreed. "That's what I told her. Who wouldn't want to come to a place like that?"

Mom showed off the other pages that detailed each cabin's offerings and price. Then there was a picture of the outside of the rec hall that hadn't been used in decades.

"It still needs a lot of work inside," Bertha said.

"That's what I'll do this winter," Ryan said. "By next season it will be ready for square dances, movie nights, shuffleboard, games, and potluck dinners."

Bertha pressed a hand against her chest, clearly in awe. She looked at Ryan's parents. "I don't know how I'll ever thank you for this website, and also the money you're investing in the place. *And* your ideas."

Mom put an arm around her. "It's our pleasure because this place gave *us* pleasure when we stayed here."

Bertha kept clicking on all the pages. Then she stopped. "Are you sure people will be okay with not having TVs in their cabins? I feel kind of bad because I have a TV in here but nobody else does."

"We come in here when we want to watch something," Ryan said. "I haven't had a TV for ten years, so I'm not missing it."

"Plus we're going to have wi-fi in the rec hall, right?" Dad asked. "And a landline there, since cell phones still won't work?"

"That was the compromise," Ryan said. "It will give people a place to check their email and make calls, but keep their cabins tech-free."

"I like that idea a lot," Mom said. "If the cabins had access, everyone would be on their phones the whole time. This way families can regulate screen time, and have evenings to spend as a family."

"The old-fashioned way," Bertha said.

It was time for Ryan to share his good news. "I know there's work to do around here this fall and winter, but I also wanted to tell you that the Wilson's down the road have hired me to do some fixup at their cabin."

"A job where you'll actually be paid!" Bertha said. Her face clouded. "I wish I could pay you."

"Stop it. You know I'm more than thrilled with the stake in the Honeycomb you gave me. I mean twenty-five percent. That's amazing."

"We're thrilled with our stake too. It's quite generous indeed," Dad said.

“It’s the least I can do,” Bertha said. “Ryan, you supply the manpower, and Roy and Kathy, you supply the funding . . .” She put a hand to her chest. “Without all of you coming into my life, the Honeycomb would have crumbled and closed. I feel very blessed.”

Suddenly, Grandpa and Lisa started singing. “‘Seek and ye shall find, knock, and the door shall be opened. Ask and it shall be given . . .’”

And the love come a ‘tumblin’ down.

Chapter 55

Jered

"Praise the Lord.
Praise God in his sanctuary;
praise him in his mighty heavens.
Praise him for his acts of power;
praise him for his surpassing greatness.
Psalm 150: 1-2

Jered looked over the food in the pantry. Tonight they were having Boxer and Polly over—and the kids. Ivy had made all sorts of appetizers, plus his personal favorite: chocolate drop cookies. He found two jars of olives and brought them out to her. "How about these? This one's stuffed with jalapenos."

She made a face. "The plain ones maybe. Get out that container of caramel dip. I'll slice some apples. The kids will love that."

Together they arranged crackers, summer sausage, and cheese on a tray. Ivy stirred cocktail weenies in one crock pot and hot cheese dip in another.

"You've made enough for a crowd," he said.

"Always best to have too much rather than too little." She washed her hands.

"I thought it would be harder than this," he said.

"Cooking?"

"Having people over."

She turned off the water. "They're friends, Jer. Friends make everything easy. We haven't entertained in ages. I like it."

Jered snuck a cracker off the tray "I do too."

Out of the blue Ivy walked toward him and slid her arms around his waist. She leaned her head against his chest. "I love you, Jered."

He was surprised by the sudden affection but kissed the top of her head. "I love you too." He gently pushed her back. "Save the thought. They're going to be here any minute."

She shook her head. And grinned. "I can't save the thought a moment longer. I was going to wait until tomorrow when the party was over and we could relax, but I just can't."

"Can't what?"

She took his hand and placed it on her belly. "Can't wait to tell you our happy news." The glow of her expression said it all.

He felt his mouth gape open. "Ive. You're not."

She nodded happily. "I am."

Jered stared at his hand, pressed against her stomach. He was overcome with emotion and fell to his knees. He kissed her belly. She drew him to standing and they fell into an embrace.

"I can't believe it. I . . . we're . . ."

"I know," she said.

He pulled back. "When?"

"April first."

He did a double take. "April Fool's Day? You're not fooling me, are you?"

She laughed and took his face in her hands. "I'm not. I promise."

He lifted her off the ground and spun her around before realizing it might not be good for the baby. He set her down gently. "Sorry. Are you okay?"

She laughed again. "I'm fine. We're both fine. We're all fine." She got serious. "I wasn't sure you'd be happy. You weren't gung ho about the idea."

He hadn't been. And his reaction now surprised him. "I'm very gung ho about it now." He touched her cheek. "I love you. Both of you."

The doorbell rang. Jered rushed to the door and swung it wide. "We're having a baby!"

Boxer and Polly gasped, then hugged them both. "Congratulations!"

The two kids looked up at the adults warily. Polly explained, "Jered and Ivy are going to have a baby."

Joshua cocked his head. "Is it a boy or a girl?"

"We don't know yet," Ivy said.

Boxer lifted their little girl into his arms. "Rachel, this is Ivy and Jered."

She was adorable with pale blond hair and pudgy cheeks.

"Hi, sweetie," Ivy said.

"Hi." She looked at Jered.

He wasn't sure what to do with a two-year-old so he waved, then felt silly for doing it.

Polly retrieved a cake carrier she'd set on the porch. "Cherry dump cake."

It was added to the other goodies.

"Quite the place you have," Boxer said as he walked into the grand foyer. "Makes our place look like a—"

"Lovely home," Ivy said, coming back from the kitchen. She took out some coloring and sticker books she'd bought. "Joshua, would you and Rachel like to color?"

"Yeah!"

She put the supplies on the coffee table and the kids dove in. Jered got everyone some iced tea and the kids had some 'Pacific Cooler' juice boxes—whatever flavor that was.

"You sure you don't want them to drink those in the kitchen?" Polly asked.

"Out here is fine." She put a hand to her belly. "I think it's time we broke in some of our furnishings."

It was time for a lot of things to be broken in.

**

After grazing on the food until everyone was full, Polly suggested putting a movie on for the kids so the adults could play cards. Joshua and Rachel snuggled amid the couch pillows to watch *Cinderella.* Thank goodness for Disney.

The friends sat around the dining table and Boxer shuffled the Phase 10 cards. "We haven't played this in ages but watch out for Polly. She's good."

"And watch out for *me,*" Ivy said. "I'm ruthless."

They began playing the game with card-talk intermixing with conversation. Polly and Ivy talked about working together on quilts. "The more hands the better," Polly said. Jered could tell Ivy was full to overflowing with joy.

Every once in a while he would remember the biggest joy of all: *We're having a baby!* Although he'd made Ivy postpone it far longer than she wanted, he was over the moon with the news. Him, a father? An astounding concept.

The ease between the four adults played out like their bond had always been there, just waiting to be tapped into. Jered purposely hadn't mentioned his music idea to Boxer. He'd spent the past three weeks arranging things with his agent and record producer. He'd had to do a bit of cajoling, but they'd agreed. A duet album had been approved.

Jered also purposely hadn't mentioned the idea until this point in the evening. They'd only seen each other the one night at Boxer's. Would they really get along well? Did their personalities mesh and meld enough to collaborate?

The answer was yes.

With a nod to Ivy—and from her—he broached the subject. "I was thinking . . ."

"Scary thing, thinking," Boxer said—which oddly affirmed their collaboration would work.

"How would you like to work together on a duet album?"

Boxer froze. He lost his handhold on his cards, spilling them on the table. "Are you serious?"

"Very. We sounded good together at the Red Rim."

"I thought so too."

"We can collaborate on the song choices and the arrangements. Everything. It's a way for me to pay you back for all you did for me."

Boxer looked at his wife. They took hands across the table. "I can't believe this. I mean, it's mind-boggling, I mean it's . . ."

"He means yes," Polly said with a laugh.

There were hugs and laughter all around and the kids joined in, celebrating with the rest of them.

Oh bless the Lord my soul.

Epilogue

Claire

One Year Later

"I keep asking that the God of our
Lord Jesus Christ, the glorious Father,
may give you the Spirit of wisdom and revelation,
so that you may know him better.
I pray that the eyes of your heart
may be enlightened in order that you may know
the hope to which he has called you,
the riches of his glorious inheritance in his holy people,
and his incomparably great power for us who believe."
Ephesians 1: 17-19

For the first time in her life, Claire was star-struck.

"You seem nervous," Billy said as they approached the concert venue. "It's just Jered and Boxer. They've been at our house. You knew Jered as a kid. I remember you saying you weren't that impressed with him."

"*That* makes me impressed." She pointed up at the marquee:

One night only! July 24 - 8 pm
The Mercy Shelter Charity Concert
Featuring
THE BOXER BOYS
Jered Manson & Kyle Boxer!

"That *is* impressive," Billy said. "Especially since all this was his idea."

Suddenly, Michelle rushed through the main doors to greet them. "Come on! Come on! The whole group's here. We have special seats."

She led them through the outside crowd, through the lobby, and down a side aisle. There, in the front row were their dear friends.

Summer and Max popped out of their seats. "Hey, Dad. Hey Claire. How was the honeymoon?" Max asked.

Summer swatted him on the arm. "Give them a minute to breathe." But she grinned. "How was Hawaii?"

Utterly perfect. Claire held out her arm as Exhibit A. "I am tan for the first time in fifty years."

"Our trip was paradise—in all ways," Billy said with a smile in Claire's direction.

She felt herself redden. But he was right.

"Sorry we eloped," Billy said. "But when you get to be our age . . ."

"Oh, pooh," Michelle said. "I'm older than both of you."

"Is Ryan here yet?" Claire asked.

Summer looked around the auditorium. "He *is* here. Somewhere." She smiled. "He has a surprise."

"Did he bring Lisa along? Or his parents? Or—"

"You'll see."

Claire searched the crowd, then saw him coming down the center aisle waving at her. He was holding the hand of a pretty woman with curly brown hair that was as tousled as his.

"A girl?" Claire whispered.

"Seems so," Billy said.

Ryan joined them and they exchanged hugs. Then he made the introductions. "Lana, this is Claire and Billy Cumberson. Claire and Billy, this is my fiancée, Lana Lawson."

"Fiancée?" Claire asked.

They grinned and looked at each other adoringly.

"Nice to meet you, Lana," Billy said.

Claire made a time-out T with her hands. "When did this happen? We all video chat every month and you never once mentioned Lana to any of us."

Lana beamed. "When we found out about the concert coming up, we decided to make it a surprise. I was there in the room for most of the chats so I feel like I know all of you."

Michelle slipped her arm through Ryan's and added some more newly-acquired information. "Lana told me she works in the library with Ryan's mom."

"Speaking of . . ." Claire said. "Did your parents get to come? And Lisa?"

"They didn't," he said. "The Honeycomb is crazy busy this summer so they stayed behind with Allen and Bertha. Lisa is leading the Friday night sing-alongs and takes her job very seriously."

"Jonette and her parents are here," Michelle said. "And quite a few people from the shelter came."

"That's wonderful." Claire felt like a proud mama, gathering her fold. "Have any of you talked to Jered and Boxer?"

"They came out for a minute when we first got here but were busy with a sound check. Ivy and Polly will sit with us." Michelle pointed toward the side aisle. "There they are." She squatted down like a surrogate grandma and let Rachel and Joshua run to her. Polly followed with six-month old Kylie in a pack on her back. Claire stroked the baby's cheek. "She has more teeth!"

"Which means she's eating everything and anything," Polly said.

Next came Ivy who carried a huge baby car seat over her arm. Claire rushed to see little Isaiah. He had his mother's copper hair and hazel eyes. "May I?" she asked Ivy. "We've been gone two weeks and I simply must get my hands on him."

Billy laughed. "Hi to you too, Ivy. Polly."

Polly flipped a hand. "We moms are used to it. We're loved for our kids."

Claire took Isaiah in her arms, touching his chin. Her heart melted when he smiled up at her.

Someone motioned to Michelle that it was time to begin. "Sit everyone," she said. "This is it."

Everyone sat in the first two rows and Claire reluctantly relinquished the baby to his mom.

Michelle went onstage and stood at a center microphone. "Hello, everyone!"

Claire looked around. The audience was full to capacity. Jered should be so proud.

Michelle continued. "I have a two-fold honor this evening Firstly, I am honored to represent the Mercy Shelter. We are in our sixtieth year in downtown Kansas City, offering safe shelter, good food, and godly encouragement to those in need. We thank all of you for coming this evening to support our work. And secondly . . . " She grinned and looked to the side of the stage. "We want to thank two very special men for giving their time and talents to make this evening possible. I present to you, the Boxer Boys!"

Jered and Boxer came onstage carrying guitars. There was no band. No huge production stage like Jered was used to. Just two men and their music.

The audience cheered and clapped. The musicians waved and nodded, then Boxer pointed to the mike "Say something, Jer."

Jered stepped to the microphone, slinging his guitar onto his back. "I may be a performer, but I warn you I'm not much of a talker."

"We love you Jered!" someone yelled from the back.

He seemed to blush. "We love you too," he said. He looked at Boxer. "This guy and I have known each other for ten years. We started out singing in bars, trying to make a living, trying to catch a break. But the biggest break I ever got was meeting up with him last year, for that's when he helped me rediscover the music I love. Thanks, man."

Boxer gave him a wink and a thumbs-up.

Jered took a fresh breath. "As you hopefully know, the two of us—the Boxer Boys—have just released our new album 'Epiphany'." He smiled. "The proceeds for all copies sold tonight will be donated to the shelter. So buy a ton of 'em!"

There was applause.

"I know you want to get to the music, but I would be remiss if I didn't give thanks to some very special people." He pointed to the friends in the front row. "A year ago we were all strangers. But then God brought us together to encourage each other, to love each other as we share our faith wherever we go." He raised his arms and drew in a deep breath. "I pray that the eyes of your heart may be enlightened as you come to know God's special plans for your lives." He lowered his arms and scanned the audience. "Do I hear an amen?"

"Amen!"

"Now let's sing!"

The next ninety minutes filled Claire's soul. It was astounding to see Jered—the man who had mocked his calling and fought it—come to life, sharing his heartfelt music with the world.

She looked down the row and watched Ryan and his fiancée swaying and singing to the songs. Ryan, the wanderer, the loner, who now had deep roots with family, old and new.

And Summer . . . the shy girl with no confidence and three jobs, now ran a community center for the elderly in Carson Creek. Summer, who was soon to be engaged to Claire's new son-in-law. If Max didn't propose soon, he'd get an earful.

Michelle sat beside Claire, proudly grinning at the fruits of her hard work. Michelle, the woman of steadfast, constant faith, who lived a life of sacrifice and unconditional love. Claire was blessed to call her friend.

Billy squeezed her hand. Billy, who'd brought her love, who challenged her, who made her laugh, and who was the best partner she'd *never* dreamt of.

He leaned toward her. "You having fun?"

She laughed with pure and utter joy. "I'm having the time of my life."

THE END

**

"Surely I am with you always,
to the very end of the age."
Matthew 28: 20

Letter to the Reader

Dear Readers:

Up until *Eyes of Our Heart* I had not written a contemporary novel since 2007—instead, focusing on writing historical fiction. Why the change now? Over the years many readers would write and ask what happened to so-and-so in one of my contemporary books. In 2019 I got the idea of following some of those characters as they felt God calling them to be at His beck and call.

I resurrected some of my old characters in the place they might be 15 years later. I revisited some of my books and decided to invite these old friends to join me: Claire and Michelle from *A Steadfast Surrender,* Jered from *A Steadfast Surrender* and *The Ultimatum,* Summer from the Sister Circle series, and Ryan from the Mustard Seed series and *Crossroads.* I had my characters. But . . . what should I do with them?

Not having a plan has never stopped me from starting a book. There are outliners and "pantsers" (those who write from the seat of their pants). Obviously, I am the latter. And so, I prayed for insight and inspiration and began . . .

With an antique pin.

I saw an old mosaic pin online and loved the look of it: doves and roses. Claire just happened to be a mosaic artist. What if she replicated the pin's design in a wall mosaic that somehow brought the characters together?

So that's what I did (Claire did). As Ryan, Michelle, Summer, and Jered felt God's call, I experienced what they experienced. As they looked for where He was working and joined Him, so did I. Truly, I didn't know what was going to happen. There was no neatly-crafted plan. Not even an ending to work toward. Nothing. I just sat at my computer every morning, opened up a chapter, prayed "Show me, Lord," and learned what would happen as the characters learned what would happen. As they discovered God in their lives, so did I. I know it sounds bizarre (if not slightly impossible) but that's the way this book came to be. And when I tried to mold it to my usual word length (<100,000 words) my editor (my greatly talented daughter, Laurel) chastised me and said, "I want *more.* Don't worry about the length. Write the book you're supposed to write." Which is why this book is 110,000 words. I hope they are good words.

Eyes of Our Heart is all about change: changing our lives by turning our focus away from ourselves toward God, who then leads us into God-sent interactions with others, which leads to a God-inspired change in *them*. And so on. The old "each one reach one" philosophy.

I realize you might read various portions of the book and say, "That kind of God-stuff doesn't happen to me." To which I reply, "Are you sure?" Many of the God-moments in this book *did* happen to me or to those I know. The trick is to open your eyes to look for Him. Though honestly, sometimes we only see His hand after-the-fact. We think, "If *this* hadn't happened, then *that* wouldn't have happened . . ." We see God's set-up for His will to be accomplished. It's the coolest thing. Watch for it!

Here are a few real-life moments I put in the book:

- When Ivy helps the old woman in the grocery store by giving her a cart, and then the woman in line... those incidents happened to me. The women's thankful responses warmed me all day.
- The table grace Ryan says: "We thank you, Lord, for happy hearts, for rain and sunny weather. We thank you, Lord, for this our food, and that we are together." That is the grace my family said together when I grew up, the one we taught our kids.
- Ryan and Lisa washing dishes and going over state capitals. My mom and I used to do that. And she'd quiz me on spelling.
- "We're leaving a house but taking the *home* with us" was something my husband said when we sold a house. It helped the bittersweet pain of it.
- Ryan feeling a nudge to tell a woman sitting in a café she's pretty. That happened to me at a McDonald's in St. Joseph, Missouri, just this year. I thought the nudge was odd, finished eating, went to the restroom to give myself time to

pray on it, and when I came out I found myself walking toward her as the two men in her group were distracted, chatting with an employee. I leaned down and whispered, "You are one of the prettiest women I've ever seen." She looked up at me and beamed. "Thank you." I'm so glad I did it. Only God knows if that woman needed to hear something nice at that moment in her life. I hope so. I hope she passed it on.

- When Lisa gave $7 to a woman in need and then found that exact amount in a pocket? That happened to our son, Carson, when he was on a mission trip in middle school. They went to St. Louis. He saw a man with a "Need money for food" sign and gave all the money he had. $7. The next day they went to Six Flags to swim and in the pocket of his swimsuit he found $7. Pretty cool, huh?
- Ryan and his parents work on the Columbine cabin. That's the name of the cabin where my parents and I stayed in 1968 in Meeker Park (just four miles from Allenspark—which both are real places.) We ended up buying a cabin nearby and still own it after all these years. Four generations have enjoyed it with more to come.
- Ryan's dad telling a friend, "You need Jesus!" I am embarrassed to admit I said that to someone in the heat of the moment. Not a good way to get a naysayer to come over to His side.
- When Summer sees the moose on the trail to Copeland Falls . . . that happened to my husband and I in 2019. They are huge animals with legs that are four-foot high. It was amazing.
- In Chapter 27 Summer has the day off from the flower shop. I had no idea what I was going to have her do in the first scene. And then a Kenny Loggins' song came to mind. Three words kept singing over and over in my head as I grabbed another cup of coffee: *This is it.* So that's how Summer came to hear that same song and be moved to action by it. Just as I was moved to action by it. I love how God works.
- Unfortunately, Summer's "blind man" story is my story. Read my blog entry: "Missing the Chance."

- When Andy, the delivery boy at the floral shop, asked Summer what "Repent and be baptized" mean, I found myself a bit stumped. So I asked some of my writer friends. The answers she gives are from them. So thank you, James Scott Bell, Robin Lee Hatcher, Stephanie Whitson, Francine Rivers, Angela Hunt, Hannah Alexander, Karen Ball, Gayle Roper, and Deborah Raney. What a godly group! The quotation "Repentance is your decision. Baptism is your pledge" is Jim Bell's and is a keeper. And *I* thought of this: Baptism isn't necessary to *be* saved, but is a response to *being* saved. So thanks to me too. 😊
- Michelle's verse emails that she created with pretty images are something I started to post on Facebook on March 20, 2020 at the beginning of the Covid-19 pandemic. Through those verse-images God's word has reached over 40 countries from Brazil to Zambia to Sweden to Bangladesh. It's encouraging to hear from so many Christ-loving people around the world! I hope to continue offering these verses indefinitely. I compiled the first 100 verses into a full-color *100 Verses of Encouragement* book and will do the same with the next 100, and the next…

My prayer for all of you is to accept your own calling from the Lord, for He is the eyes of our heart. Make it your mission to be at God's beck and call. Your life, and the lives of those around you, will never be the same.

Nancy Moser

www.nancymoser.com

"Jesus looked at them and said,
'With man this is impossible,
but with God all things are possible.'"
Matthew 19: 26

Verses

All verses NIV unless noted
Note: (P) = Paraphrased

Chapter 1:	Listening to God	John 8: 46
Chapter 2:	God vs. False Gods	1 Samuel 5: 1-3
Chapter 3:	Following Jesus	Matthew 4: 19
	Shining your light	Matthew 5: 15 (P)
	Great Commission	Matthew 28: 19-20
Chapter 4:	Gathering	Matthew 18: 19-20
	Give up everything	Luke 18: 22
	Giving cheerfully	2 Corinthians 9: 7
	Trust	Proverbs 3: 5-6
	God speaking	John 10: 27
	Living God's will	Psalm 143: 10
	Delighting in God	Psalm 37: 4
	God speaks	Job 33: 14
	Listening	Prov 8: 33-34
	Gifts	Romans 12: 4-8
	Great Commission	Matthew 28: 19-20
	Being Open	Ephesians 1: 18
	Answered prayers	Jeremiah 33: 3
	Standing firm	1 Corinthians 15: 58
	Direction	Psalm 32: 8
	Asking	John 14: 13
	Seek and find	Matthew 7: 7
Chapter 5:	God's Ways	2 Samuel 22: 31
	Human planning	Proverbs 16: 9
	Motives and Plans	Proverbs 16: 2-3
	Plans and Purpose	Proverbs 19: 21
Chapter 6:	Thinking about God	Psalm 119: 148
	Two or more	Matthew 18: 19-20
	Attributes of God	Psalm 36: 5-7
	Sharing God	I Peter 3: 15
	Hiding from God	Hebrews 4: 13
Chapter 7:	Serving others	1 Peter 4: 10
Chapter 8:	Arrogance	1 Timothy 6: 17
Chapter 9:	Repentance	Luke 5: 32
	Purpose	Psalm 138: 8 (ESV- P)
Chapter 10:	Helping	Acts 20: 35

	Rejoicing	Psalm 118: 24 (ESV)
Chapter 11:	Hunger	Proverbs 16: 26
Chapter 12:	Listening	Psalm 49: 1-3
	God's power	Mark 10: 27
Chapter 13:	Temptation	1 Corinthians 10: 13
	Testing God	Matthew 4: 7
Chapter 14:	God watching us	Psalm 121: 3-4
	Trials	James 1: 2-4
Chapter 15:	Humbling ourselves	1 Peter 5: 6-7
	God can do it	Mark 10: 27
Chapter 16:	Giving	Deuteronomy 15: 10
	Responsibility	Luke 12: 48
	Giving	2 Corinthians 9: 7
Chapter 17:	Wisdom	James 1: 5
Chapter 18:	Direction	Psalm 143: 8
Chapter 19:	Helping others	3 John 5-6
Chapter 20:	Contentment	1 Corinthians 7: 17
	Married or single	1 Corinthians 7 (chapter)
Chapter 21:	Justice	Proverbs 21: 15
	Love	I Corinthians 13: 12-13
	God's gift	John 3: 16
Chapter 22:	Beauty of nature	Psalm 84: 1-2
Chapter 23:	Listening	Proverbs 8: 33-35
Chapter 24:	Victory	Psalm 60: 3-4
Chapter 25:	Gods anger	Romans 2: 7-8
	God's ways	Isaiah 55: 8 (P)
	Truth	John 8: 32
Chapter 26:	Kindness	Galatians 5: 22-23
	Promised Land	Exodus 3: 17
Chapter 27:	Serving with joy	Psalm 100: 1-2
	Strength and work	1 Chronicles 28: 10
	First day	Genesis 1: 5
Chapter 28:	Helping the poor	Proverbs 19: 17
	Rest	Matthew 11: 28
Chapter 29:	Liars	Psalm 5: 9
Chapter 30:	Protection	Psalm 91: 9-11
	Direction	Psalm 143: 8
	Words	Proverbs 16: 24
	Children	Matthew 19: 14
	Angels	Hebrews 13: 2
	Giving all you have	Mark 12: 41-44 (P)
	Encouragement	I Thessalonians 5: 11
	Being still	Exodus 14: 14

Chapter 31:	Weariness	Galatians 6: 9
Chapter 32:	Giving	Luke 3: 10-11
	Golden Rule	Matthew 7: 12
	Love	1 John 4: 19
	God never leaves us	Deuteronomy 31: 6
Chapter 33:	Doing good	Proverbs 3: 27
	All-loving God	Psalm 86: 15 (P)
Chapter 34:	Patience	Colossians 3: 12
Chapter 35:	Helping others	James 1: 27
	God hearing us	Jeremiah 29: 12-13 (P)
	Seek and Find	Matthew 7: 7 (P)
	Singing	Psalm 100: 2 (ESV - P)
Chapter 36:	Reconciliation	Proverbs 14: 9
	Repentance	Acts 2: 38
	Love	Proverbs 10: 12
Chapter 37:	Wealth/poverty	Proverbs 13: 7
	Wisdom	James 1: 5
Chapter 38	Forgiveness	Matthew 6: 15
Chapter 39	Following Jesus	Luke 18: 29
	God's call	Romans 11: 29
	Forgetting your past	Joel 2: 25
Chapter 40	Forgiveness	Colossians 3: 13
	Body is temple	1 Corinthians 6: 19-20 (P)
	Helping the helpless	Mark 2: 17
Chapter 41	Being open to Bible	Luke 24: 32
	Purpose	Psalm 138: 8
	Wonders of God	Psalm 40: 5
	Faith	Matthew 17: 20
	Defying God	Psalm 78: 32-33
	Pride	Proverbs 16: 18
	Plans	Proverbs 16: 3
	Motives	Proverbs 16: 2
	Hope	Psalm 40: 31
	Bless the Lord	Psalm 103: 1
Chapter 42	God's timing	Ecclesiastes 3: 1
Chapter 43	Salvation	John 3: 16-17
	God speaks	Job 33: 14
	Sharing lessons	Matthew 10: 27 (P)
Chapter 44	Sharing Good News	1 Peter 3: 15
	Patience	Psalm 40: 1 (P)
	What time is to God	2 Peter 3: 8
	God's call	1 Corinthians 7: 17
	Seeing	John 9: 25

	Witnesses	Hebrews 12: 1-2
	Jesus	John 3: 16
Chapter 45	Gifts	1 Corinthians 12: 4
Chapter 46	Waiting	Habakkuk 2: 3 (NLT)
Chapter 47	Sharing	1 Timothy 6: 18
Chapter 48	Sharing the Gospel	Romans 1: 16
	Narrow gate	Matthew 7: 13-14 (P)
	Repentance	Acts 2: 38
Chapter 49	The Holy Spirit	John 14: 26-27
Chapter 50	Saving one sheep	Matthew 18: 12
	Falling short	Romans 3: 23 (P)
Chapter 51	Encouragement	Psalm 10: 17
	Well done	Matthew 25: 23
	Thoughts	Hebrews 13: 1
Chapter 52	Work satisfaction	Isaiah 65: 22-23
Chapter 53	Faith	Hebrews 11: 1
	God's attributes	Psalm 36: 5-7
	Sower/seeds	Matthew 13: 3-23
Chapter 54	Giving	Luke 6: 38
Chapter 55	Praise	Psalm 150: 1-2
Epilogue	Enlightenment	Ephesians 1: 17-19
	God with us	Matthew 28: 20

Discussion Questions

1. Chapter 2: The mosaic Claire is creating because it's "in style" falls off the wall and shatters. The mosaic God asked her to make remains safe on the wall. Read 1 Samuel 5 (the story of the Philistines who stole the Ark of the Covenant and placed it next to a statue of their god Dagon.) What parallels can you see between the two instances?
2. Chapter 3: Michelle and Claire discuss the art fair. Claire says that art is meant to be seen and Michelle paraphrases Matthew 15: 5 by saying, "We're not supposed to hide our light under a basket but let it shine for all the world to see." Light can be defined as your talent, but also your attributes such as goodness and wisdom, and also the light of Jesus that shines in you. What steps can you take to better shine your light for all the world to see?
3. Chapter 4: Summer is skeptical about going to Claire's – meeting with strangers. But what if it's important? Would you have gone to Claire's? How can Summer's courage inspire your reaction to possible God-connections in your life?
4. Chapter 5: Claire meets Billy Cumberson. She hears about his failures with the restaurant and feels she's supposed to help him. But she blows it by repeating the trite, "When God closes a door He opens a window" line. What other things could Claire have said to help him overcome his bitterness?
5. Chapter 6: Ryan feels a nudge to "stop here." He tells the truck driver that God will "get me back where I need to be if I'm wrong." Knowing this is true, what are you afraid of doing because you might make a mistake? Pray for guidance and take the first step!
6. Chapter 7: Summer is desperate to make a connection when she delivers flowers, but nothing happens. Why do you think nothing is happening with her efforts?
7. Chapter 8: Ivy comes home and tells Jered about cool moments she had, helping people. Jered doesn't seem to get it. Or does he? What do you think Jered really feels about Ivy's good deeds?
8. Chapter 11: Michelle has this opinion: "She wasn't close to anybody, not deep down where her soul lived. That spot was reserved for Jesus. He was her Savior, Christ, Lord, King, and Master. She didn't need or desire anyone else. People would come and go, but Jesus remained." How does your opinion coincide or differ from Michelle's?

9. Chapter 13: Claire doesn't want to call Billy. She wants to see if God brings them together again. Michelle says it's not right to test God. Do you believe she was testing God? Or (like she explained) was she afraid her own will would get in the way of God's?
10. Chapter 13: Claire sends Billy away because she's starting to have feelings for him and can't imagine God would work that way. Michelle suggests waiting a few days to call him. "Leave things as they are for a few days. God can fix your mistakes if it's important to Him. Let's take time to see what He does." Do you think this was good advice?
11. Chapter 15: Summer feels like she can't do anything right, and is sure the others are having great success on their mission. She feels she isn't doing enough. Do you think this is a common Christian attitude? Why?
12. Chapter 16: Michelle encourages Claire to use the "three second rule": pause for three seconds before calling Billy. Are you prone to impulsive words, actions, and emails? How would the 3-second rule help you?
13. Chapter 19: Summer still struggles to connect, which propels her on a walk, which makes her remember the man and the dumpster, which leads to her helping him. How has God ever used failures to get you on the right track?
14. Chapter 22: Summer prays, but only gives God a minute to answer before turning on the TV. How can you relate to this?
15. Chapter 23: Summer tries to explain to Andy how God's using her but gets shut down and called cocky. Even as we want people to understand our faith we can be rejected. Have you ever talked about God and been shut down? How did you handle it? How could you have done better?
16. Chapter 29: Michelle gives God credit for the "truth" billboard and Claire's thought that justice is the reason she and Billy were brought together. Of course, this isn't provable. But she says, "I like to give Him credit, just in case." What do you think about Michelle's philosophy?
17. Chapter 30: Ryan, Grandpa, and Lisa pick up Arlo, a hitchhiker. Afterward, Grandpa makes her promise never to do that. Ryan talks about being kind but wise. How would you explain this conundrum to a child?
18. Chapter 30: Once in Colorado Lisa points out that "This day seemed so long yet other days go by in a flash. Why is that?" Why is that?
19. Chapter 34: When speaking of Billy exposing the truth about his partner, Claire says, "Being a victim isn't a choice, but staying a

victim is." Do you believe this statement is true? Do you think Billy did the right thing exposing Robby?

20. Chapter 35: Ryan and Lisa talk about her finding $7—the same amount she gave away. Ryan says, Coincidences are how a non-believing person explains God's ways." What do you think about coincidences?
21. Chapter 36: Summer quotes two verses to two different people, with two different results. She figures out that it was her responsibility to share—to the best of her abilities. The rest was between the hearer and God. Do you agree? What's been your experience quoting verses?
22. Chapter 36: Summer has a hard time accepting help—a common issue with "servers." Why do you think this is? Inspired by the gifts in Romans 12 are you a Server, Administrator, Motivator, Perceiver, Teacher, Empathizer, or Giver? (you can have elements of more than one gift.)
23. Chapter 37: Michelle shares her testimony with Jonette, hoping her story of sin and redemption will help. Have you ever shared some of your faith experiences with others? Were they receptive?
24. Chapter 38: Billy and Claire confront Robby. Billy forgives him—shocking Claire. He says he got revenge because Robby now knows *he* knows and others know. "He knows what he did was wrong. Me forgiving him puts the burden on him. I for one, am free of my burden." What do you think about Billy's action and attitude? Have you ever had to forgive someone who hurt you immensely? (Should you do it now?)
25. Chapter 39: Ryan's mom and dad realize, "We do the same thing day after day and nothing changes. We don't change and we don't help others change either. We're coasting." Are you coasting? How can you ignite your faith and spur your life to move forward?
26. Chapter 39: Ryan way of living out his faith is not the same as his parents' way. How is your faith different from your parents' faith? How is your children's faith different from yours?
27. Chapter 39: Ryan's father admits he was jealous of Ryan's faith which put a damper on his own. Have you ever been jealous of someone else's faith? How can you get past that?
28. Chapter 40: Summer describes herself as an introvert: chit-chat exhausts her, she is content to be alone, and only needs a few friends. Which are you? Extrovert or introvert? How does that personality type play out in daily life?
29. Chapter 41: Jered finds out he got his big break in the music business when Boxer sacrificed *his* big chance. What do you think

about Boxer's actions? Who do you know who's sacrificed status or position for a friend?

30. Chapter 44: Summer confesses a big shame in her life regarding not helping a blind man. What big regret do you have about not helping someone in need?
31. Chapter 46: Billy realizes both he and Robby compromised their dreams by opening Billy Bobs. Now Billy has a chance to fulfill his original dream. "It's almost like God was holding it safe for me until I found it again." Have you compromised a dream? Have you rediscovered a dream God was holding safe for you? Is there a dream you can rekindle?
32. Chapter 48: Summer says, "God didn't like pushers. He liked followers." What do you think this means?
33. Epilogue: Michelle represents the steady Christian who often gets overlooked when compared to Christians who've had a "wow" transformation. Who is a steady Christian in your life? What could you do to make them feel they are appreciated?
34. Epilogue: If Michelle represents the "steady" Christian, what "type" of Christian is Ryan, Summer, Jered, Ivy, Claire, Billy...? What type of Christian are you? What type of Christian would you like to be?

About the Author

NANCY MOSER is the best-selling author of over 40 novels, novellas, and children's books, including Christy Award winner *Time Lottery* and Christy finalist *Washington's Lady*. She's written nineteen historical novels including *Love of the Summerfields, Masquerade, Where Time Will Take Me,* and *Just Jane. An Unlikely Suitor* was named to Booklist's "Top 100 Romance Novels of the Decade." *The Pattern Artist* was a finalist in the Romantic Times Reviewers Choice award. Some of her contemporary novels are: *Eyes of Our Heart, The Invitation, Solemnly Swear, The Good Nearby, John 3:16, Crossroads, The Seat Beside Me,* and the Sister Circle series. Nancy has been married for over forty-five years—to the same man. She and her husband have three grown children, seven grandchildren, and live in the Midwest. She's been blessed with a varied life. She's earned a degree in architecture, run a business with her husband, traveled extensively in Europe, and has performed in various theaters, symphonies, and choirs. She knits voraciously, kills all her houseplants, and can wire an electrical fixture without getting shocked. She is a fan of anything antique—humans included.

Website: www.nancymoser.com
Blogs: Author blog: www.authornancymoser.blogspot.com
History blog: www.footnotesfromhistory.blogspot.com
Facebook: www.facebook.com/ nancymoser.author
Bookbub: www.bookbub.com/authors/nancy-moser?list=author_ books
Goodreads: www.goodreads.com/author/show/117288.Nancy_Moser
Pinterest: www.pinterest.com/nancymoser1/boards/
Twitter: www.twitter.com/MoserNancy
Instagram: www.instagram.com/nmoser33/

Want to read Claire's backstory?

Excerpt from

A Steadfast Surrender

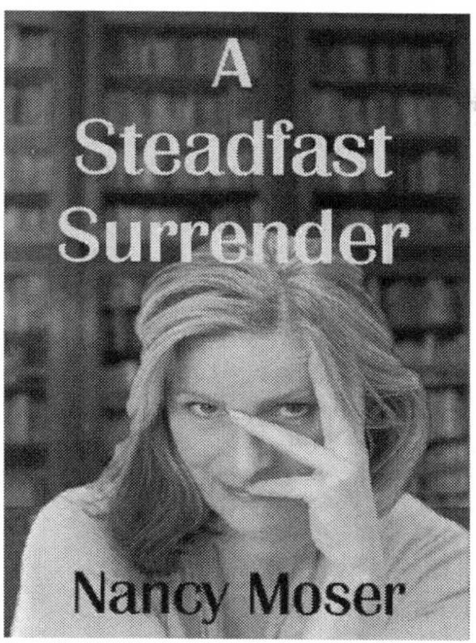

The intercom buzzed. "Claire, your husband, line one."

Ex-husband. Claire Adams's money-grubbing, selfish, two-timing, ex-husband. "Tell him I'll call him back."

"I already tried that. He says it's an emergency. He says he'll hold."

He can hold till the Second Coming for all I care.

"Claire?"

"All right, all right, I'll take it." She settled in behind the desk at her mosaic studio, closed her eyes, and tried to find the calm before the storm that was... "Ron. My two-timing ex. What can I do you for?"

"Plenty. Obviously. But beside that, I have a proposition for you."

"Haven't you done enough propositioning?"

"Very funny."

"Do you hear me laughing?"

"Are you going to dredge up the past or can I talk about our future?"

"We don't have a future, Ron."

"Don't be difficult."

She opened her mouth to respond, then closed it. Talking with Ron made her emotions dry and brittle like a slice of bread left on the counter overnight. She tapped into a verse that had been her mantra during the divorce: *"O God, you are my God, earnestly I seek you; my soul thirsts for you, my body longs for you, in a dry and weary land where there is no water."* Ron offered no water. No refreshment. No relief. Only the refreshment of God had seen her through his womanizing and her eventual surrender of their marriage.

"C.C.?"

She took a cleansing breath. "Can we wrap this up, please?"

"Don't be so quick to cut me off. This benefits you too."

She snickered.

"You like boating, don't you?"

It took her a second to register the word. "Boating?

"I want to buy a boat. I want you to pay for half."

The laugh was full now. "And why would I do that?"

"Because I'd let you use it. Like I said, you like boating."

"I *liked* boating. Past tense. Those days are over, Ron. And since you dumped me for a younger model, I think it's inappropriate for me to pay for half of a boat *she* will use."

"But, C.C., you know I've always wanted one."

Ron could make instant gratification an Olympic event. "Then buy one. But leave me out of it."

"You know I don't have that kind of money. You've always made more than me."

Ron's ego hadn't enjoyed that fact when they were married, and had taken advantage of it since the divorce. Claire was generous in the settlement, willing to give up some cash and possessions for the whole thing to be done with as soon as possible. Maybe 'that had been a mistake. "Do unto others" was hard to maintain when *others* got greedy. She sucked in a breath and steeled herself. "My answer is no."

"No?"

"Why doesn't your beloved Tiffany pay for it?" There was silence, and Claire began to laugh. "She's left you, hasn't she?"

"I kicked her out, if it's any of your business. She was an absolute leech."

"I know the feeling."

"You should see the bills she ran up."

"A disgusting opportunist."

He sighed. "So I'm alone now. All alone."

"Oh, I'm sure you'll find another young babe to keep you warm."

"Tiffany was hardly young. She was thirty."

"And you are?"

"You know very well how old I am, and my love life is none of your business. Not anymore."

But it had been her business once. Ron had left Claire because a pretty girl stole his heart and promised him a life of passion and adoration. Lola lasted thirteen months before Ron realized her portrayal of a high-living Lolita was a front for an empty bank account, which she wanted Ron to fill. Besides, Lola the Lolita liked to roam more than her Lothario.

In spite of Ron's infidelities, Claire *had* wanted to work things out. Not because she loved him so much, but because she knew it was the right thing to do. Saying "Till death do us part" in a church meant something to Claire. Yet just as it took two to argue, it took two to make up. And Ron didn't want to work at their marriage. Not after he discovered other women who made him feel young again in a way Claire couldn't. Or wouldn't.

She didn't blame him entirely. Just mostly. Claire knew she worked too much and had tunnel-vision toward her art. But in her own defense, she'd never forgotten a birthday or anniversary, she'd hung up Ron's towels without complaining, and she'd made him his favorite cheesecake that was unsurpassed by any la-di-da restaurant charging twelve-bucks a slice, even though it kept her in the kitchen way past her preferred time limit.

Claire realized Ron was still talking. "...suppose I'll have to cancel the order, though I already had a weekend planned."

"Poor baby."

"Don't be mean. With your recent success I thought you could be a little generous. I saw the article in *Newsweek* about your work."

"Generous? Don't you dare talk generous with me. Who got the good cars in the settlement? Who got the house?"

"You said you didn't want them."

She *hadn't* wanted them, preferring to start fresh, but that wasn't the point. "I have to go."

"What if we go sixty-forty?"

"Bye."

"Uh-uh, don't you dare hang up on—"

She disconnected the call and immediately longed for a nap. What she used to celebrate as Ron's spunk, she now suffered as plain old petulance. In twenty years of marriage he'd changed.

And you haven't?

She frowned. Had she? What traits had Ron found initially charming in the twenty-five-year-old Claire Adams, up-and-coming mosaic artist extraordinaire? Had her ambition and creativity turned into something less desirable at age forty-five? Had fame and money irreparably changed her?

Actually, it didn't matter whose fault it was. Their marriage was over. It still hurt like a gaping wound, and every call, every contact with Ron, added a handful of salt.

She shoved all thoughts of him aside and was actually pleased when her stomach growled. Needing and wanting to eat was a good sign. For months the necessity of food had been a burden, and she'd ended up losing fifteen pounds.

The divorce diet. If only she could package it.

Lunch and a meeting at the gallery beckoned. She stood to leave just as the line buzzed again. "Call on line three, Claire. It's your pastor."

Claire could hardly skip that one—and didn't want too. The previous Sunday they'd dedicated the mosaic altar she'd created and donated. He was probably calling to share some compliments with her. She picked up the phone. "Pastor Joe. All's well with the altar, I hope?"

"An altar fit for a King. We're extremely grateful for it."

"You're welcome."

"But I have a favor to ask of you."

"Uh-oh. I feel a request for a matching baptismal font coming on."

"Actually, I need your culinary expertise."

For a moment she was speechless. "Surely you jest."

"Oh, you'll do fine. We have the administrator of a Denver homeless shelter visiting. She's been talking at the circle meetings and will give a speech at the congregational dinner tomorrow night. She's staying at the Martin's. But tomorrow—Saturday—the Martin's have some softball function for the kids, and Molly and I have a bowling tournament—"

"How's your game?"

"I've hit three digits."

"Ooh. Strike three, you're out."

"Wrong kind of strike, Claire. Anyway, we wondered if you would entertain the administrator tomorrow noon. Have her over for lunch."

During the divorce Claire had taken solace in the church she'd previously ignored and discovered the benefits of becoming a joiner. She was now on Pastor Joe's ready-willing-and-able list of volunteers and didn't really mind. Giving back eased the pain of what she'd given up.

"You'd like her, Claire."

She sighed. "Does she have a name?"

"Michelle Jofsky."

"Wouldn't you rather have a couple do this?"

"I think she's been coupled out. An afternoon woman-to-woman would probably be a relief. She's a baseball fan, just like you. Sometimes eating pizza and watching baseball is a thousand times more satisfying than a four-course meal."

That made it easier. "Pizza I can handle. Baseball, huh? A Royals fan, I hope?"

"Cubs. You'll have to duke it out."

"I'll kick in my Christian tolerance for one afternoon. As a favor to you."

"And God."

"Who we know is an avid Royals fan."

"I'll call Michelle and tell her to come over at noon. And Claire? This is a good thing you're doing, and I'm proud of you. But . . ."

"But what?"

"Be good. Okay?"

"You're no fun."

Made in the USA
Middletown, DE
17 November 2020